TANGLE OF FATES

TANGLE OF MAGIC
BOOK FOUR

J.E. NEAL

CONTENTS

CHAPTER 1

APPROPRIATIONS

DAN VINDICO

"We're home," Aida announced as Dan shuffled his family into the living room loaded down with their luggage. Fionna lit the fire with her hand as soon as she'd laid Halia in one of the arm chairs in the living room. She was sound asleep.

Dan carried in the bassinet and another load of bags to find Fionna on her cell phone when he returned.

"Yeah, Daddy, we'll be over tomorrow afternoon. I can't wait for Nana to meet the girls and Dan." Fionna sounded thrilled.

"Aida, let's go get your bath." Dan guided Aida up the stairs while Fionna talked with her father.

"This is the very first night I get to sleep with Davi in my fairy princess bed, and I think maybe I'll put Sophie in her cradle in my room," Aida explained to Dan as he dried her off and rubbed kukui and coconut oils into her skin. "I like Aunt Kara's bed, but I like my fairy princess bed more."

"I like my bed here better than the one at Grandpa and Grandma's too," he assured her.

As Dan tucked Aida and her bunny and her blanket in her fairy princess bed, he seated himself beside her and studied her for a moment.

"I love you, Daddy, so much," she pledged, making him beam.

"I love you too, baby, so much," Dan quoted, reveling in her giggle. "Hey, Aida?" Her eyebrows lifted as she reached and placed her hand inside of Dan's. "You know when we move to Tutu and Papa's farm on Kauai, Daddy will have a different job, right?" Dan concentrated on her rhythms.

"Yes, you told me, and Mommy told me."

"Are you okay with that?"

"I think so." She refused to meet Dan's gaze. "Mommy said it won't be like what happened at Alex's house." She rubbed Davi's well-worn ears between her fingers.

"No, baby, I promise you," Dan vowed. "But it will be a little bit like what Alex's daddy does. If Daddy does his work, then people who want to hurt other people go to jail and they get some help to learn how to deal with their anger."

"I miss Alex and Alfred." Aida yawned.

"I talked to Alex's daddy a few days ago, and they're thinking about coming to visit us over Christmas. They're going to come stay with us and then go see Alex and Alfred's grandfather."

"I can share my room with Alex and Alfred."

"Uh, no." Dan shuddered slightly. "I think Halia will sleep in Mommy and Daddy's room, and we'll make the boys a pallet on the floor in the nursery." Dan willed away the stories about Rainer and Emily—that Emily had dared Rainer to kiss her when she was seven, and Rainer Lawson had fallen head over heels right then and there.

Another deep yawn contorted Aida's face, and Dan chuckled. "You go to sleep. We can talk more about Daddy's new job tomorrow, okay?"

Aida sat up and kissed Dan's cheek. "Thank you for being my daddy," she vowed in a choked whisper that fissured his heart.

"Thank you for being my baby girl." Dan wrapped his arms around her and swore to himself that he'd never let anything hurt her again.

Easing down the stairs, Dan smiled as he took in Fionna seated on the couch, cradling Halia as she drank a bottle contentedly.

"Daddy wants us to come over tomorrow for lunch. He's going to open the bakery, but Gretta is going to stay home with Nana until she's settled. Nana wants to meet you and the girls."

"That sounds good," Dan agreed. He'd certainly never deny her anything that had her smiling like that.

He wrapped his arm around her, and she cradled Halia between them. "Glad to be home?"

"So, so, so glad to be home."

"Want to talk about it now or wait 'til we're in the bath?"

Her energy tensed for a moment. "We do make really good decisions in our bathtub."

"And would my Maylea like a mug of Maylea's tea?" He reveled in the fact that his family was alone and safe in their home once more. The street lamps were lit along with soft glows coming from the other houses in the neighborhood. A sighed chuckle even escaped his lips as he noted that the Scheckleses' home was still lit up on every available surface with gaudy Christmas lights.

"You mean Aida's tea?" Fionna giggled.

"Will we have to make it Aida and Halia's tea once our little coconut is old enough for tea?"

Fionna shook her head. "The tea for Aida and me is made for Empathic Receivers. It soothes our nerves and helps relax our mind when the emotions of the world have been more than we can really handle. It helps us shield them out a little.

"Halia can't feel that like Aida and I can, so Tutu will give her the tea she used to make for my mom. A tea for Scholera Predilects to help them sort their adventures and concentrate so that they can share their knowledge and find peace."

Letting that information settle on him, Dan kissed Fionna's cheek then Halia's as he stood to fix his wife the tea.

After she finished drinking her tea, Dan and Fionna gave Halia a bath in her flower bathtub before putting her in her swaddle wrap and laying her in her bassinet.

"She doesn't really remember this is her house," Fionna explained dejectedly as they stood back from the bassinet watching Halia's chest rise and fall in rhythmic breaths.

"She's been through a lot of changes to not even be a month old yet."

Dan guided Fionna into their bathtub a few minutes later. He crawled in behind her and tried to decide where to begin. "I need to know what you felt when we were talking to Representative Kalakona."

"She tried to keep herself very shielded, which always worries me."

"Did you pick up on why she'd do that?"

"People on Kauai know that I'm a very strong Receiver just like Tutu. Some people don't like that. I didn't pick up on anything necessarily wrong. She wasn't lying. She's very controlled. She's also very afraid of something, and whatever it is, it's why she's so eager for you to command Hawaiian Iodex."

Dan nodded. "I need to ask you another question, and I'm worried I'm going to sound like a racist asshole."

She shook her head. "I highly doubt that."

"I'm a white guy, and I am well aware that many horrible things that have happened in this world were our fault. I'm sure as hell not one of those *not every man* pricks. I felt your energy tense when she was talking about being white but also being Hawaiian. I...don't understand. How can she be white and Hawaiian?" Dan cringed. He was certain that he'd said something wrong.

"That usually depends on who you ask."

"I'm asking you."

"Race is very complicated. Labels and identities are important, and they also maybe shouldn't be as important as they are. I don't know. Tribalism is how white people did some of the damage they've done. People don't understand that if they exchange who they are for allegiance to a tribe, it leads to nothing but destruction. On the other hand, we should celebrate our ancestry and the beliefs of our culture, but we're taught in a thousand different ways every day to be afraid of different. Our language and our ways of life were taken from us. They still are. Our island country was seen as nothing but a source of revenue. Horrible things were done to us. If we could somehow make people understand that every person, no matter what they look like, deserves respect and honor that would go a long way. We need people to understand that others don't have to think like we think, but that our way of life is every bit as valid as theirs. They have a right to their own beliefs, but they do not have the right to tell others how to believe.

"But as for Representative Kalakona, to most Native Hawaiians, she is not Hawaiian even if she was born there. But, how do you tell someone born in a state who's lived there her entire life that they aren't Hawaiian? What does being Hawaiian mean anymore?" Tears pricked her eyes.

"She's appropriating your culture."

"She doesn't believe that," Fionna sighed. "Am I not Hawaiian because my father is Mexican even though my mother was Hawaiian, and I was raised in Hawaiian traditions and culture? Is she not American because she married a man who is Japanese? Are Native Hawaiians whose families have been there since long before western invasion not also American because they were forced to became a part of this country? It's complicated, like I said. If they don't want to be American, can they renounce their citizenship or will they still fall under American and Realm law because Hawaii was taken as a state? Who decides where the lines are drawn? She believes she has a right to call herself Hawaiian, but I do *not* think she has that right. I can assure you that there are a lot of Native Hawaiians who agree with me. I..." Fionna grimaced.

"What?"

"I suspect she told us that because you're white."

"She assumed I wouldn't question it." Dan shook his head in disgust. "I sure as hell would never call myself Hawaiian even if we live there for the rest of our lives. I'm so fucking honored that you teach me the ways of the Hawaiian people, that Tutu and Papa accepted me as your husband, but I have no intention of trying to steal a culture. I'm just thankful that I get to live on the land and do everything I can to preserve and honor the ways of life. I can't wait to learn more."

Fionna grinned. "Yeah, people like you are our favorite kind of haoles."

"I don't want to take this job if I'll be taking it away from someone with native heritage."

"You wouldn't be. She's not going to ask any native people. She wants you. If you say no, she'll offer it to another white Shield. That's how it works. White people hold the power and then give it to other white people, but here's the thing—the Hawaiian people need help. *My* people need help. Native Hawaiians are arrested way more often and they're sentenced with much longer terms than any other race on the islands for the very same crimes. They need you to come in and try to make it fair. It's much worse in the Non-Gifted precincts, but you'd have some say there as well."

"Are you saying you want me to take the job?"

"I don't know." She shook her head. "I'm thinking a million things all at once."

"Start with one of the million things, and we'll work through them all."

"Thinking about your being the highest-ranking officer in all of Hawaii feels different to me than when you were the Chief of Elite."

"Different how?"

"I feel like I should have been really, really scared when we were talking to Representative Kalakona. I expected to want to beg you not to take the job because you could get hurt, but I don't feel scared and that confuses me."

Still not certain he understood, Dan nodded. "Are you not scared because you don't feel like I'm going to take the job, or do you think I should take the job and it feels right to you?"

"I don't know," Fionna whimpered.

"Okay." Dan drew her back to him. "We don't have to decide tonight, sweetheart. There's a lot to consider."

"I'm just very…" Her words drowned in her confusion.

"Chaotic," Dan concluded for her. She nodded her adamant agreement. "It's been insane this week. Between Guinevere's, and Katherine Bryant, and my mother, I'm not surprised we're chaotic."

Fionna tucked her head under Dan's chin, and he wrapped her tightly in the safety of his embrace.

"When Representative Kalakona said that Hawaii could give us life and you could give her safety, that makes so much sense to me. Tutu has been saying for months that Hawaii is calling the Shields. She's always right. I think maybe even with everything crazy I feel right now, you are supposed to take this job. I think you could make a real difference, but I'm so scared to say that. The way I feel and the way I think that I should feel don't match, and that's hard."

Her confession touched the deepest wells of Dan's heart. Hope flooded through his energy. She felt it instantly. "Why don't we let that settle for a day or two? Just think about it. We'll talk about every feeling you think you should feel and the ones you *are* feeling."

"That sounds good," she whispered. Her fear was palpable in her rhythms, but it didn't seem to be fear of the job. It was a fear that what had been expected was changing to what she considered unknown. "I'll talk to Tutu."

"We probably should have started with her." Dan chuckled.

CHAPTER 2

TWIST OF THE KNIFE

"Maylea," whispered from the woman lying in what had once been Fionna's adolescent bedroom. The lights were dimmed, and Dan swallowed down his discomfort and fear. Tears leaked down Fionna's cheeks as she moved to her grandmother's side. She was so much worse than Dan had allowed himself to understand. Fionna's father had been telling the truth. She wasn't going to make it much longer.

Gretta hadn't been able to accept her mother's life drawing to a close. Her desperate vows that Nana was better had been the information Fionna had clung to in the last few weeks, and Dan had taken his cues from his wife. Fionna must've been blocking out the emotions associated with death. Dan's eyes closed in defeat. Her mother's death had forever altered his Receiver.

He held Halia on his shoulder. Aida's hand was clutched in his. She was frightened as well. She didn't know the woman, but she could feel the sorrow and terror in Fionna's rhythms. Aida cringed into Dan.

"Nana." Fionna took her grandmother's frail hand in her own. Mr. Styler was standing at the door with his arm wrapped lovingly around Gretta. He didn't have the heart to leave her to open the bakery. It was a feeling Dan understood only too well.

"How are you feeling?" Fionna managed in a convulsive choke as she tried desperately not to sob. Dan handed Halia to her grandfather and joined Fionna at the side of the bed.

"You…must be…the dreamboat." Nana gave Dan a weak smile. Chuckling, Dan rubbed Fionna's back.

"Nana, this is Dan." Fionna was smiling through her tears as they recalled Fionna informing her grandmother over the phone last Christmas that Dan was a dreamboat. Nana continued to smile as Aida timidly moved toward Fionna. "And this is our little girl, Aida," Fionna continued in a heartbroken whisper.

"Hi." Aida offered her a sweet smile.

"Aida." Nana reached for Aida's hand. Panic etched Aida's features as she let Nana hold her hand. "Ella es hermosa, Maylea," Nana whispered.

Fionna swallowed back more emotion and nodded. "She is beautiful—my sweet, beautiful little girl."

Aida bit her lip. Her cheeks flushed as she blinked back tears of her own. Dan guided her into his lap. He wasn't certain if the emotions of death were something his precious baby girl had dealt with so intimately that she recognized it or if she was feeling her mother's heartbreak in her developing rhythms, but he held her to him and tried to soothe them both.

"Where is the little bebe?" Nana coughed weakly as she forced the questions out. Mr. Styler approached and handed Halia to her mother.

"This is Halia, Nana," Fionna explained tenderly as she kept Halia in her arms but placed them in Nana's embrace. Halia weighed in just a little over seven pounds. The enhanced formula was working wonders, but Nana could never have supported their tiny baby girl.

"Usted tiene una maravillosa familia, Maylea. Estoy tan orgulloso de ti," Nana whispered.

You have a wonderful family, Maylea. I'm so proud for you. Dan translated the Spanish instantly. He'd learned a great deal of the language in his dealings with the Interfeci.

"Thank you." Fionna reached for Dan's hand. He supplied it and felt her draw him in. She needed his shield. She needed his strength and his reassurances, and he would be all of that for her.

Nana's blinks grew heavier, and panic set in. Dan strengthened his shield as Fionna trembled against him.

"Mama, I think you need a nap," Gretta urged. Nana nodded her agreement as she reached and caressed Fionna's cheek, wiping away the escaping tears.

"*La muerte es parte de la vida dulce,* Maylea." Nana tried to reassure her. Dan forced himself to draw breath as Fionna turned and collapsed on his shoulder. Her grandmother's quoting the fact that death was part of life was simply more than she could handle, even if for the moment her grandmother was only taking a nap.

"Come on, sweetheart." Dan guided her up off the bed and took Halia from her arms. He led her back to the living room. After laying Halia in her bouncy seat, he moved to the couch and wrapped Fionna in his arms. He let her ruin his shirt as she sobbed in earnest.

Mr. Styler slipped into the room several minutes later. He appeared to have aged a decade in the past week.

"Maylea," he sighed. His heartbreak over her tears was evident in his tone and his features. Fionna shook her head convulsively as she clung to Dan with all of her might. She grasped his shirt in her fists, burying her face in his neck. Her eyes squeezed shut as she hid from the harsh bitter reality.

"I tried to tell you." Her father was exasperated suddenly. "You never listen."

Dan shook his head and glared at her father. He wouldn't allow her to be scolded—not now and not ever.

"She's resting," Gretta assured everyone as she moved into the living room. She was still blinking back tears as she took in Fionna. "I'll make her some tea."

Fionna did calm after several long minutes. Dan plied her with the tea and kept her wrapped up under his arm.

"I'm right here, baby," he soothed as she continued to cling to him.

"She wants to be buried in Juarez with Pops." Gretta seated herself beside Mr. Styler.

Fionna's chin trembled. Dan knew precisely what she was feeling. He recalled his own fury over his parents discussing his grandfather's impending death when Dan was sixteen. His grandfather, Dan's childhood hero, the only other Ioses Predilect in the Vindico family line, had been in the hospital for a week, and Dan simply refused to believe that he wasn't going to recover.

He'd refused to go to Georgetown when his father called him in the last few hours. Dan had gone to Amelia's instead and ignored the forthcoming doom.

As he thought back on those weeks of his adolescence, he'd always considered his reaction to his parents' discussion of his grandfather's death as youth and lack of life experience, but as he held his wife in his over-muscled embrace, he understood.

Age and life experience had nothing to do with it. It was a fervent need to deny reality and shun the truth in light of desperation for life to go on just as it always had because you didn't know any other way that it could possibly be.

Fionna calmed under Dan's constant casting. Halia began crying, and holding her seemed to soothe Fionna as well. Aida stuck close by her mother, and she allowed her family to comfort her.

Nana woke an hour later, and Fionna fed her broth and helped her rub her face with cold cream. The action seemed to bring them both solace. Dan took care of the girls and tried to give Fionna a little time to spend with her grandmother. He knew these next few days would mean everything to her.

"Daddy." Aida tugged on Dan's arm as he gave Halia a bottle. Mr. Styler paced as he watched over Gretta fretfully.

"What, baby?" Dan drew Aida to him as he balanced Halia with his other arm.

"I think we should move to Tutu's right now. I want Mommy to be happy again. Mommy is so sad it makes my tummy hurt." She began to cry in earnest. Dan's heart shattered as he tried to comfort her while keeping the bottle in Halia's mouth.

"What?!" Mr. Styler gasped. Shocked fury blazed in his eyes.

"Samuel," Gretta soothed as a broad grin formed on her previously devastated features. "It is where Maylea needs to be. I've told you this so many times. Dan loves her so much he's moving them back to the only place she's ever truly happy. It has never been here."

"This is ridiculous. Maylea needs to be here with me. You will not take her away," Mr. Styler demanded.

"I think we should discuss this later, sir." Dan gestured his head toward Aida who'd begun crying harder.

"Maylea," Mr. Styler fumed as he stomped toward the hallway.

"No." Dan blocked his way. His shield pulsed. "Aida, give Halia her bottle for Daddy," he instructed. Aida nodded and seated herself on the couch. Dan laid Halia in her big sister's arms, and she continued her lunch. Patting Halia's back gently seemed to bring Aida comfort as she cuddled Halia to her and kissed her forehead. She was a Receiver in every sense of the word. Taking care of someone she loved healed her aching heart.

"You are not going to yell at her about this. If you want to be mad, be mad at me, but you're not doing this to her, not today." Dan stared his father-in-law down.

"You have done nothing but hurt her. I held my peace long enough. I should never have let her marry you after what happened. I will not let you move her back to that godforsaken island. Only horrible things happen there."

"Daddy," Fionna gasped as she rushed into the room. "That isn't true. Don't say that." The pain in her voice was so strong in that moment it choked out her demand.

"Samuel, you will do nothing but drive her away again. You two are like oil and water. How many times must I tell you? Maylea and Daniel are meant to be. You mustn't stand in the way of her fate. She will not choose you, so do not force a choice from her. He is everything to her. Her husband and the father of her children," Gretta pled with him.

"You will not go back there, Maylea. I will not allow it," Mr. Styler commanded.

"Yes, I will, and you can't stop me! Don't make this harder than it needs to be. Halia was made on the island. I was made on the island. My daughters, and my husband, and my family need to be there and that's where we are going." Fionna trembled. Dan wrapped his arm over her. She buried her face in his chest.

"It's okay, Mommy. Please don't cry," Aida begged, but she stayed on the sofa, still trying to manage Halia.

"Halia was made on the island because of him. He is nothing but trial and torment. The baby doesn't need that island. It will take her from you," Mr. Styler drove the knife in and continued to force its abhorrent twist.

"Daddy," Fionna convulsed in horror.

"Stop it now," Dan threatened.

"Then leave," Mr. Styler ordered. "Leave now."

"Samuel, no," Gretta pled.

Fionna stared at her father in abject disbelief. "I'm staying with Nana."

"She is not yours, Maylea. Don't forget that. Why do you always want things that only brought you pain?" He threw his arm out to Dan. "Go," he commanded again.

"Fi, take the girls to the car. I'll be right there. I have a few things I need to say." Dan glared hatefully at Fionna's father.

Fionna managed a nod. Aida handed her Halia and helped her carry a few things to the car.

As soon as the front door closed, Dan was in Mr. Styler's face.

"How dare you?" he seethed. "How dare you say things like that to her? You took her away from the only things that could ever have healed her. She lost her mother and what that didn't rob her of, you took. Everything that ever meant anything to her, everything that could have given her relief, you took away. What kind of father does that?"

"I took her away because I loved her," Mr. Styler came right back.

"No." Dan shook his head. "You took her away because you wanted to control her. And your desperation to keep her safe strangled her. She did things she will never forgive herself for trying to get away from you. I take full responsibility for what happened to her in the spring. That was entirely my fault, but my God, everything I did, everything I *do*, is me trying to keep her safe. You brought her here because you couldn't stand to be on Kauai. You didn't do that for her. She can't even see what an incredible woman and wife and mother she is because of you. You took everything that made her who she is away from her. So, you go right ahead and hate me, but just remember, from the very beginning, when God himself stepped in on both of our accounts to save us from the hell we were living, know that she ran into my arms willing and ready because she was still trying to get the hell away from you."

"I said to leave," Mr. Styler hissed.

"Fine, but we are moving, sir, and if you want her to come back and see you or you ever want to see my girls again, then you need to make this right. Gretta, if we can do anything for you, please let us know."

Gretta managed a nod, but she was crying too hard for anything else. Grabbing the bags Fionna hadn't been able to manage, Dan stomped to the door.

"This is the biggest mistake you've ever made," were the last words he uttered before he slammed the door in his father-in-law's face.

CHAPTER 3

LISTENING AND HEARING

D an kept his fingers laced through Fionna's as he drove them home. Silent, harrowing tears leaked down her beautiful face for the entire ride. He supplied her with his soothing protection as he tried to think of something to say that would ease the burdens her father had heaped upon her.

Aida was just as distraught as her mother. Their energies were far too interconnected for her to be able to access peace before Fionna was able to herself.

After easing the car into the garage, Dan guided Fionna inside and then returned for Halia as Aida rushed to the couch beside her mother. Halia was sleeping soundly in her car seat, so Dan decided not to disturb her. He seated himself on the couch, not certain if it would be Fionna or Aida that would curl up in their customary balls in his lap, but either one was fine.

Fionna threw herself in his arms, and he cradled her tenderly.

"It's okay, sweetheart. He didn't mean any of that. He's exhausted and scared." Dan knew what he was saying was true even if it didn't heal the scars her father's words had seared on her heart.

"I know," Fionna managed in a pained whisper. She shuddered against him and cringed inward on herself.

"Baby, are you hurt? What happened?" His shield surrounded her without being summoned. She nodded and rubbed her hand over her abdomen. Realization surged through him.

"I'm sorry. I wasn't thinking." Dan pulled heat into his hand and rubbed her back. He'd hoped after having Halia that her menstrual cycle might improve. Before her subsequent pregnancies, they'd been horrible. She would be up all night long writhing in pain with Dan unable to do much to help.

"Will you make me some of that raspberry tea Tutu makes me for this?"

"Of course." Working quickly, he brought a mug of water to a low boil in his hand and then added the teabags from Tutu's store.

She rallied a little after the tea. Aida cuddled up beside her mama, and Dan laid a quilt over them. They were both asleep a few minutes later. Breathing a sigh of relief, Dan carried Halia in her car seat up to the bedroom to make his call.

"Aloha, man, I'm standing in what I'm hoping will very soon be your kitchen," was Kai's greeting. He sounded almost as excited to be discussing Dan and Fionna's move as Dan felt. He wished he could be there to see the plot of land that Kai and Papa had picked for the Vindicos' future home.

"Thank you for your hard work. Maylea fell in love with that house plan. I can't wait to see her in it every day."

"You can't be as excited as Malani." Kai chuckled. "But what's got you bummed?"

Assuming his tone had given him away, Dan sighed. "I was wondering if I could ask you a few things about Maylea's dad. I get the feeling I might be missing something regarding Elisabeth's death."

"I'd sure love to know what brought this on, but you need to talk to Malani. She's up at the house with Tu and the baby. Give her a call."

"Thanks." Dan assumed Malani would be the person to talk to, but he'd hoped to avoid upsetting her by dredging up painful memories.

"Are you still heading out in a few weeks?" Kai asked.

"Yeah. Fi's been planning the blessing."

"Then we better get going."

"Thank you for everything you're doing. I feel like I should be there helping."

"Nah. Malani is over the moon, and if she's that happy I'll do anything, you know. We're all excited. It's where you need to be. Give her a call. We'll see you soon."

Dan followed Kai's orders.

"What's wrong?" was Malani's greeting.

He tried to figure out the best way to respond. "How did you know something was wrong?"

Malani wasn't a Receiver. She was a Vis Virres Predilect though she was not particularly strong. "You never call me. You call Kai to ask me things, and Tutu has been brewing teas for hours and chanting."

He recounted everything that had happened since they'd arrived at the Stylers' home.

"He said that to her?" Malani gasped.

"Word for word."

"Tutu, would you mind watching Lanie for a few minutes?"

"Of course. Tell Daniel the story. He needs it to heal my Maylea. Tell him Samuel Styler may hear, but he does not listen. Their life awaits them here," Tutu commanded.

"Okay, I will."

Dan heard the screen door on Tutu and Papa's house slam as Malani made her exit.

"Where's Maylea now?"

"She's worn out after the past week of staying with my parents and then with everything this morning. She also isn't feeling well. She's taking a nap with Aida on the couch."

"That goes away when she's here. Her rhythms are always off when she's on the mainland. It makes her periods terrible. I think she was able to get pregnant again so quickly because you were here."

Fionna had never mentioned that the Kauaian rhythms regulated her periods as well. It made perfect sense though. The cysts she'd suffered, her horrible cycles... Her body was reacting to being away from the island that regulated everything about her. Her father had never understood that either.

"Hey, I don't want you to tell me anything you don't think Fi would want me to know. I just know I'm missing something."

"Just listen, okay? Maylea's not keeping things from you. What I'm about to tell you, she doesn't know. I mean I kind of think she knows, but she'd never ask Tutu or Samuel to confirm it."

"What happened?"

"Samuel never understood Tutu. He never really even understood Elisabeth. He never accepted that the way we do things here is ingrained in us as a part of our souls. But he loved Elisabeth as much as he was able and he adored Maylea. He didn't really like living so close to Tutu and Papa and them being so involved in their lives."

Dan considered that. He wondered if he wouldn't have reacted the same way if Fionna had wanted to live near her father, but that wasn't the way life had worked. He vowed to himself to never try to cut out the people who meant the world to his wife.

"He'd wanted to move back to Texas for a long time, but Elisabeth refused. They fought all the time, but Maylea never really knew. I mean she always sensed it, but Tutu and Papa kept her away from all of it. Her dad thought everything we sell in the store was some sort of witchcraft, and he was furious whenever Elisabeth or Tutu used the products on Maylea.

"When he first met Elisabeth, I think he fell in love thinking that she'd move off of the farm with him and forget her whole way of life, but that wasn't at all what Elisabeth had in mind."

Dan hated to interrupt, but he wanted to understand. "How long were they married before Maylea was born?"

"Less than a year. He blamed the ʻŌhiʻa lehua because she conceived so quickly."

Dan shook his head. "Keep going. I'm sorry I interrupted."

"It's fine. I'm glad you asked me. Tutu told Elisabeth not to go to the beach that Sunday that she died. She begged her not to go, but Samuel insisted they were going just to spite Tutu. She drowned, and Maylea fell apart. Samuel didn't understand her, and she refused to speak to him. She refused to go back home with him, refused to do anything without Tutu. He convinced himself that the island rhythms had taken Elisabeth away. So, he took Maylea away to punish Tutu and the island."

Dan was disgusted. "He went from refusing to believe in something and then he ultimately weaponized it when it served his purpose."

"Exactly. It was bad. It was so much worse than Maylea even allows herself to remember. He got her to Texas and wouldn't let her call Tutu and Papa or me. She used to wait until he fell asleep, and then call us. She would cry so hard we knew we had to do something. He wouldn't let her use Tutu's products or speak Hawaiian or talk about Kauai at all. Tutu and Papa petitioned for custody, and it got ugly. Ever since they did that, Samuel hasn't spoken to them. But Gretta stepped in. She convinced Samuel to let Maylea come back to the island in the summers and be at least a small portion of the girl she'd been. But it really messed Maylea up. I mean bad."

"She rebelled," Dan sighed. He knew some of this portion of the story already.

"She didn't just rebel. She went wild. She hated Samuel and clung to Gretta. She used to do anything she could to drive him insane, so he just got more and more strict, which just drove her more and more crazy. She ran away so many times. She'd be gone for days. She used her abilities to stay away from people who would've hurt her, but Dan, it was so bad. That's why Samuel wouldn't come back here to see you get married. That's why he's so mad you're moving back. He knows if he wants to see you, he'll have to come here which means seeing Tutu and Papa. They understand how sad he was and that in some convoluted way he was trying to protect Maylea. They don't blame him, but he won't believe that. But she needs to come back. Please don't change your mind. Please. I've been so worried about her for so long." Malani broke down in tears that shattered Dan's heart.

"I promise. I'm bringing her back. We'll visit here occasionally, but I know where my girls need to be. I'm bringing her home. You have my word." Dan tried to erase the numerous child trafficking cases he'd worked in his decade as the Chief of Elite from his mind. My God, his baby out in Dallas. He was sick.

"Thank you," Malani managed in a heartbroken whisper. "We just love her so much, and she hasn't been herself in so long. Not until she met you, and you saved her."

Disbelief rocked through Dan. He wasn't her savior. It was the other way around. "Believe me, she'll always be my conquering angel, so if this is what I need to do to make her whole, then no one will stop me."

Fionna appeared with her eyes swollen and bloodshot from her sobs.

"Hey, baby," Dan soothed and let Malani know that she'd entered the room.

"Try to get her to talk to you, and maybe try to talk to Gretta. Tutu's shouting that she's sending her a crate. It'll be there Tuesday, she says," Malani concluded with a slight chuckle.

"Thank you and tell her thanks too." Dan ended the call and drew Fionna into his chest.

"Who was that?"

"Malani."

"What were you talking about?" She asked with more tonality as she raised her head to study Dan.

"You."

Dan lifted Halia out of her car seat and guided Fionna to their bed.

"What did she say?"

"How much she loves you and how badly she wants you to move back home."

"What else did she say?" Fionna demanded. She knew. She always did.

"She told me a little bit about your dad and what your life was like after he moved you away. Things you've never really told me." Dan gave Halia her bottle and leaned to kiss Fionna's cheek. "I hope that's okay."

"I tried to tell you. I still don't understand much of it. It was awful until I met you. There were parts that were fun, and I did love being an Angel. I loved doing all of the service jobs. I lived for that, but..." She shrugged and caressed her hand over Halia's head.

"Did you ever think about moving back to Kauai before we met?"

"Not really." Fionna scooted closer to him. "Garrett got me

through the academy, and I was recruited out of Venton to be on the Angels. That seemed like something I shouldn't turn down. I had good friends, and my life seemed perfect from the outside. No one knew about Mama here, and Daddy never wanted to talk about her. Gretta finished raising me, and she made certain if I wanted to go to Kauai that I got to go. I lived at home with them for several years after I graduated. I traveled all the time with the Angels. Daddy hated that, so in my book I had everything I wanted." She shuddered as her body rejected her own rebellion.

"When I got more and more desperate and lost, I bought the house in Alexandria. I tried so hard to turn it into somewhere that reminded me of Kauai and that was me. But I didn't know who I was anymore so I couldn't. But when I was there, I was sort of happy, but my wilder days followed me there. That's when I started dating Jared. I think I was punishing myself for all the wild things I'd done. I told you I was a mess before I met you. I know you think I saved you, but that's not ever how I'll see it."

Dan smiled at her tenderly. "I wish I'd understood what you'd been going through when I was letting you save me. I feel like an asshole. I had no idea you were so miserable."

"I wasn't miserable," Fionna combatted. "When I was with you, I was happy. That's what I'm saying. You are everything to me. I can make it without Kauai as long as I have you, but I can't make it even on my island without you and our baby girls."

Dan lifted Halia to his shoulder and caressed Fionna's beautiful face. He wiped away the beginnings of another round of tears. "I want you to have both," he whispered. "You waited long enough for me to run like a mad man down a road that led me nowhere good because I was so hell-bent on revenge. So, now, let's head toward the life that's waiting on us on *our* island."

She gave him his smile, even after everything their day had held. His heart skipped several beats as he gazed down at her.

"I'm so sorry, baby, about what your dad said, and about Nana, and mostly about the fact that your father didn't see what he was doing to you. I know I can't take all of that away, but please let me be there for you and try to make this a little easier."

"Thank you." She fell to Dan's other shoulder and let him share in her burdens.

"Can I snuggle too?" Aida's face contorted in a deep yawn. She moved into the room as her parents chuckled over how sweet their little blessings were.

"Come here, baby girl."

CHAPTER 4

TRIALS AND TRIBULATIONS

To Dan's shock, Nana had made slight improvements over the weekend. Dan had called and checked on her by way of Gretta. Fionna's father was still being a prick, and Dan refused to allow Fionna to be on the receiving end of another of her father's scathing remarks. So Gretta phoned Dan, and he phoned her to check on Nana.

Fionna had a horrendous weekend. She'd suffered cramping to the point that she was in tears. Dan had phoned Adeline panicked. Adeline had assured him that Fionna's body was dispensing with the last of everything it held from carrying Halia, and that Fionna's stress levels always affected her menstrual cycles. She'd offered to call in a light pain medication, but Fionna had refused the prescription.

Dan had begged her to take it, but she'd explained, less than patiently, that pain medication affected her rhythms and that she would suffer through with Dan casting her and taking over the counter medications.

To say that he was exhausted when he arrived at Venton Monday morning would have been a serious understatement. They had one week until exams.

With a deep breath, he stepped into his senior level defense class.

The disciplinary meeting with Katherine Bryant, regarding her insanity at the lingerie shop, was during his off period.

"I cannot believe what that witch did," Ben spat. The entire class nodded their agreement.

It seemed all of his students were eager to discuss Mentor Bryant's actions with the press and the disciplinary hearing. Dan debated how to handle the situation. They went over the legalities and the options available to Dan and Fionna. They reviewed what a libel case would likely bring. There were numerous questions about Mentor Bryant's reasoning and her husband working at Venton.

Dan was deeply impressed with his seniors by the time the bell rang. He was, however, overwhelmed several minutes later. His Shield students lined the hallways holding signs up supporting Dan.

Fionna was standing in the corridor beaming as she read the posters declaring that Mentor Vindico loved his wife and Dan and Fionna forever. There were several posters denouncing Mentor Bryant as well. There were pictures of Dan teaching pasted beside pictures of Mentor Bryant in her classrooms. "Mentor Vindico would never cheat," was written under Dan's. "Our mentors should be capable of telling the truth," was written under Bryant's. Dan put his arm around Fionna and kissed her cheek, eliciting cheers from the crowd.

"You may not like the job, son, but you certainly seem to have left your mark." Governor Vindico slapped Dan on the back and gestured toward the throngs of students.

"Are you feeling any better?" Dan asked Fionna as they followed his father into the conference room.

"Much better, just still a little weak." Fionna gave Dan his smile. It seemed that having the majority of the Ioses Predilect vowing his fidelity and adoration to his wife had her elated.

She'd performed the cast Gifted women did to flush their body of menstrual fluid in two days' time instead of the customary week that the Non-Gifted had to endure, and she seemed almost back to normal.

"Dan, Fionna." Jack entered the room a minute later. "George Sapman is going to preside."

Dan wondered what Governor Sapman would decide. Of all of the governing board, he was by far the most conservative. He also didn't care for Dan's championing Jeff, and Dan had told him off when Becca had been hospitalized.

Fionna studied Dan. She'd picked up on his energy tensing as soon as he'd heard that Governor Sapman would be hearing the trial. Normally, a disciplinary hearing would be heard by the chancellor and school governing board. Since Dan's father was now serving as chancellor, that wouldn't be happening. The Crown Governor would never be asked to step in for something as mundane as a Venton disciplinary hearing. Governor Willow would also be viewed as biased to Dan as he was the Governor of Iodex and had been Dan's boss for many years.

Governor Eleanor had ties to Dan and Fionna as well since she was the governor over the Auxiliary Department, and Dan and Fionna were currently employed as the spokespeople for their international adoptions program. Governor Vanzlant, who'd taken Peterson's spot, was over the finance department and Senate banks, and would have been a viable choice had she been in town.

Dan pulled Fionna closer and kissed the side of her head. He inhaled her heavenly island scent and let it soothe him. Academy Governor Sherman and Governor Hutchison seated themselves at the conference table in the front of the room.

Mentor Bryant entered the conference room in a fitful huff. She took in Jack talking to Dan and Fionna and made a dramatic eye roll. "Jack Stariff representing you at a school disciplinary hearing. Why am I not surprised?" she sneered at Fionna.

Jack bristled, but Dan beat him to the punch. "At some point, Mentor Bryant," he drawled her name like it was poison to his tongue, "you're going to learn not to mess with me. I don't take something like an accusation that I abuse my wife lightly. I am a Shield, and I will use every resource available to me to keep her safe."

Governor Sapman entered before she could make a retort. He shook Governor Vindico's hand and exchanged pleasantries. After offering Dan and Mentor Bryant a nod, he took the seat at the center of the conference table.

"Dan, it seems your students don't like what we all saw in the papers any more than I did."

"Kids don't like being lied to, sir." The fury he'd felt as he realized what Bryant was up to in the lingerie store flooded his energy.

Mentor Bryant gave an audible huff with another eye roll. "Yes, Governor, Mentor Vindico has become very popular with the upperclassmen after giving out free advice on intercourse."

Governor Sapman looked stunned momentarily. He eyed Dan in shock. The academy governors looked equally confused.

"Let's get this done. We all have jobs to return to," Governor Sapman finally ordered.

Jack gave Mentor Bryant his customary chuckle that said nothing about this trial concerned him because he had the case in the bag. It was a chuckle Dan had heard many times. It was meant to shake his opposition's confidence whether he had everything figured out or not. It would take a person who'd been involved with as many cases with Jack as Dan had to recognize it. Dan fervently hoped that this time Jack wasn't bluffing.

"All right, Dan, I have a note that you'll be providing another piece of evidence," Governor Sapman requested.

"Yes, sir." Dan pulled his wallet from his back pocket and supplied the receipt from Guinevere's that had handwritten descriptions and prices of everything he'd purchased.

Governor Sapman glanced over the receipt but looked uncomfortable knowing what kinds of things Dan had purchased Fionna. Governor Vindico sat off to the side and offered his son a sympathetic gaze.

"Mentor Bryant, as was reviewed in the documentation you received, Mentor Vindico has filed a formal complaint against you, citing that you were in Guinevere's Lingerie and Erotic Gifts Boutique when he entered the shop last week and that you phoned the press and planned on exiting with him when he left the store.

"He phoned his wife, Fionna Vindico, and had her come to the store because he was so concerned about your plans. I would also note that it seems obvious to me, and to anyone who's even moderately aware as to what's being printed in the papers, the fact that Mrs.

Vindico must've left their newborn daughter in someone else's care in order to rush to her husband's side does give credence to his allegations," Governor Sapman pointed out while Dan tried to hide his smirk.

"When she arrived, Mentor Vindico alleges that you became an informant for the press and shared with them information about his purchases while in the store. He has just given documentation proving the story in the paper wrong." Governor Sapman held up the receipt to the school governors but didn't show them what was written there. "This also gives credence to his complaint, Mentor Bryant," Governor Sapman warned. "Do you have anything to add to that, Dan?"

"If I may, Governor," Jack leapt. Governor Sapman nodded his approval as Mentor Bryant gave another dramatic eye roll. "I do have confirmation that Katherine Bryant was in Guinevere's prior to Dan's arrival per store manager Contessa DeRyan. She ID'd a photo and did give written testimony to the fact that Mentor Bryant made several derisive comments about Dan's purchases and made several phone calls while she was in the store. Mrs. DeRyan also added that Ms. Bryant asked to see what the store calls customer cards. They have cards on their customer's preferences and sizes. The store has those records on Mrs. Vindico, although I feel it necessary to state that I shouldn't know that, nor should anyone sitting here, save Dan and Fionna. Nonetheless, Mentor Bryant had the audacity to request Mrs. Vindico's cards but was denied access.

"Mrs. DeRyan did explain to me that even Dan would not have been given a copy of the cards. Only employees of the store may see them and then use them at their discretion to help a shopper. Mrs. DeRyan did sign an affidavit to the information she provided me and was willing to go under oath." Jack shot Katherine Bryant a derisive glare.

Dan felt Fionna draw from him heavily. His heart ached. She was glowing crimson. Jack was right. No one seated at that table had any business knowing that Fionna frequented Guinevere's or what she purchased there. Fury lit like a flame through him. Dan leveled a hate-fueled glare on Katherine Bryant. His shield sizzled around him, tingeing red.

Governor Sapman did offer Fionna an uncomfortable smile. He seemed to be considering something as he turned to Mentor Bryant. "Mentor Bryant, do you have anything to say in your own defense before I begin questioning?" Even he seemed shocked by the sheer amount of effort Jack had gone to for a disciplinary hearing.

"I don't get the impression me saying anything at all is going to matter," she quipped.

Governor Sapman narrowed his eyes. "You'll find, Ms. Bryant, that I'm not impressed with martyrs or people who rely on their victim mentality to get them out of trouble. Now, if you have something to say, the floor is yours. If not, I'd like to begin questioning. I will also take this opportunity to remind you that my daughter is a student here at Venton, and as a national governor of this Realm, I can recommend you be replaced."

Mentor Bryant held out her hand. "Go on with your questions, Governor."

"Were you in Guinevere's Boutique when Mr. Vindico arrived and began shopping?"

"Yes."

"Did you phone any press agency while you were in the store with Dan Vindico?"

"I don't recall," she lied outright. A defiant smirk formed on her pursed lips.

"You don't recall," Jack challenged.

"Jack…" Governor Sapman shook his head. This wasn't a Senate trial. This was a school disciplinary hearing. "Let me say this. I may not have always seen eye to eye with Mr. Vindico when we worked together for over eight years, but it does seem to me that he would not have phoned the press himself. There were pictures of him and his wife exiting the boutique in numerous papers, so think back, because I would like an answer to my question. Now."

Dan wrapped his arm over Fionna. Katherine Bryant needed to be taught a lesson. He would never deny the fact that he had ins with most of the governing board. His own father had been a Realm Governor for thirty years. He himself had held the highest-ranking law enforcement position for a decade. It might not have ever been fair, but Mentor Bryant needed to stop trying to defy the system and realize that Dan wasn't the guy she wanted to mess with.

"Yes, I phoned the *Realm Times*."

"Why would you do something like that?" Governor Sapman demanded.

"It was high time the Realm learn that Dan Vindico isn't some innocent governor's son who should be pitied. He's incapable of following rules. He was as incapable of it when he was Chief of Iodex as he is now as mentor. He's done nothing but buck the system since he arrived at Venton and stuck his nose in things that he had no business involving himself in. It is interesting to me that since his father stepped in as chancellor, things like the fact that Mentor Vindico's amative energies class which began with seventy-five juniors and seniors swelled to almost one hundred thirty students, and no one said a word. I wonder why students would be willing to skip their assigned class to take his," she feigned confusion.

"Excuse me, Katherine, but I take offense to that implication," Governor Vindico immediately stepped in. Governor Sapman would never call down Governor Vindico, who not only outranked him in position but in decades of service. "For your information, of the seventy-five students in Dan's amative energies class, the lowest grade on the exam was an eighty-nine. As the exam is based on the curriculum, I would take that to mean that his students understood the curriculum enough to perform well on the exam. If students are skipping class and are caught, that is dealt with per Dean's rules. Furthermore, if you have a problem with my son, you are free to file for a disciplinary hearing as well."

Governor Sapman nodded. "I will also add that another of Governor Vindico's children has come before the board, and he voted to have her detained and then put in rehab for the maximum amount of time for the crime she'd committed, so I have no evidence to support the accusation that he would give Dan special favors."

Dan had never thought Lindley's wild stunts and drug use would come in handy, but he decided he might call and thank her as she just gave their father a viable example that he would never show preference to his children if they'd done something wrong.

"Dan, would you like to add anything in response to Mentor Bryant's admittance that she did call the *Realm Times*?" Governor Sapman brought everyone's attention back to the hearing.

Dan narrowed his eyes. "I fail to see the logic in her premise. If she disagrees with my teaching methods, how does her having news organizations photographing me leaving Guinevere's help her prove her point? I'm certainly not ashamed that I purchase my wife lingerie, although I would prefer to keep those purchases between the two of us."

"Point taken, Mentor Vindico," Governor Sapman allowed. "I will say this escapade you orchestrated, Mentor Bryant, is almost childish in its very essence save the nature of the store, of course. Did you intend to have yourself photographed leaving the store with Mentor Vindico?"

"No, certainly not," Mentor Bryant lied with ease.

Fionna scowled. The deception might not be apparent in her words, but it flooded her energy.

Jack went to bat again. "May I just interject that Dan is not only a powerful Ioses Predilect, but he is also an extremely rare Visium Predilect of equal power. It seems to me his abilities might've granted him a little insight."

Governor Sapman nodded as Governor Sherman made a note on a yellow pad she was keeping close to her chest.

"I cannot stand to be around Mentor Vindico or his precious wife," Bryant sneered hatefully. "Why would I want to be seen leaving a store with him?"

"Excuse me," Dan fired right back, "my wife is not the one being brought up for discipline. She is here because of the nature of the hearing and to support me which she has always done. You had no reason to attack her, and you owe her an apology."

"Oh well, excuse me, Mrs. Vindico, please accept my most humble apology. I certainly wouldn't want to upset the Angel," Mentor Bryant mocked.

Dan's entire body vibrated in fury. His shield pulsed like he'd been hit.

Fionna shook her head. "Governor Sapman, may I please say something, sir?"

"Certainly, Mrs. Vindico," the governor allowed.

"You know, Katherine, Dan and I certainly don't know you. I'd never even spoken to you until the Fall Ball. But there are things that I know just from being around you. I can feel how sad you are, and I can feel your desperation, and your jealousy, and your guilt, and even your shame. I'm a Receiver after all," she reminded Mentor Bryant gently. "I'm sorry for everything you're feeling, and believe me, I do understand that it isn't much fun for the entire Realm to think they know all about the circumstances of your life." Fionna swallowed harshly.

"I've been there, but I also know that there is so much more to you and to every situation in your life than what is being printed in the papers. So, I'm asking you, from one woman to another, from one mother to another, please stop taking out all of your frustration and embarrassment on my husband. He did not do this to you, and I'm not trying to place blame. Like I said, I know everyone on the outside sees one tiny part of the huge story and thinks they understand. But there isn't even one tiny part of this that's Dan's fault. I know sometimes it's easier to blame someone else and try and demonize them, but please stop," Fionna begged. "It isn't getting you anywhere. Ultimately, you're only making it so much worse for yourself. I don't want that for you. Whatever our differences or your feelings about me, I want you to be happy and healthy, and all of this,"—Fionna gestured her hand out to the documents lying on the table—"isn't either of those things."

Everyone in the room including Katherine Bryant was stunned. Everyone except for Dan. He gazed at his wife in awe. He kissed the side of her head sweetly. Dan had gone in guns blazing ready to crush Mentor Bryant with evidence and reason, but it was much more difficult to enact vengeance on someone who had just admitted that they genuinely wanted the best for you.

Governor Sapman raised his eyebrows in deep impression to Governor Vindico. Dan saw his father nod his recognition of his daughter-in-law's deep wisdom and empathy.

"Unless the academy governing board has any other questions, I think I'm ready to move on with what I feel should happen," Governor Sapman offered the floor up to Governors Sherman and Hutchison.

"I'm not certain what Governor Sapman will decide, Mentor Bryant, but I have a few things I would like to add," Governor Hutchison leapt. "As a governor of this academy, I must urge you to show us that you are capable of making better decisions. From what I've seen for the last few years right up to this little stunt you've pulled, I would say that unless I see a dramatic turn for the better, we will not be offering you a contract next year," he threatened.

"And I will echo what Mrs. Vindico put so eloquently. All of the things that you're going through right now lie with you and Dean alone. If you want to be mad at someone, why don't you start there. Either take responsibility for your actions and conduct yourself with maturity and decency, or you can find employment elsewhere."

He shifted his body to Dan. "Mentor Vindico, I am sorry for the embarrassment and anger that this has most certainly caused you and your wife. I will also admit to partially agreeing with Mentor Bryant's accusations toward you. I, for one, would like to hear more about your amative energies class growing to nearly double its assigned size, and I do not feel that you have a tremendous amount of respect for the long-standing rules of Venton Academy and the way things have always been done."

"You can't have progress without change. Just because something has always been done one way doesn't make that the only way or the right way," Dan defied.

"I agree with that as well," Governor Hutchison nodded. "And I would like to hear your opinions. If you'd come by my office, I have your contract for next year, and perhaps we could chat about making some changes on both of our parts."

Dan sighed. Every time he tried to keep anything in his life personal, someone announced it in public. "I'd be happy to discuss curriculum changes with you, Governor Hutchison, but I won't be signing a contract for next year."

Katherine Bryant was visibly shocked as were the school governors.

"What?" Governor Sherman huffed. "You can't quit, Mr. Vindico."

"I was going to tell you soon, so that you can begin looking for my replacement, although I firmly believe you should offer the job to Mentor Jackson. He would make an outstanding head of Ioses Order. But as Governor Hutchison just pointed out, I don't think I'm the man for this job."

He knew what the academy governors actually heard him saying was that he had no intention of changing. If they'd known him a year before, they would be just as shocked as his family at the dramatic changes he'd made.

But Dan knew that a man could never be something that simply wasn't in him. Dan was not a teacher. He was a Shield. The need to protect shaped every facet of his personality and every rhythmic pulse of his energy. He'd been put on this earth to keep others safe. Scholera Predilects were the teachers.

Governor Sapman cleared his throat and brought everyone's attention back to the hearing. "May I?"

"Please, Governor." Governor Sherman was shooting Dan disappointed glares.

"Mentor Bryant, I feel a public apology by means of both the academy newspaper and the *Realm Times* is appropriate in this case. Please apologize to the Vindicos for your actions, and let's let it rest at that. When my boys and Becca would argue growing up, my wife would usually separate them on different floors of our home. That seems fairly logical here as well. Stay away from Dan and Fionna. I think that will probably solve a myriad of problems."

Mentor Bryant nodded but she was still studying Fionna. It wasn't the hate-fueled wrath that Dan had come to expect in Katherine Bryant's glares. She seemed genuinely surprised that Fionna knew what she was feeling, and that she was willing to forgive her indiscretions and even be polite.

"And I think we'll call that a day." Governor Sapman stood and shook the academy governors' hands.

"Mentor Vindico, I for one would like to speak with you regarding your decision to leave Venton, and as a longtime opposer to amative energies classes altogether, I would like to discuss just what went on in your amative class this year," Governor Sherman ordered. Dan rolled his eyes.

Anxiety and anger rolled off of Fionna in waves. She was worried he was going to be reprimanded and angry that someone disagreed with him. Dan would never deserve her.

He winked at her. "Don't worry, sweetheart. I don't give a damn what they think."

"I just want to go home," she confessed with a sigh.

"Go on, baby," Dan urged. "I'll be there in a little while."

"Mentor Vindico," Governor Sherman spat. With a sigh, Dan eased away from Fionna and followed the governor toward her office.

CHAPTER 5
SHIELDS
~FIONNA VINDICO~

"Dan's not going to get into trouble, right?" Fionna begged her father-in-law as they headed toward his office. Exhausted, frustrated anger coursed through her rhythms. Fionna drew a deep breath and felt her body begin to soothe itself. Nothing made her angrier than someone coming after her husband.

Governor Vindico gave her his kind smile. She wanted to hug him and let him know that Dan was going to miss him as much as the governor was going to miss his son. She wasn't yet certain how, but she knew that Governor and Mrs. Vindico would be visiting them on Kauai quite often. She could feel it.

"I don't think so, sweetheart. I doubt there's anything the board can do that would bother Daniel. If the people making the offer don't have any of the cards you want, you've taken away all of their power. You've removed their options. Dan's always been good at that."

Fionna's face pulled into a smile. She loved the way pride was always Dan's father's primary emotion whenever he thought about his son. She could always feel it whenever she was near Governor Vindico.

"Kiss my grandbabies for me." He waved to Fionna.

"I will." Fionna headed out the door of the administration building.

Why does she have to feel so lost and miserable? Fionna sighed as she thought about Katherine Bryant. *I want to be mad at her, but I just feel so sorry for her.* Glancing to her left, Fionna winced slightly. There were two girls walking toward the Occamy building. *Desperation for approval* rolled off of one. *Haughty disdain* coursed through the other, and just like always, there was nothing Fionna could do to soothe either of them.

She tightened her coat around her and tried to tap into the rhythms of Kauai. *Why does it have to be so far away?* She fought back a whimper as the freezing winds lashed at her soul. Her head jerked to the right. *Lust and vulgarity* pulsed from a young man staring at her as she headed toward the car.

Fionna turned her head back to the administration building. *It's closer to the car,* she told herself as her customary longing for Dan ramped into overdrive. An energy she recognized had her receptors relaxing.

"Hey, Mrs. Vindico, how'd the hearing go?" Jeff jogged to catch up with her. Fionna smiled. Jeff Strenton had one of the kindest, most sincere emotional energy strains she'd ever felt.

"Good, I guess. Mentor Bryant has to apologize in the papers. I kind of feel bad for her though," Fionna admitted. Jeff's brow furrowed and *confusion* shifted in his rhythms.

"But that's good because then everyone will know that Mentor Vindico would never hurt you or cheat on you. That's what she wanted people to think, right?" *Justice* for what was right was drowned quickly by Jeff's *deep respect and admiration* for Dan. A broad grin formed on Fionna's face. She supposed that Jeff's marvel of her husband might have something to do with why she thought his emotion strains were so nice.

"I don't really think Mentor Bryant has any idea what she wants. She just keeps making terrible decisions because everything about her is so erratic. She's lost herself completely." Fionna tried to explain to Jeff but was aware he probably wouldn't understand. Only Dan seemed to understand her.

"I'm going home to pick up Becca. We're going to see Adeline before I have to be at work."

Fionna debated reaching out and touching Jeff's hand. *Fear and anxiety* overtook him. He was worried about the baby and worried about Becca and worried that no matter what, he just wasn't good enough.

"That's sweet of you to go with her. I know that means a lot to her. You're a great husband, just like Dan," Fionna supplied the things she knew he wanted to hear. They were all true.

"Thanks." *Hope* began to quell his *fear.* "I'll see you later." Jeff waved as he rushed toward his truck.

"Bye," Fionna called as she continued her trek to her car. Suddenly, her body convulsed. She trembled and searched the surrounding area. Her rhythms tensed and churned around her. Her heart raced, and she broke out in a sweat.

Hatred and fear pulsed in jagged arcs from behind her. Fionna spun around and swallowed back the bile that flooded her throat.

Clarence Pendergrath was moving toward her. Every muscle in Fionna's body began to tremble as he glared and paced faster in her direction. His eyes narrowed and *spite* and *vengeance* shifted from the fear in his energy strains.

"Well, well, well," he drawled. He looked so much like his father Fionna shook her head. She didn't want to see his face. It brought back too many horrifying memories. "Where's Mentor Vindico now?"

"Clarence, this isn't you." Fionna tried to soothe him. "Stop and think."

But suddenly Fionna felt her rhythms ease. The hatred and violent energy growing from the fear was muted somewhat. She was in someone's shield. Jeff, she realized. She recognized his rhythms.

"Stay the hell away from her, Pendergrath. I can have Vindico out here in about a half a second, and I would not want to be the guy messing with his wife when he gets here," Jeff threatened as he came into Fionna's vision and then stepped in front of her. He'd thrown his shield from several feet behind her.

But suddenly, Fionna's receptors lit in warning. Jeff's shield wasn't strong enough to contain her power, only Dan's was. She shook from the force.

Clarence Pendergrath's fury began to force his mind to make the disconnect that came just before people did heinous things. She saw heat begin to form in his hand.

"Clarence no," Fionna pled. "Listen to me. I know you're scared, and I know it's easier to be angry. But you don't have to be like your father. You don't have to live his mistakes. Just stop and walk away. Don't do something now that you can't take back. You won't get another second chance." *Confusion* and *sadness* coursed through Clarence. "I know you're a better man than he ever was. I know you feel all alone, but you don't have to be."

But then, Fionna saw him coming. Her Shield. Her conquering angel. Dan sprinted to them. He must've seen them out the glass doors of the building. Jeff's shield moved off of Fionna as Dan shoved Clarence back.

"You stay the hell away from my wife or so help me I will bury you right beside your daddy," he growled. *Fierce hatred* consumed Dan. Fionna hated to feel that in his rhythms, but she was so thankful he was there. Clarence recoiled in abject terror as Dan's fist flew back.

"Mentor Vindico," rang from Jeff.

"Dan, no," Fionna gasped. "He just wasn't thinking."

"Leave, now," Dan menaced. Fionna shivered. It always shocked her how the man's energy that conquered her every fear, soothed her every worry, and that had nothing but adoring love when he thought of her could look and sound so terrifying and violent.

She edged closer to Dan. She just wanted to touch his arm, to feel his strength and his love. She needed to soothe him. Clarence glared hatefully at Dan.

"Don't ever come near her again," Dan snarled.

With a defeated sneer, Clarence turned and slithered away. Dan cradled Fionna in his arms. Her heart soothed. She wanted to beg him to cast her, to put her in his shield so she didn't have to feel anything but him. Life had just been too much lately.

Stop being so weak, she commanded herself, but she tucked farther into his embrace. His energy was astounding. It was so powerful and so full of his complete acceptance and adoring love for her. Being inside of his rhythms was the only place she ever felt safe. That was the only time she ever felt truly alive. Fionna knew she could never survive without him.

"Are you okay?" he whispered. Fionna nodded her lie, but he knew. He always knew. "I didn't think so." Her body relaxed in his arms. He cradled her head to his chest and allowed her to hide herself completely in his embrace. He didn't even care that she'd just lied. "It's okay," he soothed. "I've got you." Fionna felt his powerful hand gently brush away tears she hadn't realized she was shedding. His touch was so tender and reverent she shivered from the caress. "Why don't I take you home?" His deep voice reverberated through her heart.

"It's okay. You need to work. He just wasn't thinking. He misses his dad. He's scared and he considered giving in to the vengeance."

"Yeah, I know," Dan assured her. "That's precisely why the sooner we leave the better."

She still couldn't believe he was taking her home. It was more than she'd ever even allowed herself to consider. She couldn't have Kauai and Dan, and if she had to choose, she would always choose him. Moving back to the farm and having him seemed like more than any woman could ever even dream of having.

"Hey, thank you. You've been wanting to make up for what little we did for you and Becca—well you're paid up and then some," Dan assured Jeff.

Embarrassment rolled heavily in Jeff's waves.

"No, sir. I saw the look on his face when he headed her way. I got over here as fast as I could. That was nothing. I mean, I'm a Shield. That's what we do."

"I saw him head toward the parking lot. It took me half a second to figure out that she probably hadn't gotten to her car yet. I left Governor Sherman midsentence," Dan admitted. He chuckled and Fionna smiled.

"Thank you both." She pulled away from Dan begrudgingly.

"Let me see if I can get Mentor Jackson to cover my next two classes," Dan soothed. He was so incredibly sweet. No one had ever taken care of her the way he did.

"No, I'm okay." She did feel better, she decided. "Go teach. They have exams coming up."

"You're sure?" He studied her eyes.

"I'm sure."

He gave her a nod. "I'll be home before Aida. I promise."

Jeff waved goodbye as Dan guided Fionna toward the car. The bell rang and the parking lot flooded with students.

Guilt, desperation, glee, excitement, lust, happiness, sadness, fear, anticipation, copious amounts of envy—they all swirled around Fionna in a confusing mass. She drew a deep breath and tapped in to Dan.

"I love you, Maylea. I'm so sorry, baby," he soothed. He always blamed himself for everything. She felt the *guilt* course through him.

"Dan, you saved me, once again. This wasn't your fault."

He nodded but didn't believe her. He lifted her chin, and Fionna felt warmth flood her body as her heart picked up pace, and the confusing mass of emotion around her washed away with the touch of his hand.

"I love you," she whispered.

"Me too," Dan teased her. The phrase still meant so much to her. His rhythms always lilted in happiness whenever he said it. He wanted so badly to make her understand how much he loved her even if he hadn't been able to say the words for several months. Fionna smiled as she recalled the fact that all she'd wanted was to explain to him that she knew how much he loved her, she'd just never understand how she got so lucky.

Pained concern flooded Dan's energy as Fionna climbed into the car. He kissed her. "Be careful," he pled. She knew what those words always meant when they came from him.

"I love you too," Fionna beamed. Dan closed the door and backed away as Fionna reveled in the silence.

CHAPTER 6

RESTORATIONS

~DAN VINDICO~

Dan raced inside the house, not certain what he might find. Relief flooded his energy as he took in his beautiful wife standing at the stove stirring. Halia was in her bouncy seat on the counter. She was kicking her legs and listening to Fionna speak to her in Hawaiian.

She switched languages midsentence. "There's Daddy. I told you he would be here soon."

"Hey, baby girl." Dan kissed Halia's cheek and then repeated the motion with her mother. Halia began jostling her little body with both her arms and legs, keeping her eyes locked on Dan. He unbuckled her and lifted her into his arms. Dan beamed as Halia curled herself into his chest.

He lifted the lid on the pot on the stove.

"Yum, ham and potato," he groaned as Fionna beamed.

"Halia and I went to see Nana for a few minutes today." Sadness shadowed her previously content expression.

"Did you see your dad?" Dan willed away his anger at his father-in-law, but Fionna picked up on it immediately.

"He was at the bakery. Gretta asked if I'd go check on her while they worked."

"How is she?" He wasn't certain he wanted to know the answer to his question.

"Not so good." Her eyes closed.

Nana wasn't going to outlast Fionna's father's stubbornness. "If you want to go back tonight, I'll go with you." Halia began sucking on her fingers and the side of his tie. Dan edged the fabric out of her mouth with a chuckle.

"I'm going over there all day tomorrow. Daddy can just get over it," she decreed. Fionna wasn't usually stubborn, but she also knew how precious life was and that her grandmother wasn't going to be around much longer.

Dan would never have tried to dissuade her from going, but if her father said one word to her, he'd step in.

After dinner, he put Aida to bed while Fionna gave Halia a bath in the sink and gave her a bottle. When Dan finished one of the stories in a book Fionna had picked up for Aida, called *Don't Kiss the Frog*, he tucked his sleepy little girl in and kissed her head as she fell asleep.

Fury coursed through him once again though he tried to push it away. Clarence Pendergrath's confused and infuriated expression clouded his mind. *We have to get out of here.*

The shower water in the master bathroom began to fall, and the customary debate began in his mind. He couldn't push away the temptation. She was just too sweet, and he needed to feel her near him. If she wanted to be left alone, he certainly understood, but he wanted her desperately. It was a need acute to the point of pain. His shield longed for her rhythms.

Dan checked on the girls and then closed the bedroom door behind him. Fionna was standing at the sinks completely naked. She appeared to be examining her beautiful body, but where Dan felt his heart pick up pace and his groin react to the stunning sight, Fionna's face was turned in a dejected scowl.

"My God, you are beautiful," Dan urged in a hungry groan. He let his eyes trace up and down her luscious curves. Fionna looked genuinely confused, but he knew she had to have picked up on the lust and yearning in his energy.

He loved that she knew what he felt even if she struggled to believe his words. She turned into his arms and let him hold her. "My beautiful baby. Sweet as an angel and sexy as sin." She tucked into his embrace. "You know..." Dan drawled flirtatiously, "I could help you with your shower if you'd like." He let his hands trace tenderly down her back. Her energy spiked in an instant. She trembled in his arms.

Dan let his mind race back to having her in his arms as he swayed her body with his own on the dance floor of Anglington's Bar. Unable to stop himself, he'd let his hand work down her side and his thumb caress the perfect swell of her left breast. *She should have slapped the shit out of me,* he thought wryly. But she'd trembled against him then too. Her breaths had come in quick pants, and he was done for.

"And what would you like to help me with, Commander Vindico?" she breathed. Her calling him commander in her smooth, sultry tone had Dan groaning in need. That would be his title as soon as he got them the hell out of DC. That had been their decision the night before when she'd finally felt like really talking about it.

He began kissing his way from her neck to her breasts. "If you need anything washed, I could do that, but then, I want you to get wet and dirty for me." Fionna's energy tensed in tantric waves. "That sound good, baby doll?"

"I'm already wet," she informed him.

"Then go get in, and I'll take you dirty," he commanded.

Her eyes flashed as the storm in them ignited. She spun and stepped into the shower. Dan had his clothes off in record time and climbed in behind her. He lathered his hands in the Pikake Kukui soap that Tutu made that was Fionna's favorite. He began massaging her soft skin in his pliant hands. She moaned and relaxed in his muscled embrace as she allowed him to wash away the toxic world from her soul.

"I've got you, baby doll." He knew she was tired and frantic. Her energy was chaotic. She'd been trying futilely to soothe her own rhythms. He could feel her desperation to be restored by her island. They were leaving for the foundation blessing as soon as Dan gave his last exam. It would be a quick trip, just a few days, but he knew it would help.

Pendergrath's son, her grandmother, her father, the move, the disciplinary hearing, Dan becoming the commander of a state Iodex branch, and her cycle had all worn her down. She needed her Shield. She needed to forget everything but the two of them together, and that became his single focused goal.

"I'm gonna take it all away, sweetheart," he promised as her moans began echoing off the tiled walls. "Lean back and look at me, Maylea." Her body flinched as she tried to catch her breath. She was going to let him own her body. Let him dominate her thoughts and bring her peace, allow him to take her to the depths of ecstasy at his hands. Her eyes were ravenous as she locked them on his. "I'm gonna touch you, baby doll. See if I can't take the edge off. I need you to relax for me before I fill you full."

"Yes," moaned from her as her body continued to tense in need. Dan leaned in and braced himself on the wall with his forearm as his other hand sought the throbbing rise of nerve endings, raw from desperate need, between her legs.

He gently prodded and coaxed her. He circled his index finger just along her slit. Her body contorted for him.

"Look at me," he continued to command. She was insatiable. Her body consumed his fingers as he slipped them inside of her. A gasping moan shook through her as she kept her eyes locked on his. Dan grabbed her hand. He placed her own fingers over her clit. "Show me," he ordered as he continued to seek out her release from deep inside of her.

She went wild as she began caressing herself. Certain he'd never seen anything hotter, Dan nearly lost it all from watching her. He wrapped his arm around her with a hungry growl. Grasping her backside, he let his fingers play just along the center. He knew.

She came undone. Her hands flew to his biceps and she clawed him in ferocious need. Dan's eyes rolled back in his head. The pain was unadulterated pleasure. He spun her around.

"Hold on for me, sweetheart. I'm about to fucking ruin you," he warned.

"Oh god, yes." Her back arched, and she braced her body against the tile wall. Dan grasped her hips as he jerked her back over his aching cock. He began to pump her slowly and rhythmically.

Each and every rhythm of her body edged her closer and closer to climax. "Not yet, baby doll. Not yet. Be a good girl for me," he soothed as her body began to beg for air. Her head shook back and forth. "Let it build for me." He kept his voice low and in control. He pounded harder, burying himself deeper with each pass then pulling away, watching the slick heat coat him with her nectar.

"I'm gonna," she pled frantically.

"Not yet, you're not." He continued his build. "Not until I tell you. Never forget who owns this tight, little pussy." A moan in the tenor of a scream seared through her.

"That's it. Let me hear how good it feels," Dan growled as he watched her body beg for release. Her muscles clenched tightly around him. He could hardly move. It was exquisite. "You feel so damn good. Such a good girl. Waits 'til I tell her she can come," he vowed reverently. "I'm gonna lose it, honey. You're too fucking gorgeous. You ready to give it to me," he groaned as his body throbbed inside of hers.

"Please, please," she begged and whimpered.

"You say my name when I let you come," spilled from his mouth in a low, guttural growl.

He lost his rhythm and pounded relentlessly, only capable of taking more of her.

"Please, Dan," she pled.

"Come for me like a good girl." Her immediate release drove his, and he filled her full of everything he was and listened to her moan out his name.

He pulled away after the aftershocks quaked through him, so that she could fall in his arms and let him cradle her now languid, satisfied body to him.

"Feel better?"

"So much better."

"Good but I'm not done."

He began washing away his release. A sudden thought made him panic. She picked up on it instantly.

"I decided to just set the cast every morning, remember?" She reminded him of their decision from several weeks before. With their schedule still rather insane from having a newborn and a seven-year-old not to mention Dan's work, her dance classes, designing a new home, and continued discussions on Dan taking over Hawaiian Iodex, Fionna had suggested that she set the cast every morning when she woke up. That way there wouldn't be any more little Vindicos until they were ready.

She'd declared that it would be several years before she wanted more, and Dan had adamantly agreed. His only suggestion had been that he set the cast. If he set it, he was able to add in his own soothing energies and make certain that she felt none of the discomfort that came when she set it herself.

"I knew I hadn't done it this morning," he confessed his concern.

"You left early, so I did it."

"I'm sorry. I should have asked you before we started, and I should have done it before I left. I was trying to let you sleep, since Halia hadn't woken up yet."

"It's fine. You take such good care of me. You're amazing." With that, she turned her face into his neck and hid from the pouring water and from the drowning world. As he cradled her to him, he poured shampoo in his hands and began washing her hair. He used his powerful fingertips to deeply massage her scalp until she was moaning again and beaming at him.

"Can you take some more, sweetheart?" he soothed after he'd washed and conditioned her hair. "Can you be a good girl and take more of my cum for me? I need to fill you full."

"Oh god, yes," she sounded elated. With a cocky smirk, he turned her around and took her over again.

When they were finished, Fionna shut off the water and stepped out, as Dan heated them both towels and wrapped one around her.

CHAPTER 7

SHE KNOWS

Just after two o'clock, Fionna crawled back into bed after giving Halia her bottle. She laid her head on his chest. "Something is wrong," she choked.

"What?" He sat up. "With Halia?"

"No." She shuddered. Dan's cell phone rang a moment later and his heart sank. Fionna began sobbing before he'd even answered.

"Hey, Mr. Styler," he managed the greeting as he held Fionna on his shoulder. "She already knows." Fionna's father was the last person she needed to talk to just then, and she knew why he was calling at two in the morning. There was no question of who was going to tell Fionna that Nana had passed away. She already knew. "If you need help now, I can come over, but if the undertaker can take care of everything tonight, Fi and I will be there in the morning. Please tell Gretta how sorry I am," he offered as his parting line. Tossing the phone onto the bed, Dan wrapped both of his arms over Fionna and let her sob into his chest.

"I'm so sorry, baby," became his constant reassurance. Fionna cried herself back to sleep with Dan watching over her constantly. She'd been through so many horrible, painful experiences, he couldn't stand for her to hurt again. He understood her father's desperation to protect her and terror that something would happen to her. Mr.

Styler just hadn't been able to see that in all he'd done trying to protect Fionna, he'd hurt her worse than anyone.

When Dan heard Halia grunting just before six, he heat casted the sheets and slipped out of the bed. He fed Halia and called his father simultaneously. "I'm going to take Aida to school, then when we figure out all of the plans for the funeral, I can give you a better idea of when I'll be out," he explained to his father.

"Let us know if we can help with the girls. Tell Fionna how sorry we are, but please remember that your students do have to pass their exams next week," his father gently reminded.

"I know, Dad. I'm hoping we don't end up in Juarez until this weekend, but I just don't know yet. Taking the body back out of the country will be an ordeal. You know that."

"I'll sign the papers for you. Just take care of your girls," Governor Vindico pledged.

"You know I will." As he ended the call, Dan heard Aida's footsteps rush across the hallway upstairs.

"She knows Mommy's upset doesn't she, Halia." Halia's beautiful brown eyes stared up into Dan's as she finished her bottle. Her rhythmic sucks gave him solace. He carried her back up to the bedroom. She was cooing softly and didn't seem willing to go back to sleep.

Dan grinned as he took in Fionna and Aida curled up together watching cartoons. Fionna's eyes were swollen and red. Dan handed her Halia before he climbed in the middle of all of his precious girls.

"There's my little coconut." Fionna cradled Halia to her chest right beside Aida.

"Mommy felt sad, and I said that sometimes if school makes me sad that *Supernova* makes me laugh, so we decided to watch cartoons. You and Halia can watch too," Aida explained. This brought a broad grin to Fionna's face. The sight soothed Dan's soul.

"That sounds perfect, sweetheart, and then Daddy's going to take you to school this morning, okay?"

Aida nodded solemnly. She bit her lip and reached for Dan. He pulled her closer. "Did something bad happen?" Fear flooded her tiny rhythmic pulses.

"Kind of," Dan allowed.

She turned to Fionna. "Did your nana go away?"

Fionna dissolved into a puddle of tears. Dan immediately strengthened his shield around all of his girls. Halia began cooing. Much to Dan's delight, she seemed to revel in her father's shield just as much as her mommy and her big sister did.

"I'm so sorry," Aida soothed. Fionna clung to her tightly. "I think that your nana is in heaven with Mamãe and Pai and with your mommy that went away, and they will all be best friends, and they can have dinner together, and they can say that you're the very best mommy ever, and that Aida loves you so much."

Dan squeezed his eyes shut, trying to block out tears of his own as Fionna began sobbing harder.

"I think you're right, baby girl." Dan nodded.

"Halia thinks so too," Aida pledged.

He was always unable to believe the wisdom of his precious seven-year-old.

Dan fed Aida breakfast though she only picked at it.

"It's not as good as when Mommy makes it, is it?" Dan apologized.

"I like it better than the stew we ate at the orphanage," Aida offered hopefully. Dan tried not to laugh. He was certain that was not a compliment.

As so often happens, the nighttime tears and fitful sleep did seem to bring a renewed outlook in the morning light. Her grandmother had lived a long, inspiring life. She'd made her way in the world as a seamstress, and after Gretta's father's death, she'd turned quite a few heads around the town of Juarez. Never opposed to enjoying herself in the arms of a lover, she'd lived life to the fullest right up until the time that her body had given out long before her mind or her spirit.

Dan drove Aida to McCarron and then took Fionna and Halia to the Stylers' home. He shuddered slightly as they entered. Death always seemed to take up residence within the house for a brief time. It clouded the rooms with its recollections. The guilt always made the air more difficult to breathe. Sorrow permeated the beds and the tables and chairs along with the lives left behind. It crept slowly room to room, choking out the life of the home for a brief time.

Fionna drew from him in heavy doses. Dan kept his hand on hers. They both fought the urge to turn and run away. To flee to somewhere they could draw breath more easily and pretend the sadness never existed. Wishing to somehow separate yourself from the pain was normal, Dan supposed.

"Maylea." Gretta held the customary exhaustive smile of a caretaker whose subject had gone on. That smile was always sadder than tears.

"Gretta, are you alright?" Fionna rushed to her stepmother and hugged her. Dan saw her soothing energy work through Gretta.

"I'm all right, sweetheart. Nana was ready to go. It was me who wasn't ready," she explained. Mr. Styler and Dan shared an uncomfortable glance. Dan was still furious over what Fionna's father had said to her a few days before, and Mr. Styler was still smarting over Dan's throwing Fionna's rebellion in his face.

Dan stuck steadfastly by Fionna as she helped Gretta make the funeral arrangements. Governor Vindico stopped by the house on his way to the academy to sign all of the papers that would expedite moving the body back to Mexico. After being thanked heartily for his assistance, the governor offered his polite, "I'm so sorry for your loss," and then left for work.

As Nana hadn't really known many people in the US and certainly not in Arlington, Gretta decided only to hold a wake service in Juarez in Nana's home. A family gathering would be held Friday evening and the burial Saturday. Dan thought it would probably be best if Aida and Halia stayed in Arlington, but he wasn't certain what Fionna would want to do.

They discussed everything as they headed back home to await Aida's arrival on the bus. Dan sliced up an apple and added several spoonfuls of peanut butter to the bowl as Aida seated herself at the bar.

Aida grinned and set down a half-eaten slice of apple. She threw her arms around Fionna. "I wanted to come home and hug you all day. I was worried that you were still sad."

Fionna strengthened her hold of their little girl. "I am still a little sad, but your hugs make me feel so much better."

"And Daddy's hugs," Aida reminded her.

"Definitely. But listen to me for just a minute. Daddy and I are going to go to Juarez for Nana's funeral."

"I don't know if I went to my mamãe and pai's funeral and my brothers'. I think I forgot to remember."

Dan's heart ached. He wanted the death toll his family had suffered to halt. He didn't want his girls to hurt anymore. No more leis washing out to sea, no more burials, no more visits to place flowers on Amelia's grave, but death is a part of life. He heard his father's gentle prose when he'd finally cornered Dan and made him talk about his grandfather's passing.

"It's okay, baby, even if you weren't able to go," Fionna soothed her. "They're all still with you. Right inside your heart."

With a nod, Aida clutched her chest. "I feel them," she whispered. Dan and Fionna both blinked back tears as they nodded their understanding.

"You feel them because they love you so much and you love them so much," Fionna assured her as she spoke in the present tense. Aida nodded her adamant agreement.

"So," Fionna transitioned back to her original conversation. "Daddy and I were thinking it might be better if you and Halia stay here while we're gone." Aida's face fell as she nodded her understanding. "We'll only be gone for one night. Would you like to stay with Grandpa and Grandma or maybe we could see if Aunt Kara and Uncle Zach might stay with you."

"I want for Garrett to keep me," she begged.

"I'm sure Garrett would love to keep you. Would you like me to see if Rainer and Emily might help too?"

Aida nodded. Dan rather liked the thought that his girls would be in the care of two Elite Iodex officers, one of whom he'd trained.

"Okay, we'll call them," Fionna assured her.

CHAPTER 8

HIDE AND SEEK

Will met Dan at his car the next morning. "Garrett told me about Fi's grandmother. Is she okay?"

"You know how it goes. I'll think she's fine and go off and do something, then I come back ten minutes later and she's sobbing into a kitchen towel."

Will grimaced. "Brooke's grandmother passed back in the summer. She kept insisting she was fine while she cried on Lily Ana."

"We're leaving for Juarez right after my last class Friday. I think the service might help," Dan explained as he and Will made their way into the admin building.

"Garrett said he's watching Aida and the little coconut. He's excited."

"Aida's thrilled too."

"Hey, can I ask you something?" Will changed course quickly.

"Sure." Dan noted the serious tone in Will's voice all of a sudden. He lifted a notepad with the Senate Bank logo stamped on the heading. "Do you know Mentor Grace Peyton?"

"Not really, but her office is out in the mathematics building, I think." Dan tried to recall Mentor Peyton. He remembered being introduced at the first faculty meeting of the new school year.

Will nodded. "How about Mentor Owen Crydell?"

Suddenly feeling like he was being interrogated, Dan nodded. His brow furrowed as he studied Will. "He's one of my Ioses sub-freshman mentors. Pretty decent with his classes. Likes to party on the weekends. Why?"

Will ignored the question as he continued. "How about Mentor Chase Satzman?"

"Never heard of him, but what is this all about?"

"Let me make certain that what I think is happening is actually happening, and then you'll be the first to know," Will pledged as he made his escape.

Dan had assigned a paper the week before Thanksgiving in his Histories of Defense class that was due after lunch. He collected the many thumb drives that contained the assignment.

"Monday and Tuesday will be devoted to exam review, and your exam will be next Thursday at one o'clock. Everything we've gone over this semester is fair game. If I were you, I would study," Dan urged.

"Mentor Vindico, will this be on the exam?" throbbed against Dan's skull as he drove the quiet streets of his neighborhood Thursday evening. He was certain he'd never been asked a variant of the same question so many times.

Dan selfishly wished they didn't have to pack for Juarez that night. He longed to cuddle his girls on the couch and talk about their upcoming move or just watch television.

Fionna was standing on the front porch holding Halia. Frustration tensed in her rhythms contentiously. Carrie Leslie was beside her holding Annabelle.

Dan pulled the parking brake on the Ferrari and rushed toward them. "What's wrong?"

Carrie offered him a kind smile. "I think I'm just going to mention all of this to Chris once we get the kids to bed," she explained to Fionna before she headed back across the yard.

Without so much as speaking, Fionna stomped back into the house with a fretful huff. She handed Dan Halia. "Aida and Olivia are watching *Moana* in our bedroom," she informed him as he followed her inside. She sounded angry and embarrassed.

"Okay." Dan studied her. Trying a different tactic, he held Halia out so that she was staring into his eyes. "What's wrong with Mommy, my little coconut?"

Fionna smiled, but she was still looking out the living room windows. "I'm sure it's nothing. I'm just being crazy."

Dan cradled Halia back to his chest and took Fionna's hand.

"What happened?"

"I don't know. I had this weird feeling all day." Fionna's weird feelings held a great deal more weight than most people's.

"Weird how?"

"Remember, I told you this morning that Tutu said I needed to have a Maylea and Halia day because I've just been so stressed and sad about Nana, and my hormones are still so crazy and everything," she reminded him.

"Yeah, baby, I know." Dan had been thrilled Fionna was going to allow herself a whole day of doing things to help her recenter and help her empathic receptors calm.

"I went to class and then came home," she admitted hesitantly. She seemed to think she'd done something wrong. "Halia was asleep from the car ride, so I put her in the bassinet and went to take a quick shower." Dan nodded his understanding to keep her going. "I turned on the shower water and then my phone rang. I thought it was probably Daddy or Gretta calling from Juarez. I went back into the bedroom to answer it. I know this is crazy," she fussed. Her cheeks colored rapidly.

Dan didn't like the thoughts his mind was conjuring. "Keep going."

"It wasn't Gretta's number, and it wasn't an area code I recognized. I answered the phone, but no one was there. I figured they didn't have a good connection from their own cell phones in Juarez and for some reason weren't able to cast their phones, so they were using someone elses. So, I called Gretta back, and she said it wasn't her."

"What were you wearing when you answered the phone, honey?" He forced his voice to a calming thrum and tried not to alarm his wife.

"Nothing," she confessed with a slight shudder. "I was about to get in the shower. If Daddy and Gretta weren't in Mexico, I wouldn't have even answered, but I swear I didn't think about that at the time."

"This is your home. You did nothing wrong."

"After I showered, Halia was starting to fuss so I just threw on a pair of my old Angel shorts and went to get her bottle. After I fed her, we cuddled in the bed. She fell back asleep pretty quickly. I just laid her on our bed, and I put on that papaya kukui mask Tutu sent me, and I did stupid stuff that makes me feel better." Fionna's face was glowing crimson. Her rituals, though Dan was well aware of all of them, weren't something she wanted to discuss. She shouldn't have to. "The house was getting to me so I picked up as much as I could. I cleaned out my makeup drawers, and did some online shopping, went through some cookbooks, and then I reorganized all of my lingerie. Stupid stuff."

"It's not stupid. It's what you were supposed to do today. Remember?"

"I know," Fionna agreed. "I decided in light of me allowing myself a Maylea day before we go to the funeral, I wanted some of my coffee. So, I came downstairs to fix a pot."

Dan was well aware that Fionna frequently walked around topless. It was one of the many, many things he adored about his wife.

"Honey, you're not confessing to murder. You wanted coffee. You did nothing wrong," he continued to remind her.

"I don't know why I'm so nervous. I still feel…off. Anyway, I came downstairs and turned on one of my playlists and made coffee. I flipped through some magazines I hadn't had time to look at. I kind of got into just being alone except for with my little coconut. Her emotions are so easy to feel. It gets to be a lot when you can feel everything everyone else is feeling all the time. I just wanted some time with my own thoughts."

Dan certainly couldn't empathize, but he also couldn't fathom what Fionna must go through anytime she was in a crowd of people. She'd been with her parents quite a bit the last few days, and her father's disdain over their move coupled with Gretta's sadness and longing had been extremely difficult for her to navigate.

"Halia woke up again before I poured my coffee. I went back upstairs to get her and then fixed my coffee and settled back down on the couch. I still didn't have a shirt or bra on though."

"Nothing wrong, baby," Dan reminded her again. Fionna grinned suddenly. The sight overwhelmed Dan.

"Halia kind of likes my boobs. I think she gets that from you," she informed him with a giggle.

Dan laughed. "I'm certain she does. Probably for different reasons though."

"Anyway, we were snuggling, and I was drinking coffee and listening to music and then..." she paused, and Dan finished the inevitable end to this portion of the story.

"The doorbell rang."

He tried to keep his anger at bay by reminding himself that Fionna felt she was the culprit. His shield flared.

"How did you know that?"

"Remember what I did for a living for the last twelve years or so, and what I'm about to do again as soon as I get us the hell away from Arlington?"

"You think someone was watching me? Like a Peeping Tom?"

"We'll see. Tell me what else happened." He laid Halia out in his lap. She was carrying on an adorable conversation all her own.

"Obviously, I didn't answer the door. I was gonna call you, but you were in class."

"You can always call me."

"I know, but like I said, I hadn't put all of it together yet."

Dan willed calm by staring at Halia. "If Daddy finds out some perv is trying to see Mommy or one of my baby girls, I'll string him up by his binocular cord and shove his camera so far up his ass he'll be photographing the back of his teeth," Dan informed Halia in a singsong voice.

Fionna cracked up. Halia attempted a drooly smile as she heard her mother's laughter.

"Her first word is going to be ass," Fionna warned through her laughter. "Anyway, I kept us covered in a quilt and waited a long while before I got up and went and put on a shirt. I didn't want to walk by the front door," she pointed out unnecessarily. "I cannot wait to move to the farm," she added before she continued. Dan laced his hand through hers.

"I'm getting you there as fast as I can. Once we move, you never have to put a shirt on again as far as I'm concerned." He was still trying to shake the mental images of himself choking Fred Scheckles, who he suspected was behind this.

"I ate lunch and then Halia chewed on her little moose toy while we read that peek-a-boo book she likes with the mirror. She just wanted to be held so we snuggled. We did some baby yoga and played for a little while. Then someone knocked on the back door. I figured it was Carrie because they're the only ones that come to the back door. So, I answered, but no one was there. I figured either Annabelle or Parker were playing, so I went out, but no one was out there."

"Oh my God, stop!" Dan's entire body seized in horror. "Listen to me, you do not answer the door if you are here alone unless you are certain you know who is there. Second, do not ever, ever walk outside if someone rings the bell and then runs. Ever." He willed his lunch to stay in his stomach.

"Dan." Fionna rolled her eyes. "I'm not a child." He ground his teeth to remain quiet. "So, then I fixed Halia another bottle, and she'd been awake all that time so I knew she was going to sleep for several hours. I cleaned for a while and made bottles for her for this weekend. I looked at a few home design sites to get some ideas. I put stuff on my Pinterest boards, but then Tutu called and ordered me to have some of the tangerine ylang ylang tea and to take a bath to relax. There is one sure way I can kind of make myself relax in the tub." The violent crimson blush that blazed in Fionna's cheeks was the only explanation Dan needed as to what she'd done for a little while that afternoon.

"Absolutely nothing wrong, sweetheart. Although, I am now simultaneously infuriated and turned on."

Fionna squeezed her eyes shut and seemed to have to will herself to go on. "I was in the bath with all of the oils that kind of keep me going. We haven't been taking baths at night, and I need that."

"Done," Dan agreed. He took a moment to scold himself for not insisting on that. He knew perfectly well what those baths meant to both of them.

"So, you know," she shuddered. Her face contorted in her embarrassment.

"Honey, I cannot tell you how sexy that is. Please don't be embarrassed."

"Fine, so you know, candles, book, my favorite waterproof vibe," she confessed. Dan chuckled as he nodded his understanding. "Anyway, all of a sudden I heard this clattering noise and then I swear I could hear someone talking. I got out really quick and threw on my robe, but our bathroom is upstairs so no one could have seen me unless they were up a tree or something. But Carrie told me she thought she saw someone in their backyard this afternoon. She even called the police. They sent a car out and looked around but couldn't find anyone."

Leaning back slightly on the couch, Dan narrowed his eyes, bringing the Scheckleses' home into sharper focus. He stood and moved to the large window in the kitchen. He scanned their backyard and then the Leslies' back lawn. Something caught his eye. His focus honed as his detective skills came back at a moment's notice.

"Hold the baby for me just a second."

Halia nuzzled into Fionna's chest immediately, and her little hand did in fact seek out her mother's breast.

"That's the part she gets from me." Dan pulled his coat back on and marched to the Leslies' back yard.

Chris opened their back door. "Is everything okay?" He was obviously wondering why Dan was skulking around their children's swing set at dusk.

"No," Dan seethed. He pointed to a key chain in the dirt. There was no longer grass under the large wooden play area. "Is this one of your kids'?" He reminded himself that Chris Leslie was not his number one suspect.

Chris pulled the key chain from Dan's grasp and shook his head. As he brushed away the dirt, they both studied the design. It was a metal valet key ring but one of the slip rings was detached. The letters

SDEEMU were etched in black on one side. A picture of a deranged looking Emu was on the other.

"What the…" Chris spat.

"South Dakota Engineering and Electrical Management University," Dan reminded him.

"Go Emus." Chris shook his head.

"Has Fred Scheckles been playing on the swing set?"

"Not unless he'd like to be arrested for trespassing."

"Do you mind if I check something?"

"Go ahead." Chris turned curious. Dan tugged on the support beams of the swing set. After determining that it would more than hold his weight, he hoisted himself up on the bridge section. Gazing at the master bathroom window of his own home, he shook his head. If he couldn't see in it, then Scheckles certainly couldn't as Dan stood almost a foot taller than Fred. He hoisted himself up on the top support beam and carefully balanced before standing erect.

A long string of expletives spat from his mouth as he eased back onto the bridge and then landed on the ground.

"No." Chris grimaced. "Tell me he didn't," he begged. "What is that?" He pointed to the window Dan had been gauging.

"My master bathroom."

"And Fionna was?"

"Home all day alone with the baby."

"So, now are you going to have to kill me too because we had this conversation? I swear I'll never tell anyone where you hide his body. I can't leave Carrie with all five kids, and I kinda think it might be six here in a few months."

Dan did offer a begrudged chuckle. "Congratulations. Did you want to come watch me force a confession out of Freddy just before I force his dinner back out of him?"

"Sure. I've always been a big fan of making perverts puke." Chris was genuinely nervous, Dan could tell, but he did want to see Dan handle the situation. "Let me just tell Carrie where we're going."

CHAPTER 9

SHIELD IN THE WILD

Dan slipped the key chain back in his pocket and returned to his own home. Aida and Olivia were sitting at the bar, and Fionna was fixing them pieces of pizza she'd pulled from the oven.

"What's wrong?"

"I'm going to go have a little chat with Fred Scheckles. I'll be back in a few minutes."

"Oh my god. Please tell me he didn't." She shook her head. Dan pulled her close and kissed her forehead.

"I'm going to take care of it. I'll be right back."

Fury coursed through Dan as he stomped toward the Scheckleses' home. Chris met him in his trek. Cold wet leaves sloshed under Dan's boots as his fists clenched tightly over and over. He pounded on the Fred's door.

Betty answered. She was already wearing her house robe and slippers.

"I haven't let Freddy play with the lights anymore, Officer Vindico," she vowed. Her expression was a mix of panic and bewilderment.

"Where is Freddy?" Dan demanded.

"Who's there, Betty?" Fred called as he came to the front door from the kitchen. There was stew on his shirt and on his chin. "Well hiddy there, neighbors."

"Let's have a little chat, Fred," Dan demanded.

"Is this my induction to the Neighborhood Watch Patrol? Do I get a badge?"

As Dan's head shook in infuriated frustration, he glanced around the entryway of the Scheckleses' home. There, lying on the hardwood floor, was a binocular case. On the strap was a removable slip ring from a valet key ring. Red incensed fury pulsed in Dan's shield.

"What the fuck are you thinking?" Dan jerked the binocular case off the floor.

Betty gasped and clutched her chest.

"Now, calm down, Betty. I told you, you might hear words that we don't say in Pilmore," Fred soothed.

"Where were you this morning, Fred?"

"I was at work, of course. I just got home. I stopped and brought Mrs. Chris her paper this morning on my way out," Fred reminded Chris.

"That's right, he did." Chris sounded shocked.

At that moment, the Scheckleses' sons sauntered in from the kitchen. They were both tall and thin, unlike their father in stature and size.

The youngest, who appeared to be right around thirteen, let his eyes move from his father to Dan to the binocular case. Panic flared in his eyes.

"Is this yours?" Dan demanded.

"Yeah, that's Wen's bird-watching gear. Did you need to borrow some binoculars?" Fred did sound perfectly willing to let Dan borrow the binoculars.

"Bird-watching," Dan spat. All of the blood in Wendell Scheckles's face drained quickly to his feet.

"It's December in Virginia," Chris huffed. "What birds is he watching exactly?"

"Were you out of school today, Wendell?" Dan asked.

"Yes, sir."

"Wen just got back from the Middle School Beta Club field trip last night. He was so tired I decided to let him stay home with me today," Betty explained.

"I don't think Wendell stayed home all day," Dan informed her. With that, he pulled the other half of the valet ring from his pocket.

"I didn't know you were an Emu fan," Fred gasped.

"I'm not."

Chris stepped in. "We found that in my back yard, Wen. Do you have any idea where it might've come from?" His tone held the wisdom and patience of a father that knew he held the child in question by a key chain.

"I uh…I uh," Wen stammered. "I wanted to swing. I didn't think you'd mind," he managed and then looked rather impressed with his own lie.

"I don't think that's what you were doing, so why don't you tell your parents what you were really doing."

"Either you tell them, or I will," Dan commanded.

Fred and Betty turned to study Wendell. "I was just walking around," Wendell mumbled and refused to meet his parents' eyes.

"Bird-watching?" Fred quizzed.

"Yes, sir."

Dan considered his options. The likelihood that Wendell was going to make a full confession to his parents was fairly slim. Dan narrowed his eyes and glared at Wendell.

Shrinking away from Dan, Wendell kept his gaze locked on his sneakers.

"Bird-watching isn't against the law," Fred stated stupidly.

"No, it isn't," Dan agreed. "But trying to look in my windows while my wife was in the house, ringing my doorbell hoping you'd get a peek of a few things that I'd dare say you've only seen on a screen, and then climbing up on the Leslies' swing set so you could see in my bathroom window while my wife takes a bath, those are all against the law."

To Dan's shock, Betty Scheckles gasped and then rushed into the living room. She returned with a thick magazine and proceeded to beat Wendell about the head and back.

"Betty, Betty." Fred tried to hold her back. "It's perfectly normal to be curious."

Dan and Chris scowled. "It's not his fault that Dan's wife looks like she stepped right outta one of them girly websites he keeps looking at in his room."

With that, Betty began beating Fred with the magazine. Fred managed to grasp the magazine and remove it forcefully from his wife's hand. "It's not like she's even all that modest. I told you what they were doing that night when everything went kablooey. If she just looked more like you, nobody would want to sneak a peek at her. You can't blame the boy," Fred vowed stupidly.

Dan was certain he was going to lose his mind. "I can blame the boy, just as I would blame anyone at all that tried to look inside my home," Dan roared. His fury echoed off the walls. "Let me tell you something, Wendell," he menaced. "First and foremost, you need to respect other people's privacy and their property. It doesn't matter what my wife looks like or what she does, it is not a woman's responsibility nor is it her job to get you to show her respect and obey the law. She has the right to wear or not wear anything she wants, just like you have that right. When she is in our home and obviously when she is in our bathroom or our bedroom, that is entirely private. What you did today is against the law, and if you were just a few years older, I'd press charges. What goes on in other people's homes is their business and not yours. So that is the legal side of this mess you've created. Now, let's get to the practical side." Wen managed a slight nod though he was still staring at the ground.

"That is my wife you decided you'd spy on. Mine and mine alone. Do you understand me?"

"Yes sir," Wendell muttered.

"Everything you were trying so hard to see, all of that is for my eyes only. Now, you tell me the truth," he continued his orders. "Look at me." Wendell's eyes rose to Dan's. "Did you see her in the bathtub?"

"No, sir." Wendell shook his head.

"Did you see her walking around in the kitchen and living room?"

"Yes, sir," Wendell admitted in a choked whisper. Heat radiated from his face. "But she, you know, had the baby." Wendell gestured to his own chest. He sounded thoroughly disappointed.

"Are you seriously standing there and complaining that my child was blocking my wife's breasts from your eyes?"

"No, sir." Wendell shook his head and Dan refocused.

"Did you call this morning to get her to walk into the bedroom before she was getting in the shower?"

Wendell gave a slight nod. "But I couldn't see her, honest."

"How did you get her cell phone number?"

"Dad had it."

Dan turned his infuriated glare back on Fred. "How the hell do you have my wife's cell phone number?"

"Well…I noticed it on some of your mail. It's neighborly to share phone numbers. What if we needed to call her?"

Dan ground his teeth and reminded himself that they were moving and wouldn't have to put up with Fred for that much longer.

He shook his head and refocused on Wendell. "Do not ever, ever pull another stunt like this again. Do you understand me?"

Wendell gave a heavy nod.

"I think you probably owe Mrs. Vindico an apology," Chris pointed out. They both knew that embarrassment was always the best form of punishment when it came to teenagers.

"You just march yourself right over there, Wendell MacArthur Scheckles, and you say you're sorry and that this is not how you were raised. And if you don't, I'll get out the dictionary next," Betty shrieked. Dan shuddered to think about Betty Scheckles beating her son with a dictionary.

With that, Dan grasped the scruff of Wendell's neck and shoved him out the front door with entirely more force than was necessary, but he was driving home a point.

"How would you like it if someone tried to see you like that, Wendell?" Chris started as soon as they were on the walkway. "At a time when you thought you were alone and wanted to be private?"

"My wife would absolutely never open the door topless, so you can go ahead and get that little fantasy out of your head. What would you have done if she had anyway?" Dan demanded. The look on Wendell's astonished face told Dan and Chris that he hadn't thought that far. He hadn't thought at all.

Dan halted Wen on the driveway. "You're not coming in my home, so you can just wait right there." Chris stood with Wen while Dan edged carefully through the front door.

"Isn't that the Scheckleses' kid?" Fionna was peeking out the front window.

"He would be your Peeping Tom."

Fionna crossed her arms over her chest instinctively.

"Are you serious? What did he see?"

"Nothing," Dan soothed. "Fred and Betty sent him over here to make a formal apology."

"I don't want to see him."

"Yeah, I wondered about that. I can make him apologize to me," he offered.

"No, it's fine. I don't guess it's all that different from you and the Angels program." He certainly couldn't argue, but he knew that at the time he would never have believed that. He, just like Wendell, hadn't developed enough emotional maturity or brain power in his adolescence to ever understand that the women in magazines were so much more than objects to be admired.

Fionna edged out onto the front stoop. Dan motioned to Chris and Wendell.

Wendell was woefully unable to even lift his head to look into Fionna's eyes. He apologized to her ankles. At least Dan assumed it was an apology as he couldn't really make out any of the words. As soon as he'd concluded, Wendell sprinted home. Dan and Chris shook their heads as Fionna covered her face.

"I am so not looking forward to mine being teenagers," Chris sighed.

"I don't think he even knew really what he was looking for. He just wanted to see more." Dan shook his head.

"Not helping." Fionna cringed.

With a nod, Dan wrapped his arm around Fionna. "We're heading out of town tomorrow. Some friends of ours are coming to keep the girls. We'll be back Saturday evening," Dan explained to Chris.

"Yeah, Carrie told me about your grandmother. I'm so sorry."

"Oh, thank you."

"I'm pretty sure Dan scared Wendell either straight or shitless, so you're probably good for a while." Chris tried to console Fionna. She laughed, but Dan knew she wanted to go back inside and probably crawl under the covers of their bed and cling fiercely to Dan as he casted her in his shield. These were not things that Chris Leslie would ever really understand, however.

CHAPTER 10

NIGHTFALL IN JUAREZ

The next afternoon, Fionna spent a full hour with Emily going over every possible scenario that might come up while they were away for barely twenty-four hours. Fionna trusted Emily implicitly.

The problem seemed to be that Fionna was afraid to leave the girls. Emily could feel her fear and constantly tried to reassure Fionna. But Fionna could feel that she was worrying Emily with her fear and continued to apologize and over-explain. It was a horrible, almost comical cycle.

Rainer stepped in with a smile. He'd taken the afternoon off for babysitting duties.

Garrett was picking Aida up from school and taking her to the public library before bringing her home. "Em, Fionna knows we'll take good care of Halia and Aida. Just think about how you would feel if we were leaving our baby for the first time, and I imagine it's been a rough week. Fionna, just tell us anything we need to do, and we'll do it. I promise," he soothed Fionna and Emily in one quick vow.

As the girls began hugging and laughing and crying all at the same time, Dan shook his head as Rainer joined him in the living room.

"People have made fun of her for being so sensitive her whole life,"

Rainer lamented. "But can you imagine what it would be like to feel everything around you all the time?"

"I know," Dan agreed, "and not only to feel it but to have the ability to fix it and not always be able to."

"I don't get how people don't get it," Rainer sighed.

"Okay, well, that guy"—Dan pointed to the Scheckleses' home—"is a moron, and his sons are following right in his footsteps."

"That's the genius who blew the transformer, right?"

"Yes, and his son took it upon himself to try and see my wife without clothing on several different occasions yesterday by looking in my windows."

"And he's still breathing, and your boot is not permanently lodged in his ass?" Rainer sounded dumbfounded.

"He's thirteen."

"Ah." Rainer laughed.

"If any of his family members get within, let's say, a hundred and fifty feet of one of my girls, you have my permission to blow them back home to South Dakota."

"I solemnly swear that I will not hesitate to show off all of the skills you taught me if anyone so much as looks at one of your girls wrong."

"There was a reason you were chosen for this mission."

Dan eventually pried Fionna away from Halia and out the door. They'd already gone through a tear-filled goodbye that morning when Fionna had taken Aida to school.

"I've only been to Juarez a few times," Fionna explained as Dan steered the Ferrari into one of the parking decks at Ronald Reagan.

"I was in and out of Juarez for several years. Fitz and I actually hunted a guy down and finally found him hiding in Cheve Cave. Wretchkinsides had quite a setup there. They moved a lot of drugs."

"I remember Nana kept telling me that people were killing the Non-Gifted Police." Fionna instinctively tucked closer to Dan.

"It's better now than it was, but it's still not the safest city. That's why I didn't really want the girls to come with us."

Fionna nodded. "I know. I could tell."

"Most of the police are more corrupt than the crooks, and the ones that aren't are hunted down brutally."

"Nana said it had gotten some better over the past few years."

Dan knew she credited him with making Juarez safer, but he couldn't allow himself that accolade.

"Daddy still won't speak to me," Fionna changed the subject. She must've sensed his discomfort.

"He'll come around. I think he's a little concerned about coming back to the island to visit. Being around Tutu and Papa has to be awkward." Dan recalled how uncomfortable it was for him to be around Amelia's family. "When I become the commander of Hawaiian Iodex and we get settled out there, I knock you up another time or two," he teased, making her beam. "Then I'm certain we won't be in Arlington that often, and he knows that too."

They talked for most of the flight about anything but the reason for their trip. As one of the coolant officers gave the twenty-minute warning for their approach into Ciudad Juarez, Dan began his speech. "I now get five minutes to be completely neurotic and overprotective because you are my entire world."

"You mean in addition to the two hours that you spent on the computer after the hours and hours you spent on the phone with Garrett deciding which hotel I would be allowed to stay in." Fionna chuckled. "Oh, and then an additional call to Landon."

"Yes, in addition to all of that. I don't think you really understand. I must've read a dozen hotel reviews where the reviewer claimed that they 'felt safe' and those were all in places that they were most definitely not safe. Hotels spend a great deal of money to give the appearance that they care about their guests' safety. The reality of it is that most of the hotels are run by drug lords and crime rings." Fionna drew a deep breath and nodded her understanding as she wrinkled her nose.

"I had a really nice camera stolen out of my luggage here once," she seemed to remind herself. "Okay, go on with your overprotectiveness."

"I have my brand-new badge, and I will be using it. Victoria gave it to me yesterday in what I assume is an effort to get me to sign the papers when we arrive in Lihue next week," he explained. "That will keep anything from being stolen out of our luggage. You know I'm strapped, and I will be for the entire time we are here." Fionna glanced automatically to the pistol that was in Dan's shoulder holster under his jacket. "Just please let me watch you like a hawk."

Fionna leaned and kissed Dan's jawline.

"I like it when you watch me like a hawk, and I would love nothing more than to spend an entire weekend inside your shield, so no argument."

Several minutes later, Dan was carrying their luggage off the plane. A rather abrasive attendant running the security checkpoint jerked Fionna's large Givenchy purse off her arm. Dan's eyes narrowed as he flashed his badge and moved so the pistol was in view. He jerked the purse away from the attendant.

"Keep your hands off of my wife or we're going to have a problem," he threatened furiously. The guy backed off immediately and moved farther down the line of arriving tourists.

Dan guided Fionna toward the car rental area of the airport.

"Commander Vindico," an Iodex officer that worked in Juarez greeted them and handed Dan the keys to a brand-new Camry that he'd secured.

"Thank you very much," Dan said. He'd worked with the guy years before.

"No problem, and I'm glad to hear you're getting back in the game, sir. You were the best," Officer Marcos vowed.

Dan shook his head. "I'm thrilled to be back, but I had a lot of help getting where I was." He smiled and nodded to Fionna.

"Have a nice trip, and like I said, welcome back." He waved as he climbed back in a squad car and his partner drove away.

CHAPTER II

VOWS

"How did we end up with this?" Fionna asked as Dan held open the door for her.

"Being the head of a state Iodex division does have quite a few perks."

Fionna phoned Gretta to tell them that she and Dan had arrived and were going to check into their room before heading over to Nana's home for the visitation service.

With an audible sigh, Fionna laced her fingers through Dan's.

"Are you okay, baby?"

Fionna shrugged. "Kind of."

"Can I do anything to make this easier?" He was perfectly willing to do anything at all that might make his Maylea smile again. And there it was—she turned and gazed up at him and gave Dan his smile. He felt the warmth and love of her flood through his rhythms. It was exquisite.

"Maybe after the service, we could just escape. I don't know. That's probably dangerous or something, right?"

Dan concentrated and read her rhythms. They pulsed with sadness, and confusion, and longing need. They were stressed and frustrated, but tempting rebellion coursed through her as well.

Several ideas came to Dan in that moment. If she wanted a night to just forget, a night to relax and let the world slip away, then that is precisely what he would provide for her. If she wanted to tap into her sultry feminine side and let her maternal side rest for a while in Arlington, he would help her accomplish that mission.

They could get lost in Juarez, or at least near there. He'd never let anything hurt her, and there were several places nearby that were relatively safe. Then he would take her back to their hotel room in the early morning hours and he'd get lost in her.

"If you want to go out and have a little fun here, baby doll, then that's what we'll do."

"Really? I mean it's okay and safe and everything?"

"I will keep you safe, sweetheart, and like I said, I was in and out of here for weeks at a time for several years. I think I could probably give you a little break from all of the shit going on right now."

She nodded and then raised her eyebrow. "And do I want to know what you were doing here when you weren't working?"

Dan grimaced, but she certainly knew he had a past. "Let's just pretend that everywhere I take you tonight I just stumbled upon."

"Uh-huh." She rolled her eyes.

"Only one who ever mattered is sitting right beside me in this car."

That brought his smile back to her lips. Dan could recall two women that he'd drowned his sorrows in while he worked in Juarez. He knew there were others, but there was almost always far too much tequila in his system for him to ever have even recalled their names much less their faces.

"So, you think that's okay? We can just sort of forget everything?" She needed him to assure her that what she was feeling was perfectly normal.

"I know we keep saying this, and believe me, I sincerely hope things settle down after we move, but it's been a hell of a year. I think a night off is not just required, it's damn near clichéd at this point." Another thought occurred to Dan and he smiled. "If you got to spend one night in Juarez with me, what would Nana want you to do?" That did it. He had her. She was going to let him help her let go.

Dan pulled into the loading area of one of the nicest hotels in Juarez. He offered Fionna his arm as he rolled their one suitcase behind him and kept their carry-on luggage on his other shoulder. He handed the valet the key while keeping his badge on clear display on his belt. After securing their room, Dan guided Fionna onto the elevator.

"So, this hotel isn't owned by bad guys?" she whispered as she took in the opulent decor from the see-through elevator.

Dan chuckled and pulled her closer to him. "It is actually, but the owners are currently working with the Mexican Iodex to help keep this hotel extremely safe as they get a great deal of revenue from their rental properties. The police are happy because crime here is virtually unheard of, and the Reyes family is happy because their money laundering is being overlooked. But money laundering and a few other white-collar crimes are the extent of the Reyes family's interests, so between that and their far-reaching powers and the police involvement, I think this is probably one of the safest hotels in Juarez."

Fionna's mouth hung open in bewilderment.

"Too much?" Dan grimaced, but she shook her head.

"No, but for tonight, I might just pretend that I don't know any of that."

"No problem," Dan soothed as the elevator doors opened on the top floor.

He opened the door to their suite using the key card instead of his casting since there were several hotel employees and patrons in the corridor.

"This is really nice." Fionna seemed to relax as Dan closed the door.

"It's mainly for people traveling for business."

Fionna moved to him and wrapped her arms around his neck. Unable to help himself, Dan leaned and brushed a tender, hesitant kiss across her lips. He pulled away and watched to see if she might like more. Her breath caught as she laced her fingers in his hair and pulled him back.

He moaned as he began consuming her mouth. She was so damn sweet and sexy his groin was on high alert in a second flat. She felt him harden against her, and her hand sought his strain.

"You feel so good inside of me," gasped from her with a hungry groan. Dan's body shuddered in desire.

"I'm gonna make it feel good, baby doll, don't worry. But we need to get ready for the service and then we're going to spend the whole night driving each other wild before I bury it so deep you feel me explode."

"Is that a promise, Commander Vindico?" Fionna challenged with fire lit in the depths of her eyes.

"Oh yeah, baby doll. That's a promise."

Fionna pulled away from him. She was timid suddenly. Dan's brow knitted.

"I just keep feeling so guilty," she confessed.

"For what?" Dan placed the suitcase on the stand, unzipped it for her, and then performed his customary scan of the hotel room to make certain there was no energy source in the room that shouldn't have been there.

Fionna shrugged sheepishly. "I'm here for Nana's funeral. I shouldn't be excited about getting away for a night. I should be sad."

Dan nodded his understanding. This was something he had a great deal of experience with.

He reclined on the bed in the room and pulled her beside him. "A phenomenally beautiful woman told me that life is precious and that we have to appreciate each day because none of them are guaranteed," he reminded her. "In fact, she has this tattoo right about here"—Dan traced the hibiscus flower tattoo that ran from Fionna's mound to her hip bone—"that means that we have to live each day to the fullest.

"And I know I didn't know Nana that well, but from what I've heard, I would say that if she were sitting here with us that she would tell you that life is for the living, Maylea. Trust me, funerals, and burials, and gravesites, they're all for the ones left behind not for the ones that have gone on." Amelia's headstone seared through his mind. He shuddered slightly. Fionna's soothing cast worked through him instantly.

Dan allowed himself a full minute to revel in the heavenly sensation of her energy coursing through his veins. He didn't know how he'd ever lived without it, but then he realized that he hadn't ever really lived without her at all. His life had begun the night he'd followed her home from Anglington's.

"You ready to go, baby doll?" He cradled her on his chest.

To Dan's surprise, Fionna shook convulsively. She began to cry.

"Will you just cast me for a few minutes, please?"

"Of course." Dan panicked as he set his shield firmly in place over the two of them.

She began talking. The words seemed to be her life's blood in that moment, and he wanted to hear the memories that seemed to have her trapped and bound.

"At my mom's funeral…I mean…it was just a memorial because you know they never, you know." She just couldn't seem to give voice to the words that would tell him that her mother's body had never been recovered. It had washed out to sea.

"I know, sweetheart," he assured her.

"It was just a few weeks after my fourteenth birthday, and…" She flushed and tucked farther into Dan's stronghold. "I'd just started my period a year before." Dan nodded and kissed the top of her head.

"I had all of my abilities kind of all of a sudden, but I didn't know how to shield out any of the emotions yet."

"Sweetheart, it's okay," Dan soothed. "We will lie here as long as you need."

She nodded against him, and he strengthened his shield. "I was just standing there, and people kept telling me how sorry they were. But, all I could feel was how uncomfortable they were or embarrassed, or bored, or wishing they were somewhere else. I could feel people's lust, and greed, and all of their sorrow. Everything everyone feels all the time, on top of how truly sad they were.

"So all of that, plus the insincerity that I could feel from some of them, it was all just more than I could understand or process, and I couldn't imagine how my life would go on without my mom. I didn't even want it to. I remember I was embarrassed because everyone kept talking about me like I wasn't even there and then I felt guilty that I was embarrassed." Dan held her tighter. He'd never even begun to realize what losing her mother at such a tender age had been like for his baby.

"So, I just ran." She broke down again in convulsive sobs. "I ran and ran and Malani took off after me, but I wouldn't stop, not even for her. I could hear my dad and Papa yelling, but I just kept running. I ran all the way back to the farm. I don't even know how I got there.

"I ran into Tutu's house and locked myself in my room there. I refused to come out. I let Tutu come in with me, but not Daddy. I was so angry at him. I blamed him for Mama. And then he just got so mad and decided he was taking me away. It was horrible. All the shouting and fury… It was everywhere. I couldn't escape it."

"Keep going, sweetheart. I'm right here," Dan kept up his constant reassurances.

"That's the only funeral service I've ever been to. They're horrible. Everyone's emotions are amplified because of the death. Everyone believes they're supposed to feel a certain way and if they don't sincerely feel that way it's hard to work through it all.

"I hate them because I can feel all of the emotions that people have that are normal at a service like that but that no one would ever want to admit to feeling. No one ever thinks they've done enough at the end no matter how much they have done, so regret and shame become their predominant emotions. Those are very harsh. It sort of robs everything good." Her body relaxed somewhat in her conclusion, but Dan never weakened his shield.

Her words seemed to have run dry so he began. "Sweetheart, I'm so sorry for everything that happened to you. You are the sweetest, most precious thing in the entire world, and it kills me that you hurt like that. But, baby, I think I know you pretty well.

"I think what you felt when you were fourteen was pity, and I think that's what made you run away. I'm pretty sure Nana's service will be different. It's not nearly as tragic as a thirty-six-year-old woman who was full of life and love and that was the mother to a beautiful young girl that needed her desperately," Dan explained as he cradled Fionna's face in his hand.

"I think everyone on the island knew that you and your dad weren't close, and they were worried about you. And my Maylea is so strong and so powerful she can't stand to think that she's caused other people to worry about her because she can feel their worry. They can't hide it," Dan explained. "Look at me, baby. Do you remember standing on the beach and listening to me vow to love and cherish you and take care of you for the rest of our lives?"

Fionna nodded as her brow furrowed. "Of course," she whispered.

Dan pulled her back to him as he cradled her head on his shoulder. "I'm going to lie here in this hotel room and make you a few more vows."

Fionna's head moved back until she was staring into his eyes.

"I will always be here. I will always be your Shield. I will always stand between you and this world that's taken too damn much. We will go to this service if and only if you want to go, and I will be right by your side with your hand in mine because that's how we were meant to get through this life.

"If you want to run away, I will run right beside you, and when you stop, I will be right there to hold you in my arms. If you want to be inside of my shield, then that is where I will put you. If you want to go back to the airport and fly home and hold onto our baby girls and let Aida take care of her mama and let my little coconut give you her sweet, drooly kisses, then that's where we're going. I don't give a damn what your father thinks. As much as I appreciate the fact that he did move you to me, he had his chance to take care of you, and I'm sorry, but I just don't think he did a very good job. But it's my job to take care of you now, and hear me say this, I will never let you down. I will always, always be there for you," Dan concluded his fervent vows.

Fionna sobbed uncontrollably as he held her. She let go of all of the resentment and hurt she'd been carrying since she was fourteen years old. She let Dan drown the harrowing fear and turmoil that plagued her in the safety and serenity of his shield. Her tears held the sadness and desperation she'd felt for so long, and Dan wiped them away softly and steadily until they dried of their own accord.

"Thank you," she finally managed. Dan smiled as he kissed her forehead.

"For what, sweetheart?"

"For loving me and taking care of me. I don't deserve you, but I'm not letting you go so…." She smiled.

"Good, because I can't make it without you," he vowed again.

"Now, my beautiful Maylea, would you like to go pay our respects and then see if we can't get lost in this city for a little while?"

She scrubbed her hands over her face. She leaned and kissed his cheek and then moved to re-do her makeup and get ready to go.

Dan's cell phone buzzed, and he smiled as he answered.

"Hi, Daddy," rang from the sweetest little voice Dan had ever heard.

"Hey, baby girl, are you having fun with Garrett?"

"Yes, and Rainer ordered us pizza, and then Halia's diaper leaked all over Garrett, and he said two words that we're not supposed to say because it isn't nice. And I tried not to giggle, but I did just a little bit," she confessed.

Dan bit his lips together to keep from cracking up. "Tell Garrett Daddy said to watch his mouth." He finally managed an appropriate command.

Aida began laughing. "Emily got on to him and said if he said bad words again that he had to go to his room."

"Good for Emily."

"Is Mommy there?"

"Yeah, we're just getting ready to go see Pops and Abuelita."

"Halia and I miss you and Mommy."

"We miss you too, baby. We'll see you tomorrow."

"Okay, I love you," she sang. Dan allowed himself one quick moment to revel in that fact.

"I love you too," he assured her.

CHAPTER 12

HAUNTS AND HOMES

Dan drove Fionna toward the outskirts of town. He tried desperately not to revisit the harrowing scenes that had been the backdrop to his and Fitzroy's work in the city a few years before.

He shuddered as he began amending his earlier thoughts that he and Fionna would be safe blowing off a little steam that evening. The haunting memories chafed his shield—gang markings on homes, chains on doors of buildings left in charred remains, bodies stacked on the sides of the roads. Dan grasped Fionna's hand. He just needed to feel her.

Glancing at the GPS on his phone a few times, Dan managed to drive them to the tiny, quiet neighborhood near the border. The small, square homes all had bars on the windows and appeared to be trying desperately to hold ground in the eerie calm before the impending storm.

There were several cars parked along the street in front of Nana's home. A for sale sign had been placed in the small front lawn. It joined a dozen others on the same street. Dan made a mental note to contact the head of Ciudad Juarez Iodex and have him check the house frequently. An abandoned home was a breeding ground for many things, none of them good.

Dan guided Fionna into the tiny home. Her chin trembled as she entered through the barred screened door.

"Where have you been, Maylea? I was worried," her father scolded.

"We went to the hotel and then came here. Just like I told you," Fionna defied.

"Samuel, please. Not today," Gretta sighed out her exhausted plea. Dan shot Fionna's father a warning glare. He needed to back the fuck off.

Gretta headed to the small kitchen to help several women prepare food for the wake. Dan glanced around the cramped home. It was humid and dark. Several people were praying quietly. Food from several meals that had been eaten together throughout the day had been lovingly placed on the kitchen table.

A small, frail woman grasped Fionna's forearm. She spun and smiled.

"Maylea," the woman managed in a quiet rasp.

"Hi." Fionna smiled, but she didn't seem able to recall the woman's name.

"I'm Dan, Maylea's husband." Dan stepped in to help.

The woman nodded and gave him a kind smile. "Estoy Ena, un amiga de Susanna." Ena gestured back to the open casket in the small living room. Susanna was Nana's first name, Dan recalled as he nodded and smiled at Ena. Whatever Fionna felt in Ena's energy seemed to soothe her. She and Ena embraced, and Dan's heart ached as tender tears leaked from Ena's tired eyes. They began a conversation half in Spanish half in English that Dan tried not to overhear.

Fionna joined him on the sofa a few minutes later. "I remember her now. She was Nana's best friend, and now she's here in this mess all alone. Her son wants her to move with him and his wife to Merida. She doesn't want to leave Juarez, but now she doesn't have Nana. They kind of looked after one another," Fionna concluded in a choked whisper.

"Merida would be an outstanding place for her, sweetheart. I know she doesn't want to move, but she needs to go with her son. It's a beautiful and safe city, and she'd have family nearby."

"I know and she knows. She just feels lost and so sad."

Dan kept close to Fionna. He watched over her obsessively. She seemed okay for the first hour and a half or so, but then several less than savory looking men entered the home.

Fionna shuddered, and Dan narrowed his eyes. Some of the other guests offered the small group of newcomers polite nods amid frightened whispers of conversations. Dan assumed they probably lived nearby and were looking to interlope on the meal being provided. All four pairs of eyes locked onto Fionna instantly. She turned and laid her head on Dan's shoulder. He wrapped his arms over her and set his shield firmly. The room filled with violent hues of green energy.

Fury lit through Dan as one of them called Fionna an extremely rude name and commented on her ass. But he'd learned a thing or two about letting his temper get the better of him. He didn't know if these men worked for the drug lords that had systematically taken hold of Juarez, and he didn't know how far of a reach they might have, so he clenched his jaw and said nothing.

He shifted Fionna slightly and brushed his jacket away from his side enough to reveal the Browning and his badge as he kept his eyes locked on the man that appeared to be more brazen than his cohorts.

Guests began making excuses to Gretta and Samuel and then giving Fionna waves as they made hasty retreats. The men loaded up paper plates from the kitchen table with homemade delicacies Nana's friends and neighbors had prepared and brought by. They left several minutes later, never speaking to anyone at the visitation.

The entire home seemed to relax after they left. The previous tension that choked out the pleasant memories that were being shared abated instantly.

Fionna was thoroughly worn by the time she and Dan helped Gretta clean up. The casket and body were being moved to the burial grounds the next morning just before the service. Samuel and Gretta were staying overnight in Nana's home. Dan offered to cast the house before he left, but Gretta shook her head.

"Mama lived here all alone for years, Dan. We'll be all right for one night," she assured him.

Dan insisted that he drive Ena home though she kept telling him that it was just a block away. They walked her to the door and accepted her invitation to come in. Dan wanted to make certain that everything was fine before they parted ways.

"I'm going to cast your house, Ena, and I'll come back and pick you up in the morning before the service. You can ride with Maylea and me." Dan prayed that Ena would allow this. She began crying. Fionna embraced her immediately.

"Gracias, gracias," she gushed and Dan's heart fractured. "I haven't slept so well lately. I think I'll call Isaac. Maybe I should move," she finally admitted.

"I think you should, and I really would like to talk with you sometimes. If you move in with your son and he can set you up with Wi-Fi, then I could send you emails and pictures of my girls. We could talk about Nana," Fionna pled.

Ena nodded through her tears, and Dan stepped back as Fionna's soothing cast worked over her. He longed to be inside of her heavenly rhythms, but didn't want to take any of them from Ena who needed them more.

"Would you like me to sit with you until you fall asleep?" Fionna offered. Taking care of Ena soothed her more than anything had all evening.

"No, no, Maylea. I'll be fine. You go out with Dan. Get lost in our city, but stay safe. I wonder if Matteo's is even still there. I haven't been that far in so long," Ena stated wistfully.

"What's Matteo's?" Fionna asked as it was obvious that Ena wanted to tell them. She smiled and settled on a vintage floral sofa complete with orange and crimson velvet patterning.

"Matteo's used to be a little tiny bar where the locals go. Our parents knew nothing about it. I used to go out of my parents' and meet Salvador there, when I was *joven y hermosa* like Maylea," Ena vowed as she patted Fionna's leg.

Dan beamed as he and Fionna joined Ena in her small, well-kept living room. A cat wound its way around Ena's legs, and she patted it sweetly. "My padre did not like Salvadoro, no, he wanted me to marry the banker. But I said no. I ran away," Ena regaled them with a twinkle in her eye.

Fionna leaned in and nodded. "You married Salvador because you loved him."

Dan chuckled. She reminded him so much of Aida in that moment his heart ached.

"That is right, Maylea. I loved my Salvadoro and I do to this day, God rest his soul," Ena vowed as she performed the Catholic sign of the cross with her hand. "I miss him," she admitted with a slight choke. "We worked and worked, and we got married at the church where your Nana will be buried tomorrow. When Isaac was coming along, Salvador built this home and we live here. My Salvadoro is here and my little ones they are here in this house where we raised them. And now..." She shook her head. Tears leaked down Fionna's face as she nodded and cradled Ena's hands in her own.

"The drugs they take everything good from Juarez. I don't want to leave my home. The home Salvador build for me. But now I am an old lady and I must," she lamented.

"Oh, Ena." Fionna shook her head. "Salvador isn't only here in this house. I promise you. I remember when Daddy made me move from Kauai after my mother died," she began her story with Ena listening intently. "I was so afraid that if I didn't live on my island that I wouldn't be able to feel my mother anymore. That I might forget her because I wasn't there. But she's in my heart, and I'll never forget her. And you'll never forget Salvador or living here in Juarez even after you move, because he will always be in your heart," Fionna vowed fervently.

Ena smiled through her tears as she nodded.

"Would you look at my pictures with me, Maylea?" Ena could barely manage to make the request. She seemed so hesitant and frail it broke Dan's heart.

"I would love to," Fionna assured her.

Ena moved to stand, but Dan shook his head. "Let me get them for you?"

She pointed to a small bookshelf in the corner of the room.

Dan handed her two large leather photo albums and reseated himself.

"This is me and Salvador on our wedding day. I had my little Isaac in there, but we didn't tell nobody," she confessed sheepishly. Dan and Fionna laughed as they nodded their understanding. "Look, here is me and Susanna when we were hot tamales," she declared.

CHAPTER 13

ECHO'S EVOLUTION

Dan and Fionna left two hours later after hearing stories of Ena and Susanna's childhood in Juarez before the drug lords moved in, when the city was a bustling, thriving much smaller town. Dan set a fierce shield over Ena's home and promised to pick her up at eight the next morning.

"Want to go see if Matteo's is still there?" Fionna begged as Dan opened her car door for her.

"If her directions were right, there is still a little bar there, but I think it's changed names and hands. It's actually where I was going to take you."

Fionna seemed thrilled to hear this.

After taking several back roads and trying not to see the gang markings on the sides of brick buildings with shattered windows, Dan turned down a road that was relatively free of debris and spray paint.

He parked the Camry and casted it near the tiny bar tucked beside a small grocery market. The owner was smart. For years, he'd been giving deep discounts on his liquor to Iodex officers. Therefore law enforcement was typically there in droves, and Caliente's, as it was now named, was relatively crime free.

Dan and Fitz had frequented Caliente's most every night that they worked in Juarez. The food was decent, the drinks were outstanding, and not that Dan cared anymore, but there were usually several women who didn't mind spending a few hours with an Iodex officer to help him get his mind off work.

Dan was surprised that the bartender seemed to recognize him. He smiled kindly and shook Dan's hand.

Dan pointed to a table near the back of the smoke-filled bar and kept his arm on Fionna as he guided her back. He shot several glares to men who'd begun to visibly salivate as soon as Fionna had walked in the bar.

"Dan, look." Fionna pointed to a grouping of black-and-white photos in one of the corners. They showed numerous shots of Juarez in the fifties and sixties, and there were several pictures of the very bar where they were sitting down. The large placard sign read Matteo's. There were pictures of young ladies dancing in the arms of Mexican servicemen during the war and of happy kids standing around juke boxes and dancing on the bar.

"Could we bring Ena out here tomorrow after the funeral, please? That would mean so much to her before she moves," Fionna begged.

"Of course." He couldn't help but smile. Ena delighted Fionna and therefore she delighted Dan.

"Hola, gringo. I know your face. Don't remember your name." The owner gave Dan and Fionna a kind smile.

"Commander Vindico and this is my wife, Fionna."

"You working Juarez again?" the man quizzed after he greeted Fionna.

"No, we're in town for a funeral."

"Sorry to hear that. We could use you around here, but what can I get you?"

Dan raised his eyebrows to Fionna. She shrugged. There were no menus.

"Do you still make those Golden Margaritas?" Dan asked.

"Yeah, of course," the owner scoffed. "How 'bout a platter of tripas to go with?"

Dan shook his head and tried not to grimace. "No, thank you, but a platter of enchiladas would be great."

"You got it."

Fionna settled in to the warmth of the bar. "What are tripas?"

"They're tacos filled with cow and pig intestines. They're supposed to be quite good, but…"

"Organ meat," Fionna shuddered. "No, thank you."

Dan kissed the side of her head. "I had a feeling that's what you'd say."

Cigarette and cigar smoke hung in the air, but it didn't seem to bother her. The music was playing and several couples were melting into one another and letting the tequila and rum guide their evening plans. Well over half of the people in the bar were Iodex officers just coming off their shifts and looking for a little reprieve.

"This seems like the perfect place to get lost for a while," Fionna whispered as she scooted closer to Dan. He smiled and wrapped his arm around her. Their enchiladas arrived along with a pitcher of the best margaritas Dan had ever had.

He poured Fionna a glass and then one for himself.

"Okay, before I drink this," Fionna began. Dan raised his eyebrows having a pretty good idea where this was going. "You now have my express permission to take advantage of me even if I get a little tipsy," she informed him.

Dan chuckled as he shook his head at her.

"We'll see, Mrs. Vindico." He couldn't stop the memories though he tried. He had to ask her even though bringing up their first pregnancy was certain to drown her smile. He had to take care of her. It was who he was.

The last time she'd requested a little carnal attention after she'd had a few libations was the time he'd gotten her pregnant. Dan knew he hadn't casted her that morning. She'd been in the shower when he left to take Aida to school.

He drew a deep breath. "If I should decide to take you up on that offer, sweetheart, would I need to cast you first or is that part already taken care of?" He tried to sound flirtatious and sexy in an effort to keep their evening focused on just letting go.

Fionna nodded. She glanced down at the table to keep her composure.

"I did it this morning in the shower. I really want my body to heal this time, like Adeline said. And I don't want to go through another pregnancy off of Kauai," she confessed. "It was just really hard."

"I know, sweetheart," Dan assured her. "I don't want you to, and Fi, I swear to you I'm getting you there as fast as I possibly can."

A beautiful, sweet smile spread across Fionna's lips. "I know you are. You're the best husband ever, and as much as I want to go back to Kauai, I don't want to be anywhere without you."

"I'm right here, baby doll." Dan pulled her closer to him in the tiny booth. Suddenly, a man Dan recognized sauntered to the table. He was tipsy but seemed to be able to walk and carry on intelligent conversation.

"Aren't you Chief of American Iodex, Vitrio, or something? We worked together a few years ago."

"Vindico," Dan corrected. Vitrio had been one of Wretchkinsides's thugs. He was one they'd been after while they were in Juarez. Dan had eventually caught up with him last Christmas in Vegas. He offered the Mexican Iodex officer his hand, but Fionna shuddered.

"Marriett," the man reminded Dan who nodded, but he wasn't really paying attention.

Fionna's face contorted slightly, and she began shivering. She was trying so hard not to show the man before them what she knew.

"Oh baby, I told you, you can't eat the fruit here," Dan panicked.

"Oh, is she sick?" Marriett did look genuinely sorry.

"Yeah, I think we better get back to the hotel," Dan bristled. He wrapped his arm around Fionna and willed Marriett to leave so he could call Romero and tell him he had himself a dirty cop.

"It was good to see you again, man. You should come by the precinct. Rom would love to see you, I'm sure." Marriett was doing a very good job of playacting though it was extremely brazen for him to have approached Dan in the first place. He felt like he was untouchable, and that realization had Dan's blood running ice cold.

"We're just in town for tonight. I won't have time to get by the precinct, but tell Romero I said hello."

"Will do." He waved as he made his way out of the bar.

"Are you okay?" Dan whispered.

Fionna gave a weak nod. "He's not a nice guy."

"Yeah, I got that when he was about ten feet away from you. Just let me take care of this, okay?"

"It's fine," Fionna assured him.

Dan pulled his cell phone from his pocket and threw a sound barrier shield around their table.

"Romero," was the greeting Dan received.

"Hey Rom, it's Dan Vindico. How are you?" Dan offered politely.

Romero immediately switched to English. "I'm good. I heard you were out."

"Right now, I'm in between, but my wife and I are in Juarez tonight. I just wanted to give you a call while I'm in town," Dan gave the properly worded explanation that meant he had confidential information that no one else needed to hear.

"Really?" Romero sounded morose.

"Yeah," Dan sighed. "We're out here at Caliente's. We saw a couple of your guys. I just ran into Marriett."

"Oh," Romero's tone turned relieved. "Yeah, I already know that. My wife's a Receiver. None of them get by her. I'm just giving him enough rope to hang himself, and he's leading me right to the head of a drug cartel. If he survives them after I'm finished, then he can waste away in Gongora," Romero spat. Dan nodded his relief.

Gongora was a Gifted prison near the Naica mines. The lead, gypsum, and silver deposits coupled with Gongora's being many miles beneath the earth's surface made it one of the most stringent Gifted prisons in the world.

"It was good to talk to you. If you're ever in the States, look us up," Dan urged.

"I'll take care of Marriett, don't worry."

"Great. Talk to you soon." Dan ended the call. "I'm sorry. I wanted to let you get lost and that certainly wasn't what I had in mind."

"It's fine," Fionna assured him again as they continued to sip the margaritas and settle into one another in the dark bar.

CHAPTER 14

TEQUILA TEMPTATIONS

As they finished up their second glasses and the platter of food, Fionna gave him a soft sultry smile as she slid closer. "I really just want to get lost in your arms," she whispered.

The trace of tequila on her breath coupled with the heady scent of her in the humid bar had Dan's heart racing. Suddenly, her hand was on his thigh under the table. She used the thick Mexican fabric tablecloth to cover her work.

Dan gave her a look that said he had many, many things he planned to do to her that evening and that he'd make certain she enjoyed each and every one of them. "That's it, baby doll," he urged as he leaned and began kissing and licking just under her earlobe.

The electricity and the need sparked between his lips and her skin. "If you want to leave and go back to our hotel room and let me lay you out and pound that sweet pussy then grab me right now. Make me hard and then rub me. Make me ache.

"But if you want to get lost on that dance floor first then be a sweet girl and give me a kiss. I want to taste your lips right now, but later I'm tasting all of you," he commanded.

Fionna's eyes flashed and the storm that had begun its build lit explosively. Her breaths panted as she considered her options.

Her cheeks flushed as she licked her lips, driving him wild. She leaned and in a sexy move that set him on fire, her hand located his burgeoning strain as she dipped her tongue in his mouth. He feasted on her mouth, devouring all of the energy it contained.

Before she made him unable to walk and much less dance, Dan slid away from her and out of the booth. He offered her his hand. She gave him her hungry, lust-filled grin as she took his hand and he guided her up.

Dan spun her into his arms on the crowded dance floor. "I'll let you be a sweet girl for me now," he whispered in her ear, "but later, honey, you're gonna be a bad girl for me."

He could feel her heartbeat fly in her rhythms as a slight moan she couldn't quell reverberated from her lungs. Dan wrapped her up tightly in his arms as they let the world melt away in the smoke-filled haze that surrounded them.

They swayed to the sultry Spanish ballads, melting into one another, with Dan elaborating on their plans for the evening in great detail. She shot him a sassy smirk as a song worthy of a tango began playing.

She waggled her eyebrows, and Dan managed to keep up with the sexy sway of her hips as he jerked her forward and dipped her low. He was certain the fact that she'd danced most of her life and that he could keep a beat but was by no means a dancer was very apparent.

But his Maylea was having a ball and that was all he needed. Her long, sexy leg slid up Dan's hip, and he was done for. He grasped her thigh and kept his eyes locked on hers as he dipped her again.

"Mine," he hissed in her face. Her eyes flashed in her desire as he spun her out, holding on to her hand, and then spun her back into his arms. "And I want what's mine, under me, in my bed, screaming out my name," he ordered as his hands slipped from her waist to her luscious ass as she swayed in his arms.

As the song drew to a close, she waggled her eyebrows, and Dan shot her a cocky smirk as she led him out of the bar. People held up their drinks in a toast of admiration. Any of the men in that bar would have given their right arm to have been able to take her back to their room, but that would never happen. She was his, and he was about to stake his claim.

"Pretty sexy dancing there, Mrs. Vindico," he complimented as he opened the car door for her.

"I love to dance," she informed him though he certainly already knew that much. "Especially for you."

"Oh, I'm gonna let you dance for me, honey. I'm about to take you to our hotel room and make you shake those hips right on top of me," he growled.

The rhythmic pulses of the music and the lavish spices of the liquor coursed through them as Dan dragged Fionna from the car and to the elevator. He had to remind himself that it was glass to keep from pinning her to the wall and running his hands up her dress.

After deciding that he didn't really give a damn, he leaned and began kissing his stunningly sexy wife. She reached for his strain again as the elevator climbed higher. Dan caught her hand.

"Not yet, baby doll. We're almost to the room, and then I'm gonna make you grab me and suck me. It's all for you, and I'm gonna bury it deep inside of you," he promised.

"Oh god, yes." She was on fire. Dan wasn't certain he was going to be able to contain her. The liquor had her rhythms quaking, and her need was palpable in the air around them.

Dan managed to get her into the room before she jerked his tie off and unbuckled his belt.

"Needy, baby doll?" He spun her around and hoisted her dress off in one smooth, sinuous move. He dropped to his knees behind her and slid the thong she was wearing down her legs slowly. She stepped out of it and spun, wearing nothing but a black lace bra and a pair of heels. A ravenous guttural groan echoed from Dan's chest as he traced up her inner thigh with his tongue. Her breath caught in her throat as she shuddered.

He teased her, not giving her what she wanted just yet. She whimpered as he let his tongue dance along her folds but never entered her.

"Go get in my bed, and I'll show you what this beautiful body was made for," he assured her. Her moans shattered through her in desperate need.

She stepped toward the bed, but he caught the back strap of her bra. "Just a minute." He pulled her back to him. As he released the clasp of her bra, he edged her head to the side and kissed up her neck, driving her wild. "These are mine and I want to play," he informed her as her body began to pitch and toss in desperation. "Now go." He smacked her ass.

He watched her naked body in nothing but heels as she let her hips sway dramatically as she sauntered to the bed. She lay out on her stomach, bent her legs, and crossed her feet at her ankles. Then she propped up on her elbows and gave him a look that said she wanted to be tamed.

"So fucking gorgeous. My god, there are so many things I want to do to you."

"Now," she cooed seductively, and Dan growled as he stripped and moved in front of her.

"Suck me like my good girl. I want to see it in your mouth."

Her breaths stuttered deliciously as her hand wrapped around his cock. It pulsed and demanded her attention. Dan's eyes rolled back in his head as she dragged her tongue up the thick veins. He wrapped his fingers through her silky, chestnut locks and guided her to his need. She crawled up to her knees and pulled him deep as she bathed him with her tongue. His groans echoed around the room as she continued to suck and lick him. "Be a good girl and put your hands behind your back. Then take me deep." She complied immediately. "That's it."

He pulled away, making certain he could give her reprieve as well. "Now lie back. I'm hungry," he ordered fiercely.

She flipped over on her back and spread her legs for him. He took a moment to stare unabashedly at her lips as they throbbed and dripped, so ready to be filled they ached for him.

Dan leaned over her. He dragged his tongue up her slit and then moved immediately to her nipples, throbbing and pulsating as they begged for relief. Fionna's back arched deeply as Dan pulled her right breast in his mouth and suckled and licked it fervently. He moved to her left, granting it equal attention. He worked back down her body.

"You're dripping for me like such a good girl," he panted as he dragged one finger slowly down over her opening. She cried out his name.

"Please, please," she begged him.

"Don't worry, baby doll, I've got everything you need. I'll take good care of you," he promised as her body shuddered in frenzied need of relief.

Dan began to suck as he lapped his tongue slowly over her clit. She went wild. He dragged his teeth over her lips and swirled his tongue inside of her. Dan moaned against her as her body began to buck under him. He delved deep a moment later, and the very essence of her energy flooded his mouth.

He crawled into the bed beside her.

"So hot and wet, baby doll. So fucking perfect. Now, I want you to ride me," he ordered. Fionna started to sling her leg over Dan's crotch with her hands on his chest, but he shook his head.

"No. I want to see that gorgeous ass bounce while I make you take it deep," he commanded.

Fionna's eyes flashed in voracious hunger.

"Turn around."

She spun, and Dan bent his knees to give her something to brace herself against. He positioned her over him as he stared at the most luscious ass in the world.

"Take it." He grasped her waist and penetrated the very heart of her.

Her body arched back toward him as he pounded into her. She began to ride, and Dan's eyes rolled back in his head. It was exquisite. Her lush ass jiggled with every lift of her body against him. She was sweet, delicious perfection. Dan began to buck up into her, driving himself deep with no reprieve as he throbbed inside of her.

She came in tantric waves of ecstasy.

"That feels so good," she managed in between her gasping moans.

"I didn't tell you to stop."

She pitched and tossed until his sight clouded with an erotic haze.

He cursed as he lost it all so deep inside of her she'd feel it for days. She eased off his body and fell onto his chest.

It took Dan a full minute to catch his breath as he held her in his protective embrace.

"I'm pretty sure I shouldn't have had that much fun the night before my grandmother's funeral but wow," she gushed.

Dan laughed as he let the ecstatic feeling of thoroughly satisfying his wife fill his soul.

"I do aim to please," he assured her.

"I'm very pleased, Commander."

"I hope you're not too pleased yet," he challenged.

She lifted her eyebrow in intrigue. "Why is that?"

He gestured to his still hardened strain. "I need more, and you're going to give it to me. I'll be gentle this time, baby doll. Nice and slow. But I'm still aching for you."

After another round, this one slower and more thorough, he followed her to the bathroom. He wanted to be in contact with her constantly.

She washed her face and they brushed their teeth before Dan cradled her back in the serenity of their bed. He stayed awake for several hours listening to the disturbing sounds just outside of their hotel room.

It was distinctly odd to be in the middle of a drug torn war zone and to feel completely content. It didn't matter where they were. As long as his Maylea was in his arms that was all that mattered.

He had to make certain she was safe. He set his shield in place over the two of them and felt her rhythms soothe completely as she began to drink in his protective love and all-encompassing devotion as he watched over his beautiful wife.

CHAPTER 15
THE LAST CONVERSATION
~GARRETT HAYDENSHIRE~

"Garrett," came from a soft, sweet, yawning voice behind him.

"What's wrong, Aida Mae?" Garrett sat up off of the couch as Aida approached hesitantly. He glanced at his phone. It was just after midnight. He switched off the television.

"I miss Mommy," she whispered dejectedly. Her voice caught as she tried not to cry. Garrett's heart ached.

"Do you want me to lie down with you?" He scooped her up as she gave a thankful nod. She buried her little face in his neck. Her chin trembled, and Garrett set his shield over her instantly.

"Thank you," she whispered through another yawn as Garrett carried her into her room and cradled her in the bed.

"Mommy and Daddy will be home tomorrow." Garrett tried to soothe her, but he was certain it was Fionna that she wanted.

"I know, but I feel better now because you're here with me."

Garrett smiled as he kissed the top of her head. She wiggled until her little face was under his chin, and she clung to him with force.

"Garrett," she whispered, and he felt hot tears pierce his neck.

"What's wrong, sweetheart?" He was certain she was going to ask for Fi again, but she didn't.

"I don't want to move to Tutu's without you." She began to cry in earnest. "Please, please don't make me. I don't like it when you go away." Her tears burned as they pooled through his T-shirt.

Garrett's eyes closed, and he squeezed her to him. He didn't want to promise her anything he didn't know if he could do. "I love you so much, Aida Mae, and no matter where I am, if you need me, I'll be there. I promise."

"I love you more," she vowed. "Please come with us. I need you to. Please. Please. I need you to come with us."

Among her sniffled tears, she slowly drifted back to sleep in his shield. The conversations he'd debated having over a dozen times began in his mind again. Everything began to tally, but a firm decision continued to elude him.

Dan and Dad would tell me yes. Fionna and Aida would be thrilled. Chloe would be furious. Chloe deserves somebody better anyway. I'm sick to death of DC. Mom would cry. Garrett shuddered at that thought before he continued his list. *Dan and Fi are my best friends, and I want to see Aida grow up. I've been taking care of her longer than they have. I still want to work in Brazil but that's an even longer flight. Your dad's the Crown Governor, you moron. He has his own freaking jet that you can use. Will's here. Will has his own life. The women.* Garrett grinned as he recalled the few hours he'd spent with Kalea. *If I'm still thinking about her, she was obviously phenomenal. Chloe needs me to go so she can move on. I can't take any more of her bullshit.* Of that, Garrett was absolutely certain.

He tensed as he tried not to remember the last conversation.

There was an urgent knock on his apartment door. Garrett's brow furrowed as he opened it. "What the hell is wrong with you?" he demanded of Cal. He looked sick.

"I need to talk you," he all but begged.

"Of course." Garrett gestured him in the apartment and wondered why Cal even thought he needed to ask. They'd talked their way through life. "What's going on?"

"It's Logan."

Garrett's eyes closed as he nodded. "Yeah, that girl's sweet, but geez, that's a shit ton of trauma."

Cal looked relieved that Garrett knew that. "I know, but I just walked around the lake with him. He's in love with her."

"He's barely sixteen."

"I know how old he is. I'm serious. Just listen to me." Cal began to pace. *"Lo spent his whole life being around Rainer and Emily. He wants that so bad. I'm worried..."*

"That he thinks he's found it, but he hasn't?" Garrett guessed.

Cal shook his head. *"No. I'm worried that he has. Just listen a minute. Logan isn't like me and you. He's wired different or something. He needs you to believe him when he tells you stuff and asks for your help. Just... promise me that you'll be there for him. He's already trying so fucking hard to live up to you."*

Garrett scowled. *"Why the hell would anyone want to do that? I haven't done anything. He should be trying to live up to you."*

"Man, you know that's bullshit. You cast a massive shadow. I know how much you love all of us, but Logan especially...he's gonna need you. A lot. Just...be there if I can't."

Realization drenched Garrett in icy shards of terror. His shield gave a disconcerting tense. *"I will always be there for Lo and all the rest of them, but what the hell is this about really? Why don't you think you'll be there?"*

Cal's jaw tensed visibly. *"It's uh...it's not looking good what Nic's got going on in Moscow. He's going to end up taking over the governing board."*

"Cal," Garrett choked. *"Man, tell Dad. Let me tell Dad. Dan will get you out of there. Please..."*

He shook his head. *"I'll be fine,"* he lied. *"I met someone."*

"Stop trying to distract me. I don't care who you're fucking."

Cal laughed. That easy-going, pure laughter that had been so brutally robbed from the world. *"Haven't gotten that far yet, but give me time. She's uh...she's a spy as well."*

Garrett's heart stalled. *"For who?"*

"Latvia."

"Dammit," Garrett seethed. *"Nic's got a whole lot of people in Latvia. Are you sure she's not double-crossing you?"*

"I'm sure."

"How?"

Cal smiled. *"I just know."*

"You don't fucking know. What did I tell you when you signed on for this suicide mission? I said not to get attached to anyone. Ever. It's dangerous."

"It's also lonely, Garrett. I think Logan may be right. There is someone out there for all of us. Maybe someday you'll get that, but until then, just take it from me. When you know, you know."

"That's bullshit, and you know it. Shut this down now. You don't know who this chick is really working for. She could lead Nic right to you."

"I know enough." He checked his watch. *"I've got to go. Just...for me, promise you'll can it with the shit stories of your conquests with Logan. This girl is it for him. Help him always. Promise me."*

"Fine." Garrett narrowed his eyes. *"If you won't get Dan to pull you out, then I'm going with you."*

Cal smirked. "No, you're not. You don't even know where I'm going. I love you, bro. Always have. Always will. Be mindful of that shadow of yours. It's way bigger than you think."

"Wait!"

He'd left.

Garrett had called Dan and begged him not to let Cal board whatever plane he was heading toward. Cal must've known. Dan had immediately grounded the flight, only Cal never made it to the Senate. He'd known all along Garrett would try to save him. He'd booked a private flight.

Aida shuddered, and Garrett ordered himself to think about something else. She was picking up on his terror.

His memories shifted to those horrible days when he'd fluctuated between death and life, and he'd been all alone.

He'd refused to tell anyone his name. He didn't want his parents showing up in Brazil just to watch him die. He didn't want his family in the country with the men who had murdered two of their sons. But, by some miracle, Garrett had survived. He'd rallied in that hellhole of a medical clinic where that tiny old woman had somehow managed to take him. His shield had sustained him.

He fought the memories, but holding Aida brought them back in crisp clarity. *She was crying too hard to ever remember that it was me that took her to that orphanage. I should have just told Mom and Dad. They would have raised her, and she never would have had to live there. It all worked out for the best though. She's so happy here with Dan and Fi. But when they aren't here, she wants me,* Garrett reminded himself.

And in that moment, the decision cemented in his mind. *Of all people, Dan would understand.* Garrett tried to convince himself to just tell someone what had happened. *Dan certainly can't complain about why I went. He dedicated his entire life to vengeance before he met Fionna. Not that I blame him.* Garrett eased his fingers over Aida's sweet face, brushing her hair from her mouth. She snuggled farther into his embrace, and Garrett squeezed his eyes shut.

He clenched his jaw as he tried to dam the haunting memories that weighted his soul and marred his life.

The dirt rose off the road and seemed to evaporate in the acrid humidity before Garrett's eyes. He wiped the sweat from his brow as he pulled his hat lower and tried to blend in to the tiny bar forty miles outside Rio.

"Cerveja, gringo," called a man that was selling Brazilian beer out of the trunk of his car.

Garrett shook his head and let his hand discreetly check the pistol in his pocket. He moved to a back corner near the men he was after. Dressed in dirty jeans, a worn cotton shirt, with a broad band cowboy style hat, Havaianas, and sunglasses, he blended in well.

He hadn't shaved in nearly a month much to his mother's irritation. But he had a plan, and he wasn't going to get caught. The call had come. Pravus had surfaced outside of Rio, and Garrett had spewed forth his lies with ease.

"I just need a break, Dad. Few friends and I are gonna hit Cancun and kick a few back."

"Garrett, if you need to talk about what happened to Cal, or Emily, or anything at all, that doesn't make you weak, son, it makes you human," his father had pled with him.

"I'm fine. I just want a vacation." He'd looked his father in the eye and lied.

"When are you coming back?"

"I'll be back when I get back. Don't freak," Garrett sniped just before he'd boarded the plane under his name and headed to Cancun.

He'd covered his tracks well. He'd mailed his license and badge back to his apartment in DC from the hotel he checked into in Cancun. Then he'd changed his credit cards and fake IDs in his wallet to take on his alias and boarded a commuter plane to Rio.

Garrett ordered a beer from the waitress that was eyeing him. He winked.

She blushed and grinned, and he'd gone right back to listening to the conversation two tables over.

Rojas's cell phone rang. Nervous glances moved quickly around the table.

Garrett couldn't quite make out the rapidly spoken Portuguese, but suddenly, the men were leaving.

He threw several Brazilian coins on the table. He was certain it was more than enough to cover the beer he'd ordered but hadn't yet received, and he followed the men. Cal had joined Iodex because of Garrett, and Pravus's days were numbered. Cal's last words to him speared through his mind again. "Be mindful of the shadow of yours. It's way bigger than you think."

They climbed in a taxi, and Garrett immediately leapt in one that had pulled over to provide travel to a couple on vacation.

"Sinto muito," Garrett had apologized then ordered the driver to follow the other cab. He'd thrown three hundred American dollars over the seat and promised more if the driver didn't get caught.

The driver was skilled but not fast enough. The shack was in flames before Garrett could get to the men. He'd had the cab driver drop him several blocks beyond where Rojas had pulled in.

Garrett shuddered again as he recalled the heat from the flames singeing his beard as he sprinted toward the tiny shack. *It was constructed entirely of cheap resin wood and it was gone in seconds. A woman had run out of the house, and Garrett raced to her.*

"Minha filha, minha filha." She'd pointed to the picture in her hand. She'd been shot along with her husband and sons, and Garrett couldn't heal her fast enough. There was too much smoke in her lungs, and she was vomiting blood.

She was a Receiver. Her energy bled from her in deep fuchsia waves. She knew Garrett wasn't working with the men that had just murdered her family.

"Please," she choked out in English. "My baby," were the last words Aida's mother had managed as Garrett held her as she died.

"I'll take care of her," he swore to her as she drew her last breath. Having no idea what to do, Garrett left the woman there when he heard a little girl calling from down the road. He grabbed the pictures clutched in the woman's hands and ran toward the cries for Mamãe. There she was. The little girl from the photos. She was barely managing to carry a bucket of water.

Garrett lifted her up and tried to ask her about her family, but she only understood a few words in English.

"My nome, Garrett," he explained.

She'd nodded. "Aida," she'd pointed to herself with tears leaking constantly out of her frightened brown eyes.

He walked her for miles, for days. He carried her most of the way, until they came upon the nuns outside of Holy Rosary. Aida had clung to Garrett.

He was shocked that she hadn't fought with him or tried to get away. He hadn't known then that she was a Receiver. She could feel that he was desperately trying to take care of her. He'd filled up his canteen at a running stream, and he plied her with water. He'd given her all the food he had in his small pack. She'd been starving.

"Her family has been murdered. I can't take care of her." Garrett had tried not to sob as he'd handed Aida over to the nuns. They'd reassured him that they would care for her, and he'd managed to leave late that night by promising himself that he would find Pravus and Rojas and end them, and then he would come back as often as he could and take care of Aida.

He didn't sleep. He didn't eat. He did nothing but hunt. He located them in a tiny inn just outside of Queimados.

Naftan left the room, and Garrett met him in the parking lot. He'd left the body in a dumpster and waited.

Rojas came out an hour later looking for Naftan. Garrett moved behind him and fired, but Pravus had followed him.

Aida shook her head in her sleep as the searing pain that shot through Garrett's groin shattered his memory.

"Shh, baby girl, it's okay. I've got you," Garrett soothed her back to sleep, but the memories wouldn't rest.

He'd woken up several days later in some kind of aid clinic. A priest had been praying over him, and Garrett had tried to sit up, but the pain was too crippling. When he'd finally regained the ability to walk and think at all, a Gifted medio from London that volunteered in the clinic had come to his bedside. There was one large room, and operations, new births, and a great deal of death were all taking place around them. Garrett recalled the harrowing, shrieking screams.

"We didn't think you were going to make it, now did we?" the medio seemed to ask himself. Garrett hadn't known what to say so he'd said nothing

at all. "Your guardian angel, Mr. Simpson," he'd said as he studied Garrett's chart, and he suddenly remembered his alias, "was an eighty-year-old woman with a mule which she used to bring you here," he'd explained wryly. "Had I gotten to you earlier, perhaps we wouldn't have to have this conversation, but like I said, we weren't even certain you would be alive a week ago." Garrett wondered what was coming next. Arrest was his first concern, but the medio seemed to have no idea what he'd been doing just prior to being shot.

"What's wrong with me?" Garrett managed the first words he'd spoken in a week's time. His tongue rejected the movement. His teeth began to chatter as he shook. The medio immediately set another cast and eased Garrett's strain.

"You were severely dehydrated and half-starved when you arrived. Your energy rhythms were so weak I hardly knew you were Gifted at all. We removed the bullet, and I've restored your organs to the best of my abilities. Everything works just the way it was meant to. There's just one complication I can't seem to correct. You were just too far gone when we got you here. Are you married, sir?"

At the time, Garrett had actually laughed when the medio explained that he was effectually sterile and wouldn't be able to have children. He'd considered sending Pravus a thank you card. Garrett hadn't wanted children, but he'd always enjoyed having a beautiful woman in his bed. The more the merrier had, after all, been his mantra for the last several years.

Two days later, after enduring near constant casts, Garrett had flown to New York. His Uncle Tad had met him at the airport and taken him back to his and Nathan's apartment. Garrett had never shared the diagnosis. He had visited a medio in New York but the diagnosis was the same.

He'd told Tad and Nathan bits and pieces of the story, but they'd asked no questions. They'd nursed Garrett back to full health, without his parents or siblings ever knowing what happened. They'd plied him with chicken noodle pho from Bep Ga and double patty American cheeseburgers from the Empire Diner when he was well enough to desperately need to put some weight back on. Eventually, they'd talked him into going back to DC and starting his life over without Cal.

He'd taken their advice and returned home, but he'd immediately made plans to volunteer back in the orphanage the following month. Eventually, Logan had finished the job Garrett had started.

At thirty-one, the weight of the diagnosis was more of a burden. Chloe's beautiful body and naughty smile flashed in his mind. Sex with Chloe Sawyer had always been a blast, but life with Chloe was never something he'd really wanted.

He heard Halia start to cry and recognized Emily's quick footsteps as she moved to the nursery from across the hall.

Drawing a deep breath, Garrett edged away from Aida so that he could study her sleeping form. Logan was fine now. He was healthy and married and so freaking happy it delighted Garrett. Logan had made peace with what he'd done. Garrett had talked him through it all summer long until he'd finally understood that he couldn't undo what he'd done and that it was okay if he didn't want to. He was his own man now, and Garrett had other promises to keep.

"I promised your mama I'd look after you, baby girl. So, tomorrow I'm talking to Daddy and I'm going with you to Kauai," he whispered his vow to her, and the peace that had eluded him for weeks finally settled in his shield.

CHAPTER 16

PANCAKES AND PLEAS

~DAN VINDICO~

Dan fell asleep in the early morning hours. As the sunlight gave reprieve to the dreaded darkness of night in Juarez, a delighted grin spread across his face before he opened his eyes.

Fionna's soft warm curves were tucked against him. Her back was to his chest with them both lying on their sides. She was tucked under his chin, and his arm was slung over her. Fionna's breast was very conveniently located near his hand, and Dan took advantage of the opportunity to feel his wife up before they got up to get ready for the funeral. He heard her sweet giggle as she reached her right hand back and located the part of his body that was on high alert and hoping for her attention. Dan gave a shuddering moan as she caressed him.

"Something long and hard woke me up," she sassed deliciously.

"Can't really say I'm sorry about that."

She giggled again, but then tucked farther into Dan's body. He could feel the sadness that threatened to permeate her energy again.

"I'm right here." His shield bled from his pores and encapsulated her.

Relief flooded through her as she let him block out the world.

Dan rubbed his hands tenderly up and down her body. He tried to massage away some of what the day was certain to hold.

Dan's cell phone rang on the bedside table. He kept Fionna tucked on his chest as he eased his other hand to the phone.

"It's Garrett." He tried not to panic as he answered.

"They're fine don't freak," was Garrett's greeting. Dan chuckled.

"Okay." Relief was evident in his tone. He casted the phone so Fionna could hear as well.

"I was just wondering if it would be okay with you and Fi if I hung out for a little while after you get back tonight. There are a few things I need to talk over with you." Nervous tension punctured his words.

Dan's brow furrowed. Something was definitely up with Garrett. Fionna picked up on it immediately as well.

"Of course. You can stay as long as you want. Hell, move in. Aida would be thrilled," Dan assured Garrett. He laughed heartily.

"I may take you up on that at some point. All right, I'm making Aida Mae some of Dad's pancakes. She's stirring the batter, so I better run." Garrett seemed to want an escape.

"Uh, sure, tell her I love her. We're heading to the funeral in a little while and then to run a quick errand before we catch our flight," Dan explained.

"No problem. See you tonight," Garrett vowed quickly and then the line went dead.

Fionna sat up and shared a concerned expression with Dan.

"I don't know, baby." He answered the inevitable question before it exited her lips.

"Well, something is wrong."

"Yeah, and it sounds like he's going to tell us when we get back, so we'll do whatever needs to be done to help him." He owed Garrett his life many times over. Will and Garrett had been Dan's closest friends all through childhood. Garrett had been friends with Fionna since they'd all been at the academy together. He'd flown to Brazil dozens and dozens of times and worked at the orphanage where Aida lived.

He was the reason the Angels worked there as part of their service. He'd stayed over night after night sleeping on Fionna's couch when she was scared to be home alone before she'd met Dan. He'd even beaten the shit out of some jerk who'd tried to lock Fionna in a room when she refused to sleep with him.

He'd flown to Brazil and picked Aida up so she could be in Rainer and Emily's wedding. That was how Dan and Fionna had ended up meeting and adopting their precious little girl. There was absolutely nothing Dan wouldn't do for Garrett.

"I hope he's okay until we get there," Fionna panicked.

"Fi, relax," Dan guided her. She nodded. "Now think about Garrett. What do you feel?"

Her eyes closed in concentration. "Nothing bad has happened. I don't think," she explained, and Dan allowed himself to breathe. "Maybe something a long time ago. I can't quite feel it."

"What emotions is he currently feeling?"

"He's nervous, really nervous, with a little fear mixed with relief, which is how people feel when they're going to say something they've needed to say for a long time. Whatever it is, it feels like I'm going to be really happy about it, but there's so much sadness too. I'm worried. Maybe we shouldn't go to the service. What if he needs us right now?"

"We'll do whatever you want, but we'll be there this evening. He sounded okay for the moment. I'm sure you'll get a better read once we're back home, but for now let's get ready to go and then we'll figure out what's up with Garrett."

CHAPTER 17

A STITCH IN TIME

An hour later, Dan released the cast on Ena's home and knocked on the front door.

She appeared, clutching a rosary and dressed for the funeral. Fionna explained to Ena that she and Dan had gone to what used to be Matteo's, and that they wanted to take her back after the service.

She cried tears of joy as she nodded into Fionna's embrace.

"Isaac is coming to the service. He loved Susanna too, but he wants to take me back home with him. Maybe he will come to Matteo's with us," she pled hopefully.

Dan sincerely hoped that Isaac would be agreeable as he guided Ena into the passenger's seat and drove her to the church where the funeral was being held.

"Are you all right, Maylea?" Ena asked as they proceeded into the church.

"Oh, yes, ma'am," Fionna lied. "I just can feel everyone's sadness, you know."

Ena shook her head. "No, what you must feel is thankful that you had your Nana and that she got to be with you while she was here and that she lived the life she lived. Tap into the celebration and leave the mourning behind. She has gone on to a better place, just like your mother and my Salvador," she assured.

Fionna nodded as tender tears leaked from her eyes. Dan wrapped his arm around her as he settled her on a pew.

True to Ena's word, the service was a celebration of Nana's life. Gretta spoke and recalled wonderful moments with her mother growing up. Ena told about Susanna's antics when they were young and then when they weren't so young.

Samuel even retold the story of picking Nana up at the train station after he and Gretta had decided to marry and move to DC so that Maylea could attend Venton Academy. The service wasn't formal, and Gretta urged Fionna to share a recollection of her own. Dan squeezed her hand and willed her strength as she nodded and stood to move near the casket.

"I'm so sorry. I don't know how to say all of this in Spanish." She bit her lip but then smiled. "I was fourteen when I first met Nana, when we lived just outside of Dallas. That's when Daddy met Gretta," she explained and offered her stepmother a sweet smile.

"Nana used to take the train to come and visit us. And my mom taught me to sew Hawaiian quilts, but I couldn't bind them. So Nana began teaching me how to sew them even better, so that she could bind them for me. She taught me so much," spilled from Fionna's heart right out of her lips. Dan smiled as he watched the memories heal his Maylea.

"Nana used to tell me that life is like a quilt. Sometimes the fabric isn't quite right. Sometimes we miss a stitch or two, but when the quilt is complete, more of it is beautiful than not. And that if we lie in its warmth and remember the good times that it will have been worth every missed stitch and all of the times that the fabric was wrong, or even the times that the binding wears thin. It will work its way into the beautiful pattern at just the right time." Fionna's eyes fell to Dan and she gave him her smile. "And you know what, Nana was right," she concluded with a nod. She kissed her hand and patted the kiss onto Nana's folded hands as she returned to Dan's side.

After the recollections, a priest led everyone in a brief ceremony and then they proceeded to the graveyard.

After the service, Ena regaled Dan, Fionna, Isaac, Samuel, and Gretta with recollections as they sat at a table in Caliente's. Iodex officers moved in and out, some of them joining in the memories of Matteo's.

Dan helped Isaac load boxes of Ena's possessions and her cat along with her suitcases into his car, and they waved as Ena was driven to her new home in Merida. Dan and Fionna helped Gretta and Samuel begin packing up Nana's things. Gretta gave Fionna a few of Nana's quilts and other things that had meant a great deal to her.

CHAPTER 18

CONFESSIONS

At nine o'clock, Dan pulled the Ferrari into the garage, still wondering what Garrett wanted to talk about as he tried to will away his exhaustion.

He guided Fionna into their home to find Garrett reclined on the couch, with Halia sound asleep on his chest, while he watched football.

"Aida tried to stay up. I promised you'd come kiss her when you got home. Rainer and Em cut out just a few minutes ago," he explained in a whisper. Dan and Fionna nodded and slipped into Aida's room to give her a good night kiss.

"Hi, Daddy." She yawned, half-asleep.

"Hey, baby girl," Dan whispered as he sealed heat in the quilt that covered her.

"Garrett feels like when your tummy hurts," she managed to inform Dan before she was out completely.

Dan and Fionna shared another concerned glance and pulled Aida's door closed as they moved back down the stairs.

"Em fed her like an hour ago," Garrett explained as he carefully handed Halia to Fionna.

"Okay." Fionna placed Halia in her bassinet and returned. "Now what's wrong?" She seated herself beside Dan on the couch.

"You want a beer?" Dan sensed that Garrett needed to relax a little.

Garrett shrugged. "Yeah, sure, since I'm off babysitting duty."

Dan and Fionna sat staring at Garrett as he seemed to will resolve from the air around him.

"This is kind of a long story, I guess," he began.

"We're not going anywhere, so just start whenever you're ready." Dan had a great deal of experience hearing confessions, and Garrett Haydenshire appeared to have a lifetime's worth of secrets he needed to share.

"The Governor and Lillian don't know any of this. There's this one medio who works in London, and he's the only person who knows one certain part, so I'd like to keep it that way," Garrett requested though it was more of an order.

"Done," Dan agreed as Fionna nodded her understanding.

He turned to stare Fionna down. "If you could not freak, that'd be really great."

Dan bit back his chuckle.

"Garrett, just tell me whatever it is," Fionna pled. Dan could feel the harrowing fear in Garrett's shield, so she certainly could.

He turned his eyes back to Dan. "Do you remember a couple of months after we buried Cal?" Garrett ran his hands through his hair. "And we got intelligence that Naftan and Rojas had been found murdered. We suspected that Pravus had killed his own men."

"Yeah, I remember." Dan's brow furrowed as he studied Garrett. "Brazilian Iodex found Naftan in a dumpster, and Rojas was nearby on the side of the road."

"Yeah," Garrett agreed. "Only…uh…Pravus didn't kill them."

Dan braced to hear the forthcoming explanation. "Okay."

"Let's see here." Garrett backtracked suddenly. He explained how he'd told Governor Haydenshire he was taking a few weeks off. How he'd used Iodex computers and printers to make his own fake IDs, as soon as they'd gotten word that Pravus was back in Brazil. How he'd gone as far as to plan out how to cover his tracks and blend in. He explained the promises he'd made to Aida's mother and how he'd known the photographs, that were currently in frames in Aida's bedroom, were at the orphanage. Fionna sobbed convulsively as Garrett continued.

"So, I took care of Naftan and Rojas, and uh…Pravus thought he'd taken care of me." He grimaced. "I ended up in one of those aid stations, and somehow, I survived. I really don't think I thought I would live. I figured if I murdered them, Em and you would pick up on it,"—he gestured to Fionna—"so I don't think I ever really planned on being back home." He shrugged. "Anyway, they healed me up for the most part."

Dan let Fionna cry into his chest as he nodded. "For the most part?" He caught the part that had Garrett's muscles visibly tensing.

"It was a pretty basic medical clinic, and I was mostly dead when I was left there, so everything works, but I can't…" He gestured to his own crotch and then to Halia in the cradle, and Dan let the shock and understanding work through him.

Fionna moved to Garrett as she wrapped him up in her embrace. He held her tenderly and let her continue to cry. "I'm fine. I swear." He tried to reassure her as she cradled him to her.

"I'm so sorry I never picked up on it. I should've known, so I could've told you that it's okay. I'm just so sorry," Fionna managed through her sobs. "I should've helped you talk through it all. Energy is darkened by intention, so I would never have felt anything dark from any of that. Your intentions were good, but I should have helped you more. I'm so, so sorry."

"Fi, it's okay. I'm fine."

"No, you needed me, and I wasn't there."

"You were there. The fact that you didn't know made me feel like I…don't know…wasn't a terrible person, maybe. I needed you to be who you've always been for me and you were. You've always been there whenever I've needed you. You let me stay at your house for weeks after he was killed. You saved my life."

"You are not a terrible person," Dan vowed. "Look at what you did for Aida. Are you sure about everything though? Maybe a different medio or…?"

"I don't even want kids, but I really, really do want to help take care of Aida." He shot Dan an urgent, pleading look. "So, now that you know I've committed murder in the first several times, I was hoping you'd hire me on at Hawaiian Iodex because I promised her mom. I just want to be there for her always, you know." His voice snagged on what must've been desperation.

Fionna turned her pleading, sienna eyes on Dan as she clung to Garrett.

"Of course," Dan agreed instantly. "But I'm not just hiring you on. I'm making you my partner, and I think Fi and I would really like you to be the girls' godfather."

"Please," Fionna managed in a heartbroken plea.

"Yeah, of course." Garrett couldn't get his agreement out fast enough. "Thank you."

"Garrett." Fionna clung to him. Her cast worked through him, soothing his frantic rhythms. "Is that why you won't just ask Chloe to marry you? Because…" she began but her voice was choked out with renewed tears.

"No," Garrett scoffed. "Chloe doesn't want to leave the Angels and move to Kauai, and she needs someone else. I do not want to be married to anyone, most especially her."

Fionna paused, and Dan knew she was wading through Garrett's emotions. "Okay." She seemed to feel he was telling the truth about Chloe. "But Tutu can help you, and just being on Kauai, it might heal you…if you ever did want to have kids."

Garrett shook his head. "It doesn't work like that."

"Fi, baby, come here." Dan beckoned his wife back to him. She eased away from Garrett, still giving him sorrowful gazes. "I'm going to tell you this once, and I swear I'll never bring any of this back up, okay?" Garrett nodded through his scowl. "There were several hours after she got shot,"—his body convulsed from the memory—"after they told me she was going to be okay, they also said they weren't certain she would ever be able to have children. They weren't sure she could carry them with the scar tissue. Adeline was able to fix everything, but that would never have deterred me.

"It would never have changed the way I felt about her or have made me not want to spend every second of the rest of my life with her, so if

122

on any level you think you might owe Chloe at least the chance to decide for herself what she wants to do, don't decide that for her. You've been going back to her for fifteen years. There has be something to that."

"I've been going back to her for fifteen years because she never wanted anything more out of our relationship than I did. Okay? I get that's not the way you're wired, but marriage, the family deal, all of that. I don't want any of it. I should never have told you that part. All I want is to work for you again. We're an unstoppable force, and I miss that," he admitted, making Dan grin. "I want to help you raise Aida, and I'm sick to death of DC. I want out of here. You, of all people, know what it's like to live here as a governor's son."

"I'm so happy you want to come with us!" Fionna headed back to Garrett's arms. He gave a genuine chuckle over the juxtaposition of her vow and her tears.

Dan hoped Garrett would think about what he'd said, but he would keep his promise and never bring up what had happened to one of his best friends ever again.

"We're thinking of moving as soon as I get the disaster cleaned up at Venton. Maybe you could come with us next weekend for the foundation blessing. I was planning on signing my contract. It's Hawaiian tradition that the Gifted people serving the lands sign the contracts there, so you could sign yours as well. I'll have Victoria draw it up tomorrow." Dan gave Garrett hope and a plan and something he could think about besides the horrors of his past. Dan knew that was what he needed at that moment.

"That'd be good," Garrett agreed.

"And you can stay on the farm," Fionna pled. Her urgent tone had Garrett agreeing.

"I guess I better tell Sorenson and the fam before I go signing a contract, but yeah, that sounds great. Thank you."

"There is no one else I would have as my partner and that I would have looking after my girls, all of them." Dan gestured his head to Fionna.

"Yeah, well, I loved two of them first. Don't ever forget that."

"You have my word."

"All of us love you so much," Fionna gushed. She sounded a little like Aida.

"I love you too, baby," Garrett vowed. "Do you think your grandparents would mind me staying there until I find a place on the island?"

Dan and Fionna both felt the excitement and peace that the plan had given Garrett.

"They just expanded the farm to twice the size it was when you were there. You're staying there forever. Aida needs you every day and so do I. But you do have to start calling me Maylea."

After strategizing the best way to run Hawaiian Iodex and what their lives might be like on the islands, Garrett left three hours later. Dan checked his watch. He had a phone call to make before he could really process what they'd just decided.

Josh Riker answered on the first ring. "I am so ready for you to be out here putting up with this crap we get from the representative's office," was the frustrated greeting.

Dan's brow furrowed. "Okay, uh, listen, I was just wondering if you'd given any more thought on what you want your position to be since I'm going to be running Iodex for all of the islands and not just Kauai?"

"Yeah, man, I thought about it. I'll keep running Kauai if you're okay with that, but I really don't want to work for the state."

Relief eased the tense set of Dan's rhythms. "That's fine with me. Thank you."

"Need to learn to say mahalo if you're coming to Hawaii." Josh laughed.

"Mahalo. You're right. I'm sorry. Been a long, long day."

"Catch you later."

Dan and Fionna let the stunned disbelief that had morphed into forms of understanding wash through them as they moved to their bedroom.

"Will you take a bath with me?" she asked.

"Of course." Dan was eager to talk as well.

"I just can't believe I never felt any of that from him. He's been my best friend for almost fifteen years," spilled from Fionna's mouth as she reclined against him in the tub. "If I'd felt it, I could've helped him more. I should have been there for him. He's always there for me."

"It's something he just dealt with. He went to Tad and Nathan's and healed, and he put it away and then he didn't have to think about it. He told himself Pravus hadn't taken away anything he'd wanted, and he continued to fight." Dan knew how Garrett had handled the situation because that is precisely what Dan would have done. "I think the fact that you didn't feel that in his energy gave him a lot of peace, so it helped him more that you didn't treat him any differently."

"He stayed on my couch for weeks after Cal died, and I tried so much to help him. I fed him and casted him so he could sleep. I stayed with him constantly. But after that, he wouldn't talk about it anymore. Then all of a sudden he tells me he's going to Cancun. I knew he was lying…but I had no idea where he was really going. I didn't want to say anything to Mrs. Haydenshire. She'd been through so much, and I knew she couldn't take anymore."

"That's probably about the time he went from devastated to furious. That's when he made his plans."

"All of the stupid papers announcing that Halia was his." She shook her head. "On top of it just being so insane, it had to have thrown it all back in his face."

The comment Dan had made so haphazardly sitting in the bar a few weeks before Halia's birth, when he'd been teased for getting Fionna pregnant on their honeymoon, seared through his mind. *"Hey, I get the job done."* Nausea roiled in his gut. How could he have said something so pompous? His jaw clenched as he shook his head.

"I know Garrett like the back of my own hand." He let his thoughts take flight on his tongue. "The last thing he would want is our pity. He wants to be a bigger part of Aida and Halia's lives, and we both want that as well. Let's start there. I think you might be right. Maybe after he's lived there a while, he'll let Tutu help him. We both know the Kauaian rhythms are healing, even if you aren't from there. I think Garrett needs Aida and us, and I know we need him. We need to root our family there."

"Garrett has always been a part of our ohana. It kills me he went through that. I can't believe he never even told Will."

"Like I said, he put it away and decided not to think about it. We adopted Aida, and I think that brought him a lot of peace. But we decided to move her almost five thousand miles away, and it all got to him again," Dan lamented.

"You're amazing, you know that?" Fionna whispered as she let Dan cradle her in the warm water.

"Oh yeah, I'm so fucking amazing I allowed myself to be so consumed with my own vengeance, I didn't know that one of my best friends was in such a bad place he went on a suicide mission to Brazil alone." He would never forgive himself for that. Ever.

"Would you have gone with him?" Her face held no traces of judgment only of deep remorse.

"Yes." Dan saw no reason to lie to her. "If I'd been with him, someone would have had his back. If I'd gone with him, Pravus would have met his maker years ago. If he'd gotten hit, I could have gotten him help faster." Dan tried not to think of how drastically different all of their lives would've been if Pravus hadn't survived Garrett's mission.

CHAPTER 19

PARTNERS

Dan paced in front of his History of Defense class as they took their exams. Garrett was picking Aida up from school and bringing her to the airport. They would be in Lihue by nightfall since they'd been given the Crown Governor's jet for their use.

Dan glanced out at his students. He tried not to chuckle at those who were writing everything they'd ever heard on the subject each question covered and at the ones who were praying for the words to magically appear on their test sheets.

The final papers of the semesters were on thumb drives sitting on his desk.

Dan was pacing because of the lunch appointment he had in an hour. Governor Haydenshire had phoned Dan and requested to take him out to lunch. Garrett had told his parents that he'd been offered the job as deputy commander of Hawaiian Iodex and that he was going to be moving to Kauai. The Crown Governor knew his children well. He had to have known there was more to this than Garrett's excuses that he wanted out of DC and that he wanted to work for Dan again.

Dan would never betray Garrett's trust, and he would never retell his gruesome story, so lunch with the governor was certain to be awkward to say the least.

They would be back in town Tuesday and then the Fitzroys were coming to visit. Dan had helped Fionna and Aida decorate the Christmas tree Monday night. Aida was ecstatic over all of the festivities.

Fionna had wrapped the book set and a few of the accessories that would go with the doll Aida had asked Santa for. The board games, friendship bracelet kit, and a unicorn stationery set were all placed under the tree along with a few gifts for Halia. She'd done this while Aida was at school Wednesday. They'd waited eagerly for her to read her name on the tags. She'd always been a little uncomfortable receiving gifts, but Dan and Fionna were too excited not to hope she would be thrilled with her presents. Aida had seated herself in front of the tree and studied the gifts.

"Mommy, did you mean to write Aida on all of these?" she'd asked on the verge of panic.

Fionna had nodded sweetly. "They're for you from me and Daddy," she'd gently explained.

"I think you're only supposed to have one, because I don't think I have enough money to buy you and Daddy more than one thing," Aida had managed before tears began falling from her eyes.

Dan had promised he would take Aida shopping for Mommy and Halia and that he would give her the money for the gifts she wanted to get. Fionna had promised to take her shopping to buy gifts for Dan and Garrett. This had helped some, but Aida was still concerned.

Fionna had suggested that Aida could help out around the house and earn some money to spend on gifts. Aida had leapt into this with great gusto. Dan had eaten a peanut butter and jelly sandwich his little girl had lovingly packed for him as a snack that morning instead of telling her that he was having lunch with Governor Haydenshire.

Dan and Garrett had sat down with Aida to help her write her letter to Santa. The entire letter requested items she wanted Santa to bring to the orphans in Brazil. Garrett had finally gotten her to admit that she would like the doll Dan and Fionna had ordered for her before Halloween, but Aida had insisted that the presents for her friends at the orphanage were much more important.

Dan, Fionna, Garrett, Emily, Rainer, Logan, Adeline, and the Haydenshires had purchased dozens upon dozens of Christmas gifts that Garrett would be delivering to the orphans on Christmas day.

The buzz of the bell shook Dan from his reverie.

"Exam papers on my desk. Have a wonderful Christmas break. I'll see you January fourth for our last term together," Dan commanded.

As he collected everything, Dan moved back to his office to lock everything up. His father followed him.

"The press got wind of you and Garrett signing your contracts tomorrow in Lihue. Victoria's office is flooded with phone calls, but she wasn't certain how you wanted to handle your decision to name Garrett your deputy commander," Governor Vindico prodded.

"Representative Kalakona was thrilled when I told her I was hiring Garrett. He's an outstanding officer. He's one of our best friends. On Sunday, he will officially be my children's godfather. I don't know why anyone would find any of this difficult to understand."

"You know, you and Garrett were a matched set growing up and all the way through Iodex. Stephen and I do have a little experience knowing when you're conveniently leaving out large pieces of the yarn you're spinning for us."

"Gotta go, Dad. I have no doubt Governor Haydenshire will continue this lecture for you at lunch. We'll be back Tuesday," Dan assured his father as he raced out of his office.

The pent-up air escaped Dan's lungs in a fretful huff as he cranked the Ferrari.

"Round two," he lamented as he made the turn on Venton Drive.

Garrett phoned Dan just as he made the exit to the Pentagon. "I was in Dad's office getting the third degree when your dad called and invited himself to your lunch. I decided I'd come along as well," he explained with a chuckle.

"Good. If worse comes to worst, at least I'm not outmanned, but you know I'd never say anything." Garrett had shared a dark, tattered piece of his soul, and those were the very hardest to share.

"I know. I just thought if you're actually going to have a deputy commander, I should probably show up and be your partner. Teach you what that's all about," he harassed.

When Dan had taken over the National Elite Squadron, he'd let everyone know that he worked alone. Things had changed, and Dan had learned a tremendous amount in the last year.

Dan and Garrett continued to talk just as they always had until they pulled in the parking lot of Frye's. They seated themselves at the booth Governor Haydenshire preferred.

"Seems our lunch meeting for two has attracted a few additions." Governor Haydenshire studied Garrett.

"We're Iodex officers, so the whole divide and interrogate thing we have all figured out," Garrett sneered. "We invented it."

"I wasn't going to interrogate anyone. I wish you felt like you could tell me whatever happened that has you deciding you'd like to quit your current job and move almost five thousand miles away."

Governor Vindico slid into the booth just then. He must've left right after Dan.

Garrett drew an exaggerated breath. "Let me go through this long list with you yet again. First of all, it is Hawaii. I'm really good with being paid twice what I make now and getting off every day around three or four to go surf and camp. Dan and I are the best damn Shield team there ever was or will ever be. My best friends and my goddaughters will be there. I'd kind of like to see them grow up."

"So would I," Governor Vindico quipped.

Garrett continued, "I'm sick to death of DC traffic, smog, and winter, and with my every move being recorded because I'm the Crown Governor's son, no offense. On top of all of that, the average temperature being between sixty-five and eighty-five every day and being on an island where the women have no real issue being topless sounds like heaven to me," Garrett concluded.

Dan laughed but wondered when he should break it to Garrett that topless women weren't exactly the norm. He suspected Garrett knew that but was trying to shock his father into silence.

"I don't know, son, you've never seemed to have any trouble getting women here in DC to take their tops off for you." Governor Haydenshire wasn't backing down, it appeared.

As Dan and his father didn't typically have conversations quite that blunt, they shared a quick glance, eager to hear Garrett's retort.

"Yeah well, I've seen all DC has to offer. I'm looking to expand my horizons," Garrett dared the governor to continue.

"Garrett," Governor Haydenshire scolded. "I am thrilled for you to move to Kauai and to work with Dan again. I know the two of you are a force to be reckoned with. I want you to be happy and fulfilled in your career and in your life, but I know there is more to this. I don't understand why you're not being truthful with me." His plea held more than a note of pain.

Dan and his father both shifted uncomfortably.

"Dad, I swear to you, this is what I want to do for me, okay?"

"What about Chloe Sawyer?"

Dan wondered if the Haydenshires had assumed Garrett would eventually settle down and ask Chloe for her hand.

"What about her?"

"Have you told her you're moving because, believe me, it's going to be in the papers tomorrow."

Garrett drew a quick sip of his Dr Pepper and nodded. "I did tell Chloe I was moving, but like I told her and have told you a dozen times now, I'm not moving until Dan and Fi are ready to go, so it could be months. Hell, it'll probably be summer. I don't know why you're freaking out about this now."

The governor paused and studied his son with a great deal of thought before he asked, "Is Aida your biological daughter, Garrett?"

Dan's mouth hung open in shock.

"What?!" Garrett gasped. "No!" He stared at his father like he'd lost his mind. "If Aida were mine, I sure as hell wouldn't have let her live in an orphanage all that time. I would've brought her here. I would be the one raising her. My God, *you* raised me. How could you think that?"

And in his response lay the final piece to the puzzle. Dan choked on the bile that flooded his throat as the picture formed complete in his mind.

Garrett always thought he should have tried to adopt Aida, or he should have brought her home to his parents and made some excuse, done anything but left her in that orphanage.

He couldn't have brought her home. That would have placed him in the area at the time of Rojas's and Naftan's deaths. He would have been brought up on suspicion immediately.

Dan sat beside Garrett in a booth across from their fathers and let the stunned disbelief wash through him. Garrett couldn't see that he'd saved Aida's life. He blamed himself for her having to live in that orphanage even knowing the orphanage was better able to provide for Aida than her parents had been. They were all starving because of Pravus's sick extortion racket that he ran all over South America.

He took what very little money they had before he murdered her family in cold blood when they weren't able to continue paying. Dan couldn't allow Garrett to go on hating himself for everything that happened in Brazil so many years ago. He refused.

Waves of horror and nausea washed over him as he considered what would have happened to his precious little girl at four years old if Garrett hadn't been there. If she'd stumbled upon her home engulfed in flames and her family dead, she would have tried to go in. It was who Aida was, and she had no means of taking care of herself. She would have looked for her parents. Had Garrett not been there, Aida wouldn't have survived. If the fire hadn't robbed her of life, she would have starved. Their closest neighbors were miles away, and no one had means or strength to get her to that orphanage—no one but Garrett. If he hadn't followed Pravus and his men, they would have taken her life as well.

"All right, fine." Governor Haydenshire nodded his defeat. "Your mother and I want you to do whatever you find fulfilling in this life. We want to help you accomplish your dreams and your goals. If moving to Kauai is what is next on your horizon, I would never stand in your way.

"In fact, I will do anything in my power to make your life in Hawaii the best it can possibly be, but let me say this, I know there are things that have happened in your life, things that you have done, that you don't think we would ever be able to forgive you for, and you're wrong. You could never and *have* never done anything that would make me not love you or not be proud of the man that you are.

"I already know, and I knew it when it happened. Recently, I figured out what you've been dealing with ever since. All I can hope is that at some point you'll be willing to tell me what I already know. It would mean a great deal to me to know that you trust me enough to let me hear it from your mouth." Governor Haydenshire set his challenge and then with a slight headshake. He sat back having said his piece.

Dan stared steadfastly at the table as he began to understand that Governor Vindico was the only man seated at their table that day who had no idea what had happened to Garrett.

"I'm fine, Dad," Garrett continued his lies.

CHAPTER 20

SWORD DUEL

At four o'clock, Dan scowled as he took in the awaiting press at the Senate.

"Oh, good grief." Fionna tried to cover Halia with another blanket. Dan set down the suitcase he was carrying and helped her arrange the blanket so that nothing but Halia's sleeping form on her mother's chest was visible to the dozens of cameras.

"You seem to bring the press out in droves." Victoria Kalakona sounded oddly thrilled as she joined Dan, Fionna, and Garrett while they trudged toward the awaiting doom.

Garrett had his bags in one hand and was holding Aida's hand in his other. He was also loaded down with Aida's Disney Princess backpack and bags full of toys. Dan was carrying his and Fionna's luggage and Halia's car seat. Fionna was carrying Halia along with several other bags hung on her shoulders. They looked like they were either moving or had become pack mules as a side gig.

Rep. Kalakona was overjoyed that two of the Realm's highest-trained, tested, and proven officers were set to work for Iodex in her state. She beamed and waved like a pageant queen as they approached the reporters and photographers.

"Fionna, Fionna, Fionna," chanted from every direction. "Are you in an open marriage?"

"Dan, can you tell us why you've decided to get back in law enforcement?"

"Have you named Garrett Haydenshire your daughters' guardian because he is Halia's actual father?"

"Fionna, are you in an open marriage with these two men?" chanted from multiple reporters.

Fury blazed through Dan like a dropped match in lighter fluid.

Fionna's mouth fell open, but then she began to laugh in disbelief.

"You know, I should've seen *that* coming." Garrett shook his head and rolled his eyes.

"Representative Kalakona, can you tell us what prompted your decision to recruit Officers Vindico and Haydenshire for Hawaiian Iodex? Does this have anything to do with the Suen Ma crime family who has recently purchased land on Oahu?"

"Garrett, Garrett, Garrett." It was endless. "What was the Crown Governor's reaction when you told him you were opening the Vindicos' marriage and would be raising their daughters with them?"

Dan spun and glared at the reporter who had asked the last question.

"Let's get a few things straight," he spat viciously. Fionna sighed as she stopped and stood by Dan.

Garrett nodded his agreement and stepped forward. "Listen up. I am not now nor have I ever been romantically involved with Fionna. She is his only wife. He is her only husband," Garrett stated slowly as if he was speaking to someone extremely unintelligent. "These are their daughters." He held up Aida's hand that was still clasped in his own and then patted Halia under her blanket.

"The Vindicos are very dear friends of mine, and Aida and Halia are my goddaughters. I will be Dan's deputy commander in Hawaii, but those are the extents of our relationships," he concluded.

Dan and Fionna nodded their adamant agreement.

"I so do not sword duel," Garrett huffed under his breath as they headed to the awaiting jet. Dan had to laugh.

"Uh yeah, and I do not share. I'm fine with you being Uncle Garrett to my girls. Thrilled really, but Fi is all mine."

"No issue there," Garrett assured him.

The Crown Governor's jet was a serene getaway when they finally boarded. Aida's eyes lit as she took in the lush accommodations. Fionna seated herself on one of the cushioned couch areas and let Dan help her get Halia arranged. Aida released Garrett's hand and rushed to her mother. As they took off, Fionna was in heaven heading to her island while snuggling with Aida and Halia as the plane climbed in the sky.

The representative and her aide took a seat near the front, and Dan gestured for Garrett to join him in back seats near the girls.

Garrett grinned at Fionna covered in her children and laughed. "They look like cats."

"Yeah, listen to me for a second," Dan guided. Garrett's brow furrowed as he nodded. "You know my girls are my entire world. And the two biggest ones there," he gestured his head to Aida and Fionna. Aida had engaged her mother in a kunik kiss. They were rubbing noses and giggling and then Halia nuzzled her head under Fionna's chin. "They need each other. They don't do well apart. If you hadn't followed them," Dan whispered making certain no one but Garrett could hear him. "If you hadn't done what you did, that beautiful little girl who means the world to both of us, she wouldn't be here. And that means my Maylea would be missing a huge part of her soul and her spirit. So, you just remember that when you get to thinking you're the bad guy and maybe you should have done something different.

"When you move with us to Kauai and you hang around the farm, you'll hear this over and over, but you'll also realize that it's true— everything happens for a reason and everything happens in its own time. You've got to let that doubt go, because you did everything right. Stop believing your own bullshit. You saved her. You saved Fi, and you've saved me more times than I can count. And then *she* saved all of us," Dan vowed as he gave a single nod to Aida. Garrett drew an audible breath as he studied Aida and Fionna as they seemed to revel in one another. He finally gave a hesitant nod.

"She's amazing," he whispered.

Dan nodded. "Yeah, and she's here with us because of you."

Aida beamed at Dan and then leaned to whisper in Fionna's ear. Fionna helped her unbuckle her seatbelt. Aida whisked into Dan's arms and climbed up in his lap.

"I'm so happy you're moving with us," she informed Garrett as she lay on his shoulder while she remained in Dan's lap.

Garrett kissed the top of Aida's head. "I'm glad I'm moving with you too, baby girl. You'll have to show me all the fun stuff we do when we live on Kauai."

"Okay!" Aida sat up. Her eyes lit. "There are so, so many things."

Dan and Garrett grinned as she continued. "First, you get to play on the farm, and Papa will let you ride on the tractor with him, and let you pick any flowers you want, and Tutu will let you make all kinds of things in her workshop. And if you want to stick your hands in the goo and squeeze it because it feels gushy, she will say, "Yes my little e ku'u aloha, you may squeeze." Aida giggled in delight over her great-grandmother's general policy of letting Aida do just about anything she requested.

Garrett laughed at her outright.

"And you get to swim in the ocean, and you can maybe take me to my dance classes sometimes and see me hula." Aida wiggled in Dan's lap in effort to show how she shook her hips. "And Uncle Kai can surf and so can Mommy now that Halia isn't in her tummy anymore and she's out here to play with me. And you can go on the paddle boards and get shave ice and it's the most yummy. I like the mango kind with ice cream too. And there's lots of roosters, but they're not as much of the fun parts.

"And you can play in the waterfall, and sometimes Papa will turn on the sprinklers by our house, and you can play in them. Mommy lets me play in them after we come back from the ocean because you can take your swimsuit off and get all of the sand off of you before you take a shower. And you can take baths outside, and Mommy will put flowers that float in your bath if you want, and Tutu will put oils in your bath that make your skin not itchy anymore, and they smell so good. And Daddy gives Mommy baths there all the time and everyone is happy there, and my tummy almost never hurts there. And there's almost no thunderstorms ever, maybe only sometimes. And I haven't ever gotten to see Mommy surf yet because God sent me to live with Mommy and baby Halia to live in Mommy's tummy almost at the same time." Aida sounded fully confident of what she was informing her godfather.

Dan raised his eyebrows in effort to show his earlier point. Garrett gave a slight nod of acceptance as Aida continued. "And sometimes it's very funny, because when Mommy doesn't wear her shirt when she's on the farm sometimes because you don't have to because it's private, but if Papa sees her, he shakes his head at her and says, 'Maylea, go cover up. You're driving that boy lolo, and I need him to work.'" Aida waggled her finger in her impersonation of her grandfather. Dan squeezed his eyes shut as Garrett cracked up.

When he regained the ability to do anything but laugh at Dan, he shook his head as he gazed at Aida adoringly. "I love you, Aida Mae."

Aida threw her arms around Garrett's neck. "I love you too, so much, so much!"

She fell back against Dan's chest and sighed contentedly. Garrett was still chuckling over her story when Aida decided she wanted to play on the iPad and went to retrieve it from her backpack.

"So," Garrett leapt as soon as Aida was out of earshot, "I've always felt when it came to other guys' wives the look but don't touch policy worked well. You know, you can admire the view but not purchase real estate."

Dan shuddered visibly. "I function better under the policy of—if you admire my wife's rack, it might be the last thing you ever see."

"Uh yeah, man, I'm sorry to tell you this, but I've seen them so, so many times. I may have seen them more than you have if I'm being honest." Garrett gave little effort to hide his goading grin.

"If what you're about to tell me is going to make me change my mind on you becoming my baby girls' godfather, stop talking."

Garrett laughed again as he shook his head. "I sure as hell didn't spy on her. I'm not some kind of perv. We've been best friends for fifteen years. I'm not sure if you know this, but Fi is pretty comfortable with her body and herself. She walked around topless in front of me all the time. I certainly never complained."

Dan fought the possessive fury that bubbled in his gut.

"Deep breath, Vindico," Garrett harassed. "And..."—he waited while his smirk spread farther across his face—"exhale."

Fionna was watching Dan and Garrett. She laid Halia in her car seat and popped a kiss on top of Aida's head. She fell into Dan's lap.

"What did you say that made his *I am now going to choke something violently* face come out?"

"That I've seen your headlights on more than one occasion, but never turned on the high beams," Garrett explained.

Fionna shook her head. "Don't tell him things like that. He gets all possessive and crazy and then I have to take him to the private room on your Dad's jet because I get all turned on when he's like that," Fionna came right back. She stuck her tongue between her teeth as she began laughing. She had no issue harassing Garrett.

Garrett held up his hands in defeat. "That is way more information than I needed. Thank you." Dan gave Garrett a derisive chuckle as he cradled Fionna in his lap and kissed her.

CHAPTER 21
LONE WARRIOR

Fionna pointed out about halfway through their flight that Kalakona and her aide were uncertain if they should interrupt the extreme ease with which all of the Vindicos and Garrett related with one another.

Fionna shifted seamlessly into the role of Commander of Iodex's wife. She gradually included the representative in a conversation. They all began discussing the differences in life in Hawaii versus that of life in DC.

Fionna's rhythms would tense around the representative, but Dan never got a chance to ask her what she was feeling.

"Halia and I are wearing the bracelets that you gave us," Aida hesitantly informed Victoria.

"They look very pretty on you and your baby sister," Ms. Kalakona assured her.

"Do you know my Tutu?"

"Not well, but I'm sure they're excited you and Halia are coming back to live on the farm."

Aida nodded her agreement. "Did you know I have four names, and Mommy has four names and Halia too?"

Garrett, Dan, and Fionna all watched her explain the way her world worked to the Senteon Representative.

"I didn't know that, but I do know that names are very important. Will you tell me your names?" Victoria asked.

"Yes, ma'am. My name is Aida Santos Hanai Vindico. And Mommy's name is Fionna Kalani Halia Vindico, but everyone that lives in Kauai calls her Maylea and that makes her feel very happy, so I think that's the most important one."

Fionna and Dan chuckled as did Victoria.

"I think you're right, and that you are a very smart little girl."

"Thank you." Aida blushed from the compliment. "Halia's name is Halia Elisabeth Amelia Vindico," she concluded.

Victoria's eyes rose to meet Dan's for a moment as she nodded her understanding and extended a smile to Fionna.

"Are you going to come to the farm with us?" Aida wondered.

"No. Not today." Victoria shook her head. "Your Daddy and…" she paused as she glanced at Garrett. "What do you call Garrett?"

"I call him Uncle Garrett because I love him very much and he loves me very much, and he takes very good care of me. I can feel how much he loves me when he hugs me like this." Aida proceeded to give herself a tight hug.

Dan elbowed Garrett. He grinned and gazed at Aida like he'd never love anything as much as he adored her. Aida continued, "But, sometimes, Mrs. Haydenshire calls him Garrett Alexander Haydenshire if he did something and he's in trouble."

Garrett laughed as he nodded his agreement. He stood, hoisted Aida into his arms, and sat her in his lap.

"I love for you to call me Uncle Garrett, baby girl," he assured her. The representative watched Aida and Garrett intently. Her expression was unreadable.

Fionna beamed at both of them. "Do you know what Alexander means, Aida?"

Aida shook her head but was intrigued. She laid her head against Garrett's chest to listen.

Fionna's neck contracted in a harsh swallow before she answered. "Alexander means the lone protector." Her voice caught before she could go on.

"And steadfast shield and conqueror," Victoria added for her. Fionna nodded as she smiled at Garrett.

"And Garrett means strength of the spear," Fionna concluded.

He was visibly moved but did a good job hiding his emotion. Halia began fussing from her car seat, and Fionna stood to retrieve her.

"She wants Daddy," Fionna informed Dan wryly. He beamed.

"That's because she's my little coconut," he drawled as he took Halia and the bottle Fionna provided him.

"Do you know what your names mean?" Aida quizzed Victoria hesitantly.

Victoria smiled and seemed pleased she was getting to know the Vindicos better. "Victoria is my first name and it means the winner or victor, and Mara is my middle name," she explained.

Aida's brow furrowed. "I don't know what that means."

"It's not a Hawaiian name. I'm not sure why my parents liked it. In African it means spotted land."

Fionna tensed. "It also means nightmare," she whispered to Dan.

Victoria didn't seem to notice she'd spoken at all.

"Aida means helpful visitor, and Hanai means precious chosen child," Aida explained to Kalakona. "And Daddy says that's because I'm his very, very precious little girl." She beamed and wiggled in Garrett's lap.

The plane touched down in Lihue in just over four hours. The Crown Governor's jet flew faster than any other.

"We'll meet you tomorrow morning at the Iodex office for the official signing," Victoria restated the plans before everyone exited the plane.

"We'll be there," Dan assured her as he began gathering up all of the luggage.

"Tutu, Papa, I'm home," Aida called as Garrett carried her out of Malani's Jeep. Dan and Fionna gazed at one another over the precious sentiment.

"Me too," Fionna whispered as she laid her head on Dan's chest and let him hold her tight just for a moment.

Tutu and Papa were overjoyed with her declaration as they rushed to greet them. Tutu's hand lingered in Garrett's a moment longer than anyone else's. Dan knew she was reading him, but he didn't let on. She studied him intently when he was distracted with the girls.

A little while later, everyone was settling in to the large dinner Tutu and Papa had prepared. Tutu, Papa, Malani, and Kai had spent an extra few minutes doting over Aida before they almost fought over who got to hold Halia first.

Garrett struck up a conversation with Papa about places to live near the Lihue Iodex precinct that would effectively become the satellite office for Hawaiian Iodex.

"Why don't you want to live here with me?" Aida sounded devastated.

Garrett stopped talking abruptly.

"Now, if my moʻopuna wants you here, we'll build two houses if you don't like the guesthouses." Papa smiled with the customary twinkle in his eye.

He liked Garrett. Dan could tell. Garrett had come to Kauai for Dan and Fionna's wedding, but he'd only been on the island for less than twenty-four hours and hadn't spent any real time with Tutu or Papa.

"She's not the only one," Fionna begged.

"If all three of our moʻopunas want you here, then I insist that you live here with us," Tutu stated confidently. Dan understood that she already knew Garrett would stay on the farm.

"I couldn't do that, ma'am, not without paying rent or something."

Tutu shook her head. "My island has called you to protect it. You living here is the least we can do. Besides, Maylea, what are the rules for living on my farm?"

Fionna laughed as she swallowed down a bite of food. "If you live on the farm and Tutu makes you tea, then you must drink it. If she gives you something for your bath, you must use it. You must take time each day to walk in the waters of Kauai, to relax, and fully breathe in the air. You should observe the energy and the beauty around you, even if it's raining," Fionna continued with Tutu nodding her on. "And most importantly, you must understand that the land belongs to the earth, and no one pays to live on the farm. If you live here, you help work the farm or you work in the shop and that is the only payment allowed," Fionna concluded but Tutu shook her head.

"Unless…" Tutu urged.

Fionna rolled her eyes. "Unless you are Mano Forsyth who Tutu warned me not to get involved with, and I didn't listen," she huffed.

The table lit in laughter. Dan shook his head and pulled Fionna to him, letting her hide in him.

As everyone quieted, all eyes turned to Garrett.

"How does that sound?" Tutu encouraged.

"Remember, I'd really like to work from here a good bit. It'd be great if you were close by," Dan upped the ante.

Garrett hemmed. Dan could tell he was overwhelmed by the gesture.

"I grew up working a farm," he allowed, "so that I can do. Don't tell my dad, but I kind of like it. You're sure you don't mind me living here?"

"We would be honored. You will become an important part of our ohana. I already know this," Tutu vowed. "Maylea didn't mention my other recommendations. We want you to live aloha ʻāina, Garrett. We want you to honor the the land and the ways of life here, so it will sustain you. You need to be filled physically, emotionally, and spiritually, so that your spirit will be balanced. You need to eat the foods of our islands, walk the waters, breathe the air, rest, like Maylea explained. But I also feel that you need to engage in long, satisfying lovemaking, and let our island heal your spirit. Things are just a little off, I believe. There is very little my island cannot heal."

As no one else at the table found it odd that Tutu announced this at dinner, it was only Garrett that choked on his water.

"Uh…" Garrett shot Dan a shocked glance.

Dan chuckled and nodded. "You get used to it," he allowed.

"I'm…good with all of that. I'm not sure I can take care of that between now and Tuesday, but I'm not above trying." He smirked. Everyone laughed both at his embarrassment and his quick wit.

"The island rhythms have many, many plans for you, my baby boy," Tutu informed him. "So many plans."

"You'll get used to that too." Malani shook her head at Tutu.

"Tutu," Fionna scolded. "Maybe we could let him eat his dinner before we completely freak him out." Dan noted the excitement in her eyes.

"Maylea, the rhythms move when the time is right. You know this. You can feel them moving now. They have brought all of you back to me, and I intend to care for each and every one of my babies." She held her hands out to everyone seated at her table. "And you, my precious little Halia, we will raise our island girl just like her mama and her big sister." Tutu lifted Halia from her bouncy seat.

Dan and Fionna had already noted how Halia seemed more alert and smiled more readily as soon as they'd landed on her island. But as Tutu lifted her, Halia's head jerked to the side and her eyes sought Dan.

"Yes, Daddy is right there, baby girl." Tutu chuckled as she handed Halia to Dan. She was able to read her instantly just like Fionna.

"Hey, baby." Halia cuddled into his neck. He turned her forward as she began trying to look around. Aida leaned over to see her baby sister.

"Hi, Halia," she cooed as she tickled Halia's belly gently. Halia gave her big sister a broad, fully formed grin and began to coo excitedly.

Fionna swooned over the obvious adoration her girls had for one another.

CHAPTER 22

TEA PARTY

They walked Garrett around to all of the guesthouses. Papa insisted that he look them over and choose where he would like to live, even though they wouldn't be moving for a while. Garrett had in turn insisted that the guesthouses were perfectly fine and that he would never allow a second house to be built just for him.

Papa had barely been able to contain his knowing grin at that announcement, and Dan wondered just what the island had in store for Garrett.

Fionna opened the door to the guesthouse they'd stayed in during Dan's first trip to the farm. "This one only has one bedroom, but the porch is amazing. It's my favorite bed swing of all the guesthouses."

Malani nodded. "Maylea and I used to stay here when we had sleepovers," she recalled with a broad grin. She was carrying a sleeping baby Lanie on her shoulder but was also holding Aida's hand. Dan smiled as he thought of all of his girls being with Fionna's best friend and her little girl each and every day.

"That sounds interesting," Garrett teased Fionna. She swatted his stomach as he ducked away from her and laughed.

Garrett glanced around the guesthouse, but Dan could tell he wasn't that particular. Being given free room and board made him feel he shouldn't be picky.

"Papa and Tutu will want you to pick somewhere your spirit feels at peace," Fionna explained. She must've picked up on the confusion in his energy. "They won't think you're being picky. Try to really feel the energy in each of the homes and then decide which one to make yours."

Dan smiled as he watched Fionna Vindico from Washington, DC, slowly melt into his beautiful island girl, into his Maylea.

Garrett cornered Dan in the kitchen. "I don't know if I'm more freaked out by everything I've heard since I agreed to move onto these people's farm that I barely know, or by the fact that somehow this doesn't feel that weird. I mean, that woman's nuts, right? And I'm like, hell yeah, give me a furnished house."

Dan had to try and quell his laughter as to not awaken Halia.

"I hear you, but trust me, if you just go with it, you'll be happier than you've ever been before," Dan vowed when he regained the ability to talk. "She's not nuts. She's a genius."

"Pretty sure she's a witch," Garrett harassed.

"Just go with it."

"She just told me to chill every day, play in the ocean, not work too hard, and that she doesn't care if I bring girls over with reckless abandon as long as we have long, fulfilling lovemaking sessions." Garrett cracked up as he quoted Tutu. "I'm going with it. Trust me."

He walked around the small square home. There wasn't much to it, but Dan pointed out the fact that it had a decent-sized kitchen.

"Yeah, but Fi's going to feed me, right? She's gonna have to pick up for when I won't be eating at Mom and Dad's."

Dan rolled his eyes as he followed Garrett into the only bedroom in the cottage.

Fionna and Malani were lying on the bed swing on the screened-in back porch. They were lying perpendicularly with Fionna's head on Malani's stomach, and they were laughing. Dan laid Halia beside Lanie on the large queen-sized bed in the bedroom. Aida was busy playing in the kitchen.

"And approximately how many times in the past ten seconds have you contemplated getting in the middle of that?" Garrett gestured his head out to Malani and Fionna.

Dan shook his head. "I'm not dignifying that with a response. Not all of us are wired like you."

"Uh-huh, about ten times. That's what I figured."

Dan rolled his eyes again. "Hey, you know Papa builds all the beds here. They're incredible."

"Yeah, I remember." Garrett recalled the night he'd stayed on the farm before Dan and Fionna's wedding. "Hey, this is not where the little coconut was created, is it?" He pointed to the bed where the babies were sound asleep.

Dan shook his head but decided Garrett could be taken down a notch or two. "Nah, but we practiced here a lot."

Garrett scowled. "I'll get new sheets."

Dan laughed again and shook his head. "Tutu has strict requirements on how one sleeps best, and, trust me, she is once again, one hundred percent correct. You have to use these bamboo sheets that they get the bamboo for from The Big Island and then they have spun by a guy that lives on the North Shore. One thin comforter and two quilts that Tutu hand sews. You wash them once a week and then line dry them. I swear it's the best damn sleep I've ever gotten."

"You are aware you sound like some kind of hippie cult recruiter, right?"

Garrett was in for quite the culture shock, and Dan couldn't wait to watch him eat his words.

Garrett moved out onto the porch. "And we bathe outside because…?" he asked Fionna and Malani who had been giggling mischievously just moments before. Garrett was standing beside the gigantic outdoor bathtub on the back porch. There were huge tubs on all of the screened-in porches on Papa and Tutu's property.

"Because it's relaxing, and you can breathe in the island air which has healing rhythms," Malani answered. "Papa will plant bushes and flowers or trees right beside your porch that match your rhythms. It's amazing how well it works when you're relaxed and breathing in the very things that your energy needs."

Fionna nodded adamantly. "And it's romantic. You can see the stars and the moon if you take your bath at night and all of the flowers and the farm during the day. And it helps you sleep after you've relaxed in the tub."

Dan realized that the reason Papa and Tutu had rather insistently encouraged Garrett to go ahead and pick out his new home was so that they could plant whatever they'd felt his rhythms needed near his hale.

"Your hale is your center." Fionna sat up and shared more of her life and her spirit with the guy who'd been her best friend since she was fifteen. "It's the biggest part of what balances your spirit."

"Uh-huh." Garrett smirked.

"You'll see," was Fionna's retort.

"There's another one-bedroom down the path that way," Malani tried to help. "And there are three two-bedrooms. One is where Dan and Maylea live now, but once they move into their new house, you could move in there."

"Tutu wants everyone to have their own place of peace, so if your family comes to visit, she would give them their own guesthouse," Fionna added.

"Then I can't imagine why I'd need more than one bedroom," Garrett assured. "I already feel like I'm putting your family out."

Fionna shook her head. "Papa would much rather have a little help around the farm than your rent money."

Dan followed Garrett back into the kitchen. Aida had taken out several pots and pans and was pretending to serve dinner to Davi the bunny and Sophie. She'd set the table with empty glasses, silverware, and plates.

"Here, Daddy, I made purple grape juice tea." She thrust an empty mug into Dan's awaiting hand.

"Yum, my favorite." Dan pretended to sip the tea. She giggled delightedly.

"Dude, dishes too?" Garrett cringed. "I don't have to buy anything?" He sounded even more uncomfortable as he gestured to the fully stocked kitchen.

"If you want to buy kitchen stuff, I'm sure you could. And you'll probably want to upgrade the TV and speaker system and everything.

You might want a desk." Dan tried to make Garrett feel a little less like he was taking advantage of Tutu and Papa's generosity. "I think they just want you here. We all do. The girls are thrilled. Remember, if the commander and deputy commander of Hawaiian Iodex both live here, a few blocks from one another, that makes this farm pretty damn safe." Dan tried to point out what Garrett would be giving back. "You can use your big new paychecks to wine and dine some new hottie so you can work on that other requirement of Tutu's."

"Hotti*es*," Garrett emphasized the plural portion of his correction. "It was kind of a bitch going from Elite Squadron pay back down to liaison pay."

"My understanding was that with the cost of living difference, you'll be making more than you were when you were on the squadron."

"Yeah, why is it that you understand that when you actually know the real reasons I'm moving out here but Dad doesn't?"

"Uncle Garrett, I made you purple grape juice tea too." Aida thrust a mug into Garrett's hand.

"Thanks, Aida Mae." Garrett drew a long pretend sip as he joined Dan in the tea party. "This is delicious," he assured her before he turned back to Dan. "Did you ever see us, like, running Hawaiian Iodex and drinking purple grape juice tea with your seven-year-old back when we were graduating from the academy?"

"You know, I definitely did not." Dan laughed.

Fionna and Malani's laughter reached them from the porch.

After sharing a knowing grin, both men thanked Aida for the tea and headed toward the back porch.

"But I really, really want you to teach me." Malani was laughing hysterically.

"Well, I need a pole." Fionna joined Malani's giggling. Dan smiled automatically at the sound.

"Somebody need a pole?" Garrett sauntered out to the porch with a goading smirk.

Malani rolled her eyes. "Oh, you and Kai will get along just fine."

"Hey, I aim to please."

"Yeah, you'll get used to Garrett too," Fionna assured.

CHAPTER 23

DEBTS AND GRATITUDE

Despite Garrett's doubts about the way of life on the farm, Dan and Fionna shared a knowing grin when Garrett seemed to surprise even himself as he chose the other one-bedroom cottage. It would actually put him closer to Dan and Fionna's new home which Aida was excited about.

"This one just kind of reminds me of Mom and Dad's beach house. I don't know. It's weird," Garrett said almost to himself. Dan nodded but didn't comment.

"Daddy." Aida rushed back into the guesthouse Garrett had decided to make his home. She was dragging Papa along by his hand.

"What, baby girl?" Dan lifted Aida up as Papa laughed heartily over her exuberance.

"Did you know that it's Christmas here too? And Tutu said I can help decorate their Christmas tree tomorrow after we go with you and sign something."

Dan chuckled as he nodded. "That sounds like fun. And tomorrow we can go see where our new house is going to be." That was the part of the entire day he was most excited about.

Tutu joined them in the guest cottage. "I had a feeling you would like this one, Deputy," she commented knowingly.

"Mrs. Iona, please call me Garrett, and I really appreciate this, but I feel like I need to pay you something."

"Then you must call me Tutu. Everyone does. You have already paid me more than I would ever be able to give you in return. You have been an excellent friend to my Maylea. You took care of her when none of us were able. I believe you had a hand in finally showing Dan and Maylea the way to one another, which was of course always what was meant to be. As I recall, there was a time back in early spring when you were the only one she allowed to care for her."

Dan tried not to feel the bitter fist of regret as it clenched tight in his gut. When Fionna had been pregnant the first time and was terrified to tell Dan, it was Garrett she'd called and him who had held her and let her cry. It was him who had wrapped his shield around her after the test came back positive.

Tutu moved on quickly. "You brought all of our family our most precious Aida. She has brought healing and peace back to our family I wasn't certain we would ever have again after Samuel took Maylea from us. And you cared for Aida until the time was right for Dan and Maylea to care for her. You continue to care for her and our little Halia. And now you have come to my island to care for my people, to keep us safe, and to preserve our way of life, so if anyone owes anything, it is I to you and not the other way around."

A harsh swallow tensed Garrett's neck. He didn't seem to know how to respond to the truths Tutu had laid before him. "I'm honored to be here," he stammered. "Really. I can't thank you enough."

"And we are honored to have you on our farm and as part of our ohana," Tutu assured him as she patted his face and gazed at him. Garrett grinned sheepishly for a moment. "Oh, how my island longs for you to be in her care. So many, many things she has planned for you, my warrior."

"When we all get to move to Papa and Tutu's farm," Aida asked in the lull in conversation, "can I sometimes spend the night with Uncle Garrett like I do with Tutu and Papa?"

Fionna giggled as she removed the empty bottle from Halia's mouth and began burping her.

"Sure, baby girl, as long as he doesn't have anyone else spending the night." Everyone laughed as Garrett waggled his eyebrows.

Tutu glanced at Garrett with a knowing look in her eyes that intrigued Dan. "My sweet Aida, how would you and Halia like to spend the night with me and Papa tonight? We could show her how we have tea parties, and I have a feeling your mommy and daddy might like a whole night to themselves."

Aida's eyes lit in delight. "Can Halia and I please, please spend the night with Tutu and Papa, please, Daddy?"

Dan shared one longing glance with his wife. All thoughts of Garrett and new Iodex positions evaporated as he considered having an entire night to worship his beautiful wife's body and then to let her sleep uninterrupted wrapped up in him. Fionna nodded. She gave Dan looks that threatened to make him combust.

"Sure, but you'll have to help Tutu and Papa with Halia, okay?" Dan remembered he was supposed to be answering his daughter's question. Garrett was laughing at him outright.

Tutu chuckled and shook her head. She lifted Halia into her arms.

Fionna warned, "She'll wake up every three hours and want a bottle. It's kind of exhausting."

"Maylea," Tutu scoffed. "I think we can handle Aida and Halia and let you have a night off."

Suddenly Halia gasped and cooed as Tutu cradled her tenderly. "That's right, my precious kekei. We'll have a good night, won't we?" Halia's eyes were locked on her great-grandmother's, and she seemed perfectly at ease in her capable hands.

A few minutes later, Tutu and Papa waved goodbye as they headed back toward their hale with the girls. Papa carried the girl's bags and looked thrilled to spend the evening with his great-granddaughters.

"So," Garrett leapt as soon as they were out of earshot, "I was thinking we should sit down and hammer out how we want to set up the innerworkings of Iodex here, since there will be so many branch offices on all of the islands and since we'll be running the main branch from here instead of from Honolulu," he teased. "There's going to be a lot of planning. We may be up all night."

"Not tonight, Haydenshire." Dan let lust etch his tone as he drew Fionna into his body.

Garrett laughed. "Yeah, well, why don't you two head on down to your hale," he quoted the Hawaiian word for home, "and not get that started here."

Mischief lit Fionna's features as she stepped away from Dan. A broad grin formed her lips.

"We'll let Garrett get settled into his new hale, and I have lots of plans for you, Commander Vindico," she chanted, "but you have to catch me first." With that, she took off. The screen door slammed as she raced away.

Garrett shook his head. "Are you seriously going to chase her?"

"To the ends of the earth and back again." Dan gave her a decent head start and then took off in a heated sprint.

CHAPTER 24

SKEPTIC'S SHIELD

Dan's body gave a shuddered groan as he felt her move. A broad grin spread across his face before he ever opened his eyes as he reveled in the exquisite sensation. The early sunlight gave weak light to their room.

Dan was lying completely naked in the soft serenity of their bed, and Fionna's hands were drawing teasing patterns up and down his shaft. He pulsed and began to pant as he gazed down at her.

"My god, I love it when you wake me up like this, baby doll," he vowed as she continued her slow torturous moves. Her hair was tangled from their voracious lovemaking the night before and from her long, languid slumber without having anyone awaken them all night long.

Its silky tresses brushed across him as she worked. Her cheeks had their healthy glow that came from being on her island. She'd worked her way down in their bed so her face was mere inches from his strain, and her eyes were locked on his as she played. Her breaths teased his sac. Dan's eyes rolled back in his head as she swirled her index finger in perfect circular patterns up his shaft and then traced his head as he throbbed in her face.

"You hungry again? You need to be taken care of?" he growled.

She moaned as she gave a heavy nod. Dan was absolutely certain he was the luckiest man alive as her tongue flicked over his head. He reached down and softly caressed her beautiful face with his thumb as he cradled her cheek in the strength of his hand.

Her pulse picked up pace in her rhythms. The yearning and desire ignited inside of her as he slowly traced his hand down the side of her breast. Her nipples throbbed and begged for his attention. Dan reached and pulled her upward until her soft chest melded into his muscle.

He eased Fionna onto her back and brushed her lips with his thumb. They were swollen and eager for his kiss. He moved over her, positioning his body between her thighs. He throbbed against her mound as she groaned in anticipation of him filling the hollow empty space that was desperate to be full and belonged to him alone.

"So damn beautiful." He leaned and began his hungry feast. He dipped his tongue between her lips, letting their souls join as their tongues danced and swirled inside of her mouth. She pulled away and gasped for breath, and Dan continued downward.

He kissed a fiery trail of lush kisses across her neck and collar bone as she arched her back. Then he kissed and licked the salty dew that had gathered between her breasts as she'd slept. A hungry growl echoed from his lungs as he feasted on the energy rolling off of her.

He watched her as he traced and teased around her nipples with his index finger never touching them. Her eyes begged and her body pleaded for relief. The dark brown tips of her breasts were drawn tight for his mouth to ease their strain.

"Suck me," gasped deliciously from her in a desperate pant.

Dan moaned from the directive and then fulfilled her wishes.

"Is that what you need, baby doll?" He let his tongue lap over her right nipple. He swirled it around her, feeling it throb and pebble against his tongue. Fionna panted as a hungry moan escaped her.

"Or is this what my good girl needs?" Dan soothed as he moved to her left breast and drowned it in his mouth. He sucked and pulled until she was writhing in the bed beneath him. As he sucked, he let his hand drift down her body. He edged slightly to the side and separated her soaking wet folds. Her body spasmed as the air reached the tightly coiled nerve endings that were raw in their need to be touched.

Dan pulled his mouth away from her breast as he slipped his fingers inside of her.

"My god, baby. You're still so tight and wet. No matter how hard I fuck you, you are so fucking perfect," he groaned in ecstasy. "Such a good girl for me."

"Take me. I need more. I dreamed about you all night. I ache," she begged. Dan's shield pulsed from her wanton words. He would never be strong enough to deny her the ecstasy of the two of them as he made them one.

"You're still so tight, Maylea." He swirled his fingers inside of her trying to prove his point. "I think you need a little more first."

"Take me," she continued her pleas. "I want to feel it when I walk."

Dan's entire body tensed as he moved back over her and braced himself on his forearms as he rubbed her clit with his head and then prodded at the very perfection of her. "You won't just feel it when you walk, baby doll. I'll take you so hard you get wet just thinking about it tomorrow." He tried to prepare her for the force as his need leaked just inside of her lips. He remembered suddenly and summoned to cast her. She was still closed from the evening before, so he released the cast and then dropped low.

"Please," spilled from her lips once more as her body contorted, and he pushed inside of her.

A shuddering gasp tore from his lungs as her body began to open for him.

"That's it, baby, just a little more," he coaxed as he pushed harder, and as she began to give way, he plunged her depths.

"Yes," groaned from her as she met his unrelenting thrusts. Dan kissed her and matched the rhythmic thrusts of his pelvis with the eager strokes of his tongue in her mouth. He felt her swell. Her energy pulsed in jagged arcs. Her temperature rose.

"It's coming, isn't it? You can't hold it back. I make it feel too fucking good, don't I? Now, let it go for me," he ordered and she lost it all. Her body trembled around him as she broke. Her orgasm consumed her, and he fought to keep from exploding himself. "Good girl, now, I want another one," Dan urged as he began his rhythmic thrusts again.

He grinded against her body as she bucked into him pulling him deeper. He held her thighs, making certain his cock rubbed past her clit with each pass.

"Dan, I'm gonna," she warned of the second, but her breath washed from her before she finished.

"Just let them keep coming. Keep giving them to me," he ordered as he thrust and pulled away and dipped low again.

But it was too much. Her body's consumption of his felt too damn good, and as the second orgasm shattered through her, Dan's body convulsed, and he filled her full of everything inside of him.

When she stilled, he fell to the bed beside her and wrapped his arms around her as he guided her onto his chest. He panted as he kissed the top of her head.

"I love you," he vowed and felt her smile against him. "I love to see you here. It's incredible. I love to be here with you." He was unable to stop professing how overwhelming his love was for her.

"I love you too. And thank you for bringing me back here. I think you're the incredible one."

They lay in the peaceful sunrise that drifted into their hale from the screened-in porch and watched their energy as the erotic, spiraling shapes danced around them. Fionna pulled the covers back over them and cuddled into Dan's embrace. He smiled as he cradled her to him. Being her Shield would always be the thing that meant the most to him.

"Can I ask you something?" she whispered in the serenity of their afterglow.

"Anything."

"You know how Garrett kind of acted like Tutu is crazy and everything," she sighed. "And I know, it does sound crazy." Dan knew she'd tried not to let Garrett's skepticism bother her, but it had hurt her feelings. "Why didn't you think it was crazy when we were here after we'd gotten engaged and after the miscarriage and everything?"

Dan considered. "Honestly, the only way I know how to explain it is that I never thought it was crazy because of you. I'd hit rock bottom. You'd almost gotten killed. We lost the baby. I was so far gone I didn't think I'd ever surface, and just like when you took me out of that bar, literally my very own angel, I would have followed you anywhere. You brought me here and you'd given me everything because you gave me you. I could feel your energy in the island, and I could see you in Tutu and I believe in you. Garrett doesn't have that. His skepticism is a part of his shield, and it will take a little longer to melt away. But it sounds like Tutu has plans for Garrett."

"The island has plans for Garrett," Fionna stated confidently. "It just let Tutu know about them."

CHAPTER 25

MEAN WHAT YOU SAY

At a quarter to ten, Dan helped Fionna out of Malani's Jeep and then lifted Halia into his arms. Aida leapt out and held Fionna's hand as she took in the media circus outside of the Kauaian Iodex building. Garrett and Dan shared an uncomfortable glance as they both wondered why Victoria Kalakona was putting on such a show of their signing. That was bizarre.

Fionna's face fell. "Why are there so many reporters here?"

Garrett shrugged. "Looks like Kalakona arranged it."

"She is very proud," Fionna sighed, "and very, very fearful."

"Of what?" Dan asked.

"I don't know. I only know the emotion."

"Nice." Garrett gestured his head to two brand-new Hummer EV Edition 1 SUVs complete with the Hawaiian Iodex signage. They would essentially be able to run their cars with their own energy.

"I told you there were perks," Dan reminded him as they headed toward Victoria who appeared to be setting up for a full-blown press conference.

"What the hell is this about?" Garrett asked through his teeth.

"I wish I knew." Dan shook his head.

Dan and Garrett were both in suits, and Fionna was wearing a long flowing sundress complete with a hibiscus flower in her hair.

Aida and Halia were once again in matching dresses both with hibiscus flower headbands fixed in their hair as well.

Fionna was still a little irritated that Halia had slept from midnight until six with her great-grandparents. Tutu had pointed out that the Kauaian rhythms soothed Halia just like they soothed Fionna and that after her bottle, she'd slept quite well.

"Man, it's December and it's seventy-five degrees. After this, I'm putting on shorts and going to the beach. How did we never think to move here before?" Garrett sounded thrilled as he offered Representative Kalakona a polite smile.

"Now, Dan, we were hoping that you might answer a few questions and maybe say a few words of reassurance after you sign," Representative Kalakona explained though it was far more of an order.

Dan nodded his begrudged agreement. He'd certainly given his fair share of press conferences when he was Chief of Elite, but he would have liked some warning.

"Maylea." A man and woman approached. The woman was trying to restrain an irrepressible little boy who appeared just as determined to get down and walk as his mother was to keep him in her arms.

"Malie, how are you?" Fionna beamed as she embraced the woman. "Josh." She hugged the man with her that was dressed in a Kauaian sheriff's uniform. Dan smiled. "This is my husband, Dan, and our girls, Aida and Halia. Dan, this is Josh and Malie Riker."

"Nice to finally meet you in person." Josh shook Dan's hand.

"You too, and I really appreciate everything you're doing for us. I promise I'm getting us out here as quickly as I can."

"No problem. I'm happy as long as I get to be a cop, and I get to play with my kids each afternoon. As long as we're out on the beach around four or five most days, I just appreciate the promotion." Josh couldn't seem to get out the appreciation or the terms of his agreement quickly enough.

"Believe me, I'm with you. I plan on picking Aida up from school myself most days," Dan assured Josh.

"Who is this?" Fionna grinned at Josh's son as he wriggled in his mother's arm.

"This is Akoni, and this"—Malie turned and seemed to pull a little girl who appeared to be just a year or so younger than Aida out from behind Josh—"is Everly," she concluded.

"Here, give him to me." Josh extracted his son from his weary wife's arms.

Fionna chuckled. "How old is he? He looks just like you."

"Eighteen months," Malie supplied. "And he looks so much like Josh people wonder who his mother is."

Everyone laughed as they nodded their agreement.

"Hi, my name is Aida." Aida stepped toward the Rikers' little girl.

She shrunk back into her father. "Aloha," she managed in a choked tone.

"Very shy," Malie mouthed before she leaned downward. "Everly, Aida is going to go to your school next year, and her daddy is going to work with your daddy. Aida might be up at the precinct as much as we are." This did bring a timid smile to Everly's face as she nodded.

"Well, if it isn't the Rikers. I saw your mother yesterday at the store, Josh. How's the diaper rash?" Tutu moved to the small gathering and beamed at Akoni.

"It's already gone, Tutu." Malie smiled. "Thank you for your help. The coconut oil and the oatmeal bath did the trick."

"It always does." Tutu patted Akoni's back.

"I thought the kids had finally pushed Malie over the edge when I got home. She and Mama had Akoni in a wash bin sitting in oatmeal," Josh teased.

Garrett and Papa joined them after speaking to the other members of the Kauaian Consul.

"Josh, this is my deputy commander, Garrett Haydenshire," Dan announced as he stepped back so Garrett could shake Josh's hand.

"Nice to meet you," Josh supplied, but Dan was watching Fionna. She bristled as she took in Josh's energy as he shook Garrett's hand.

Dan gestured his head to the side as he repositioned Halia slightly. Fionna eased away from the Rikers.

"What did you feel?" Dan whispered as he tried to blend into the crowd. This wasn't an easy task since everyone there seemed to be eyeing him speculatively.

"Concern and worry and a lot of jealousy." Fionna sounded angry. Tutu noticed their whispered conversation, and with a knowing grin, she stepped in.

"Deep breaths, Maylea. Why does he feel that way?" she guided, but Dan already had his suspicions.

"I don't know. He doesn't even know Garrett," Fionna fumed.

Tutu shook her head. "You're letting your love for Garrett cloud your vision. If you'll listen to the island, it will tell you how to defend him."

Dan stepped in. "He may not know Garrett, but I know cops. He's worried I'm going to start replacing Hawaiian Iodex officers with my friends from DC. He's scared some of his friends might be out of a job."

Tutu nodded and looked very pleased with Dan's assessment.

"They are also worried that you won't honor the traditions of Hawaii. You come with a bit of a reputation, Daniel. You and I know how Maylea has soothed your spirit and your soul, but they don't know this yet. Part of your job will be to reassure them and to get them to lay down their concerns and welcome Garrett to our island. It is, after all, where he was meant to be. My island is calling all of the fiercest shield warriors."

"Dan, we're ready," Rep. Kalakona called from nearby.

He handed Halia off to Fionna and joined Garrett at the front tables as the cameras moved in.

"They're a little bit worried about you, so make sure they know you want to be here," Dan urged through his teeth.

"I know. Papa told me. I may not get Tutu's spirit stuff, but I am honored to be here. I really do respect their way of life. I'm not here to step out of line or to try to turn this into the mainland. You know that," Garrett vowed.

"I'm about to let you tell them that."

Representative Kalakona stepped to the mic. "Ladies and gentlemen, aloha. It's so nice of you to come out today. If you'll just gather around, we want to welcome Commander Vindico and Deputy Commander Haydenshire to our noble lands. We're going to get right down to business. They'll be signing their contracts and then I'll swear them in. Then we'll have the ceremonial leis, and Commander Vindico will be taking a few of your questions."

Dan swallowed harshly. He let everything that had happened to him in the past thirty years spiral through his mind as he signed his name on the contract.

He and Will and Garrett playing on Haydenshire Farm. The camping trips in the back fields. The Playboys, the beers, the talks both derisive and serious. Amelia, Wretchkinsides, dozens of other women. Garrett trying desperately to get through to him, to get him to stop drinking, to stop using, and to be human again. Garrett pulling the pistol out of his hands. Garrett escorting Fionna into that bar. Garrett handing Dan the white lei to place around Fionna's neck as he vowed to love and adore her forever. Garrett carrying Aida out to the gathered crowd on Haydenshire Farm. Garrett smiling as she ran into Fionna's arms.

"I solemnly swear," he began. He could see Fionna at the front of the crowd gazing up at him. He could feel her love from twenty feet away as she cradled their baby at her breast and held their precious little girl's hand, as they watched him vow to protect her home and her lands.

"To protect both Gifted and Non-Gifted alike. To keep these lands safe and sacred as they have always been. To honor the traditions of Hawaii and be her steadfast Shield in the relentless storm." Dan and Garrett concluded succinctly as they followed Representative Kalakona's prompts.

They bowed as freshly made leis were placed around their necks. Representative Kalakona handed them their badges and then held up the keys to the Hummers. They both laughed as they took them and smiled for the crowd.

Representative Kalakona stepped back up to the podium.

"A few words, Dan," she urged.

Dan's mind went blank as he stepped up. "Aloha," he offered. "All I'm coming up with are bad Western movie references from the movies I used to watch with my grandfather," he offered wryly and the crowd laughed, much to his relief. "I am truly honored to be here.

My wife and I are thrilled to be back on her island." He bowed his head to Fionna who was beaming up at him.

Pride was etched on her features and it filled Dan's soul. *Every guy ought to have a moment where he looks out into a huge crowd and the only face he sees is his wife's staring up at him with that much pride,* he thought as he blew her a kiss, and she laughed sweetly.

"I meant every word of the vow I just made to you and to your lands. I want Hawaii safe, and we are determined to make certain that the beautiful ways of life that you've created here will last and be honored." Garrett nodded alongside him. "I want my girls to grow up in the traditions of Kauai. I thank you for giving me this tremendous opportunity," Dan concluded and Victoria stepped back in.

"We'll take questions from the press first," she directed.

Dan moved back to the podium. He nodded to a woman in red on the front row. "Commander Vindico, can you tell us how you came to the decision to rework the entire Hawaiian Iodex structure and why you brought Deputy Commander Haydenshire here with you?"

"Certainly." Dan offered everyone a kind smile. "Representative Kalakona has worked tirelessly to serve and protect the Gifted people both here on Kauai and on all of the islands," he worded his answer carefully.

"When Commander Kingston expressed his desire to retire, she approached me about taking over Hawaiian Iodex. I am honored to serve these lands. I know we're changing things up just a little bit, but it's only to better serve both the officers who work with us and the people we serve. I'm trying my best to make this the best Iodex in all fifty states," Dan assured the people he was set to serve.

"Deputy Commander Haydenshire is by far the most outstanding officer in the field today," Dan vowed, and Garrett grimaced slightly. He didn't want the accolades for his work any more than Dan did. "Together, along with all of the men and women already working so diligently for the state of Hawaii, we will be able to keep the lands safe and thriving for the good of everyone."

A man Dan recognized from one of the major Gifted news networks shoved his way to the front of the crowd. Without being called on, he began. "Can you tell us, Commander," he sneered, "does your appointment have anything to do with the recent merger between the Capacona drug cartel and the Suen Ma family and their land purchase on Oahu?"

Dan swallowed as the job began to settle back in his bones, and the familiar need to set his shield out over his family swam in his multiple rhythm strains.

"I can tell you that I have been briefed on all of the crime and the concerns on all of the islands and that just like the officers that held office before Deputy Haydenshire and myself, we will not stand for it and we will be steadfast in our protection of the citizens of the state of Hawaii."

Another reporter stepped up and offered Dan a smile. "Care to, once and for all, clear up the paternity issues over your youngest daughter, Halia?"

Dan smirked as he and Fionna shared a glance. It was a pretty good ploy to get Fionna to reveal Halia for the cameras.

"You know, Mrs...." Dan paused as the woman supplied her name.

"Sanders."

"Sanders," Dan repeated. "It's long been my belief that people will believe whatever they've decided is their version of the truth, but for those of you who have ever seen my baby girl, I don't think there's any question as to whom her daddy might be."

Garrett and Fionna both nodded adamantly as everyone laughed.

Another reporter leapt to the mic. "This question is for Deputy Haydenshire."

Garrett nodded as he stepped forward.

"This question has two parts," she began with another nod from Garrett.

"First, can you tell us how the Crown Governor reacted to you moving to Kauai to take post in the state Iodex office, and second, can you tell us of your knowledge of the Hawaiian traditions and ways of life?"

Garrett cleared his throat. Dan gave him a slight nod. This was his chance.

"I think my parents were a little surprised. I've been affiliated with some department of the National Iodex Office in DC for the past eleven years, so this is certainly a change. My parents have always shown all of us their unwavering support, so that was there as well and will continue to be there. I have no doubt.

"As for the traditions and ways of life in Hawaii, that is one of the primary reasons why I want to move here and work for you. I know I haven't been on the lands near as much as Dan and Fionna...sorry, Maylea," he quickly corrected and tried not to grimace. "But I have great respect for your ways of life, and I'm hoping to get to experience this great culture even if I don't share its heritage." He gave a slight nod to Fionna.

"I did participate in the Vindicos' wedding ceremony, and tomorrow, I'll become Aida and Halia's godfather at their blessing ceremony. I have nothing but the utmost respect and admiration for the lives we share here on Kauai, and I want to serve and protect the people and the land and your ways of life," Garrett vowed. "I want to learn from all of you if you're willing to teach me, and I am beyond honored to have this opportunity." The relief from the crowd was palpable. Victoria looked overjoyed with Garrett's responses.

After a few more questions directed to Dan on whether or not he would be hiring any other officers from outside of the islands, Victoria opened the questions up to the crowd. An attractive young woman, with a great deal of encouragement from her cohorts, stepped up to the mic.

"I was just wondering if Deputy Haydenshire is still single and needed someone to show him around the island?" Challenge was alight in her eyes, and her hopeful grin had Dan laughing.

"I'll have to let him answer that one." He stepped aside.

Garrett gave his customary, cocky smirk as he moved back to the mic. "Is that an offer, sweetheart?" he flirted shamelessly. The woman nodded. "Come talk to me after this is over." Garrett winked at her, and she looked like she might faint from her excitement.

Dan shook his head in disbelief as Garrett waggled his eyebrows.

Several minutes later, Victoria stepped up and thanked Dan and Garrett for their service, urged everyone to welcome them to the island, and then dismissed the crowds.

Dan held up the keys to the brand-new Hummer he'd been given and grinned at Fionna.

"You think Malani and Kai might take the girls back home for us so I can take my beautiful wife for a ride in my new car?"

"I think that might could be arranged." Fionna beamed as she cradled Halia closer and leaned to kiss Dan's jawline.

"Might do a little of that too," he informed her wryly.

"I was hoping." As the girls were handed off to Tutu and Malani, Dan waved to the remaining crowd as he opened the door to his new Hummer for Fionna.

"We can't be gone too long. Tutu is having Josh and Malie over for lunch," she warned as he cranked the enhanced motors and a broad grin spread across his face.

"No problem," Dan assured her.

Garrett had the woman who'd asked him out leaned up against his own new Hummer.

CHAPTER 26

LET'S DANCE

A little while later, Dan gave Halia her bottle while he sat at the table trying to eat intermittently and hold his baby girl.

"I hope I'm not being too forward, Commander Vindico," Malie began hesitantly.

"Please, call me Dan," he urged.

"Mahalo." She nodded. "We were just kind of worried, I guess, that you might be looking to replace Josh. I'm going to lose my job, so we were panicking, even though Tutu said you would never do that," she tried to explain what Fionna had picked up from Josh when he'd met Garrett.

"I have no intention of replacing anyone. I promise."

"Malie, I didn't know you weren't dancing at Miss Leialanie's anymore." Fionna looked concerned.

"I've been there for years, ever since I graduated, but she's retiring and moving to Oregon with one of her sons. Unless she finds someone to buy the studio and run the classes, we're all out of a job in a few months."

Aida's head jerked up from her meal as devastation cast her features. "Why isn't Auntie Leialanie going to teach anymore?"

"She's moving, sweetheart," Fionna explained, but then Dan saw it in her eyes. "Do all of the teachers want to stay?"

Malie nodded. "Definitely, and she'd just hired this girl a couple of years ago that grew up on Oahu, but she studied in New York. She's amazing. I've never seen anyone dance like her. She's been teaching all of the advanced classes. She takes care of her grandmother here. I don't know what she's going to do without a job."

"I'd buy it and let Malie run it, but I just don't have the money," Josh lamented.

Malani and Fionna shared an excited grin. Dan chuckled as he watched Fionna's hopeful eyes land on him. "If that's what you want, baby," he immediately vowed.

"I don't know how much she wants to sell it for." Malie tried not to sound hopeful, but it perforated her tone. "She's always turned a profit. I do know that."

"I don't know when we're moving back exactly, but I'll call Auntie Leialanie after lunch. Dan and I will talk this through." Fionna sounded ecstatic and Dan was thrilled she was so happy.

Owning a studio would further tie them to the people and the lands of Kauai. Malani was bouncing in her seat as was Fionna. Tutu was shaking her head at both of them.

"If you need a little help, we're glad to pitch in," Papa offered quietly, making certain no one could hear him but Dan.

"I think we might go in on that with you." Kai chuckled. Fionna and Malani were already in a whispered discussion of how they might run a hula studio.

An hour later, Dan and Fionna were sprawled on the swing bed on their back porch with Halia between them. Kai and Malani were on the porch swing across the room, and Aida was playing in her nearby garden with a few friends that she'd made the summer before that Tutu had invited over for her.

Malani's brow furrowed. "She said if we bought it, she would cut the price that much?"

"Yes," Fionna sighed. Dan kept his hands running through her soft, silky hair. He was trying to calm her rhythms. Her nerves were getting the better of her.

"Why?"

"You were like her favorite student, Malani, and she adores Aida."

"Yeah, I'm sure it had nothing to do with you, Maylea." Kai shook his head at her.

"Do we really want to do this? Because I've been feeling like something big was coming for a while, but I kind of thought it was you moving back. Maybe it's this too." Malani still seemed overwhelmed by the entire idea.

"The question is why didn't I feel this?" Fionna studied Dan.

"Baby, there is so much change going on all around us, I'm not sure you've been able to discern any one thing in particular. On top of that, Miss Leialanie clearly hadn't even considered you as a potential buyer. Nothing in her energy would've triggered your receptors. She had no idea we were moving back.

"But you do love to dance, and I've never actually seen you hula, but I assume you are even more skilled at that than at the dances I have seen you perform. People know you and trust you, and even if they don't know you, they know Tutu, so you have built-in loyalty. You have teachers in place who people trust. You already have clientele. The only concerns I have, and they are fairly mild, would be that if you two are launching your own business and I'm running Iodex and we're all helping run this farm, I don't want any of that to take time away from us or the girls," Dan laid every thought of his heart out for her knowing that she would understand.

"That would be one of the good things about us doing this together. If we manage to keep all of the teachers in place, then we only have to find instructors for the classes Auntie Leialanie was teaching. As long as we can handle the front end stuff, we don't have to be up there all the time." Malani pointed out the perks of acquiring a business that already had employees. "The halau isn't even open every day."

Dan nodded. "I'm just thinking out loud, but do you think there might be classes some of the parents might want to take? Are there grown women here who'd like to learn to hula that might not have as kids? That would give them something to do instead of just waiting on their kids or leaving to run errands before they have to be back. Having the parents in the building would be less liability."

"That's a great idea," Malani sounded impressed.

"It definitely is." Fionna brushed a kiss across Dan's lips. It startled him slightly. "You're amazing."

"If they start making out, I'm leaving," Kai harassed as Malani began giggling.

"I haven't actually danced hula in years." Fionna's worries came back in an instant.

"Malie and I will give you a few refresher hula courses," Malani assured her.

Dan wished that Kai and Malani would leave. He knew that Fionna felt the pressure to decide something, and he wanted her to be able to relax and really think about what life would be like if they purchased the hula halau.

"Hey, you know what we haven't done in years?" Malani eased forward on the swing. Fionna's eyes lit, and Dan felt her rhythms trill in excitement.

"And we can now 'cause we're not knocked up," she squealed.

Malani nodded as Kai laughed.

"They're out in the back workshop. I cleaned them up for you," he informed Fionna and Malani.

"Thank you." Malani hugged Kai and kissed little Lanie who was sound asleep on her daddy's chest.

"Surfing, right?" Dan guessed. Everyone nodded excitedly.

"Where's Garrett?" Fionna asked. "He was wanting to go to the beach."

"He's on my laptop trying to figure out where to take Carmindy this evening," Dan informed her. Fionna rolled her eyes and shook her head.

"He could've just asked."

CHAPTER 27
SURFER GIRL

A little while later, Dan and Garrett were seated on the sands of a locals only surf beach. Fionna had explained that the surf was gentle enough there that she and Malani could have fun and relearn after their pregnancies.

Dan found it mildly humorous when Kai pointed out that both he and Garrett's brand-new Hummers were equipped with board racks on top.

Halia was sleeping on a quilt under a vast umbrella and her father's watchful eye. Aida had requested to stay on the farm with Sarah and Harper, so they could keep playing. Fionna was paddling out on her board. Dan's breath caught as he watched her graceful form revel in the ocean that had raised her.

The waters continued to rise, but she paddled on, searching for the perfect wave. Dan stood when he could no longer see her from his seated position. A broad grin spread across his face as she pulled up to her knees and then leapt up. He could see her beaming smile from the shoreline as she rode the wave in. He grimaced as she lost her balance on her next ride. She intersected the wave. She emerged a moment later, grabbed the board, and headed back out.

"She's good," Garrett allowed.

"Maylea, hell yeah," Kai scoffed as he waxed his own board. "She was the best before her dad took her back to the mainland. That was her thing. She could've done the Mavericks or anything else, but he couldn't stand it. He wouldn't let her back in the water," he lamented. "She *is* the water, you know." He shook his head. "It messed her up bad. Gonna take her a long time to remember who she really is."

After a few more turns where Fionna repeatedly tried to perform a cutback and came down more than she succeeded, she rode the board in beaming.

She secured her board, complete with hot pink hibiscus flowers painted on it and Maylea written down the center, and took the towel Dan handed her. She hoisted the zipper of the thick swimsuit top down and peeled it off of her. Dan bit his tongue as she seated herself beside him and Halia wearing nothing but a bikini bottom. Garrett chuckled at Dan and shook his head. Kai didn't seem to think this was odd in any way as he lifted his board up and raced into the tide waters while Malani rode in a large wave and was jumping up and down as she dragged the board toward them.

"Did you see that?" she chanted.

Fionna grinned. "Yes, and I'm jealous. I can't even cut it back anymore."

"I thought you were great," Dan vowed.

"I need new skegs and pads," she explained. "Thank you for bringing me out here. I've needed to do that for a long time." Dan tried to discreetly lie beside her and block her chest from view of Garrett.

"So, when can I get a few lessons, Maylea?" Garrett continued to chuckle at Dan trying to mesh his extremely protective and possessive nature with the way life worked for his island girl. Fionna leaned up on her elbows much to Dan's chagrin. She gave him a sweet grin as she caught the emotions of the war that had begun in his mind.

"I'll teach you whenever," she promised. "I got Dan up twice in Sydney, and we were only out there for a few hours."

Garrett chuckled. "Come on now. I know you've gotten him up way more than that." He laughed as he leapt up and brushed the sand from his hands. Dan rolled his eyes.

"Care if I try?" He gestured to Fionna's custom-made hybrid board.

"Go for it. Just don't wreck my board, or I'll get Dan to beat you up," she sassed.

Dan laughed as he shot a cocky smirk to Garrett.

"Right." Garrett rolled his eyes and then carried the board out to the water.

"I'm sorry. I didn't think about my top," Fionna apologized. "It's not a big deal, right?"

"It's okay. Just caught me off guard, I guess."

"Garrett's seen them a bunch of times, and I didn't think you'd care. You didn't seem to mind when I was on the beach with Logan and Rainer," she reminded him hesitantly.

Dan let his mind work backward for a long moment. That was a lifetime ago. Fionna topless on Manly Beach at the very beginning of their relationship. Dan hadn't minded Rainer and Logan seeing her. They'd both been extremely respectful and they were ten years her junior. Dan finally admitted that occasionally, even after all they'd been through and all of the confessions that had been made, he did still see Garrett as a potential competitor. It was ridiculous.

Dan ridiculed himself. Garrett Haydenshire was an outstanding officer and an outstanding human being. He was Aida and Halia's godfather and one of Dan's best friends. *Get over yourself, Vindico. You're being a prick,* he commanded as he maneuvered himself so that he could rub his hands up and down Fionna's back and brush kisses in her salty hair. He reminded himself of what her father had done to her, how he'd taken away the people who meant the most to her, the people who healed her. He refused to ever even fathom such a thing. He just had to convince his shield of that.

As Halia slept on and Kai gave Garrett surfing lessons, Fionna rolled to her back, and Dan engaged her in a rather heated make-out session.

"If you'll move the baby, I'll dump water on them," Garrett harassed as he and Kai returned from his lesson.

Malani giggled as she shook her head at Fionna. "It's nice to see you making out on the beach with a guy who actually deserves you."

Fionna pulled on one of Dan's T-shirts. "We need to get back. Aida wants to decorate the tree, and I want to go see the new part of the farm," Fionna urged. Dan lifted Halia up to his shoulder, and she took in the brilliant blue water and the sands of her island. She began cooing her excitement, much to her parents' delight.

"That's right, my little coconut. You love it here, too, don't you," Fionna gushed as she moved her face directly in front of Halia's. Suddenly, Halia gave her a big, open-mouthed, drooly grin, which elicited the same reaction from everyone else.

CHAPTER 28
HOUSE AND HOME

"Daddy!" Aida raced into Dan's arms as he pulled up to Tutu and Papa's a little while later. "Harper and Sarah just went home, and Sarah invited me to spend the night if it's okay with you and Mommy," she begged. Dan was always astonished by the differences in Aida when she was in Kauai. She was so much more confident and willing to be away from Fionna for long periods of time without worrying.

"We'll have to ask Mommy."

"Ask Mommy what?" Fionna lifted Halia's car seat out of the Hummer.

"Aida wants to spend the night with Sarah tonight." Dan tried not to sound disappointed. He loved that Aida already had friends who would be in her school next year, and if Fionna and Malani purchased the hula studio would be their students as well, but he'd wanted to spend the evening with his girls.

"And Sarah probably can't do it another night while we're here because she'll have to go to school Monday," Fionna tried to remind Dan of why Saturday night was the only evening Aida could stay over with Sarah and her family.

Dan gave a begrudged nod.

"I'll call Sarah's mommy and tell her Daddy will drop you off in a little while. Maybe you and me and Daddy and Halia and Uncle Garrett could go get some shave ice first," Fionna suggested. Aida threw her arms around Dan's neck.

"Thank you," she trilled, and Dan squeezed her tightly.

The Christmas tree decorating was put off until the next evening. After everyone went for shave ice, Malani gave Garrett a few good places he could take Carmindy to have a little fun that evening.

After Dan dropped Aida off at Sarah's house, just a few miles from the farm, they loaded Halia into her stroller and decided to take a leisurely stroll around the farm and out to see the newly acquired acreage.

"Papa said they hadn't gotten as much done on the foundation as they were hoping," Fionna eased. She was afraid Dan was going to be disappointed, and truthfully, he was, though he would never have admitted that. "I wish everyone would tell me whatever the big surprise is. It's making me crazy."

"What?" Dan had no idea what she was talking about.

"There's something Tutu and Papa and Malani and Kai know. I can feel their excitement and them trying not to tell us. Whatever it is, they want to surprise us, so I haven't asked."

"I have no idea, sweetheart. I've noticed that Papa gets a look in his eye every so often. He seems excited."

"He *feels* excited too."

They worked their way past one of Tutu's greenhouses and continued beyond the other guest homes. They came to the back of the farm several minutes later and took in the area of land that had been cleared to become the Vindicos' new home. The pier foundation had been started, but not much else had been done.

"Let's keep going," Fionna urged. Dan studied her. Something seemed to be driving her forward though she was still holding his hand as he pushed the stroller.

"I kind of think I do want to buy Miss Leialanie's," finally spilled from her mouth.

"I already knew that. I was just waiting on you to tell me." He stopped on the path and brushed a kiss on her forehead.

"And you're okay with that?" She seemed to pick up the pace involuntarily.

"Of course," he assured her. "I want to help do whatever needs to be done. I want it to be everything you want it to be."

She grinned, and in that moment, she felt truly loved. He sensed it in her rhythms. Dan reveled in her slight shiver of elation. But something was still pulsing in her energy strains. It seemed to be driving her forward toward something. She moved magnetically northeast.

The lush acres passed by, and suddenly, they were upon it.

"Wow!" Fionna's mouth fell open. "I think this is where the former owners lived before they sold and moved to the mainland. I didn't know it was so nice."

Dan pushed the stroller up the concrete driveway onto a travertine tile flooring that made up the large lanai on the east side of the house.

"Tutu said for us to walk up here," Fionna whispered as she gazed around the expansive lanai. It led to three sets of French doors. Dan tried one knob, and it opened. He lifted Halia into his arms and carried her into the vast open kitchen and living room portion of the home.

"Look at this kitchen," Fionna gasped. She summoned and lit the recessed lighting throughout the rooms.

"Wow," Dan agreed. The kitchen housed a massive island complete with a polished stone counter top. Dan's brow furrowed. The countertops were the exact granite Fionna had picked out and had in the file for their new home.

There were two ovens along with an eight burner stove top. The room bled seamlessly from the living room out onto the lanai. There was an octagonal breakfast nook, but it was obvious that most of the dining would naturally be done outdoors on the lanai.

Dan moved through the living room into a small room just off of the front door entryway. It held floor-to-ceiling bookshelves along with another set of French doors.

"This would make a pretty nice office," Fionna commented as they shared a knowing grin.

"It would." He walked Halia down a long hallway. There were three guest bedrooms, two of which were connected to a bathroom with a double sink vanity. They continued on and peeked in two large storage closets in the hallway. The last room at the end of the hall was a very grand master suite. It had a teakwood ceiling and opened onto another massive, covered lanai.

"Dan, look!" Fionna slid the glass doors to the side and stepped out to reveal not only one of Tutu's recommended outdoor tubs but also a fireplace and a swinging sleeper bed. This portion of the home was secluded by canopy and ʻŌhiʻa lehua trees. The other end of the lanai met the lanai off of the kitchen.

"Honey, do you think maybe the new foundation didn't quite get done because Papa's been working his ass off up here?"

Fionna blinked back tears. "Can you feel it?" She closed her eyes in concentration. "Can you feel the energy here? It feels like home."

Dan couldn't feel the emotional energy there, so he did the next best thing. He took her hands and read her rhythms.

"The girls wouldn't have a playroom," he pointed out though he knew it wasn't necessary.

"The girls have a farm and dozens of the most beautiful beaches in the world."

Dan headed into the master bathroom. He smiled as he pointed Fionna to the closets off of the bath.

"They're huge." She spun in one of the walk-ins. "And look at this shower." She opened the shower constructed entirely of clear glass panels.

"I'll get a show even if you don't let me in the shower with you," Dan teased.

"And when have I ever not let you in the shower with me, Commander Vindico?"

"Never, so let's keep it that way."

"What do we think?" Tutu's voice called from the hallway.

Papa was chuckling as Dan and Fionna moved out of the master bathroom.

"You have to let me pay you for this. I know you upgraded everything here." Dan gestured to the massive, tiled shower and the granite countertops along with enough drawers to hold the inventory of hair and beauty products Fionna loved.

"You two buy the hula studio, furnish this place, and move my grandbabies back as soon as you can, and that's all the payment I'll take," Papa vowed.

Fionna threw her arms around her grandfather's neck and squeezed. "Thank you so much. I can't believe you did all of this." She blinked back tears.

Papa cradled her face in his callused hands. "This is right where you're supposed to be." Dan understood that Papa hadn't necessarily meant only that Fionna was supposed to be on Kauai. At that moment, her grandfather wanted her safely back in his arms. Halia pulled her body back and leaned toward Fionna. Dan beamed as he chuckled at his wife's delight as she gave Papa another hug and turned to take the baby.

Halia immediately nuzzled her face in Fionna's neck and curled up in her mother's arms.

"She's so happy." Fionna was overwhelmed suddenly by what she was feeling from Halia.

"And she wanted you to know that," Tutu vowed as she patted Halia's back.

"Wait, why did you break ground on the other area if you knew we'd end up here?" Dan asked.

Papa laughed. "Many, many things to come."

CHAPTER 29

STORMS AND WILDFLOWERS

"Let's go pick out your room." Fionna carried Halia into all of the available bedrooms. "Actually, we should let Aida pick hers first," she amended. Dan nodded his agreement.

Halia lifted her head from Fionna's shoulder. She seemed to study her new home.

"So, we can have the home blessing tomorrow instead of the foundation blessing, or we could just do the girls' blessings and then bless your new home when you move in," Tutu offered.

"I want to move in now." Fionna spun Halia around inside of the room that Dan was fairly certain she wanted to make the nursery. Halia's gasp made everyone chuckle.

Dan let the peace of already having a home right where he wanted it satisfy his soul. "We could do a little furniture shopping tomorrow and maybe start getting this ready to be our home."

Papa chuckled. "I don't have your bed finished yet, Maylea. Give your Papa a little time."

"Are you kidding me? I can't believe you did all of this." She gestured around the expansive home again.

"It had most of the things you said you wanted. The hardwood was in great shape. I knew my Maylea wanted a big kitchen, so replacing everything in there was most of the work and getting the big soaker out on that lanai and hooked up. The fireplace was already there, but I was hoping to get my girls back to their island before the summer." Papa winked. Dan tried not to let the pressure continue to mount. "You can bring him too." Papa slapped Dan on the back.

"Thanks." Dan laughed.

Suddenly, the overcast skies released a deluge of rain that beat against the house. Dan turned immediately to Fionna. Tutu instinctively reached for Papa's hand, and Dan smiled. As powerful as she was, she was still a Receiver. She could feel the volatile, violent energy of the weather, and she wanted the man who had always been her solace in the storm.

The unpredictability of storms bothered all Receivers. They weren't accustomed to not knowing what might happen. Thunder and lightning were so rare in Kauai, Fionna didn't often worry there, but they were just coming out of the rainy season and it seemed Mother Nature had one more storm to bring to Kauai.

Dan wrapped his long muscled arms over two of his baby girls. He kissed the top of Fionna's head and grinned as Halia grasped his T-shirt in her tiny hand and snuggled herself between her parents.

Dan wondered how long the storm would last. They would get drenched if they tried to run back to their guesthouse now. A rare round of thunder echoed in the Vindicos' new home, and Dan's cell phone rang in his pocket.

"Oh, my poor baby." Fionna drew Halia back to her chest as Dan answered. They both knew who was calling. Dan just had to figure out the best way to go and get his baby girl.

"Hey, Mr. Alana," he answered. "I'm on my way."

"My Kaitlyn is a Receiver too," Sarah's father explained. "We tried to talk her into staying, but I know if one of my girls was away from home and she wanted me to go get her, I would be upset if no one called. She's up in Sarah's room with her, but she's just barely holding back the tears."

"I'll be right there," Dan vowed.

"I'll tell her you're coming."

Fionna was bouncing Halia to sleep and staring out at the storm, extremely concerned. "How are we going to get back to a car?"

"You stay up here. I'll run back. It's fine," Dan assured her. "As soon as I have Aida, I'll come pick you up." He hated to leave her, but he knew she wanted him to go and get Aida. "Actually, why don't I go get the Hummer, and we can all go get her."

But suddenly a Hummer pulled into the covered carport area of their new home.

"Malani said you were up here," Garrett explained as Dan let him in the side door. "I kind of figured you might like a ride back down before I go pick up Carmindy."

"Thank you." Fionna braced Halia on her shoulder and threw her other arm around Garrett's neck. He cradled them both in his fierce embrace. "Aida's scared of the storm, and she wants to come home."

Garrett's entire demeanor changed in the length of one heartbeat. "I'll take you all back and go get her."

"Thanks, but you don't have to do that. I just appreciate your getting them home safe and dry. You go have fun. I'll get Aida," Dan assured him.

"Nah, Carmindy doesn't get off work 'til seven anyway. I've got time."

A few minutes later, Dan climbed in his own newly acquired Hummer, and he and Garrett headed to a small section of homes that made up a loosely formed neighborhood a few miles from the farm.

"I take it you aren't building a new house. You're moving up there?" Garrett asked.

"It has everything we need, and Maylea loved it," Dan explained. "Papa let me go on and on about what she wanted in the new house. I even sent him her choices for colors and countertops, and then he created it there."

"He's one hell of an Occamist," Garrett commented.

"That's for damn sure."

"Do you always call her Maylea when you're here?"

"I get used to hearing everybody else call her that. When we're back in DC, I only do it when we're alone. But Maylea is more Fionna than Fionna. It makes her happy," Dan added as he let Garrett in just a little bit deeper, gave him more allowance than just about anyone else when it came to the steadfast shield he kept over his precious girls.

"Wildflower, right?" Garrett recalled.

"Yeah." They pulled into the Alanas' short driveway and leapt out of the Hummer. Garrett followed him up to the front door through the driving rain.

"Daddy!" Aida raced to Dan as soon as they stepped into the foyer. Unable to hold in the emotion she'd been trying so hard to keep at bay, she began to tremble in Dan's arms as tears leaked from her eyes.

"Poor little thing." Sarah's mother patted Aida's back.

"I'm sorry about this," Dan apologized as he cradled Aida tightly to his chest.

"No, it's fine. Kaitlyn was the very same way when she was Aida's age. She's not much better now, truthfully." Sarah's mother gestured in their cozy living room where Kaitlyn, Sarah's older sister, was cuddled up on the sofa under a quilt with her phone and a cup of tea. Every time thunder shattered her concentration, she would shiver involuntarily.

Kaleo Alana frowned. "Now she texts her boyfriend when she's scared instead of telling me," he grumped.

Kaitlyn's mother shook her head at her husband. Dan and Garrett just offered kind smiles.

"I'm sorry you're scared. Maybe you can spend the night next time you come home," Sarah offered sweetly.

Dan smiled down at her. "That might be sooner than we thought. I just have a few loose ends to tie up back in DC, but we already have a house here. I'm trying to get us here as quickly as I can."

"We're thrilled to have you and Maylea back on the island and to know that you'll be keeping all of us safe. I tell you, I have to turn off the news now after I hear everything going on in Honolulu and Kahului." She shook her head.

"We'll try to put a stop to most of that," Dan vowed with Garrett nodding his head adamantly.

"You must be a very special little girl, Aida, to have your daddy and your Uncle Garrett come get you. Not everyone gets the commander and the deputy commander to pick them up." Sarah's mother chuckled.

"Yeah, if we're not careful we're going to have like a Mayberry thing going on here," Garrett teased.

"You know that makes you Barney, right?"

Everyone laughed as Garrett's head fell.

"Aida, tell Sarah mahalo for inviting you," Dan urged. Aida's head lifted off of his shoulder.

"Mahalo. I'm sorry that my tummy hurts. Would you like to come to my house instead?"

Dan bit his tongue as having an extra little girl for a sleepover hadn't really been what he'd had in mind.

"I kind of don't like the storm either," Sarah fussed. Her father chuckled and nodded.

"I think we'll just see you tomorrow at your blessing, sweet girl," he assured Aida.

"Thanks again." Dan cradled Aida to his chest and rushed her out to the Hummer.

CHAPTER 30

THE LEGEND OF THE WOLF AND THE LION

A few hours later, the storm had waned to a steady drizzle. Aida was sound asleep in her bed, and Halia was being rocked to sleep. Fionna laid her in the bassinet and then joined Dan and her grandparents out on the screened porch. She crawled onto the swinging bed with Dan, and he began pulling his fingers through her hair as she reclined in his lap.

Papa was thoughtful, and Dan was eager to hear the impending wisdom that seemed to accompany the storm. Dan and Fionna both cringed as Garrett's Hummer drove past their home just a little before ten.

"He got shut down." Fionna wrinkled her nose as she whispered the obvious conclusion. Dan nodded. He pulled Fionna closer instinctively and offered a silent prayer of thankfulness for her. He'd never wanted to live that life in the first place. Deep down he'd always wanted what he had right now. The most phenomenal wife in the world and two beautiful daughters. He would never know how he'd gotten so incredibly lucky—so incredibly blessed, he corrected.

Garrett never seemed to mind playing the field, and he certainly scored far more than he struck out. He tended to view women as all the same, although he was partial to blondes with a heavy rack.

Papa gestured his head to Garrett's passing Hummer. "We have a lion who believes himself a lone wolf." Dan and Fionna both leaned in to listen. "The battle inside of him has waged on so long it's almost destroyed him."

"Garrett's not a lone wolf. He has a huge family, and he has us," Fionna argued. But then she grew quiet and thoughtful. "What do you mean? What almost destroyed him?"

Papa smiled at her with a twinkle in his eye. He nodded his agreement of her assessment as he began to explain.

"He comes from the most powerful pride, the most noble, but he separates himself out of shame. Inside of him, the wolf he's turned himself into fights the lion that he is. The fierce battle of spirits tears him apart. The wolf will never win the battle. A wolf will never beat a lion. The wolf knows that the only way for him to survive is to use his cunning deception to outwit the lion and separate him from his pride. So, he convinces the lion that he doesn't deserve his family. Then he makes him believe that he's not a lion anymore at all, that he's a wolf. The lion believes the wolf's lies and tries to discipline himself for mistakes none of the others in his pride would blame him for. He tries to turn himself into a wolf. He sets out on his own, trying to escape the lion inside of him. He lets the shame rule him. Tough life outside of his pride, but the ones who survive let the wolf convince them that they like it better that way. The wolf tells them they deserve for it to be tough. But the lion lives on inside of him."

"So, you don't think he'll ever have family of his own or believe that the one he does have loves him? That we love him?" Fionna's heartbreak was evident in her tone.

"I didn't say that, Maylea. I didn't say that at all," Papa vowed. "Lone male lions are often very attractive to the lionesses. Lone wolves as well. They'll snap and growl at all of them, but they're not looking for a pride. They don't believe they deserve one. Gifted legend says that unless the female seeker knows the dances of both the cunning wolf and the noble lion, they won't give them much attention."

Dan's brow furrowed as he continued to listen intently. The Haydenshire crest was the lion, known for strength of family, courage, valor, and nobility. The wolf crest had a dual meaning—both bravery and loyalty but also chaos and destruction.

"Lone lions have lots of seekers, that's the female lion interested in becoming their mate. But until the one that's meant to be comes along, the lion doesn't care. As soon as he sees her, the other seekers no longer matter. When the seeker that has something none of the others have—the one who knows how to dance with the lion and how to outwit the wolf—makes her show, you'll see the wolf become the lion he always was. It'll happen in an instant. He'll protect her where he hasn't looked after any of the others. When the time is right, then only then, you'll get to see the dance.

"You must have just the right seeker and then all the others will fall away in a single beat of his fierce heart. He'll only have eyes for her, and their dance will light the sky like the fires of our volcanoes. They can't be cooled by the water. They can't be cooled at all. She'll show him the way back to his pride. She'll teach him who he really is. She'll slay the cunning wolf of shame, and he will defend her above all others."

CHAPTER 31

BLESSINGS

The next morning, Dan's eyes opened hesitantly as tiny, wet fingers reached and grasped his morning stubble.

"Hey there, baby coconut." He cradled Halia whom Fionna had laid upon his chest. Her head was lifted, and she was cooing happily as she smiled up at him. Fionna giggled as she crawled back into bed.

"She slept again. Here she sleeps. Please don't make me go back home," she whimpered, and Dan sat up slightly so he could wrap his girls up in his arms.

"I'm sorry, baby, I swear I'm hurrying." He knew she was only joking, but he was eager to get his family moved and to start their new lives.

"I know. I was only kidding." She certainly hadn't meant to heap on more pressure. "What kind of furniture do you think we should get? I have lots of ideas." Her trilling excitement rolled in her rhythms and made him grin.

"The kind where I can lie down and all of my girls can crawl up in my lap."

She beamed and kissed his cheek and then Halia's. Halia leaned toward Dan's chin with her mouth wide open in an effort to give her daddy a kiss as well. Dan and Fionna laughed as she gummed his jawline.

After breakfast, they took Aida to see their new home. She required a little prompting to claim one of the bedrooms.

"But my fairy princess bed is at my other house," she fussed.

"Papa is going to build you a new bed like the one in the guesthouse, but we'll pack up your fairy princess quilt and your sheets and your unicorn pillows and bring it with us, so that when we move it will all be ready for you," Fionna assured her.

"And all of my books?" Aida was approaching panic.

"Of course, baby. Your toys and your books and your pictures, and all of your very special things," Fionna continued to soothe her.

Aida began investigating the house in more detail. Fionna spread one of Halia's quilts on the floor in the expansive living room to let her play on her back while they measured windows and walls and discussed life in their new abode.

"Mommy!" shouted from Aida in her new room. Dan and Fionna raced toward her.

"What's wrong?" Dan panicked.

"Nothing." Aida looked shocked that Dan thought something had upset her. Fionna clutched her chest. "Look!" Aida opened the closet door. Dan grinned as she revealed the walk-in closet. Half of it was suitable for hanging clothing, but the other half was bookshelves with cabinets underneath and a bench seat for reading.

Fionna grinned as she sat in the closet with Aida. "I think Papa thought you might like your very own special reading spot and a place to play."

"I need to tell him thank you so much."

"He'll be up here in just a little while, and you can give him big hugs."

"I will give him lots of them."

"Hey, maybe you and Davi, and Sophie, and the doll that you asked Santa to bring can play house in here too."

Fionna had explained how important it was for Receivers to have spaces where they could be entirely alone, without having other people's feelings intruding on their own. He knew Tutu must've had Papa build Aida her own special spot for just her and her feelings.

Aida looked overwhelmed by the thought of playing with all of her favorite toys in her new closet. "I'm not sure Santa is going to bring me that doll because it costs lots of money and has lots of dresses and they're expensive too," she hesitantly explained to Fionna.

Dan's eyes closed as he tried to fight the images of Garrett's tale that crept back into his mind. His precious baby girl's home in flames, her parents shot in cold blood, and him carrying her to an orphanage.

Fionna lifted Aida into her lap. "I think you have been such a good girl this year and that in your letter to Santa you asked for things for other people and you only asked for one thing for yourself which was such a nice thing to do. So, I think maybe Santa will bring you your doll because he wants to give you a very special Christmas gift."

"I don't want to hope for it though just in case," Aida explained. Dan's heart ached as Fionna nodded her understanding.

Suddenly, they heard Halia's babbled cooing from the living room. Dan leaned out of Aida's room and began laughing. Fionna followed him into the living room to find Garrett doing push-ups over Halia. Every time he lowered himself, he would kiss her cheeks. She was visibly thrilled and smacking him in the face.

"Daddy just left you in here. What if you escaped or something?" Garrett chastised Dan in a singsong voice.

"She's not really mobile, so I'd say the likelihood of escape is fairly slim." Dan smirked. "Ask Uncle Garrett how badly he struck out last night, Halia?" Dan guided, using his own baby voice.

Garrett laughed and then leapt to his feet. He reached down to hoist Halia up into his arms. The quick motion had her gasping.

"It was bad, baby girl," he explained. "She was all, so where do you see this relationship going, and I was all whoa there, I see this going to my bed or to your bed and not much farther. That was not what she wanted to hear, and Uncle Garrett wanted nothing to do with meeting her dad or going to have dinner with her family. So, Uncle Garrett took her home way quick and went to buy himself a few electronic upgrades for his new house." Halia cooed as she heard

Garrett's soothing voice and kept her eyes locked on his. She seemed to love her godfather just as much as her big sister did.

"Did Uncle Garrett ever think she might've been the one?" Fionna challenged.

"Tell Mommy there is most definitely not a *the one*," Garrett spat incredulously.

"Never say never," Dan vowed as he took Fionna's hand and tried to soothe her frustration with Garrett's rather abrupt views of dating and women. She of all people knew that was how he approached dating, but Papa's lone wolf tale from the night before had gotten her hopeful.

Garrett rolled his eyes. "Man, you married the only one worth having. The rest of us just make do with the leftovers."

"Oh, right, so you wanted to marry me?" Fionna rolled her eyes.

"Uh no, but I was trying to keep Danny Boy off my back for a while. I just left Lillian Haydenshire's incessant chatter about me settling down. I don't need him picking up her banner."

"Fine. I'll keep my mouth shut," Dan pledged though he was almost as eager as his wife to see if Papa's prediction might ever play out.

A few hours later, Dan and Fionna stood among Aida's flower garden with their precious baby girls. Halia was dressed in the long white gown that Fionna had worn during her blessing, and Aida was wearing a matching white taffeta dress with puff sleeves that she thought was the most beautiful thing she'd ever worn.

Garrett stood steadfast by Dan's side holding Aida's hand. Malani stood by Fionna with Halia cradled in her arms. They were surrounded by the few families they knew on the island and close friends of Tutu and Papa as the Kahu began the ceremony.

Halia's face turned up to Dan in a scowl as Garrett took the Ti leaf dipped in blessed water from the mighty Pacific and touched it to her head. Aida's head bowed forward as Garrett performed the same task with her. Halia's little hands attempted to wipe the water from her brow, which Malani patted dry for her. After the ceremonial chanting and several prayers offered over their children, Dan and Fionna fed the girls each a tiny bite of poi. Halia moved it around in her mouth for a moment before pushing it back out with her tongue.

Everyone chuckled as the Kahu continued. Garrett and Malani pledged to care for the girls' spirits and to keep them tied to the lands. Dan and Fionna repeated the baptismal vows to their daughters and then joined in with everyone as a final prayer was spoken in Hawaiian.

Everyone gathered at Tutu and Papa's for lunch and then helped decorate the Christmas tree. Aida was thrilled with the fact that Papa helped her string flowers for garland just like he'd taught her to create leis.

Dan and Fionna left the girls in the care of Garrett while they went furniture shopping for their new home. That evening, Dan and Kai watched with pride as Fionna and Malani signed their names on the purchase contract to own and run Miss Leialanie's Hula Halau. Fionna used all of the rather substantial check she'd been given the year before when she was named Receiver of the Year by the Professional Summation Organization.

Dan assured her repeatedly that he'd never thought of that money as theirs and that he wanted her to use it for her new career. Talk immediately began on changing the name of the studio and when to host a grand reopening.

"We should have the teachers over for coffee before you go back to DC," Malani suggested.

"Oh, that's a good idea. We want them to stay, and I need to get to know them," Fionna agreed.

Tutu suggested that they invite the people set to become their future employees over for dessert and coffee the following afternoon.

CHAPTER 32

THE SEEKER

Dan was thrilled that Fionna was so excited about her new profession and that it would allow her to do something that she loved and be able to have Halia there on the premises when she was working. Tutu had also informed Fionna that Halia was welcome to stay with her and Papa whenever Dan and Fionna had to be at work.

The following afternoon, Dan helped straighten up the farmhouse while Fionna prepared delectable tapas style desserts, and Malani made pot after pot of what was affectionately called Maylea's coffee. It was Fionna's favorite, and Papa always picked her up some from the farm where it was grown.

Malie and Josh arrived eager to help. They both seemed relieved that Malie would still have a job, and Josh wanted to get to know Dan and Garrett a little better as he would effectively become one of their right-hand men.

Dance instructors began arriving. There were seven in all, and Fionna already knew most of them. The eighth had phoned to say she was running late, but would be there after she checked on her ailing grandmother with whom she lived. She was the instructor who had trained in New York and who taught all of the advanced classes. The way the other instructors spoke about her, Dan assumed she must really be something.

Fionna and Malani explained a few of their plans to the instructors and asked for their opinions on how to make Miss Leialanie's even better than it had always been.

"I'm so sorry." The last instructor arrived just a few minutes after everyone began talking about improvements and what would make the classes even better. "I'm Kaimi. It's so nice to meet you. I'm so relieved you're going to keep Miss Leialanie's open."

Fionna beamed. Dan could tell that whatever emotions she was feeling from Kaimi, that she trusted her and liked the energy she felt in her rhythms.

Kaimi was relatively petite and most definitely built like a dancer with impressive thigh muscles. Fionna seemed as excited to learn from Kaimi as Kaimi was that she would be able to continue working in Kauai, so that she could look after her grandmother.

As the party began winding down, Malani and Fionna thanked each person individually for coming over and for being willing to give them some time to get the studio reopened.

Aida burst into the house suddenly with Garrett hot on her trail. Her face was flush and she was laughing as Garrett scooped her up and put her on his shoulders.

Dan laughed and shook his head at them. Garrett was supposed to keep Aida occupied until the party was over. Papa followed them in, chuckling at Aida's exuberance over Garrett racing her around the farm.

"And this is my little girl, Aida, and her newly minted godfather, Garrett Haydenshire, who is going to be Dan's deputy commander," Fionna introduced Aida and Garrett to Kaimi.

Garrett offered Kaimi his hand, and in their brief touch Fionna's eyes goggled. She turned to Dan. Her mouth hung open. "Dan," she gasped as she grasped his hand. "Dan!" she urged again and shook his arm. He managed a nod as he watched.

"It's...nice to meet you," Kaimi stammered.

"Uh, yeah." Garrett nodded but couldn't seem to drop his gaze from her deep copper eyes. He kept her hand clutched in his palm much longer than was necessary. "You too," he added after a rather long pause.

Tutu and Papa had been helping Kaimi care for her grandmother, so they both knew her well. Papa gave Maylea a wink. "Kaimi," he drawled with a knowing grin. "You know, Garrett, names are important here. In Hawaiian, Kaimi means…the seeker."

"That's right," Kaimi agreed as she seemed to regain a little of her composure. She gave Garrett one last glance and then seemed to force herself to check her phone. Disappointment colored her features.

"I better go. My car's been acting up, and I wanted to try and get by that quick mechanic shop before I go home. I need to pick up a prescription for Nana too."

"I'd be happy to look at your car for you," Garrett leapt. "I'm a decent mechanic, but if I can't manage it then I could follow you to the shop and give you a ride to the pharmacy and then home."

Dan bit his lips together as Fionna's mouth hung open in shock. That was the most attentive Garrett Haydenshire had ever been with any woman.

"Thanks, but I don't want to put you out. I don't really have a lot of extra cash so…" Kaimi fumbled uncomfortably.

"It's fine. You don't have to pay me. Just let me take a look at it and see what the problem might be."

"If you're sure it wouldn't be any trouble."

"None at all." Garrett set Aida on the ground and gestured toward the door. Kaimi beamed as she turned in front of him.

Papa chuckled. "And the dance begins…"

CHAPTER 33

LION'S ROAR

~GARRETT HAYDENSHIRE~

B cup, maybe a C on a good day, short, and brunette—what the fuck are you thinking, Haydenshire? She is definitely not your type. Some highly annoying part of his brain kept insisting that she wasn't for him, but she was the most beautiful woman he'd ever seen. He didn't understand it.

Garrett tried to command his own thoughts. It was an exercise in absurd futility though, it seemed.

He popped the hood on her car and listened to her tell him that it didn't crank more times than not. He wished she'd just keep talking about the car or the weather or anything at all. Her voice soothed him. Suddenly, he could breathe when it felt like he'd been drowning for years. Fresh oxygen tempted his parched lungs and steadied his frantic shield.

She stared at him expectantly, and he remembered that he was supposed to be helping her.

He nodded. "Your battery leads are corroded." He gave her what he hoped was a cocky smile.

"I, uh, don't really know what that means," she confessed.

My God, she's adorable. Garrett shook himself slightly.

"It's not a big deal. I can fix it for you. I just need a Dr Pepper."

"Oh, right. Because you're so hot. I mean…it's…uh…hot out here, and you're working on my car." Kaimi cringed as her dark olive skin streaked with heat. Garrett bit his lips together. Her pallor took on the look of a deep juicy peach, one he was certain he wanted a bite of. His mouth watered, but the war in his mind waged on. *What the hell?*

"I have some here." She pulled a six-pack from a small sack of groceries in her backseat. She chilled it and handed it to Garrett.

He chuckled and began wondering what Kaimi's plans were for the evening since she wasn't going to have to make a trip to the mechanic.

"It's for the battery." He hoped he wouldn't further her embarrassment.

"Batteries like Dr Pepper too?" she managed in a mortified whisper as she squeezed her eyes shut for a second. Garrett couldn't quite halt his laughter.

"I tell you what, why don't I give the battery a little Dr Pepper, get it cleaned up for you, and then we'll go get a drink after I'm done. I'll take you by the pharmacy first." He was unable to stop the words from exiting his mouth.

Kaimi stared at him in stunned disbelief. "Really?"

"Sure." Garrett gave her another smirk as he let his eyes smolder over her body. *She does have a great ass and I just bet what's between her legs makes up for her lack of tits*, he reasoned with himself. *She's a dancer. Wonder if she'd like to shake those luscious hips in my bed. Probably pretty damn flexible,* he thought savagely.

Garrett casted the car battery and made certain it wasn't going to spark before he poured the cola on a rag and wiped the leads. "You'll have to tell me where you like to hang out since I'm new around here."

Kaimi grinned at him, and Garrett's heart tripped over the next few beats. There was a light in her copper eyes that he swore could light the darkest, most terrifying places in his soul. "No problem."

"Garrett!" Dan shouted as he raced out of the house.

Garrett and Kaimi spun simultaneously.

"What's wrong?" Garrett asked.

"Uh.." Dan shook his head. Whatever had happened had his snarl forming rapidly on his lips and his shield flaring. "My house was vandalized. My neighbor just called. They shattered several windows including every window on your Highlander. The girls are staying here. I can't have Aida seeing this, but I think we need to leave now," Dan commanded. He glanced at Kaimi and looked momentarily annoyed that she was standing there.

"I take it we know the guy that did this." Garrett already knew the inevitable answer.

"The word murderer is burned into the grass in my front yard along with several expletives, so I have a pretty damn good guess."

"I'm so sorry," Kaimi managed. She edged closer to Garrett. His shield sought her in earnest though Garrett had no idea why. He also couldn't stop it. Every wave of his energy pulsed toward her.

He suddenly understood that Dan was scaring her. He just couldn't fathom why someone scaring her absolutely infuriated him.

He narrowed his eyes at one of his closest friends and shot him a warning glare. He bared his teeth. His nostrils flared before he realized what he was doing. His muscles tensed and his shield sizzled ominously. He fought back the bizarre desire to roar, to defend his territory, to let everyone know that he would never allow her to be frightened. The beast trapped in his mind snarled and paced. He would readily destroy anything that set out to do her harm. He'd tear it limb from bloody limb.

He shook off the insanity that seemed to be taking up residence in his chest and amplifying out from his shield. "All right, fine. Let me fix this for her. You go get packed, and I'll call Dad. His jet is still here since he wasn't going anywhere. We'll leave as soon as I'm done," Garrett commanded as he edged between Dan and Kaimi. He kept her shielded with his body. *Get away from her.* Garrett tried and failed to regain control of his own thoughts.

Dan seemed to have realized that he was being a little forceful. He nodded and tried to offer Kaimi a smile, but he was just too angry.

Dan Vindico

"Uh, maybe we can get a drink next time you're in town," Kaimi stammered hopefully, and Dan let the guilt add to the volatile cocktail of hatred and fury that gurgled in his gut.

"Yeah, sure. Can I get your number?" Garrett sounded almost humble. It wasn't a tone of voice Dan ever heard from Garrett as he gazed tenderly at the woman before him.

"Yes!" Kaimi sounded like he'd just asked her if she'd like to become a princess of the Realm. Dan wondered if that wasn't precisely what he'd just done. "Uh…." She fumbled around in the handmade cloth bag that was slung across her body. "Here." She pulled a pen out. As Garrett wiped his hands on a rag, she grasped his right hand. Garrett's shield lit in unadulterated delight, and Dan found it odd that he was grinning.

She bit her lip and blushed violently as she wrote her cell number on his hand. Garrett chuckled as he promptly transferred the number into his own cell.

"I'm gonna go get ready." Dan realized that he was getting on Garrett's last nerve as he turned and sprinted back into the house. Fionna held Aida who was clutching her stomach. Dan felt the fury and tried desperately to fight the all too familiar vengeance that threatened its chokehold once again.

"I want to go with you," Fionna informed him.

"No," Dan soothed. "Stay here with the girls. Let me get this cleaned up and then you can come home, okay?"

"Maylea," Papa whispered. It killed him to see her upset almost as much as it did Dan. He scooped Aida up into his arms so that Fionna could fall into Dan's.

"I'm so sorry." Dan couldn't believe that he was still apologizing for the actions of Wretchkinsides and all of his cohorts almost a year after the man's death.

"It's not your fault," Fionna assured him. "I just can't believe he did this. I honestly don't think he did. This had to have been planned. I didn't feel anything like this when he was near me the other day."

Dan's shield formed without him even consciously forcing it from his hands. It encapsulated her. "Just let me get everything cleaned up and then I'll fly back out here and fly back with you if you want. I'll do anything, sweetheart. I'm just so sorry," he whispered as he let her hide in his arms.

CHAPTER 34
EFFIGIES

An hour later, Dan boarded the Crown Governor's jet with Garrett. "I cannot fucking believe this," he spat as soon as the doors were shut.

"Landon called. They fingerprinted everything they could find. They've done energy scans. There's nothing there. He's waiting on us to land. He's going to try and get a little sleep, but Dad told the pilots to crank it." Garrett sighed.

"We're not going to find anything. He's just like his old man, and I'm sure the press is already all over it."

"Didn't think about that." Garrett grimaced.

Dan could tell he was distracted, but he didn't comment. Even with all of the shit going on, he was genuinely excited about Garrett and Kaimi although he supposed not much was going to happen with that until they actually moved. Dan added that to his determination to get his girls back to their island as quickly as he possibly could.

"What made you not cast the house?" Garrett finally asked the question Dan knew had been churning in his mind for the last hour.

"My moronic neighbor keeps messing around my house. He intercepted my shield the last time we were in Kauai, and I don't know how he survived it. I'm not looking to add more names to the list of men I've killed."

"Hey baby, we just landed. I'll call when I get to the house," Dan soothed into his phone.

"Is the press at the airport?" she asked.

"Yeah, they're out there. Let me go get this over with."

"Be careful. I love you."

"I love you too." He stepped off the plane.

"Commander Vindico, what is your reaction to the rather extreme vandalism of your home?" screeched from a reporter as soon as Dan exited the jetway.

"Do you believe this has something to do with enemies you made when you were Chief of Elite here in DC or is it perhaps a warning about the position you just took in Hawaii?" rang from another.

Dan swallowed back the bile that flooded his throat. It was the first time he'd prayed that this was Clarence Pendergrath and not some future enemy.

"I have no idea." He and Garrett flew to the Mercedes, and Dan threw it in reverse.

Twenty minutes later, Dan eased out of Fionna's car as shock surged through his entire body. His shield set of its own accord.

"Holy shit!" Garrett gasped as he took in the damages. Iodex had blocked off the street so the reporters had been halted at the entrance to the subdivision.

Portwood, Ericcson, Rainer, and Logan exited the black Expedition right behind Dan.

"Your neighbor turned off the water before he called the police." Landon pointed to the shattered window panes on the large transomed window in their dining room. The garden hose was still hanging where it had been shoved through the jagged glass.

Chris Leslie offered Dan a sorrowful gaze as he walked over from his house shaking his head. "I saw the fire from our bedroom window. I dumped water on it and then saw the hose, so I shut it off as soon as I found the hookup. But I'm sure your dining room hardwood is in bad shape."

Fred Scheckles was suddenly upon them. "If I'd already been

inducted into the neighborhood watch patrol, I would've been keeping a closer eye out, but I'm pretty sure I did see the getaway car."

Dan and Landon both rolled their eyes.

"Can you give us a description?" Landon seemed to feel he should follow procedure.

"It was black."

"Oh, well, that should be incredibly helpful," Garrett huffed under his breath.

"Anything else? Did you get a plate?" Dan demanded.

"No, I couldn't see the plate, but it was one of those real fancy kind of cars. Kind of like yours only nicer."

Dan ground his teeth. "It was a Ferrari?"

"No, I don't think so. It was one of those real fancy British kind of cars. You know, like what Bond drives only newer and fancier."

Realization shimmered in Dan's shield. "An Aston Martin? Like a Vanquish, maybe?"

"Dan, we seized everything the Interfeci had after the takedown," Landon reminded them.

"That you knew about," Dan and Garrett spoke simultaneously.

"Okay," Landon nodded, "but we did seize the Vanquish."

"Trust me, he had more than one," Dan huffed.

Logan nodded. "We printed everything. He wore gloves, but your neighbor is right. We did get some black paint chips off the garage door. Clarence doesn't have a car registered to him though, so no matter what comes back, it's probably not going to help."

"Yeah, well, he learned from Daddy not to register his getaway cars."

Dan forced himself to look away from the words Mother Fucking Murderer that were burned into his front lawn to the garage door that had been driven into with a car and smashed to pieces. The back end of the Ferrari was dented, but the Agusta hadn't been damaged, much to Dan's relief.

Spray paint was covering most of the driveway explaining how Fionna was a whore who deserved to die. There were spray painted X's over most every window. Garrett's Highlander that had been parked in the Vindicos' driveway had both windshields and all six windows smashed in. There were chiseled marks in most of the black paint that looked like they'd been made with a knife.

"We're certain this was Pendergrath?" Rainer quizzed. He was always very thorough and careful not to make assumptions. When Dan had been his boss, he'd appreciated this fact about Rainer, but that was before Dan had been the victim.

"I'd say the murderer thing kind of gives him away." Garrett gestured to the front lawn.

Landon stepped in. "Get your insurance guy out here, and then we'll help you get this cleaned up. I assume the girls will be staying in Kauai until there are no longer curse words about their mother written on the driveway." His fury was evident in his tone.

As he couldn't think of anything else to do, Dan phoned the Senate Employee Insurance office and was promised that an adjuster was already on his way.

By three o'clock that afternoon, Dan, Jeff, and Rainer were digging up the huge, burned section of the lawn. Logan had taken the large amount of cash Dan had supplied him and gone in his father's work truck to purchase new sod. Landon, John Ramier, Mitch McCoy, and Ryan Tuttle were pressure washing the windows and driveway. Garrett, Will, and Chase Barron were drying out the dining room carpet with heat casts and scrubbing the wooden furniture that had gotten wet. A window and door company had already given Dan an estimate on replacing the garage door and all of the broken windows. They were standard sizes and were to be replaced by Wednesday and then painted before the weekend.

Governor Haydenshire and Dan's father had been by twice to offer assistance, but they were hearing a trial that afternoon. As school was out until the new year, Clarence Pendergrath was nowhere to be found, though Governor Haydenshire himself had gone to several places around town to look for him. They couldn't do much more than question him, but Dan planned to force a confession by sheer strength of will as soon as he found the little prick.

Dan had phoned Sam. He and Garrett were taking the Ferrari to his shop the next morning. Garrett had the Highlander towed in as soon as he'd been cut a check for the estimated damages. Sam had already located windows from a previously wrecked Highlander that he was using to replace Garrett's.

Dan ordered a dozen pizzas and went to purchase copious amounts of beer as evening dawned and the cold set in. Dan and Garrett taped boards over all of the windows in an effort to keep the house from freezing in the Virginia winter.

Rainer broached again. "I'm still not certain it was him. He's a prick, don't get me wrong, but something about this isn't right. If he wanted to avenge his dad or whatever, wouldn't he have tried to do something more along the lines of Pendergrath's old work. The Interfeci would never have done something like this. They were much cleaner. Everything they did was methodical. And the press made sure everyone knew that you were out of town signing your contracts. I still say it could have been anyone."

Dan bit back a vile remark. He forced himself to think for just a moment, to tap into his secondary Predilect. Rainer Lawson, more than anyone else, knew about living in the shadow of a father. He probably could relate to Clarence Pendergrath more than he would ever want to admit. Maybe he was right, Dan allowed. But, then again, maybe he wasn't.

CHAPTER 35

WOUNDS

~GARRETT HAYDENSHIRE~

Garrett hit send and then immediately wished he could somehow suck the text message back into his phone. *You had half a conversation with her, moron, why are you texting her?* He told himself that there was something about her and that he would obviously want someone to hang with for a while once they moved. He didn't want to intrude on Dan and Fionna constantly.

Garrett had hard and fast rules about texting women, and he'd just broken all of them. He rarely texted first. He only responded to texts, and he only responded if they'd had an exceptionally good time and he was looking for a little more action. Chloe was the only exception to the rule thus far. *But Chloe was Chloe.*

He also did not text for several days or even weeks if he wanted to go out again or just see if she wanted to come over and play a little. He certainly did not text a girl he hadn't even gone on a date with yet. *You're just off because you're at Dan's house.* Garrett finally decided that was it. He and Dan had come to the conclusion that he should just sleep in the Vindicos' guest room as he would need a lift to Sam's the next morning and then home since he didn't have a car. But the stutter of his heart when his phone chirped scared the hell out of him. He couldn't get the phone back out of his pocket fast enough.

was the beginning of the response. Garrett couldn't stop smiling.

Garrett's heart was thundering, and he couldn't stop grinning like a dumbass. *Okay, Haydenshire, you gotta get it together.*

"Hey Dan, you care if I borrow the Mercedes for a little while?" Garrett asked.

"It's fine," Dan sighed. He was still furious over what had been done to his home and wasn't that great of company anyway.

Garrett touched Chloe's name on his contact list.

"Hey, what are you doing?" he urged. She invited him over for a while, and he ordered himself to be interested, though absolutely nothing in him really was.

"Yeah, I'll be there in a few," Garrett assured her as he took the keys off the table by the door and waved to Dan.

Dan Vindico

Dan glanced at the clock when he heard his front door ease open. *You used to do the very same thing, so you can just stop being a judgmental prick, Vindico,* he ordered himself as he turned uncomfortably in the bed. How could it only be two in the morning? He couldn't sleep without Fionna beside him. He needed her soothing energy, her luscious, naked curves wound around him where her rhythms would flow into his skin all night long.

He wanted to feel her hot, steady breaths on his chest. He wanted to grope her and let his fingers prod and coax her until he drove her over the edge, and she unfurled in his hand. The all-encompassing,

218

earth-shattering feeling of Maylea coming, of all of her energy surging around him rocked through him. He fought the audible whimper that threatened to echo from his lungs. *Garrett is in the guest bedroom,* he reminded himself as he pounded his fist into his pillow for the third time and attempted to command his body to sleep.

~

Dan couldn't help but smile as his boots hit the gravel the next morning. Sam was shaking his head as he waltzed toward Garrett. The soothing familiarity of the oil and aftershave in the air had Dan calmer than he'd been since he'd gotten the call from Chris Leslie the day before.

"Any man that busts up another man's home and then his car, that's low," he vowed.

"Hear, hear, old man," Garrett agreed as he shook Sam's hand.

"Boy, you've got more Trojans in that box than the five and dime," Sam chastised Garrett with a smirk as he shook his hand. Dan assumed Sam would've had to pull the dash panel to replace the front windshield. Therefore the glovebox would have been opened and probably removed.

Garrett laughed and nodded. "Been to the medio one too many times to forget that again." Dan figured that Garrett's rather lax condom usage from years before came from the fact that he couldn't get a woman pregnant. He'd been healed several times by medios for STDs and had finally learned his lesson.

"Boy, did you ever think it might be nice not to have to plastic wrap Garrett Jr.? That maybe having a nice meal when you get home and curling up with the same set of curves would feel good?"

"Definitely not," Garrett balked as he and Dan laughed over Garrett Jr.

"Just ask Big Man here," Sam urged. "Not a bad life when your wife meets you at the door with a sweet kiss and then those baby girls curl up in your lap before you put them to bed and then bed Miss Amazing Wife, now is it?"

"It's my idea of heaven," Dan vowed. "But he won't listen to me."

"Uh, uh, uh, uh, uh." Sam shook his head as he began examining the dented back end of Dan's beloved Ferrari.

"I suspect it has less to do with the fillies he keeps in his pasture than the fact that he just hasn't found the one that won't be saddled, but he wants desperately to wear his." Sam hit the nail on the head just like always.

"Uh, no way, old man." Garrett huffed. "I'm good with the ride as long as the filly's cute."

Sam studied Garrett for a long moment. "Mr. Haydenshire, your daddy came out here worried sick about you."

Concern tensed in Garrett's shield. "Oh, yeah? What'd he say?"

"He wants to know why you're moving so far away. Feels like maybe you running from something."

"I'm not running away."

Sam nodded. "I told him not every runner is running away. Sometimes runners gotta run. Not every move is bad or good. Sometimes it's just a move that might get you somewhere else. And even if you are running away, there might be something at the end of the line that turns out to be what you were running to."

"Maybe." Garrett shrugged. "If you can get him off my back, then I'm good with whatever you tell him."

Sam shared a quick glance with Dan.

"All right, I buffed all the marks out of that Toyota of yours. I'll give it a paint job. If you still want to sell her in a few months, let me know. I'll find you someone. But can I give you one more piece of advice 'fore you run off to Hawaii?"

"You know I'll be back to see you all the time."

Sam nodded but didn't really seem to believe that.

"Listen to me, there isn't a wound that the right woman can't make better. You've been looking for a bandage for a long while now, but you aren't looking in the right places. Find the one that wants the wound more than she wants the ride. She'll have the salve that you've been needing all along. And most likely, you've got a little of the salve she's been needing too," Sam concluded.

Garrett's brow furrowed, but he didn't seem to have a comment for that. Sam began his work on the Ferrari.

"Has my sweet baby girl seen this?" Sam gestured his head to the Ferrari.

"No, sir," Dan vowed. Sam and Aida had a very special bond, and Dan appreciated the way Sam worried over her. "All my girls are still in Kauai. I would never have let them see the house the way it was."

"Boy, trouble just seems to find you, don't it?"

"I'm praying it lays off after the move."

Sam summoned and began reshaping the dented metal with his hand. "It seems to me that whoever took out their dislike did it when you and my girls weren't home. People that want to strike when your back is turned are only powerful when you aren't looking. You'll catch them. I can tell. Nobody gonna mess with our girls and you let them get away. That isn't in you, but you've got to focus. You've got too many irons in too many different fires. Fix your problems here. Don't move them with you," Sam advised. "Make use of the people willing to help you, Big Man. You aren't supposed to do this on your own. Seems to me that's a lesson you need to learn before you go out there."

CHAPTER 36
METER DUTY
~GARRETT HAYDENSHIRE~

Garrett's cell chirped in his pocket. Hope sprang up from his gut though he tried to beat it back. He saw her name and the battle was lost.

> You're the only person I can ask this. I'm in the studio with Maylea giving her a hula lesson. Malani and I talked her into teaching us to pole dance, but she swears she's never stripped. That can't be true. She's like a pro. :)

Garrett shook his head as he laughed out loud even though he was all alone in his squad car Tuesday night. He glanced back at the traffic he was supposed to be monitoring. Sorenson hadn't taken his rather abrupt and still pending resignation well. He'd been assigned night shift traffic detail. Garrett allowed himself a moment to envision Kaimi wound around a pole with her eyes locked on his, wearing very little. He went as far as to envision her stripping down to a G-string in his lap and him jerking that luscious ass back over his cock before he answered.

> Maylea only strips for Dan, trust me. But, where do I sign up for this class

Garrett typed quickly, then in a moment of what seemed to be fated stupidity he added *baby* to the end of the question before he hit send.

Dan Vindico

Wednesday night, Dan was pacing in the living room. The window installer had just been paid and made his exit. Fionna and the girls were flying home the next morning.

Dan had spent the last two days driving himself insane. He needed to figure out who was behind the exam scandal and the drug test swaps at Venton so that he could get his family as far away from Virginia as he possibly could. As school was out until January, there wasn't any way to gather evidence, and Dan didn't have anything to go on.

Fionna and Malani had used her extended stay to work on the dance studio, and Kaimi had given Fionna a few refresher hula lessons in exchange for Fionna teaching her what she'd learned in her pole dancing classes.

Much to Fionna's chagrin, Kaimi hadn't mentioned Garrett in all of their time together, but Tutu had assured Fionna that when the island's rhythms moved Garrett Haydenshire, it would be explosive and everlasting.

As it currently stood, Dan would pick Fionna and his girls up from the airport the next afternoon and then the Fitzroys would be arriving the following morning. They'd delayed their trip a few days so Dan could repair the house.

Fionna was frantic over not being home to prepare for their visit, but Dan had assured her that Fitz and Maddie and the boys had visited him numerous times and that they would be shocked at her hospitality as he'd never had much to offer them other than a hotel room and American restaurants.

He forced himself to start grading the final exams on his laptop and then begin reading the same regurgitated shit that his students had formulated as their last term papers of the semester. Dan's brain throbbed in his annoyance. *Why the hell did I ever take this job? I hate it and I'm horrible at it.* He sighed as he plugged in the next thumb drive.

A deep yawn shook Dan from the banality of his current profession. He scrubbed his hands over his face and looked at the clock on the laptop. He'd worked off and on for most of the night. It was nearing five in the morning. Suddenly, his cell phone chirped. Dan leaned in the bed and grabbed the phone.

> Are you up? I miss you.

Was the text from Fionna.

With a grin, Dan shoved the laptop away and called her.

"Hey baby," he soothed. "What's wrong with my girl?" He could hear the delight in being his in her sleepy, languid response.

"I just miss you. I want you. I can't sleep unless you hold me."

"I need you too, baby doll. I need you so damn bad," Dan assured her. "We've got to get out of here. I can't take this anymore."

"I know. Halia is so happy here. She misses you like crazy, but it's like she understands now that you'll hold her tomorrow. The rhythms here keep her calmer, and she's just happy. I don't know how to explain it exactly."

"I know, sweetheart. I talked to Sam yesterday when he fixed the Ferrari. I'm going to see if Fitz will help me while he's here. I'm obviously missing something. I've got to get this mess cleaned up at Venton and get the house on the market." Dan explained the plan he'd been formulating since he'd pulled into the driveway and had taken in his children's home covered in an effigy of hate.

"I still want to help," Fionna reminded him. Dan understood how all that had happened had resharpened everyone's focus and centered everyone's driving desire to be on their island. Without pretense and having no idea what her response might be, Dan couldn't seem to halt the words as they poured from his hungry lips.

"Hey, Fi."

"Hmm?"

"What are you wearing, baby doll?" he urged out the clichéd

phrase. Her adorable giggle was the first sound he heard, but then in the pursuant pause he could hear her breath pick up pace.

"Nothing," she whispered, and a groan Dan couldn't halt thundered from his lungs.

"Are you in the bed?"

"Yeah," she assured him. "Tell me what to do."

"Turn the camera on your phone on. Let me see that beautiful body. I need to see you, baby doll." He let his eyes take in the picture for a solid minute before his hand sought his own strain and he began his instructions.

Fionna fell into Dan's arms the next afternoon, and he devoured her mouth, consuming her heatedly for several minutes before he greeted his children. Aida giggled as she watched her parents' passionate greeting in the airport.

Dan hoisted her up into his arms and hugged her fiercely. "And what are you giggling about, baby girl?" he teased her. This only succeeded in making her laugh harder.

Halia's eyes locked on Dan as soon as Fionna turned her car seat toward him. Making certain that Aida felt his all-encompassing love, Dan kept her hand in his as he scooped Halia up onto his shoulder. She gave her sweet coo as Dan kissed her cheek.

An hour later, Fionna was zigzagging around the kitchen, debating what to feed the Fitzroys the next evening. "You just don't cook French food for French people, honey."

"Why don't we just go out? I don't want you going to a lot of trouble. I just want you to relax. I haven't seen you in days. Come sit down with me," Dan begged. He couldn't get their tryst via phone from that morning out of his mind, and he wanted his hands on her body for the rest of the day until he got the girls to sleep and then showed her exactly what he'd been thinking about during their phone call.

Garrett Haydenshire

"Are you fucking kidding me?" Garrett spat as he stared down his boss. "I'm the best damn detective on this force, and you want me to play meter maid in front of the Mall!"

"You came in and announced you're leaving, Deputy Haydenshire. I've got people out there that are committed to this force. If you want to keep getting a paycheck from the District, then yeah. You take your ass out to your squad car and go check the meters," Sorenson commanded spitefully.

Garrett spun and let the curse words spew as he slammed the office door and stomped out to his car.

> Sorenson just fucking gave me meter duty because I gave my pending resignation.

He texted Dan, certain that he would share in his acrimony and maybe even give Sorenson a call. Sorenson deeply respected Vindico. Dan had been his boss for the past decade.

> Call me crazy, but I get the idea you don't like meter duty :)

"Shit." Garrett revved the engine on the squad car. He hadn't sent that to Dan. He'd been reading the few texts he and Kaimi had shared over the past couple of days and hadn't realized he'd left those messages open.

With a sinking feeling swirling rapidly toward his groin, Garrett touched Kaimi's name and listened to it ring twice before she answered. The sound of her voice had his heart vibrating rapidly.

"Hey, sorry. I thought I was texting Dan."

She giggled. A harsh swallow tensed Garrett's neck as he reveled in the sound. His cock stirred, and his shield sizzled oddly around him.

"Why do you hate meter duty so much?"

Figuring he owed her some kind of explanation, Garrett chuckled. "Let's see here. I used to be the top officer below Dan on the Elite Squadron. I dropped back down to a Gifted liaison because I hate

Elite hours and always being on call, but meter duty down on the Mall is just crap. He's pissed because I'm leaving, so I guess this will be my life until I move out there."

"Oh, I see," Kaimi sassed. "You think you're the shit."

"I am definitely the shit, sweetheart. Just wait. I'll show you."

"Will you now?" she came right back. She wasn't going to take his crap it seemed.

Challenge lit through his veins, and desire tensed in his shield. It seared through his soul and took up residence in his heart.

"What exactly is so bad about meter duty on the Mall?" She sounded intrigued.

He certainly didn't have much to do for the next eight hours, so he quickly decided he might as well chat with Kaimi. Her voice soothed his soul like nothing ever had.

"There are, like, twelve hundred metered parking places down on the National Mall. Most tourists are smart and take the Metro in, but the ones who aren't inevitably fight over the free spots on Ohio Drive. Half the time the metered spots are all visiting dignitaries or Non-Gifted government officials who think *they're* the shit. They're usually taking people to see the monuments or whatever. They will inevitably let the meters run out, but I can't ticket them because it would cause some kind of freaking national incident. So, basically I get to sit in my car bored out of my mind for the next eight hours except for the times I'm dealing with a fender bender on Ohio because three idiots want one spot or the times I get yelled at by Non-Gifted tourists who want to tell me all about how they shouldn't have to pay to park because taxes."

"Gotcha." Kaimi sounded genuinely disappointed for Garrett. "I have to go teach a bunch of six-year-olds an ancient Kahiko dance for the Christmas festival, but after that I could call and entertain you with my wit and banter for a while," she offered and then giggled. She was the cutest thing Garrett had ever heard over the phone.

I think Logan may be right. There is someone out there for all of us. Maybe someday you'll get that. Cal's voice continued to echo in the recesses of his mind.

"Sounds like an excellent plan," fell from his mouth without him consciously deciding to say it.

"After that, I'm going camping with some friends of mine." She sounded thrilled.

"You camp?" He was thoroughly intrigued.

"All the time. I love it. We're going up to Anini Beach tonight. We'll have killer waves up there this time of year, and the tourists leave at dusk so we have the whole beach to ourselves."

"Is that so?" Garrett forcibly bit his tongue to keep from asking if any of these friends were guys. He couldn't understand why he would care.

"Yeah, it's great. If you like to camp, I could take you out there after you move. It's nice and private."

Garrett loved the sound of that. "I love to camp. My brothers and I practically lived out in the fields on our farm in the summer." The words continued to flow rapidly from Garrett's mouth. He couldn't seem to make them stop as he steered the car toward the parking lots around the Jefferson Memorial.

"That sounds like so much fun. How many brothers do you have?"

Garrett chuckled. He couldn't recall ever meeting a woman who didn't know all about his family. "One of my younger brothers was killed in the line of duty, but I had eight and two sisters." He continued to shock himself. He never talked about Cal with anyone. The conversation he'd had with Dan and Fionna the night they got back from Mexico was the most he'd spoken about Cal since his death.

"Wow," Kaimi gasped. "I'm so sorry about your brother, but that must've been so cool to have grown up with so many kids."

"It had its moments, but it was pretty cool. My parents adopted Rainer Lawson when he was fourteen, after his dad was assassinated, so he was always around as well." *My God, shut up. She doesn't want to hear your freaking life story. Get off the phone.*

"I would've loved that. My nana raised me because my mom was only seventeen when I was born so…." There was desperation in her pause, and Garrett's heart ached for her.

"Wow."

"Yeah. Not that you care or anything." Her voice shook slightly.

"I do care. I care very much. That must've been tough." Though the reasoning was absolutely incomprehensible to himself, all he knew in that moment of absolute truth was that he desperately wanted her to keep talking.

CHAPTER 37

IN A NAME
~DAN VINDICO~

"Please tell me you are fu…" Dan bit back the word when Aida entered the kitchen. Fitzroy started laughing. "Kidding," Dan concluded.

"Not kidding, my friend, and not only am I not kidding, but you deserve this for balking at my offer last April and then turning around and taking the job in Hawaii," Fitzroy sneered into the phone. Dan rolled his eyes. He'd been expecting that.

"Nothing at all deserves me having to expose my daughters and my godsons to dinner with Arthur and Marion, especially when Marion thinks she's entertaining a foreign dignitary."

Fitz continued to laugh. "She called Maddie. What was she supposed to say? She's not going to be rude to your mother."

An audible humph was Dan's only response. Fionna was studying him closely. She could feel his acrimony as it rolled in his rhythms, even as she stood across the kitchen from him.

"Fine, whatever, I'll tell Fi." Dan finally accepted his own fate and that of his precious girls. "We'll see you in the morning."

"Alex has been talking about seeing Aida nonstop," Fitz continued to goad Dan.

"I'm hanging up now."

"What was that all about?" Fionna wrapped her arms around his neck. Her soothing pulses worked through him. Dan reveled in the heavenly sensation before he answered.

"Apparently, my mother phoned Maddie and informed her that it would be impolite for the Fitzroys to visit America and not visit one of the governor's homes. So we are all having dinner over there tomorrow night."

"But Fitz and Maddie have been here tons of times before, and you didn't eat over there, did you?"

"Of course we didn't. I don't like to subject my friends to my parents. But you're not seeing the big picture here. My parents are going to try and convince Fitz to help them talk us out of moving."

"Ah." She sighed.

Dan smiled. Fionna was probably the least manipulative person he'd ever known. She would never pull the stunts his mother attempted or even think of such things, therefore she was somewhat unprepared to deal with them.

Garrett Haydenshire

"My level of coffee addiction is probably against the law in most conservative states. You'd have to arrest me." Kaimi giggled over her own confession. Garrett laughed as he continued to loop around the Mall.

"I doubt you're worse than Fionna."

"Who's Fionna?"

Garrett took a moment to relish the fact that he'd just brought up another woman's name, and Kaimi didn't seem threatened in any way, just genuinely curious as to whom she might be. But he chuckled over his own misstep.

"Sorry, I meant Maylea. I swear, I will never get used to calling her that."

"Oh right. Nana told me Maylea was her *inoa ewe*. I just forgot her other name."

"What does inoa ewe mean?"

"It's a name given to you by the person who knows you best. It's

232

based on something in your spirit. Maylea just seems like it should be her name, you know. It's so her."

"That's what Dan says too. I guess I pretended that I got it, but I'm not sure I do," he confessed and immediately called himself an idiot. He couldn't seem to make himself shut up. "She's not particularly wild, except maybe with him." He didn't care what Fi and Dan did in the bedroom, but it seemed odd her family would call her wild.

Kaimi laughed again. *I swear I could listen to her do that forever.* The thought seared through his mind, thundered in the recesses of his heart, and lit the deepest, darkest places of his soul. That insane sensation of wanting to roar coursed through him again.

"It doesn't mean she's wild."

"What does it mean then?" Garrett rolled his eyes as a kid dumped an Icee on the path a few feet from his car. His parents began trying to clean it up so Garrett drove on.

"Names here are really important. Inoa ewe are usually seen as even more important than the name you were given at birth. Wildflower totally fits her. Her mom probably saw that as soon as she was born. I mean, she's completely beautiful inside and out. And it seems like she'll make any place where she is beautiful while she's there, but wildflowers can't survive without the sun. They have to have that. As long as she has that then she can keep on lighting the world and sort of drinking in the wild air, you know." Hope rang in her explanation. He sensed that she wanted him to believe what she was telling him. "Like taking over the hula studio and expanding the classes we can teach. She saw a need and she wants to make people's lives good. She wants Aida and Halia to have beautiful lives here, so she stepped in and planted herself there. She's kind of amazing."

Garrett smiled automatically. "She is that," he agreed as he thought about Fionna and Dan adopting Aida in a moment's notice. "I don't know about the sun thing, but I do know she can't survive without Dan."

"Right." Kaimi sounded thrilled. "He's her sun. He's her light. She could grow between cracks in concrete as long as he's with her."

"You sure it's not just that Receiver Shield thing?" For some reason, he found discussing this with Kaimi fascinating though he'd never given Fionna's nickname much thought before.

"There is also that, but it's so much more with them."

A sudden thought occurred to Garrett. "What do your names mean? I don't even know your last name."

She giggled, and Garrett could almost hear her blush from five thousand miles away.

"I'll tell you, but you have to promise not to laugh."

"Or what?" Garrett teased.

"Or I won't tell you, and then you'll be sad. You'll be like, there was this girl, Kaimi, and she didn't even know that you have to let your car battery drink Dr Pepper, so she's kind of an idiot, but now I don't even know her last name. I'm so sad." Kaimi dissolved into fits of laughter at her own teasing, and suddenly a part of the fabric of Garrett's life began to unravel and tear. The malignant and mortal poisoning of his soul began to ease and calm as it washed away. The endless taunting of his own mind grew silent.

She soothed his pain with every laugh. Her voice restored him more than anything else ever had. Garrett joined in her laughter, certain she was the cutest thing he'd ever heard.

"Okay, I will not laugh…much…at all." He grinned as she laughed harder. "Unless your name is like Kaimi Pubert Scrotum, or something like that, and then I make you no promises," he continued to harass her. She was laughing hysterically at this point, and Garrett was woefully unable to stop grinning.

She finally managed to breathe and formulate words. "My last name is not Scrotum. Believe me, I would have been all over changing that one. My full name is Kaimi Caprice Adara Walyuo."

"Yeah, what's with the two middle names thing?"

"It mostly depends on what they mean, and my grandmother named me. That generation does it more often, I think. But, Maylea added Halia on her own after her mom died."

"Okay, so what does Caprice mean?" He felt like he'd just been assigned some fantastic new case that he wanted to learn everything he possibly could about.

"Caprice means unpredictable like the wind."

"And Adara?"

"Ugh," she whimpered, and Garrett continued to grin stupidly.

"Come on, tell me."

"According to my Nana, Adara means…"

"Means…" Garrett echoed.

"Beautiful virgin," she forced out by sheer strength of will. Garrett laughed at her outright.

"You promised you wouldn't laugh."

Garrett tried to halt his laughter and decided flirting was definitely the way to go. "The beautiful part is true. Is the second part as well?"

"Neither part is true, and if you're one of those guys who gets off on being a girl's first, then I'm hanging up and you can lose my number."

Garrett was shocked at her adamance. Panic sizzled through his shield. "Hey," he soothed. "I'm not like that, okay? I've done that before, but it wasn't something I particularly enjoyed. I was just teasing you. I shouldn't have asked." He would've said anything to make her laugh again.

"Sorry, I know you're not like that. Bad memories, I guess," she confessed, and fury tumbled in his gut. He'd find the guy that had relished in taking that from her, and he'd let the idiot know just what he thought of that.

The thought ricocheted in his mind. He'd never cared who'd done that with any of the dozens upon dozens of other women he'd been with. So long as it wasn't him, he was fine with it.

"Like I said, my mom was only seventeen when I was born. I kind of think my Nana was hopeful if she named me Adara it might stick."

A million questions pulsed in Garrett's mind. He wanted answers to them all.

"What does Kaimi mean, and don't think I didn't catch the fact that you said you weren't beautiful, which is total shit."

She laughed again, and Garrett's heart regulated once more. It usually annoyed him to no end when women downplayed their looks in order to gain compliments, but Kaimi seemed very confident in her belief that she wasn't beautiful. All Garrett wanted was to make her see that she was.

"Kaimi means the seeker, but I think Nana just liked the name, because other than my appointment to Juilliard, I've never sought anything at all."

"You danced at Juilliard?"

"Uh, yeah," Kaimi admitted in a slight whisper. "I quit when Nana got worse, and I came back to Oahu. We found out about Tutu, and I got a job working for Miss Leialanie, which I really do love. Tutu has helped my grandmother so much. I love living here and working at the studio, but I wouldn't have minded finishing at Juilliard. I only had a year left of my study program."

"I'm sorry you didn't get to finish." Juilliard was probably the one Gifted dance school that the Non-Gifted knew more about than any other academy. To be asked to dance at Juilliard meant Kaimi was something pretty extraordinary. It was one of the only schools in the world where both Non-Gifted and Gifted students both attended. The Gifted program always meant that they attended four of their six years at a Gifted academy and then for their final two years they can attend Juilliard.

CHAPTER 38

RECEIVERS PORTENT

~DAN VINDICO~

Dan grabbed Fionna's hand and spun her up against the wall of their hallway. "Mine." He pinned her between the wall and his body as he consumed her lips with greed. She broke the hungry kiss with her eyes blazing in a storm of voracious need.

"Take me to bed," she commanded as she reached and grasped his strain through his jeans. "Then take me hard." She grabbed his hand and jerked him toward their bedroom door.

His mouth watered as he watched the sway of her hips. He moaned as she leaned to move his laptop off their bed. She set it on the floor and then turned and grasped his hands again. Dan jerked his wrists from her grasp and began groping her breasts, tugging and pulling the fevered flesh before he consumed her with his eager tongue.

"I need you," she urged.

"I know what you need, baby doll. You're gonna take it hard for me like my good girl."

A shivered moan escaped her lungs as she turned and grasped the pile of thumb drives. But her mood shifted instantly. She dropped the drives like they'd burned her hands. All thoughts of carnal pleasures and of dipping himself into the heavenly nectar of his wife evaporated from the air around them.

"What's wrong?" Dan approached panic as Fionna shuddered and backed away. She paled.

"What are those?" she demanded. "Why are they in our bed?"

"Those are my students' thumb drives, sweetheart." He scooped them up and dropped them back in the Velcro pouch all the Venton mentors had been given for transferring the drives from their students. Dan couldn't fathom why she'd reacted that way. Any guy that had a hundred and fifty thumb drives of porn had a very serious problem, and that was the only plausible thing he could come up with. "What's wrong?"

"Those drives feel really, really dark. They've been casted over and over again. I can feel it."

Stunned disbelief rocked through Dan.

"What?" he gasped. She stared at the bag like it contained a nest of vipers. "Fi!" Dan's mind was at war suddenly. A confusing tidal wave of euphoric joy and panic fought for dominance in his brain. "You just broke the case."

"I did?"

"I'm going to get them out of here and then I'll call Jeff." He explained the next steps as the joy began to ebb out the panic his shield had pressed into his mind. "Don't touch them again."

Dan was careful to keep the bag sealed and away from Fionna. It would have taken a Receiver as powerful as his phenomenal wife to have picked up on a casted object. It was almost a perfect system. But whatever had been done to the drives was physically painful to his baby, and Dan wouldn't have that in his home. "I'll change the sheets," he promised. Her adamant nod gave credence to his concern.

"Hey Jeff, it's Dan. Are you working tonight?"

"No, sir. Bec and I were just lying around. She can feel the baby move now," he announced proudly.

"Pretty cool, huh?"

"It's awesome." Jeff sounded absolutely thrilled.

"Hey, would Becca be up to your coming over for a little while? I think Fi just broke the exam case wide open," Dan explained.

"Seriously?"

"Yeah." Dan hoped that Jeff would be on his way soon. He needed his tech expertise to figure out the drives.

"Sure, we'll be over in just a few."

Garrett Haydenshire

"How was your class?" Garrett answered his cell on the first ring. He was tired of trying to figure out why he was acting like a complete moron, so he decided to just go with it. Talking to Kaimi was quickly becoming an addiction.

"Oh, you know, one little girl cried. One wet her grass skirt, and one mom yelled at me. So par for the course I would say," she sighed.

"But you usually teach the advanced classes and adults, right?" Garrett recalled the things she'd revealed about herself before she'd gone to teach her class.

"Yeah, and Maylea and Malani want me to do an advanced kahiko hula class that Miss Leialanie would never let me do. But I have to wait until they get back and actually take over. I'm really excited about it. But the Christmas Hula Revue is next week, and I'm off tomorrow because I'm going camping, so I picked up a bunch of other classes today to help out."

"Hey, can I ask you something kind of personal?" Garrett eased. He'd given up on trying to halt anything at all from flowing from his own mouth.

"I guess."

"Wasn't there anyone else who could have taken care of your grandmother long enough for you to finish at Juilliard? Your mom or dad or someone?"

Kaimi gave an audible sigh and seemed to give herself a moment to decide whether or not she was going to let Garrett in.

"Not really," she finally confessed. "My mom still lives in Honolulu, but she and Nana don't speak. She left as soon as I was born, so I didn't really see her that often. I did more as I got older but still not much. I used to go stay with her occasionally when Nana and I lived in Honolulu. I worked up the courage to ask her about my dad once. She could narrow it down to three guys. They were all just out of basic training and here on leave before going on a float in the Pacific. Two of them are Hawaiian, but I don't know where they live now. The white guy was killed in Afghanistan several years ago, but I seriously doubt any of them want me investigating them too much."

"I'm sorry," he managed.

"S'ok. Like I said, I tolerated New York, and I loved dancing at Juilliard, but I love my islands way more. I liked Oahu, but Kauai is my favorite. Tutu has helped Nana so much, but even Tutu can't really stop the cancer. She can just slow it down and make Nana comfortable." Kaimi choked, and Garrett's heart stuttered out of rhythm.

"Hey, I didn't mean to bum you out," he apologized. She'd been so excited about going camping and he'd just ruined her night. He lambasted himself.

"It's okay," she immediately assured him. "I kind of feel better all of a sudden for some weird reason."

"I hope you have fun tonight...baby," Garrett tested the waters. He could almost hear her smile from five thousand miles away.

"Thanks. I hope it doesn't rain. I'll send you pics of the bonfire."

"Yeah, do that," Garrett pled. "I'd love to see you."

"I wish you were here. We'd have so much fun." She spoke hesitantly as if she'd had to force her mind to allow the words.

"We would have fun. I'm holding you to that offer to take me camping once I move out there."

"I can't wait!" she trilled. "Hey, Garrett?"

"Yeah..." He tried to control his emotions and contain the awkward uncomfortable feelings that kept swirling in his soul. The way his name sounded on her lips did so many things to him that he wasn't sure which to focus on.

"Maylea doesn't know all that stuff about my parents. Would you not tell her, please?"

"Of course, but just so you know, Fi would never think less of you for that and neither do I."

"Thanks," she whispered. "Would it be okay if I called you

tomorrow when I get home? I don't want to get on your nerves, but I really like talking to you."

"If you don't, then I'm gonna call you."

"Okay." She sounded so excited it delighted him.

"Have fun tonight, baby," he urged.

"I will, bye."

What the fuck? The phrase seared through Garrett's entire being. It beat against the recesses of his mind like a ricocheting pinball. Every place in his body the ball struck seemed to somehow change him. He had no idea who he was or what had happened to him. The only emotion he was able to understand in that endless moment was sadness that she was off having fun without him and that he would have to wait until the next day to hear her voice again.

Dan Vindico

Jeff pulled a tiny screwdriver from his pocket and popped open three of the thumb drives on Dan's kitchen table. Becca and Fionna looked on.

"All of these have already been graded," Dan assured Jeff as he pointed to the pile he'd made that could be popped and studied.

"Unbelievable." Jeff shook his head. "I mean this is like way evil, but it's also incredibly brilliant."

"Who did it?" Dan tried not to sound as demanding as he felt.

"Give me just a minute." Jeff casted the drive he'd opened and forced Dan's laptop to show the information on the drive. His face fell as he dropped the cast on one drive and moved to the next and then the next. He shook his head.

"It's on all of them," he gasped in disbelief.

"What does that mean?" Becca touched his arm tenderly as she rubbed her other hand over her swell. Jeff gave her an adoring grin.

"Hang on, baby," he soothed. "Can I see mine?"

Dan dug in his bag to the thumb drives he hadn't yet graded. He handed Jeff the red plastic thumb drive with his initials and class period written on a small piece of white tape. Jeff performed the same move and then shook his head.

"It's on mine too," he gasped. "Mentor Vindico, I swear."

Fionna reassured him, "If you'd done this, I would have known a long time ago."

Dan began to pace. "You were right. The entire thing with the test vault was to throw us off."

"There's the worm right there. Look." Jeff pointed to Dan's laptop screen. "It's scanning every document on your computer, every email, everything, and sending it back somewhere. But it doesn't activate until the thumb drives are plugged in. That's why I couldn't see it when I checked your laptop before. That's why even when the mentors were forced to make all new exams, they were still selling them as soon as they were made."

"So, how do we catch them?" Fionna asked.

"We write a responsive cast," Jeff answered. "But its gonna take me a few days. The people who did this know what they're doing, and any other information might get slung back. I think I could encrypt something that might at least show us where they are running this from." They watched Dan's screen flash and change rapidly with every move of Jeff's hand.

"So, if we figure that out and then the drug test swaps…" Fionna visibly held back her glee.

"We can move," Dan assured her.

Jeff tried to hide the disappointment on his features as he offered them a kind smile.

"You just have a few more weeks, right," he reminded Jeff that both of them were leaving.

"Yeah, Bec's going to finish at home. I'm going to schedule all of my second semester exams for the end of January, and then I can just work, which will actually be really relaxing."

"Take my laptop to write the cast," Dan urged. "I assume you need a little more power than yours, right?"

"I'll try to get it done fast, but it would actually be better coming from yours anyway. Their system will already recognize it as an accepted source."

"Would you mind if I sat down?" Becca whispered to Fionna.

"Of course not." Fionna guided Becca onto the couch and fixed her a glass of water.

"Bec." Jeff left the computer and the drives instantly.

"I'm okay, just dizzy. I still can't be up and around too much."

"Do you want me to call Adeline?" Jeff asked.

"No, I'm okay."

Dan and Fionna tried to blend back into their own kitchen as Jeff's shield spun up and out over Becca as he sat beside her on the couch in the living room.

"Poor thing. She's so scared." Fionna sounded crestfallen.

"He's got her," Dan soothed. "And take it from me, he will take care of her."

Becca fell asleep a few minutes later, and Jeff worked on Dan's laptop from the kitchen table until she woke up an hour later.

"I'm so sorry." Becca was on the verge of abashed tears.

"Why are you sorry?" Dan asked. He assumed that it was him that she was embarrassed to have fallen asleep in front of and not Fionna and certainly not Jeff.

"Let's go, baby." Jeff leapt. "I'll get it done as fast as I can."

"Take your time. I certainly have no idea how to do what you're doing, so you run the show, Officer Strenton. Tell me what I can do to help."

Sam's words from Tuesday morning rang in his mind. *"You aren't supposed to do this on your own."*

CHAPTER 39

THE FANTASY AND THE FINDINGS

~GARRETT HAYDENSHIRE~

"Hey." Garrett sighed as he answered Chloe's call. He summoned to turn on his television. "Not tonight. I'm beat," he lied and she knew it. "I'm gonna hit the sack," he furthered his deceit. "K bye." He ended the call before she could start bitching and grabbed a beer from the refrigerator.

He fell onto the sofa and popped open the box of takeout from Chang's. A minute later, his cell chirped from the coffee table, and Garrett nearly tossed the Mongolian beef on his carpet in effort to see the text.

He chuckled at the slide show of self-portraits done by Kaimi. There was one of her holding a dandelion she'd set on fire. It glowed in a million different hues and lit her beautiful face. Her lips were pursed as she blew the flames away. Garrett let himself fantasize about those lips. Kissing them, licking them, sucking and dragging his teeth over them. His body shuddered as he envisioned them wrapped around his cock, sucking him off.

The next was a shot of Kaimi in a tiny, yellow triangle bikini top and cutoff shorts that were unsnapped and so short they hardly existed at all. She was wearing a cowboy hat and was leaned up against some girl Garrett didn't know. There were two guys in the shot as well that he instantly hated.

Following that was a shot of her on one of the men's back being given a piggyback ride down the beach. Her head was thrown back and she was laughing. Garrett's jaw clenched as he moved on. There was one of Kaimi in the sunset. She had a long sarong draped over her arms. The bathing suit top was gone, but the thin material of the sarong blocked her ever so slightly from his starving eyes.

His cock throbbed, aching and needy, as he took in the wildfire in her gaze. She couldn't be tamed. It was written on every feature of her petite body. In the blink of her copper-brown eyes, in every strand of her short brown hair, in the tip of her tiny nose, in the curve from her collar bone down to her breasts, in the dip of her abdomen, the muscles in her legs that could only come from years of dancing, and the swell of that luscious ass. But Garrett didn't want to tame her. No, he wanted to indulge her wild being. Her beautiful, unpredictable perfection—he wanted to own it but never, ever to tame it.

The last photo made a broad grin spread rapidly across his face. She was positioned on a quilt on the beach. There was the corner of a tent in the shot. She'd curled herself up the best she was able in order to still be able to take the selfie. After she'd taken the picture, she'd drawn a line to the empty space beside her on the quilt.

"If you were here, I'd be warm," was written on the picture. Nodding, Garrett tried to imagine what being curled up beside her on a quilt would be like. All he wanted was her alone and underneath him. His shield craved the connection. It pounded against his muscles in some kind of punishment that he wasn't with her, protecting her. He didn't give a damn where they were just so long as there were no intrusions and he was deep inside of her.

"I don't want you to be cold, baby. Do I need to catch a flight now or can you wait for me for a few more weeks?" Garrett typed back quickly. He prayed she'd tell him to come back, that she wanted him, that she needed his body next to hers as badly as he needed to hear her voice, feel her breath on his skin, and to see what kind of things he might could set on fire for her.

He wanted to consume her, to inhale everything she gave up for him. He wanted to bury himself so deeply inside of her neither of them could even hope to feel where she stopped and he began.

246

She sent another picture as her response. It was a shot of her from inside her tent. She was topless, lying on a sleeping bag and on full display this time. Her hand was extended from her lips as she blew him a kiss. *"Good night..."* was the only message.

Garrett flipped the photos back to the one of her blowing the dandelion. His hand slipped down his abs and popped the snap on his jeans.

Dan Vindico

Fionna whimpered as Dan slid from the bed.

"I didn't mean to wake you up, baby. I'll be back in a little while."

"I want you to stay with me," she fussed sweetly.

"I want to stay with you too, but maybe whatever Will called this meeting about will help me finish up with all of the crap at Venton and we can get on with our life in Kauai."

Fionna yawned and sat up in the bed. The sheets and quilt fell away from her bare chest, and Dan let his hand trail over what she'd revealed. She laced her fingers over his and then proceeded to knead her own breasts as they moved against his palms.

"Fi," Dan panted as he tried desperately to remember why he was supposed to be in his father's office in twenty minutes.

She gave him her sultry smile that said she needed to be taken and owned.

"I've got to go, baby doll," he begged. She poked her bottom lip out in an adorable pout, and Dan ached for her. He leaned and breathed a kiss on her lips. "I love you, Maylea." He let his thumb spin over her bare nipple. It rose to meet his touch. It begged and pleaded for his attention.

Halia's stuttered grunts of frustration were the only things that had Dan able to move away from his beautiful bride. Fionna pulled on one of his T-shirts and went to greet Halia as Dan kissed her once more and headed to the Senate.

"I'll pick up Fitz and Maddie and the boys at ten and then we'll be home," he called as he headed out.

Dan raced into his father's office, barely making it by eight.

"Son, so nice of you to join us," Governor Vindico scoffed. Dan rolled his eyes, but he was pleased to see the color back in his old man's face. The governor looked like a new man in fact. Only working the job he'd actually earned and that he actually wanted instead of trying to carry on two more than full-time positions for the past week or so seemed to have restored him.

Will chuckled at the governor's quip as he flipped through several file folders.

Governor Haydenshire came in several minutes late and carrying Abigail.

"I'm sorry. My house is a little hectic what with the entire Australian Royal Family in to visit Adeline and Logan for the next week. Lillian is worn out, so Abby Hope is going to help me run the Senate for a little while before I bow out and head back home," he explained with a sigh.

Will beamed at his little sister as she shot her arms out toward him. He lifted her out of their father's grasp. Abigail's hand formed tightly around Will's knuckle as she stared at him expectantly.

"You're sad," he quizzed thoughtfully. "Oh, because Lily Ana isn't with me," he guessed. Abigail gave a heavy nod. Abigail Haydenshire was the only known Gifted child with Downs Syndrome and was also the only Receiver on the planet that could communicate at ten months old by pushing her emotions onto others. She performed this most easily with her family, and she was very rarely verbal. She would show them her emotion, and they would guess what was making her feel that way. Emily was by far the best at guessing correctly.

"Okay, you stay here and play with Dad for a little while and let me get some work done and then I'll take you home and you can play with Lily Ana, okay?" Will negotiated. Governor Haydenshire smiled as Abigail nodded again.

"Thank you, son. Now why don't you and Abby tell us why you've called us all in here this morning," the Crown Governor directed.

"Here, Dan's good with Receivers." Will handed Abigail to Dan and then returned to his folders. Abigail studied Dan speculatively, then she seemed to decide that she both remembered him and liked him before she tucked herself under his chin and touched his neck. Dan concentrated on what she wanted. "Oh." He realized almost immediately. She was seeking his powerful shield which he provided her. She turned to listen to her oldest brother talk. Dan grinned and cradled Abigail to him as he listened as well.

Will drew a deep breath. "We've completed the audit of Venton, but I think you're going to have to write Dan a big bonus check if we're going to keep this from getting out in the press and catch the culprit."

"What did you find?" Governor Vindico leapt.

"It's not so much *what* we found as whom," Will replied cryptically.

"Okay, whom then? And why is Dean putting so much money back into Venton?"

"My original premise was that he was using Venton money either to buy someone's silence or to give to Katherine Bryant, and then he was trying to pay it back, and truthfully, that is what it was set up to look like, but it isn't him and it isn't her. What I found doesn't seem to have anything to do with why Wilshire is putting money back into the Venton accounts. I don't think they're related."

Will handed out paycheck stubs made out to a Mentor Chase Satzman.

"Mentor Satzman"—he held up one of the copies—"doesn't exist. Well, that's not entirely accurate. The man exists, but he hasn't taught at Venton in several years. Two years ago, he showed back up receiving a full-time paycheck twice a month for over two years. Mentor Satzman lives on the south side of London. One of you will have to send out London Iodex to arrest him if that's how you want to handle it. But he, or someone impersonating him, has been drawing a three hundred and fifty thousand dollar paycheck every year for the past two years," Will concluded as his eyes glanced from Dan, to his father, to Governor Vindico. "Wilshire had donated four hundred and seventy-four thousand dollars and sixty-three cents at the time he was suspended. The two numbers don't seem related at all."

Dan's father was rubbing his temples and shaking his head in abject disbelief.

"I'll go to London," Dan immediately volunteered. "I'll find this idiot and bring him back here. No one will ever have to know about this."

"Daniel, your badge gives you carte blanche over law enforcement within the state of Hawaii," Governor Haydenshire pointed out. "You cannot fly to London, beat someone over the head, put them in cuffs, and drag them out of the country. And William, you just said someone could be impersonating this man, did you not?"

"Could be," Will allowed.

"All right, Arthur, if I may," Governor Haydenshire edged in.

Governor Vindico nodded. "Please do. I clearly haven't done anything right when it came to Venton in the past several years."

"I don't think that's true, but Dan, why don't we give this a few days? I know the Fitzroys are coming in to visit you and Fionna. Maybe after Christmas you and Garrett could fly to London for a night, see if you can't locate Mentor Satzman, and see what you can find out. If you know he's stealing the money, then you can call in London Iodex, but if he's not, then we need to figure out who is getting an extra paycheck before we turn this over to any branch of Iodex. Otherwise, I am afraid your jobs aren't going to get any easier."

Governor Vindico nodded morosely.

"We'll take care of it, Dad," Dan assured him. He couldn't believe that someone had been walking out the door with that much money every year.

"We still don't know why Wilshire was making those huge donations. I'm sorry, sir. Nothing in the books explained it," Will sighed.

"You found this. Believe me, that's something," Governor Vindico assured him. "Did this guy teach here at some point or did he only teach at the satellite campus in London?"

"He only taught in London. In fact, he might've been there when Rainer was there for those few weeks. If that helps or he even remembers him," Will recalled. "It was actually pretty ingenious. The accounting is all done here in DC, so none of the accountants ever saw this guy on campus. His name showing back up on the payroll probably didn't look odd to anyone."

CHAPTER 40

FRENCH FOOD AND FITZROY

~GARRETT HAYDENSHIRE~

"Hell yeah, I'll go to London with you. Better than playing meter maid for Sorenson," Garrett scoffed. He was thrilled to have an actual mission, and he forced himself to admit that he wanted to help Dan get through the shit going on at Venton so that he could get back to Kauai and get Kaimi in his arms. He just needed to get her out of his system. At that thought, his shield sizzled against his own skin and he cringed. He closed his eyes to try to regain control of his shield. It seemed to be waging war against him.

He clenched his jaw and willed repose. "Just get Dad to call the chief. He's furious with me and being a total prick," Garrett ordered Dan. The alarm he'd set on his phone began buzzing.

"Hey, I gotta go do something. I'll talk to you later. Tell Fitz and my girls I'll stop by tomorrow." Garrett ended his call. It was seven in the morning in Kauai. He grinned.

Good morning, beautiful. How'd you sleep?

He typed into his phone. His heart flew as he awaited a response.

That evening Garrett stomped along the concrete outside of the Non-Gifted National Archives building. Sorenson had sent him to play security guard there for a group of Vietnam War veterans visiting the memorials that day.

Garrett certainly didn't mind helping veterans, but they were the only tourists around, and the likelihood that the group of men all over the age of seventy-five were going to get out of hand seemed doubtful. At seven o'clock, the group running the tour waved to Garrett and thanked him for his help as they returned to the buses. Garrett helped the men back onto the bus, climbed back in his squad car, and grinned as his phone rang.

Dan Vindico

"And sometimes if you don't like what Grandma fixes for dinner, then you get to have a peanut butter and jelly party with Mommy and Daddy after Grandma goes to bed." Aida was explaining this to Alex and Alfred. Fitz was chuckling as he helped Alfred into his coat.

"Why wouldn't you like what your grandmother made you?" Alfred asked.

Dan glanced at Fionna as they both wondered what would come out of Aida's mouth next.

"Sometimes different people like different things," Aida prosed politely.

Dan grimaced as he led everyone outside. Fionna lifted Halia's seat into the car.

"Poor kid looks just like you." Fitz laughed again as he shook his head.

252

. . .

Garrett Haydenshire

"Okay, boxers or briefs?" Kaimi giggled out her question.

"You wondering what's in my briefs, baby?" Garrett continued to tease her. He desperately wished he could see the deep blush that his comment certainly elicited.

"Answer the question, Deputy."

"Briefs. Nothing fancy. Boxers can't keep me contained."

"I am rolling my eyes so hard right now."

"Just wait. I'll show you, but it's my turn. Thongs or G-strings?"

"Are those my only choices?" she scoffed with another delighted giggle.

"As far as I can see, yeah."

"Since there have been no guys who have been seeing my underwear in the last several years, neither. I've resorted to the sad, sad, land of those white cotton underwear that they sell in packs of five at Walmart. If I don't get some action soon, I'm going to start wearing character panties again, I swear."

Garrett shook his head. "We'll have to see what we can do about that before it reaches the land of Barbie panties."

Dan Vindico

"Now, Daniel, if you're so determined to go back into law enforcement, it sounds to me like accepting Jean Paul's offer to be his partner in French Iodex would be much more prestigious than being the Chief of Hawaiian Iodex. I mean France is a whole country," Mrs. Vindico asserted herself just as appetizers were served.

Dan wasn't certain if he was more disgusted by what she'd said or what she was serving. She'd dug out the fondue pot she and the governor had been given for a wedding gift. The pot, however, was not heating the cheese evenly, and whatever concoction of oily, cheap cheeses Mrs. Vindico had chosen were burning into a bubbling heap on one side of the pot and were still solid on the other. To combat this, Dan's mother was trying to cast it with a heat cast that was entirely too much. It was like eating molten lava on burnt toast squares.

"I did appreciate Fitz's offer, but my wife and my daughters need to be on Kauai, and quite frankly, Mom, that's where I want to be as well. They need someone to try and bridge the gaps there between the residents and the tourists. It can get contentious. On top of that, there are several drug cartels that see Hawaii as an ideal way station in the middle of the Pacific. They need to be stopped now before they get a foothold. I want to work with Garrett again, and I want him to be a part of my girls' lives. We are moving to Kauai. I wish you and Dad could be happy for us."

Maddie was appalled at the lack of decorum between Dan and his mother. Fitz seemed amused. Fionna continued to try and soothe Dan by casting him discreetly. The children were politely trying to eat the burnt toast squares with the horrible cheese mixture, but their scowls were showing through their breeding.

"Fionna, darling, tell us about your new dance endeavors. I'm so thrilled for her. I know you must be," Maddie stepped in.

The governor and Mrs. Vindico stared at Fionna blankly.

"Uh," she stammered and Dan stepped in to save her.

"Fi and Malani just bought a hula studio a few miles from the farm. They're going to expand it and teach classes themselves," Dan explained to his parents.

"And when Fitz and Maddie visit us in Kauai, Maddie said she would come talk to the students about dancing for the Moulin Rouge." Fionna's excitement was evident in her tone.

Dan's eyes closed as he tried to block out the image of his parents' horrified expressions. Dan had never told his parents what Maddie had been doing when she and Fitz had met, fallen in love, and gotten married. As prestigious as dancing at the Rouge was, and as talented as the dancers are, he knew his mother relegated it to stripping, which was just one minuscule step above prostitution in the book of life according to Marion Vindico.

Maddie beamed. "Fionna has such wonderful plans to expand their customer base. It is wonderful exercise. She has wonderful instructors in place. She will be bringing some of the sensuality missing here in America to the people. It will be great!" She was genuinely thrilled for Fionna and wanted to help her.

Mrs. Vindico stared in horror from Fionna to Dan and back. "We are not missing sensuality. We are not missing anything at all. Just what kind of dancing will you be doing? Will this be like the Moulin Rouge? Daniel, your father is a Realm Governor." Mrs. Vindico's eyes goggled to the size of plates. She tried to draw deep breaths that came out as hissy convulsions.

"I'm not certain what that has to do with my wife's future career," Dan informed her.

He was instantly taken back to the morning he'd called his parents to inform them that he and Fionna were marrying in one hour's time. His mother made the very same shrill, shrieking sound, only this time as he was within arm's reach. She proceeded to smack the back of his head with her hand. His shield pulsed furiously. Dan stood with his teeth bared as he stared down over his mother.

"Dan," Fionna panicked.

"Do not hit me," he growled.

"Daniel, have a seat," Governor Vindico commanded. "Marion, let's eat, now."

"You can't hit Uncle Dan. He's a superhero," Alex defied. Fitz plastered his hand over his son's mouth.

Fionna was horrified that Dan's parents were so appalled. "It's only hula. I promise. But Kaimi is going to teach some kahiko classes so some ancients as well."

Dan was furious at his mother's audacity, and the Fitzroys were growing more and more uncomfortable by the moment.

After Dan seated Fionna, he threw back his own chair and fell into it with a great deal of fury. Aida slipped behind him and touched the back of his head in the approximate place that Mrs. Vindico's fingers had landed.

"I'm so sorry, Daddy," she whispered just before she gently kissed Dan's thick brown hair. "I got a spanking once at the orphanage. I don't think people should do that because you're not supposed to hit someone especially if they didn't mean to do anything wrong."

Dan added outrage to the fury coursing through his veins. "She got spanked?!" he shouted at Fionna. He debated flying to Brazil and letting the nuns know just what he thought of that.

"Dan." Fionna's eyes closed in abject defeat. "Please."

"I knew you would probably be missing French food by the time you arrived here, so I went all out," Mrs. Vindico managed her rehearsed speech though it was spoken through her clenched teeth.

"Yes, because it's been approximately twelve whole hours since they left Paris," Dan sneered. "And I'm certain whatever your offensive interpretation of French food is, it's certain to offer us all comfort."

"Daniel," Governor Vindico roared.

It wasn't his father's acrimony that had Dan backing down. It was the tears that pricked his wife's and his little girl's eyes that had him drawing a deep breath and trying to relax.

Mrs. Vindico ignored Dan thoroughly as was her custom since he'd learned to talk and therefore challenge her.

"Jean Paul, red or white?" Governor Vindico moved to the wine bottles on the side bar.

"Red is fine. Thank you, sir," Fitz offered kindly. He and Dan shared concerned glances. Neither was certain how the evening had gone so poorly so quickly. The governor poured everyone a glass of wine. Dan shook his head as he noted that his mother had picked out seven-dollar California wine to serve to the Chief of French Iodex, not that Fitz would care. Maddie tried to hide the slight purse of her lips as she tasted what was certainly the worst wine she'd ever let slide by her very refined French palate.

"I found this recipe for a corn and broccoli soufflé in a favorite magazine of mine, and I figured that would be lovely and French-y." Mrs. Vindico slid back into her hostess routine. "It called for something called gruey-air, which I discovered is some kind of cheese, but I decided since you're in America you should like American cheese. It really is the best, of course, and I imagine not something you have access to in Paris." Mrs. Vindico had gone to a great deal of thought to be so obscenely offensive.

"You made a soufflé with American cheese?" Fionna seemed to pray that somehow the answer would be no.

"It's Gruyère," Maddie corrected Mrs. Vindico as she stared at the odd concoction that was revealed in a gargantuan casserole dish.

Mrs. Vindico ignore her completely as well.

She turned on her daughter-in-law instead. "Yes, Fionna. Two cans of corn, a bag of frozen broccoli, crushed soda crackers, seventeen slices of cheese, and margarine," she announced.

"Dear God." Dan shuddered in horror.

"That sounds lovely, Mrs. Vindico," Maddie lied outright.

"It does. Let me serve it, Marion." The governor took the small spatula from his wife.

"My son and daughter-in-law don't seem to enjoy my cooking, but I certainly hope you like it, Jean Paul."

When the governor served square sections of the bizarre casserole that was being passed off as a French soufflé, a cloudy liquid leaked all over everyone's plate.

"She forgot to drain the corn," Fionna explained under her breath.

"Honey, the only thing in this dish that is actually food might be the broccoli, and it's burned to a crisp," Dan huffed under his breath.

"Oh, and I found this French Dijon mustard we can dip it in." Mrs. Vindico rushed to the refrigerator and withdrew French Dijon mustard that was mass produced in Pittsburgh.

"Papa," Alex whined as he took his first bite.

"Alexander," Fitz growled. "I will own you, son."

Aida leaned and whispered to Alex. "I can make you peanut butter and jelly at my house, and we have two kinds of chips." He nodded appreciatively as Dan and Fitzroy tried not to laugh.

"Fionna, just how exactly do you intend to run a hula studio and care for your daughters while your husband gallivants around Hawaii running the Iodex there?" Mrs. Vindico demanded as soon as everyone began pretending to eat their dinner. Dan narrowed his eyes in on his mother.

Fionna patted Dan's leg in order to keep him from lunging across the table at his mother.

"Aida will be in school. The studio is for children and adults, and we'll have a very nice care program for the little ones whose mommies are taking classes. Aida will be taking classes herself in the afternoons. We don't really believe in working excessively long hours on the islands. The studio isn't even open every day. Malani and Kai will be there. My grandparents will be there. Garrett will be there, and of course, Dan is also their parent. I don't think it will be a problem. Aida loves her hula classes, and if she wants to join Kaimi's advanced classes when she's older she can do that, but it will be up to her how often she wants to be at the halau."

"Hula is very fun, and you get to have shave ice at the end sometimes, and you get to meet lots of friends, and wear very pretty costumes, and it's my very favorite thing I think," Aida gushed in an effort to defend her mother.

"Hula, much like all dance, is a lovely combination of heart, and soul, and movement of the body. It brings peace to the mind and health to your being," Maddie vowed.

With an audible scoff, Mrs. Vindico returned to the kitchen to present dessert. Dan breathed a sigh of relief when he heard his mother tear open a cardboard pie box and then the customary pop of the hard plastic shell.

"Lemon Meringue." Mrs. Vindico threw the frozen pie on the table and then began serving instant coffee. Everyone had seconds of dessert.

CHAPTER 41

OFFERS AND OFFICERS

~GARRETT HAYDENSHIRE~

Garrett rolled his eyes for the fourth time in a five-minute period.

"I just worked twelve on, and now I'm on call tonight?" he challenged Sorenson.

"Hey, you were just saying that you didn't have anything to do," Sorenson chanted derisively.

"That's because you keep sending me out on shit detail like some kind of newbie beat cop."

"You're on tonight. Keep your phone on."

Garrett slammed his chair up against his desk, grabbed his jacket, and fled the precinct office.

He glanced at his phone as he cranked the car and headed to his apartment. He hadn't been to hang out with Chloe, and she was getting bitchy. Garrett just didn't want that anymore. *I'm moving as soon as possible. She needs somebody else to fuck around with.*

Kaimi's text chime went off, and Garrett smiled automatically. He forced himself to wait until he pulled into the apartment complex parking deck to read her text. They'd texted all day every day for the past week and a half and then FaceTimed whenever they were both off. They never seemed to run out of things to say. She was the most fascinating human he'd ever known. Everything she said somehow mesmerized him. He no longer had thoughts that didn't involve her. His shield was completely preoccupied with her safety. It was becoming physically painful to be without her. It was…almost like she was the object of his shield.

How was work?

His entire being eased.

Spent twelve hours filing reports made by other officers. I seriously cannot wait to move.

Filing could have been fun. You know like if you decided to sing the alphabet song out loud every time you filed something.

Garrett cracked up from the thought alone.

Will definitely do that next time.

If you were here right now, what would we be doing?

Garrett allowed himself a long minute to think about that. His heart thundered and his breaths picked up pace.

Whatever you wanted as long as you were in my arms and in my bed.

Their texts over the past few days had gotten decidedly more sexually charged, and he wasn't backing down now.

What if I wanted you in my bed?

He could almost hear the sass in her tone without her having to have spoken the words.

Your bed, my bed, counter top, beach, lounge chair, pool, bath tub, I don't give a damn.

Garrett had never laughed so loud over a text, and in the echo of his laughter he realized how empty his apartment was and how lonely it was to laugh alone.

I want was her reply, and the two words spoke erotic volumes directly to Garrett's groin.

Garrett called Dan. "Sorenson is getting worse. Can I help you speed this up at all?"

"Fitz and I are going over some of the stuff Jeff gave us. Come look it over with us, and we can talk about London." He must've heard the desperation in Garrett's tone.

"I'm on my way."

When Garrett arrived, Aida raced into his arms.

"Hey, baby girl." He scooped her up and swung her around.

"Alex and I are playing house," she informed him. Fitzroy's boys reminded Garrett just a little too much of him and Will. He didn't like the idea of his baby girl playing house with anyone, much less a destined player.

"Is that so?" Garrett shot Dan an irritated glare. He nodded his unspoken agreement.

Jeff Strenton was seated at the dining room table behind Dan's laptop. Governor Sapman's daughter, Becca, was lying on the sofa. Fi and Maddie were fussing over her, and Halia was asleep in her swing.

"What do we have? I cannot keep working for that moron." Garrett joined Fitz and Dan at the table.

"Sorenson's always been like that. He's great until you want to go play for another team. I tried talking to him, and he informed me that

I needed to go fuck with Hawaii, that there was real police work to be done here." Dan rolled his eyes.

Fitz joined in their acrimony. "Yeah, that's a good policy. Let your best officers do your shit jobs because they're moving. Then they move or quit, and you wish you had them back for whatever time they're here."

"Yeah, well, I don't want to be here much longer, so how can I help?" Garrett needed to focus. He had a life waiting on him, and it wasn't here.

"My first three tries came right back. Whoever did this is a deviant genius," Jeff began explaining. "So far, I can see everything they're getting off the mentors' laptops, but I can't seem to locate where the information is going."

"Are you going to tell the mentors to stop using the thumb drives?" Garrett asked Dan.

"Dad could, but I'm pretty sure that would put a stop to this before we catch these idiots, and we want them caught."

Jeff's eyes lifted from the screen. "Truthfully, one way to make this work would be for you to hand these back out and then have everyone assign another quick paper due back in a few days. I could recast the drives but embed my cast so it's hidden. Then we could wait and see what we find out."

Fitz smirked and extended his hand to Jeff. "I know we just met, but Jean Paul Fitzroy, Captain of French Iodex. Have you and your wife ever considered how great life is in Paris?" He smirked.

Jeff blushed violently as he laughed.

"If his in-laws don't quit showing up at his house every day, he might take you up on that." Dan made certain Becca couldn't hear him.

"Think about it. Four-hour plane ride between you and them. It's hard to just show up unannounced," Fitz continued to harass Jeff.

"Don't tempt me, sir. Her dad showed up yesterday morning at six o'clock. My first day off in two weeks, and then he got mad at me because I took too long to answer the door. Becca heard us arguing and came in the living room in my T-shirt and that really set him off."

Laughter and head shakes went around the table.

"When are we hitting London?" Garrett broached as the laughter quieted down.

"I'd like to go the day after Christmas, but I hate to leave Fi with the girls by herself," Dan lamented.

"I could fly up from Rio," Garrett offered. "Or I'm due back in Christmas night, so I'd just want to sleep a little before we leave. Hey, Rainer knows this guy we're looking for, right?" Garrett recalled the conversation he'd had with Dan and Will the night before.

"Yeah, he was in his class, but Rainer was only in London for a few weeks, and that was several years ago."

"Yeah, but he knows what he looks like. So, we take Rainer with us and dump Em here to help Fi with the girls."

"I'll meet you up there and help," Fitz offered. "It's only a twenty-minute flight for me." Garrett knew that Fitz was probably bummed Dan was moving even farther away and wanted to work one last case together.

"We might want to ask Rainer and Emily about that," Dan pointed out.

"Are we sure it's this mentor guy?" Garrett continued his inquisition as he tried to concentrate on anything but the picture burned into his mind of Kaimi topless and blowing him a kiss.

"No," Dan sighed. "But it's the best lead we have, and I still don't know what Wilshire was donating all of that money for. It seems like they should be related, but neither of us can find any evidence proving that." He gestured to Jeff.

Garrett nodded his agreement. Something about London didn't set well.

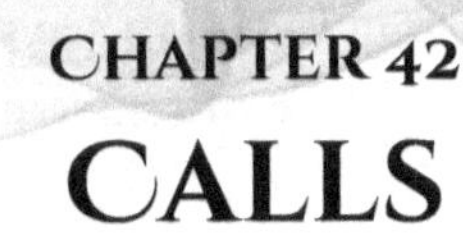

CHAPTER 42

CALLS

A couple of hours later, Garrett fell into his bed. He touched Kaimi's name on his FaceTime list.

"Hey." She was lying in her bed, and a desperate hunger washed through Garrett's shield. "I was just going to call you. I just got Nana to bed. She's running a fever." He could hear the fear that haunted her voice.

"Is that normal?" Garrett considered calling Adeline. He knew nothing about what Kaimi's grandmother was suffering from, but he wanted to help.

"It happens occasionally. Her body's responses to the cancer and the treatment. She's just so weak."

"I'm sorry, baby."

"Yeah, me too. I was just thinking about you," she confessed in a sudden change of flow.

"What were you thinking about?" Garrett tried to hide the desire and hunger that perforated his tone. There was an intimacy in her sweet voice that night. An unfulfilled desperation to be protected and adored, cradled and worshipped. Garrett longed to meet her every need. His shield ached for her. It burned against his skin in desperation. It wielded a brutal punishment that Garrett wasn't near her. "You can tell me." She seemed frightened to go on.

"I was thinking about how bad I want your hand between my legs," she finally choked out the needy confession. He couldn't halt the thunderous growl that tore from his lungs.

"My god, Kaimi, baby, I want to see you. I don't care if it's for a night or, hell, just an hour. I just want to kiss you and touch you. I haven't even gotten to hug you. I need to see you," he begged.

"I know." She was on the verge of tears, and her devastation sliced through him brutally.

"Do you want to come to Brazil with me next week for Christmas? I go down there every year and work in an orphanage. It's the one where Aida lived before Dan and Fi adopted her. I'm taking a bunch of gifts down there. It's so cool to see their faces when they get gifts on Christmas they weren't expecting," Garrett pled out his invitation. He wanted Kaimi to know the many sides of his often confusing life. He wanted her to help him heal them all.

"Wow," she gasped. "Are you like some kind of saint or something?"

"I'm definitely not, but I would love for you to come."

"That would be amazing, but I can't leave Nana, and I'm kind of terrible with kids," she admitted in a pained whisper.

"That's not true," Garrett vowed. "But I'm coming there after I get back from London."

"Really?" Her voice shook in her hopefulness.

"Really." Nothing would keep him away.

They talked for another three hours about nothing and everything. She told him about living in New York and about the wildest thing she'd done once she was thousands of miles away from her extremely overprotective grandmother.

He told her about a few of his escapades, leaving out any unimportant details, which he quickly determined were most of them. They'd discussed him living on Tutu's farm, and she'd assured him that he wouldn't be imposing and that he would only be two miles from her front door, which, to Garrett, was the best feature the free house had yet.

He realized how many days he'd wasted in monotony and how much he wanted her to be a part of his days.

Garrett told her about the Wretchkinsides takedown and what Dan and Fionna had gone through and how they'd come to adopt Aida. They discussed his family and how he'd grown up.

She explained how life had worked in Honolulu for her and how she much preferred Kauai though she hadn't figured out why other than the fact that she didn't like big cities. New York had ruined her, she'd decided. Garrett agreed with the sentiment and told her how cool it was that she liked to camp and that he thought she was beautiful despite the fact that she rarely wore makeup.

When he could hardly hold his eyes open, he promised to text her at their usual time the next morning and fell into a deep sleep.

Just after sunrise, his cell rang in the bed beside him.

"Haydenshire," he managed through a deep yawn as he tried to rub the sleep from his eyes.

"Hey," Kaimi managed in a stuttered whisper just before she began sobbing.

"What's wrong?" Garrett kicked off his sheets and located jeans before moving to his laptop to check flight times.

"I'm at the hospital," she finally explained.

"What did they say?" He prayed she wasn't there all alone with her grandmother either dead or dying.

"They just got her stabilized, but I have a bad feeling. Tutu came up here. She's sitting with me. I just...I wanted to talk to you." Garrett redacted every skeptical thought he'd had about Fionna's grandmother as she was currently sitting with the woman who meant more to him than anyone else in the world at one o'clock in the morning in Kauai.

Garrett shook himself. He didn't need flight times. "Okay, baby, let me call my dad. I'll use his jet. I'll be there in just a few hours." He tried to keep his voice calm and reassuring.

"You don't have to do that. I just wanted to talk to you," her voice trembled out her lie.

"Kaimi, I'm on my way." He wasn't taking no for an answer. If she had a bad feeling, then something was up.

"Thank you," she whispered before another round of choked sobs took over.

"Kaimi, sweetheart, he can't come if he's on the phone with you," Garrett heard Tutu guide Kaimi. "Go sit with Olina. She's asking for you."

"I'll be right there. Just hang on, sweetheart." Garrett ended the call and touched his father's name on his screen.

"Dad, it's me!"

"What's wrong?"

"I need to use the jet, please."

"Why?"

"I need to go back to Kauai, like right now. A friend of mine needs me," he confessed. Calling her a friend felt wrong. She was so much more than that, but truthfully, they hadn't known each other very long, and Garrett had no idea how to explain their relationship.

"You already have friends in Kauai?"

"Yes!" Garrett fumed. "Dammit, Dad, please. I need to get out of here. I'm worried about her. Something's wrong."

"When are you coming back?" Governor Haydenshire remained calm and steadfast just like always.

"I don't know. I just need to go now."

"All right, son. I'll call Pete, but it'll take them a little while to prepare."

"Thank you," was Garrett's parting line.

He threw what he hoped were both matching and clean clothes into a suitcase. With a slight shudder, he grabbed the dry cleaning bag that held his suit. He tossed a protein bar in his mouth and raced to his Highlander.

"Haydenshire, good. You're in early. I was just looking over the schedule for the next few weeks. I can't let you off three days at Christmas. Men who are going to be here in January want to spend Christmas with their families, so you can work," Sorensen informed him.

Garrett narrowed his eyes and shook his head. He was going to Brazil for Christmas, and Satan himself wasn't going to stop him.

"I quit," he stated firmly.

"What?"

"I," Garret drawled hatefully, "quit." After tossing his badge on Sorenson's desk, he eyed his boss defiantly.

"You can't quit."

"Just did." He gestured to the badge. "I'll take the next few months and help a guy who actually knows how to run a police force take down another criminal ring. Then I'll move and become the deputy commander of Iodex in the great state of Hawaii, and you, Officer Sorenson, can kiss my ass." Garrett set his service pistol and holster on the desk and spun to make his exit.

Stunned silence was his farewell as he marched out of the police precinct.

CHAPTER 43

HORRIFYING MOMENT OF PERFECTION

Four hours later, Garrett sprinted into Wilcox Memorial Hospital. He casted the elevator and had it flying to the fifth floor in a matter of moments. As soon as the doors opened, he took in Kaimi sobbing on Fionna's grandmother's shoulder. She lifted her head as she saw him. Her eyes were bloodshot and almost swollen shut, and Garrett was certain he'd never seen anything more devastatingly beautiful as she fell heavy into his arms.

"I'm so sorry, baby." He cradled her head to his chest and kissed the top of her hair. She'd added in a few red highlights since the last time he'd seen her. He hadn't noticed them on the phone the night before. He surrounded her entire body in his muscled embrace as Tutu gave him a knowing smile. Suddenly, Garrett felt it. His world fell into perfect accord in that one horrifying moment of perfection.

"It was just a few minutes ago," were the first words Kaimi was able to formulate. Garrett wished there was some way he could have been with her. Her fists knotted his T-shirt and somehow eased the vicious grip his entire fucked-up life held around his throat.

"I know, sweetheart. Papa called me."

"I don't know what to do now," she confessed as another choked sob overtook her.

Garrett nodded. He remembered that feeling only too well.

"I'm so sorry to tell you this, Officer Haydenshire, but your brother Cal was killed in the line of duty last night outside of Reutov. The woman he'd been seeing, Brynn, his body was found on top of hers. I'm sure he was trying to protect her." Garrett would never forget.

Suddenly, in that confusing and terrible moment where death and life swirled much too closely, Garrett knew what she should do. He stepped back slightly and cradled her face in his powerful hands. He wiped away her tears with his thumbs as he gazed into her beautiful eyes.

"You should do this." He leaned and brushed his lips across hers. "All I wanted for a week now was to kiss you," he informed her in the split seconds that their lips parted and then sought each other's again.

When Garrett finally pulled away to draw breath, Kaimi buried her face in his chest and he cradled her tightly.

"Miss Walyuo, we just have some papers for you to sign," a hospital employee approached hesitantly. "I'm so sorry for your loss, miss."

Kaimi turned to the woman, and Garrett grasped her hand. He just needed to keep her skin next to his. She turned back to him and smiled through her tears. He saw it in her tender gaze. He saw it and he wasn't afraid. He wanted the love she was timidly trying to hide but was unable to conceal.

Dan Vindico

Dan rolled his eyes as he answered his cell. He was certain he knew where this was going. "What?"

Sorenson wasn't going to call Dan up and bitch about one of his closest friends and his partner.

The shouting began instantly.

"Wait, what?" Dan gasped. "He quit?"

"Who?" Fionna mouthed.

"Garrett."

Fionna's mouth fell open as she lifted her own cell from her purse.

"No, I don't have any idea what's going on, but I imagine you treating him like your lackey intern, after he's been in eleven years and has earned every meritorious promotion available, not to mention being named Officer of the Year three times for risking his own life to save someone else's, might've had something to do with it."

"He's not answering." Fionna was approaching panic. "Is this what I've been feeling?"

Dan's brow furrowed, but his phone beeped. "I've got to go. The Crown Governor's calling, but it sounds to me like you just lost your best officer."

"Yes, sir," Dan answered the next call.

He sat in the Starbucks near his home with his wife and daughters in stunned disbelief. They'd just dropped Fitz and his family back at the airport for them to continue their journey to visit Fitz's father for Christmas.

"He flew to Kauai." Dan finally processed the information Governor Haydenshire was giving him. "No, I have no idea why, sir. He didn't tell me he was going."

Fionna's expression represented Dan's feelings perfectly. She was thoroughly shocked but extremely hopeful.

She touched another name on her phone, and Dan saw her fingers cross. He chuckled as he tried to reassure the governor that he was certain Garrett was fine, and that he would figure out what was going on.

"Tutu," Fionna gasped and then checked her watch. "Is Garrett there?" A broad, delighted grin cast Fionna's beautiful features. "He's with Kaimi!" Fionna was on the verge of dancing around Starbucks. "Oh, I'm so sorry. Is she okay?" Fionna's face fell suddenly. "Tell her we're thinking of her. But Garrett is there now, and he's with her?" Fionna restated her question.

Dan casted her phone so he could hear as well.

"I don't understand your surprise, Maylea. You felt the rhythms churning rapidly when you were here, did you not?"

"I did. I was just afraid to believe," Fionna confessed.

"He got here just a few minutes ago, and he's had her in his arms the entire time. The island is rejoicing. I can feel it. So much in store for these two precious souls."

"That's so sweet."

"Maylea, he's your best friend. I don't know why you sound astonished," Tutu scolded. "Olina was waiting, clinging to life, because our sweet little Kaimi had no one but her. When the time was right and she knew that Garrett would step in and care for her precious granddaughter, she let go. The time had come."

"I'm so happy for them and sad for her. I'm confused."

Dan was still beaming as he wrapped his arm around Fionna and kissed the side of her head.

"They're going to need you and Daniel. If this is going to work, we must listen and follow the guidance we're being given," Tutu warned. "Their road will not be an easy one."

"We're listening, and we want to help," Dan vowed into the phone, making Fionna beam at him.

Garrett Haydenshire

"I know it's stupid," Kaimi whimpered as she fell back against the seat in Garrett's Hummer. Papa had driven it to the hospital for him when he picked up Tutu. "I still can't believe you're here." She kept staring up at him like she was afraid if she looked away he might disappear.

Garrett chuckled as he laced her fingers back through his own. He couldn't really believe it himself.

"I keep telling you it's not stupid. It's totally logical," he corrected her again. He was unable to hide his concern. Kaimi was exhausted and terrified and devastated. Her rhythms were running frantically. Garrett longed to soothe her, but wasn't certain how or where. She didn't want to stay in her apartment. It had also belonged to her grandmother, and Kaimi didn't want to deal with that just then.

"How about this, let's take a day or two and just hide out, okay? Your grandmother wanted to be cremated and buried at sea, so that's going to take a little while. Let's skip the farm for now. If you're sure you want me hanging around constantly then let me just rent us a place wherever you want for the next few days. Let's really get to know each other, and let me help you deal with all of this," Garrett pled out his plan. He forced himself to drown the desire that kept pulsing in his shield.

Not now and not for a while, Haydenshire. Shut it down. That's sure as hell not what she needs right now.

"You're just sort of like my own personal guardian angel," Kaimi whispered as tears threatened imminently again.

"Shh, it's okay." He leaned and cradled her on his massive shoulder once again. Garrett kissed her temple and let her cry. There was nothing he could say or do to make the pain of losing the only person who had ever been there for her better.

"I'm sorry." She shuddered against him.

"Baby, why are you sorry? It's okay to be sad." He assured her one of the many things he'd learned as he'd watched Rainer lose his father, and Amelia be taken from Dan, as he'd watched his parents and siblings grieve Cal, as he himself had gone through all he'd lost, and what losing a child had meant for Dan and Fionna. "Do you think you'll be okay to go back to the apartment and pack a few things and then let me see where we can stay?"

Kaimi nodded against his chest. She pulled away suddenly and studied him. He smiled at her and wiped another round of tears away.

"Why do I feel so safe with you? I don't even really know you."

Garrett nodded, but she did know him so much more than most.

"I don't know what's happening here, sweetheart." He decided the truth was the only real option at their current juncture. "But I want to find out. We don't have to do anything at all the whole time I'm here. I just want to talk to you and really discover what we've got here, because I don't know about you, but whatever this is, I need it. I need you, but there's a lot of stuff we need to talk about first." He had to tell her. He couldn't keep falling in love with her knowing that he would be taking something away from her.

"I don't want to think anymore. I just…I don't know what I want," she finally admitted. Garrett gave her another tender smile as he nodded his understanding.

"Do you mind if I take the wheel for a while then?" He was perfectly willing to back off if that's what she wanted. Relief played in her deep copper eyes as she gave a timid nod.

Garrett drove her to the tiny apartment she'd shared with her grandmother. He followed her inside and stayed with her while she tried to pack.

"I don't know where we're going," she fretted.

"Okay, why don't we figure that out?"

"And you're not gonna, like, murder me when we get wherever we're going, right?" She tried to play it off as a joke, but there was concern in her rhythms.

"Come here just for a minute." He guided her to her bed. He sat beside her as he took in the room. There wasn't much to it. A small, white wooden bed with hot pink and green floral sheets and a quilt. A small dresser that housed photographs of Kaimi leaping through the air on stage wearing a black leotard and tights. Her jewelry box was beside that. The room was messy with clothes stashed in several corners and slung over the chair. There was an old sewing machine in the corner and the beginnings of what appeared to be a quilt under the needle. Several different kinds of grass skirts were laid out near the closet.

"I know this whole thing is crazy," Garrett assured her. "And like I said, we don't have to do anything the entire time I'm here. I just want to spend a few days with you, get to know you, and let you get to know me." He tucked a few stray hairs behind her right ear. "And I get that it's pretty much been a really shitty day already." This elicited a small genuine smile. "So let's talk about what you do know, okay?" He desperately wanted her to trust him. Her concern that he would hurt her wounded him deeply. Kaimi nodded and scooted closer to him on the bed.

"Would you hold me while we talk, please?" she begged. "Please," she asked again before Garrett could even respond.

"Of course, sweetheart." Taking things painfully slowly and refusing to allow himself even another kiss until he was certain she trusted him, Garrett wrapped his arms around her. "Is it okay if we lie down?" he asked softly. He didn't want her to do anything that might make her uncomfortable. She nodded sheepishly, and Garrett reclined in her bed and pulled her onto his chest. She clung to him fiercely, and he strengthened his hold.

"I would never ever hurt you. I swear."

"I know, I don't know why I said that. I just…."

"The person who always looked after you isn't here anymore, and it's a little scary out there all alone." Garrett didn't have to guess. He knew. She nodded into his chest. "You don't have to be alone. But here's what you know," he went on quickly. "You know I just took an oath to help run Hawaiian Iodex, so maybe I'm not too bad of a guy," he pointed out and earned a slight giggle. "You know my dad is the Crown Governor. You know Dan Vindico is one of my best friends, and he's a pretty good guy. You know Maylea and I have been friends for years, and you trust her." He continued and could feel her relax slightly in his tender embrace. "I'm going to call Dan and Maylea in just a second and ask where would be a good place to take you so they'll know where we are."

"I trust you. I just don't know why this feels so different," she interrupted him. She sat up abruptly and grabbed tissues from a box near the bed. She wiped away her tears and blew her adorable nose. When she finished, she curled back up on his chest. It was where she belonged. Garrett had never felt so complete as he did in that moment. "Just stay right here, sweetheart. I'm gonna call Dan and then we can get out of here if you want." She nodded but never weakened her grasp.

"Hey, man, I need a little help." Garrett noted that Dan was chuckling as soon as he'd said hello.

"If you're out there with Kaimi, I'm gonna tell you to figure that one out on your own."

"Funny." Garrett rolled his eyes. "She wants to get lost for a couple of days before the service, but I have no idea how to do that here."

Dan was silent for a long moment.

"Dan?" Garrett prompted.

"Sorry. I'm both in shock and trying to think. The only place I know that would be perfect would be where Fi and I stayed on our wedding night. I can ask Fionna for other options, but she's on the phone with Tutu. You take the Kaumualii Highway out toward Polihale Beach. It'll become a dirt road, but there's nothing around for a mile or two. You'll have to take in your food unless you want to drive back out to eat. I'll call and get you a reservation if you want."

"Thanks, that sounds perfect." Garrett was shocked by Dan's overt willingness to help.

"No problem, and Garrett, Fi's elated for you. Don't screw this up, man."

"Yeah, we'll see. I'm sure as hell trying not to."

"Get her packed up. I'll get you a reservation and send you better instructions."

CHAPTER 44

REVELATIONS

Garrett ended the call and shifted slightly so that he could cover Kaimi in her sheets and quilts. She was shivering. He kissed the top of her head and then let heat spill from his pores. She reveled in the serenity and the warmth of him.

"Are you okay?" he whispered, and she nodded hesitantly. She lifted her swollen eyes to his. They tempted him as she let her hand move softly up his chest. The touch was heavenly even through his T-shirt. His eyes closed as he tried desperately to forget what she'd said she was thinking about the night before when he'd called her. He brushed his hand over her cheek as she moved closer.

"Will you kiss me?" she finally asked.

"Are you sure that's what you need right now?" he managed though he fought with every fiber of his being not to lay her out and crawl over her. He could make her forget everything bad that had happened, give her reprieve for at least a little while.

She nodded, and her breaths began to pant in desperation. Garrett angled his head to the side and felt the electricity sizzle between them as their lips met. Her lips parted, and he moaned in her mouth as he dipped his tongue to hers. Suddenly, he felt it, and the overwhelming sensation rocked him to the core. She drew from him, deep and needy —it was exquisite.

Their energy began to spin in desperate desire to be joined. Garrett's hand moved of its own accord. He was woefully unable to stop it as it sought her right breast. She trembled as he hesitantly traced over it through her shirt. Copious amounts of erotic energy filled the air around them. It vibrated and shook with their need.

Suddenly, Garrett jerked his head back as a thundering roar tore from his lungs. Her hand grasped his strain. He pulsed fiercely as he began to give in to her desires. Kaimi's eyes flashed as Garrett's growl echoed around her. He slipped his hand under her shirt, desperate to feel her satin skin as he groped her. She released his cock and unbuttoned and unzipped her own shorts.

"Please, please," she begged in fervent need.

"Baby." Garrett shook his head, but she grabbed his hand and shoved it in the white cotton panties she was wearing. Garrett had seen and had his hands in every possible kind of panties there could be, but none of them had driven him as wild as what he was currently looking at.

He traced her hesitantly. The energy from her mound was pulsing and throbbing. The nerve endings were raw in their need to be cared for. The dark hair, that was usually waxed, gave direction to his fingers.

He tenderly traced her inner lips as a hungry moan escaped her. He couldn't stand the temptation. He couldn't deny either of them the pleasure. He dipped his fingers inside the heavenly perfection of her. He'd dreamt about it every night since he'd met her. To touch her, to feel her pull him deeper, but the reality was more than he could ever have imagined. "Do you have any fucking clue how many times I've jacked off thinking about having my hand right here?"

"Oh god, yes," she urged him on. Every single time he'd gotten himself off to the thought, it had been nothing compared to the perfection of her. It had clearly been a long while since she'd been opened. She was tighter than anyone he'd ever felt. A shuddered growl echoed from him as he imagined how incredible it would feel to push himself inside of her.

"Do you want me to cast you, baby?" Garrett couldn't stop himself.

He just wasn't that strong. He let his fingers move deeper and brushed his thumb up and over the spot that would have her dripping wet in moments, he hoped. She was throbbing in need. But she halted and pulled away slightly. Her mood seemed to shift rapidly yet again. Garrett eased his hand away. He would never force her to do anything at all.

She shook her head as tears began flowing rapidly down her face. Garrett was stunned. He'd never seen anyone move so rapidly through different emotions.

"What's wrong, baby? I swear we don't have to do anything." He was certain he'd pushed it too far.

"You don't have to cast me," she finally managed in a heartbroken sob. Fury just started to swirl in Garrett's rhythms, but he knew Fionna like the back of his hand. She wouldn't have told his story, certainly not to someone neither of them knew well.

"Okay." Garrett sat up and tried to think of what to say next. "Would you prefer to do that?" He wondered if she didn't like guys casting her. But Kaimi shook her head and took the tissue Garrett provided her.

"I know what's going to happen," she managed in a stuttered breath.

"Well, good, because I sure as hell don't at this point." Garrett's abject confusion finally broke through his desperation to let her work through her grandmother's death at her own pace.

She broke down completely, and Garrett's heart shattered into a million irreparable pieces. He pulled her back to him, but she was tense and trying desperately to block him out completely.

"Kaimi, honey, please just tell me what you're thinking," he finally pled. "I'm sorry. I shouldn't have touched you. Not today. It's too much. I get it."

She shook her head. "I'm going to tell you this, and at first you're gonna be like 'hey, that's great. It's no big deal.' But then I'm going to really fall in love with you, and I won't be what you want," she vowed adamantly.

"That isn't true, and can I at least have a chance before you decide that I'm going to break your heart?"

"No, because," she choked out a sob. "Because I'm already falling for you."

Garrett reeled as he tried to convince her to talk. "Listen to me," he commanded. "I'm falling for you too, okay. Hard. Harder than I ever have for anyone. So please, please just tell me whatever it is. I want to know."

But Kaimi shook her head with her chin trembling. "I can't. You're going to leave, and I can't. Not today."

Garrett stood and started pacing. "I quit my job," he finally admitted. "I quit my job and didn't even think about it or care because nothing in the world was going to keep me from coming here when you needed me. Call Fionna and ask her. I have never ever cared about anyone enough to do something like that. So, just please, tell me whatever it is." He sank back on the bed and held her hands in his. "Please," he echoed.

"You quit your job?!"

"Yeah," he whispered. "So please."

"Can you get it back?!" she gasped.

"Uh…" Garrett shook his head as his oddly confusing day began to take its toll. "I told Sorenson he could kiss my ass just before I left, so I'm going to go with no."

"Oh my gosh." She shook her head, but he saw the hope as it began to conquer the drowning fear in her eyes. "Uh, okay." She shivered and he pulled her closer.

"Just talk to me. Anything at all. I'm not going anywhere. Tell me whatever it is that has you so scared, baby. I want to make it go away."

Her chin trembled again as she nodded and closed her eyes.

"You know I told you how young my mom was when I was born," she admitted as hot tears flowed over her fevered cheeks. Garrett nodded but was afraid to speak. He was concerned she might stop talking.

"Right, so, uh…she wasn't really able to kind of be pregnant with me as long as you're supposed to. I only weighed like a pound and a half when I was born because I was so early. They didn't really think I was going to live. And I mean, I have all of the Gifted Energies and everything, but I'm not very strong in my Predilect."

Garrett pushed his strength and his calm through her hand. She let her eyes close again, and she drew from him deeply. His heart thundered from the heavenly sensation.

"Thank you," she whispered as she reached for a well-worn stuffed animal frog that was hidden beneath the covers of her bed. Garrett grinned. He was certain she was the most adorable thing he'd ever laid eyes on.

"Who's this?" He gestured to the frog. She rolled her eyes as her cheeks blazed. She smiled through her tears.

"Ringo," she admitted. Garrett nodded as he gazed down at her. She was almost a foot shorter than he was, but all he wanted to do was to cradle her tiny frame in his strong embrace.

"Anyway, so, because of that I'm not the way I'm supposed to be," she managed though her voice was strangled and terrified.

"Okay." Garrett wrapped his arm around her back and kissed the side of her head.

Kaimi seemed to force herself to go on. "I didn't really develop right, I guess, and for a while, they thought I might get better, but I didn't, and the dancing might've made it worse." She fumbled as Garrett continued to supply her soothing peace through his hands.

"Made what worse?"

Kaimi raised her head to look him in the eye. "I can't be casted, and it hurts really, really badly if I try to or someone else tries to."

His brow furrowed. He wondered what on earth would cause something like that.

"And," she dropped her gaze to Ringo as she played nervously with his tag, "I don't ever have to be casted...because..." She shuddered in his arms. Garrett waited patiently. "I can't ever have kids."

His heart stopped abruptly as he lifted her into his arms and seated her in his lap. He wasn't certain where to begin or how to explain to her what had happened to him. He didn't want to terrify her, and telling her that he'd hunted down and murdered several people in cold blood seemed like a good way to scare the shit out of her, but he couldn't let her sit there after that confession and not tell her his story.

"Hey, shh," he soothed. "It's okay, sweetheart. And believe me, I am not just saying that." He lifted her chin with his index finger until she was gazing into his eyes. "There's a really long story I need to tell you before we take this any further. Because I'm doing this different this time. I want you to know everything about me before I kiss you again and especially before I take you to bed." Kaimi gave a slight nod. His reaction seemed to surprise her. "Do you want to talk here, or do you want to get packed and get a little farther out, just the two of us?"

"Wait, there's one more thing," she begged. Garrett nodded for her to go on. "Sometimes I…sort of hurt, and I can't do it as often as most guys want to do it. And sometimes I have to stop in the middle. Tutu gave me some stuff that's supposed to help and heal that part, but I haven't really used it much because I haven't been with a guy in so long," she concluded dejectedly. "Most guys usually head for the door right about now."

Garrett shook his head. "Yeah, well, most guys are fucking morons. I'm not going anywhere, but before I tell you my story I want you to know that what you just said wouldn't have made me not want to be with you in every possible way. What I'm going to tell you has no bearing on how I feel about you. And if after I tell you all of this, you still want to be in a relationship with me, which by the way is not something I have ever said, then we will go as slowly as you need to go and do whatever you need to do. I'll be so gentle, baby, I swear to you. I would never hurt you."

Kaimi gave him a hesitant nod.

Suddenly, there was a knock on her front door. She furrowed her brow, and Garrett helped her stand. He followed her back through the living room, still astonished at her confession.

CHAPTER 45

SHIELDED STORIES

"Oh, hey," she sighed as she opened the door to reveal a guy that Garrett recognized from one of the pictures she'd sent from the campout at the beach.

"Are you okay?" He shot a glare at Garrett.

"Yeah, I'm all right. We're just getting out of here for a couple of days before the service. I kind of want a break, you know."

"Yeah." He turned to Garrett. "Shaun Westin," he informed rather pompously.

"Garrett Haydenshire." Garrett shook Shaun's hand. He chuckled as Shaun tried to out grasp him with his firm handshake. Garrett flexed, and Shaun took a small step backward. Garrett shot him the customary male look that said he could crush him without even having to work up a sweat.

"How'd you meet Kaimi?" he ordered as if Kaimi wasn't even in the room. She rolled her eyes.

"Garrett's the new deputy commander of Hawaiian Iodex, remember?" she reminded him indignantly.

"Oh right. Kaimi, can I talk to you in the kitchen for a minute?"

"For a minute."

Garrett rolled his eyes as Shaun began giving Kaimi the third

285

degree. The apartment was relatively small, so he could hear every word.

"So, you're just gonna go off with this guy right after your grandmother died?" he scolded, and Garrett's blood began to boil.

"I did everything I was supposed to do at the hospital. Miss Leialanie told me to take off a few days. What's your issue?" she bit back fiercely.

"You don't even know him," Shaun rebuked. "That seems flighty even for you."

Garrett stepped into the kitchen with his eyes narrowed in on Shaun.

"Sweetheart, are you okay?" he asked without ever dropping Shaun's glare. He grasped Kaimi's hand and guided her into his protective embrace.

"I want to go with you, now," Kaimi defied.

"Go grab your stuff and we'll get out of here. I'll see Shaun out," he threatened.

Shaun rolled his eyes and shook his head. "Whatever, Kaimi, call me when you get back so I know you're all right." He slipped past Garrett and to the front door.

"Nice to meet you," Garrett chanted as he slammed the door. Kaimi began laughing as she rolled her eyes.

"Shaun would be one of those guys who couldn't get out the door fast enough after I told him what I told you." She breathed out her explanation. "But I wasn't actually bummed because I only told him because I knew he would react that way, and he wouldn't back off."

"Shaun's an asshole. Why are you still hanging out with him?"

"He started dating my friend Starren, and she's crazy about him. We kind of all hang out in a group."

"Are you ready to go?" He wanted to get her out of there and off by themselves. He wanted to share his life with her.

A half hour later, Garrett was listening to his phone direct him to the cabin that Dan had secured for them. A text came in as he ventured off the paved highway.

Hey, be careful. That is where Halia was made. Have fun, Dan texted.

Yeah not too worried about that, Garrett thought as he tried to decide how to explain himself to Kaimi. He pulled the Hummer up to the long pathway and leapt out. He opened her door for her before grabbing the duffle bags she'd packed.

"Wow, I didn't know there were guys that did that."

Garrett smirked. "You need to up your standards, sweet girl. Some of us were raised right."

He guided her up onto the expansive wooden deck of the cabin that was set in a mountaintop bluff that overlooked the pristine beach below. They looked around the small chalet, and Garrett set her bags by the bed that was in a cove near the sitting room.

Kaimi smiled though exhaustion plagued her eyes. She took Garrett's hand and pulled him back out onto the deck. He seated himself on a double chaise lounge, and she fell into his arms.

"Okay, what were you going to tell me?"

He nodded as he drew a deep breath and tried to steady himself. "Promise me if I say anything that scares you, and you want me to take you home, you'll tell me."

Kaimi nodded and tried to hide her concern.

"You know I told you that one of my brothers was killed while he was working for Iodex overseas," he reminded her. She nodded again and kept her tired eyes trained on his. "The man that killed him was the same guy who killed Aida's family and Dan and Fionna's first child." He tried to give her some reason why he'd done what he'd done. "But basically, I was really fucked up after Cal died. He'd joined Iodex because of me and always looked up to me or whatever," Garrett choked. "The last thing he said to me has fucking haunted me for years."

Kaimi laid her head against his chest and closed her eyes. She hugged him tightly and gave him courage to go on. "Pravus surfaced just outside of Rio for the first time since Cal had been killed. I went down there, mailed my badge and stuff back, and went after him," Garrett admitted and then stopped talking abruptly. He was desperate for some reaction.

Kaimi lifted her head. "So, what you're saying so far is don't mess with your family." She grinned sweetly, and Garrett found it odd that he was chuckling and that she was smiling up at him.

"Something like that, my family or my girl." She closed her eyes as glee cast her features. He told her how he'd found Pravus and his men and what he'd stumbled upon. Her hand flew to her mouth as he told the story of Aida's mother.

"Oh my gosh. That's just awful," she gasped.

"Yeah. It was that. Uh anyway," he picked the story back up. "I took her to that orphanage that I told you about where I go work. And I tried to take care of her so I gave her all of my food and water and everything. I don't know how I did it, but I went on like that for a couple of days before I found Rojas again." He cringed. "I, uh…" He tried to draw breath but his lungs seized tightly.

"You found them, and they aren't being horrible, evil people anymore," she filled in for him.

"Something like that. Only I got two of them, and Pravus got me."

Panic flooded Kaimi's rhythms. "What did he do?"

"He shot me in the groin and left me for dead." Garrett grimaced.

"Oh my gosh. Are you okay? I mean, you're here, so you're okay, but probably also not okay. How can I help you?" She squeezed him again. "Let me do something."

Cradling her close, he beamed at her. "I'm okay now. I was taken via donkey to one of those free aid stations. They have several of them in Brazil. They didn't think I would make it, and I'd mailed all of my identification back home so no one knew where I was from or who my parents were. But, obviously,"—he gestured to himself—"I did survive. Only we kind of have a similar problem." Kaimi was still settled in his arms and didn't seem frightened, so he went on. "I can't make babies. I was too dehydrated, and my energies were affected badly. Where the bullet entered did a significant amount of damage, and I wasn't healed quickly enough. I can do everything just fine, but kids are not in my future."

"Wow," Kaimi whispered.

"Not a lot of people know any of that."

"I'm so sorry," she finally managed.

Garrett shook his head. "Are you okay with all of that?" He just needed her to say that she wanted him as much as he wanted her.

Kaimi sat up and gazed into Garrett's eyes as she gave him a sweet smile. "I'm okay with all of that as long as you promise if I ever go to Brazil with you, I don't have to ride a donkey." She grinned, and Garrett knew then and there that he would never love anything more. He doubled over laughing as he nodded his agreement.

"I promise."

"You're kind of amazing, you know?" she edged as his laughter abated. "The way you went back and looked after Aida and what you did, what you went through. I'm so sorry."

"No, baby, what I did was wrong, and it didn't bring Cal back. I almost lost my parents another son. But I think I've learned my lesson. It made me a better cop, hopefully a better person."

"Can I ask you something?" She leaned back into his chest.

"Anything."

"I don't know anything about being with an Iodex officer. Do you have to do that a lot? Have you had to kill other people?" She swallowed as she made her inquisition.

"Not often. But along the same lines and as long as I'm laying it all out for you, I did kill a guy last year. We were in pursuit, and he'd kidnapped my baby brother Keaton. A week before that, he nearly killed my mom and my baby sister." Garrett sighed as he tried to erase the image of Keaton begging for Emily and Vasquez choking him.

"Oh my gosh!" Kaimi brought Garrett back to the present.

"Yeah, the Haydenshires had a hell of a year."

"I voted for your dad," she informed him.

"When I get you to DC and introduce you to the whole massive gang of them, you tell him that."

"You really want me to meet your family?" She sounded simultaneously thrilled and terrified. Garrett kissed the side of her head again. He was unable to keep his lips from her adorable face.

"I'll keep you safe, baby. And they're all good people. I'm the black sheep, trust me. When my mom sees how crazy I am about you, she might, like, drop another kid though. You never know."

Kaimi giggled. She seemed to be just as delighted to be in Garrett's arms as he was to have her there. Her energy continued to shift in confusing patterns though. He was trying desperately to learn what caused her rapid mood changes.

"Are you sure they'll be okay with me? You're the Crown Governor's son, and I don't even have a family now," she choked as what the beginning of her day had held took its toll once again.

"Hey." Garrett lifted her chin. "My family will love you. And I know how fast this is going, but I do want you to meet them because I want to be with you and only you for a long time if that's okay with you." He was fairly certain she wanted the same thing, but his heart stuttered out of rhythm as he awaited her answer.

"I'm so afraid to tell you how much I want that," she finally admitted. "I don't understand what's happening. How can I already be so crazy about you that I'm terrified to think about you leaving again? How do I go on like that? I'm just…"

She paused, and in the breath of her admission Garrett supplied, "Scared."

She nodded, and he pulled her back to his chest. "Life is pretty scary, but if you'll just give me half a chance, I'll prove to you that I'm not leaving. I will have to go back to DC, but if you want, you can come with me. I swear to you I will be back out here for good as soon as I help Dan with this mess going on at Venton. I owe him that, or I would just stay out here with you now."

Kaimi was silent for several long minutes, and Garrett tried to keep his panic at bay. He was terrified over what she was going to say.

"I think I'm more afraid not to try than I am to just tell you to go away so I don't get hurt. But Garrett, please, please don't hurt me. I've been taking care of Nana for years and working sixty-hour weeks to afford everything. I can't take much more."

Garrett squeezed her tightly into his protective embrace. "I won't," he whispered.

She seemed to allow herself to believe him at least for the time being, but he knew her doubts were going to continue until he proved himself to her.

"Hey," he urged as he decided to accept the unspoken challenge and prove his love to her. "Again with the whole crazy fast thing, but would you fly home with me after the funeral and meet my family and then go to Brazil with me? I really want you to see the orphanage and meet the kids. I promise no donkeys," he teased her. "Please. It would mean a lot to me."

"Really? I mean you want me to do all of that with you?"

"I really do."

"Okay," she agreed hesitantly. "Are you sure your parents won't be freaked out about my mom and everything?"

"Believe me, you don't have my brother Logan's wife beat by ten miles, and they adore Adeline. One *kind of don't want to think about it* thing that I'm going to go ahead and tell you," he eased.

"Oh no," she approached panic again rapidly.

"Shh, breathe," he soothed. "Dan and I are flying to London right after Christmas, as soon as I get back from Rio. Things in London could get a little dicey, so will you be all right flying back here by yourself, or you can go stay in my apartment, or with Fionna and the girls, or even on my parents' farm." He offered her any option he could come up with, wanting her to know that he planned to be true to her alone.

"Uh," she stammered uncomfortably. "I'll be fine, and can I wait a little while to decide? I don't really know what this week is going to be like. I'm gonna have to call my mom and tell her about Nana, and this is just kind of a lot. I don't even know where to begin with Nana's stuff."

"If you want me to call your mom, I will. I'll do anything I can to make this easier for you." Garrett's vow seemed to touch the deepest wells of Kaimi's soul.

"Thank you. Thank you for quitting your job and coming here, and bringing me out here, and telling me everything. And just being here and being you. I'm sorry. I know I'm acting completely crazy. I swear I'm not usually quite this insane."

Garrett was certain that was true to a certain degree, but he would never want her to change.

"How about I pick you up and carry you inside this romantic little chalet where apparently my youngest goddaughter was created," he scoffed just to hear her sweet giggle once again. "And we crawl into that bed and sleep for a little while. Then I'll get us some food, and we'll just hang out." Garrett knew she didn't want to make any more decisions for the moment. He hoped she trusted him enough to let him really take care of her.

"You're really willing to sleep with me before you sleep with me?" Her doubt wounded him.

"I want to take care of you. And I don't know about you, but I didn't get a lot of sleep last night. I was on the phone sweet-talking this smoking hot dancer chick I'm trying to get with, and the time zone change is fucking with my head."

She was beaming for the moment. "If you really want to take care of me, it would be rude of me not to let you."

"It would be cruel, sweetheart." Garrett lifted her up into his arms. Her grace was evident in the way her body folded against him.

"When am I supposed to be sad?" she asked as he set her on the rubbed wood flooring beside the cozy queen sized bed.

"I don't want you ever to be sad, but it'll come, and I'll be there for that too." Kaimi nodded as she seemed to accept that sadness would be a part of her life for quite a while after her grandmother's death. "It won't ever go away, but the worst of it will pass with time."

She nodded but seemed to want to reject the information. "I meant to buy new panties for you to see," she lamented.

But Garrett's mouth had gone completely dry as she'd just dropped her cutoff shorts without warning.

"Trust me it's what's inside that counts." He stared unabashedly at the white cotton underwear she was wearing. He moved to her and kissed her forehead before he pulled her closer to him. She lifted his shirt but wasn't tall enough to get it over his head. Garrett gave her a signature Haydenshire smirk as he winked at her and hoisted it off.

"Wow. Cool ink," she gushed as she took in all of his intricate tattoo work on his chest. "I only have one," she admitted as she stared in awe at his chest and biceps which were covered in black ink.

"Can I see it?" Garrett waggled his eyebrows, wondering where this tattoo might be that he'd never seen. She laughed and nodded. With that she hoisted her shirt off and Garrett moaned.

"Damn, you're gorgeous," he vowed reverently. Euphoria spun in her rhythms. She could see his desire as it tensed in his shield, and it visibly thrilled her. She bit her lip as she unclasped her bra and let it fall to the floor.

"K, I just need to do one thing before you make me lie in a bed with you like that and just sleep." He grasped her waist and pulled her closer. He let his index finger trace from her earlobe down her neck. Then he tenderly brushed his thumb over her right breast, which had him amending his preferences on women in a heartbeat as it swelled from his caress.

She trembled in his arms as he forced his hand to move on. He glided down her abdomen that was clenched tightly in anticipation. He halted at the intricate belly button ring that was formed of tiny beach shells that he suspected she'd collected and crafted into the ring herself. He caressed the tender skin around her navel with his thumb and then moved his hand back up her until he cradled her chin in his palm and devoured her mouth.

When he finally released her, they were both gasping for breath but wanted to remain in contact. She held his hands but turned to the side to reveal a large tat that went from the top of her backside up to the side of her right breast. It was a picture of a twisting feather in Maori styling. Two Hawaiian words were written along the feather —lele aku.

"What does that mean?" Garrett whispered as he ran his fingers delicately over the feather.

"It roughly translates to fly away."

"Holy shit," he whispered.

"What?"

With that, he turned to show her his back. Just over his right shoulder blade along the large image of a ferocious dragon in flight was the Latin word *profugio*. "It roughly translates to fly away," he explained.

"Wow," she gasped. "How did you…? I mean, you didn't know. But how…did this happen?"

He had no answer for that, so he guided her into bed with him. He positioned her on his chest and pulled the soft sheets and blankets over them as he cradled her in his protective embrace.

"Do you still want to fly away?" he asked with no expectation that she would say no. He knew she wasn't to be tamed. He just wanted to fly with her if she would let him.

"For the first time in my whole life…no." She answered readily as she curled up beside him and let him soothe her to sleep.

CHAPTER 46
THE DANCE OF THE SEEKER

Garrett shifted slightly as he felt the emptiness beside him. His shield tensed in concern. He leaned up and smiled as he took in Kaimi crawling back into bed.

"Are you okay?" His own rhythms eased as she cuddled back onto his chest.

"You do know that girls use the bathroom, right?" She giggled, and Garrett laughed.

"I was aware. I just try not to think about it," he teased, hoping to hear more of her laughter. "Do you want something to eat, sweetheart? I'm starved."

"I'll make you a sandwich. Nana loves my chicken cheesesteaks," she trilled. Her face fell. "Well, I guess Nana *loved* my chicken cheesesteaks." Her voice trembled, and Garrett closed his eyes as he held her to his chest. A moment later, his powerful shield encased Kaimi in his orb. His energy was filled with soothing calm, adoring love, and tender care. His bands tensed constantly in elated rhythm that she was inside of his shield.

"Wow," Kaimi whispered as her heartbeat began to fly and her breaths quickened. She inhaled his love with every gasp of her lungs. Garrett's breaths were ragged as well.

The only other woman he'd held in his shield was Fionna, and this was a very different kind of love. He'd never cared for someone so much. If he'd ever casted anyone else, it would have let them feel his rhythms so intimately he'd never allow that. His inattention and disregard would have been readily apparent. "If I just lie here forever, will you keep doing that?" she begged.

A broad grin spread across Garrett's face, and his heart thrilled from the very idea.

"There are other ways I can get my energy into you, sweetheart. Whenever you think you might be ready to try that."

"Are you sure you really want to do that with me?" she managed in a heartbroken whisper, and Garrett released his shield.

"Listen to me for a minute, please. I don't think I fully understand what needs to happen in order for you to feel and enjoy our love life to the fullest extent, but I want to learn. I want you to tell me each and every thing you need or want, and if we try a few things and you need to stop then we'll stop. I will do whatever you need me to do."

She nodded and he went on. "Baby, I hope what I'm about to tell you doesn't make you want to fly away again, but the whole murder discussion went fairly well so maybe this will too," he wagered hopefully. Her brow furrowed as he continued. "I've had a lot of sex in the last few years, and I swear this isn't a line or some shit I'm just telling you, but I don't just want to have sex with you. I want to have a relationship with you, and I certainly want there to be a strong physical part of that relationship, but for all of these years I've pretty much been an ass that only thought about what I was getting out of the sex. But right now, lying here with you, for the first time in my life all I care about is making you feel good and showing you what you mean to me, however that needs to be done." Garrett lifted Kaimi's chin tenderly with his hand. "Okay?"

She nodded, but something was still wrong. She wouldn't look him in the eye.

"Not okay," Garrett supplied for her as he began to panic again.

"No, it's okay." Kaimi sighed. "It's just hard to explain."

"How about this…" Garrett leaned forward and brushed a tender kiss across her cheek that had her smiling for just a moment. "How about if I go get us some burgers or something and then we can just sit out there and talk?" He gestured to the large deck that was going to offer them a stunning view of the sunset. Kaimi's hands flew to her face, shocking Garrett.

"Hey, what?" He placed his own hands over hers in an effort to guide them away from her head. "You're too pretty to cover up that face," he coaxed, and she rolled her eyes.

"At some point I'm going to say something, and you're the one that's gonna fly away."

"Not going anywhere. I just want you to talk to me."

"Okay." She shrugged. "But I brought that stuff from my fridge, so let me make the sandwiches because that's part of what I have to tell you."

Garrett's brow furrowed as he nodded and watched Kaimi crawl out of the bed. He wanted her so badly he could taste it. He knew a thing or two about drawing out a lovemaking session, and though he'd had his fair share of quickies, the thoughts of spending hours guiding her body softly with his hands and his tongue before he opened her up for himself, however slowly she might need, had his chest vibrating in hunger as his body and his shield begged to be one with hers.

"Can I help?" He tried not to think that if he helped her make dinner it would move the talking along. Garrett did desperately want to know what had her so worried, but he also wanted her back in that bed and under his body. He wanted her under his shield. He wanted to be a tempting harbor for her, to draw out the pain and inflicting horrors of her day and replace them with his adoration and his tender care as he prodded her and coaxed her body to all-new heights.

"I don't really know how to make anything but sandwiches," was her concerned reply. "I'm an Occamist so you'd think I'd be a really good cook. I just never really learned how."

"I love sandwiches. If you think about it, they're the ideal meal," he assured her and earned himself a smile.

After Garrett chopped mushrooms and onions and watched Kaimi sauté them and then grill and chop the chicken, they settled out on the deck once again. This time they faced one another instead of her reclining against him.

"So, Miss Kaimi Walyuo, what can I do to make my baby smile?" The delighted grin that formed on her face whenever he called her his flooded Garrett's rhythms with equal portions of elation and desire.

"See, this is just so weird for me," she began suddenly. Garrett wiped his mouth with a napkin and nodded. "Because all of this stuff that I'm about to tell you, normal people never even have to think about. Or they talk about it after they've been together or are committed to each other or moving in together or whatever, and then you can pull out your weirdness. You know, like I have to wax my upper lip once a week or I look like Tom Selleck or something like that."

Garrett laughed at her outright as he shook his head. "If that's the extent of what you think is weird, then let's go on to how freaking delicious this sandwich is because I don't care."

Kaimi's eyes lit excitedly over his assessment of her cooking. "It's good, right?"

"It's outstanding, sweetheart."

"But I don't actually wax my lip all that often, and that isn't the end of my weirdness unfortunately."

"Just tell me."

Her shoulders fell as she nodded. "If this is way more work than you want to put into a relationship, believe me, I get it. There's a reason I haven't had a lot of boyfriends."

"Stop beating yourself up for whatever this is and talk to me."

She studied him for a long moment and then nodded. "Here goes." Her terror cut him to the quick. She really didn't think he would ever love her because of whatever was wrong. "I don't eat beef or pork partly because I don't like to think about sweet little piggies and cows being butchered, but mostly because they make all this stuff that's wrong with me much, much worse. Tutu says it's something about enzymes that I don't have or wasn't born with or something. I didn't really understand what she was saying." She sighed and her body braced for rejection that certainly wasn't coming. "I went out with this guy in New York once, and he force-fed me half of his filet at this swanky restaurant, and then I had to go to the hospital because I was so sick later that night."

Garrett's body tensed. "Did you tell him you didn't eat that?"

"He said it was ridiculous and that only mindless children were vegetarians. I said I wasn't a vegetarian, but he never really listened to me anyway."

"Baby, other than my fury over the kinds of guys you dated before me, and my sorrow for you that you can't have bacon," he teased, "I can't see how this would be any big deal. If I convince you to come stay with me on the farm and I decide to cook dinner before you get home from work, I won't make steak, burgers, or pork chops. Done. My understanding was that here on this island in the middle of the Pacific, there's a fair amount of fish. And I grill a kickass fish. As long as I can still kiss you and make out with you after I've eaten burgers or steaks, I'll do that at work. If I can't, I'll get you to make me these sandwiches for lunch." He lifted his cheesesteak in exaltation. He wasn't backing down, and the longer he stayed in her presence the more he wanted to be with her forever.

"Really?" she gasped. "You really don't care?"

"Honey, I quit my job and confessed murder to you. What else do I have to say or do to get you to see that I'm in this? I know it's crazy fast, but I'm here, and I want you just the way you are."

"Wow." Tears formed on her long eyelashes. "No one's ever wanted me like that," she confessed as she raised her tear-filled eyes to his.

"Well, I'm here, and that's what I want."

"Before you decide that, here's the ickiest part." She sighed and Garrett listened again. "I almost always have to be in a relationship with someone before we sleep together because I have to tell them what I told you about me before I go to bed with them, which means I haven't really done the fun, fast, one-night stand, just have sex for the sake of sex kind of sex," she explained confusedly. "I don't...even know how to go about that."

"Trust me, you haven't missed much." His own admittance shocked him. Everything he'd known about himself had changed so rapidly he hardly recognized himself. Garrett had sex often and had on more than one occasion indulged himself in two women at one time if they were both into it.

He prided himself on bringing pleasure to his partners, but he'd never cared who he was putting it in as long as it felt good. Now, he was sitting across from a woman he could actually see himself getting down on one knee for, and it didn't frighten him. He was desperate to make some claim of ownership to a woman that clearly had a difficult time having sex, and none of it had him turning tail and running.

"Just talk, sweetheart. Tell me everything I need to know, and then if you want to wait, we'll wait. If something doesn't feel right, we'll stop."

Kaimi gave him a small, sheepish grin as she nodded. Her reluctance had Garrett's heart aching to reassure her. "I need a lot of foreplay. Way more than most guys are willing to do." Her body gave a slight shudder, and she stared up at him like she'd just informed him that she had in fact committed some heinous crime.

"I like foreplay." He winked at her as she relaxed slightly.

"And Tutu says that if I use this stuff she gave me every time I have sex it will get better each time and will continue to improve over time. That it will help me heal. It's like a lube, and it did kind of help, but I've only used it twice and I was alone when I used it." She squeezed her eyes shut tightly.

Garrett's body seized in desperate desire and need. "Can I have like two minutes to fantasize about that before you go on?"

She began laughing as her rhythms eased beside him. "You're the greatest guy ever."

"Not true, but keep going. I think I can listen and run those images through my mind at the same time. If I start moaning, just ignore me," he teased just to hear her laugh again.

Unable to help himself, Garrett cradled her face again and drew her near. His body ached. A fire burned low in his groin, one only she could quench. He kissed her and traced her beautiful lips with his tongue until she let him in. He began sucking her tongue hungrily as a breathy moan escaped her mouth. Garrett pulled away, forcing himself to hear everything he needed to know before he set to work. He'd fly to the moon if he had to in order to set her free, but he needed to know each and every thing she required so he could fulfill her every fantasy and every desire.

"Did you bring this lube with you, sweetheart, or do we need to make a drive out to the farm?"

"You don't mind using it?" she quizzed hopefully.

Garrett's brow furrowed again. "You like it?" he asked, and she nodded. "And it makes you not hurt?" She nodded again. "And it makes everything better for you?"

"I think so. It was kind of incredible, but like I said I've never used it with a guy." She blushed deeply. His beautiful peach, luscious and glowing, was as anxious for his love and reassurances as she was to be picked and sucked and devoured.

"Then why the hell wouldn't I want to use it?"

Her breath picked up pace as she shrugged. "I don't know. Some guys get all offended, but they don't know a lot about how to get a girl…."

"Wet," he provided for her. She cringed and nodded. "Trust me, honey, I can take care of that as well. I'll find a way to make your sweet little pussy weep for me. Or I'll fill you full of my cum and then take you all over again."

She trembled and stared him down with dark, ravenous eyes. "Sometimes I need a break in the middle, and sometimes I have to go a few days between sessions," she confessed as she edged closer. Her body's magnetic need was pulling toward his. His shield craved her. Garrett shoved their paper plates away and dragged her in.

"Then we'll stop, and I'll hold you or kiss you or run my hands up and down your gorgeous body until you're ready for more. We can make this last all night, sweetheart, but my god, I want you. I want you under me. I want to show you how you should have been treated all this time. I want to show you what you mean to me." He growled in ferocious need. She leaned up on her knees and pushed her breasts in his face as he moaned heatedly. Her hand grasped his throbbing strain again.

"You're so big. I'm scared," she gasped out the apex of her concern and her fear, as her breaths began to quake and pant from her body.

"We're gonna take it nice and slow. I'm not going to do anything until I know you're ready. Let me take care of you. I won't do anything you don't want. Let me open you up for me. I'll be so gentle, baby. I would never hurt you." He kept up his adamant reassurances as he carried her to the bed.

With that, he hoisted off the T-shirt she'd thrown on. With a hungry growl, he crushed her body back to his and devoured her kiss-swollen lips. His hands slid quickly to her bare breasts as he began to massage and grope her eagerly.

"You know that feeling when you just want a guy to throw you on the bed and take you hard? I want that so bad, but I know I can't do that," she kept up her fearful admissions.

Garrett quieted her with his own mouth. He lifted her up onto the bed without breaking the forceful kiss.

"Every time you tell me what you can't do, I'm going to kiss you like that and then I'm going to show you what you can." He guided her back and dispensed with her panties. He threw them on the floor without a second thought.

Her swollen lips were far too enticing for him to look at anything else. He softly let two fingers trace just beside her slit. She bucked and moaned her adamant approval. Garrett flung off his shorts and briefs and joined her on the bed. She was writhing beside him, so eager for him to satisfy her cravings.

"I'm gonna start with my tongue, baby. I'm gonna work you over with that, suck you with something soft and so damn hungry first, and when you're ready, I'll let you feel just how hard you make me." He explained how the next few minutes or hours, however long it took, would work.

Her eyes rolled back and her body contorted. "Yes," echoed from her soul.

He began his ravenous kisses at her neck. He worked his tongue and his lips down her body, drinking in the craving carnal energy that spilled from her pores.

His hands sought her breasts again as he groped her to prepare them for his mouth. He swirled his tongue over her left nipple, and she groaned in ecstasy. He sucked and drowned it in his mouth as she began to quake and thrust. Her fingers wrapped around his cock as it throbbed and bounced against her thigh.

"That feels good, doesn't it, baby?" He sucked the erotic energy from her breast. "I can get you off just like this," he promised. "But it doesn't just feel good here, does it?" He guided her and assured her that he knew how to take her to the depths of ecstasy even if she couldn't go there as quickly as she might like.

"Relax for me, and feel it. You can feel it here too, can't you?" He let his fingers dance along her slit again as her moans echoed all around him. "When I suck those sweet tits, it makes you throb right here, doesn't it? Makes you clench nice and tight for me. Makes that sweet little clit throb. Makes it so fucking needy for me. Makes it ache for me to fill you, doesn't it? Tell me."

"God, yes," she groaned.

"I'm gonna make you wait 'til I know you're ready." He continued his plans just before he pulled her right breast with his mouth and sucked her fervently. "Feel it, sweet girl," he ordered. Her body was spun so tightly she couldn't remain still. Her fingernails dug into his scalp as she pulled his head in for more. It drove him wild.

"Yes, yes!" She began to give in and concentrated on how his tongue on her breasts made her pussy wet and desperate to be full.

"That's it. Just feel it." He moved to her left and began his work again. Garrett slid his bottom teeth along her left nipple as his saliva moistened and soothed their strain.

"Oh god," gasped from her as her body bucked off the bed for him.

"So fucking sexy, sweet girl. You're so hungry you drive me wild. I'm gonna give you what you need. I'm gonna take good care of you." He moved his mouth lower, swirling his tongue over the sweet, salty skin of her stomach until he lapped it around her navel and let it dance over her belly button ring. His name panted from her lips as she spread her legs without him having to ask.

The voracious growl he'd caged for too damn long thundered from his chest.

He let his fingers ease her lips apart.

"I've waited so damn long. Every fucking night, all I could think about was how bad I wanted to taste you."

She throbbed as her body just began to give its slow, ravenous drip. She took longer to get wet. He understood a little more now. That was why she hurt if some prick didn't do his job and decided to go ahead with everything. But he'd never let her hurt again. He would always take his time and worship her before he allowed her to soothe his own needs.

Garrett's tongue thirsted for her. He made slow, tedious patterns with the tip of it as he began to seek out the liquid perfection of her. Her body tensed, and her temperature began making its climb. Took just a little longer than other women he'd been with, but Garrett had never tasted anything that soothed his soul the way she did. He lapped at her like a parched beast who finally found a mountain spring.

He delved deeper, slowly spun his tongue, then brought it back out to lap at her clit. He sucked her lips, slid his teeth along them, and then started again in a pattern that had her head shaking back and forth as he pushed her to the brink.

"So sweet, baby," he gushed as her body began to tremble and her legs shook violently. She whimpered out his name. Her rhythms came in tight, needy pulses. She lifted her head and stared down at him.

"Do you like to watch me, baby? You like to watch me get your sweet little body ready for me?"

She managed a haggard nod. His cock fucking wept for her, but delight filled his rhythms as he discovered what he suspected was a largely unacknowledged kink.

"That's my sweet girl. You keep watching me. Every time I look up I want to see you looking back at me." With that, he stared her down and circled his tongue around her clit and then suctioned his mouth to her, claiming ownership, giving her exactly what she wanted. He pulled his mouth away. "Look at me," he demanded and she readily complied.

He licked his lips, pulling the creamy evidence of her hunger into his mouth. "You're almost ready now, aren't you? Ready to fill my mouth and let me drink you." He had her. The violent orgasm shocked her as her body groaned and spasmed. She clawed at the sheets.

He grasped her hips firmly so he could consume everything she gave up for him. He dragged his hand over his mouth and moved back beside her on the bed as he cradled her to his chest. She was gasping for breath and couldn't keep her body still. He let the tantric waves crash through her.

As he waited, her rhythms spun all around him. Her moans were still pouring from her chest, and Garrett groaned in the ecstasy of watching what he'd just elicited from her.

"Taste yourself in my mouth. Taste how fucking good we are together." He devoured her lips, and she opened for him as he swept his tongue through her mouth. His cock ached. He burned for her. He swore he was going to fuck his way through the mattress if he didn't get off soon, but he forced himself to ask, "Want a little break?"

"I've never had one like that," she confessed as she shivered in his arms. Garrett tried to hide his smirk.

"I'm gonna do things tonight you'll never forget," he assured her. "That was just the beginning." Another rapacious moan shuddered from her delicate body. Garrett kept his hands roving over her soft skin as he tenderly held her to him. When her breathing normalized, he traced his hands back over her, feeling the wet heat begin to gather between her legs again.

"Are you ready, sweetheart? Ready for just a little more? I'm gonna go nice and slow, and you tell me if something doesn't feel good," he guided her softly. She nodded and her body began its needy writhes beside his.

Working thoughtfully, Garrett circled her opening with his index finger as he let his other hand tease and barely touch the most sensitive spots on her inner thighs and tempt the swollen rise of her mound. Her entire body tensed as she gripped the sheets below her. Feeling her come around him was going to be absolute heaven, Garrett knew, but he commanded himself to wait. He switched to working with his ring finger and slipped it gently up inside of her.

"So nice and tight, sweet girl." His eyes rolled back in his head. She was exquisite. She was so tight around his fingers he couldn't fathom what that would feel like around his cock. His body begged to feel it, but he denied himself everything and focused solely on her. He brushed by the magic spot, and she came up off the bed, her body begging for more.

"That's it, isn't it, sweet girl? It's right there. Don't worry, baby, I'm gonna be careful," he assured her as her eyes flashed in desperation and in fear. "I know it's tender, isn't it? Needs to be loved more often.

Needs more attention. I'm going to take care of everything you need for as long as you'll let me." He soothed out his plea that she might be his forever.

He continued his slow rhythmic work as he stroked tenderly over the tightly coiled nerve endings that would ultimately have her flying. But he timed his strokes so that he didn't overwork them or cause her any pain. She widened dramatically after several minutes of work, and he groaned.

"More, please, please," she pled and he pulled his hand away. He grabbed the screw-top jar she'd laid on the bedside table.

"This is it, right, baby?" he soothed. She nodded as her body continued to pitch and toss, so eager for his touch. He dipped two fingers in the salve and entered her again slowly. "There you go. My sweet girl loves to be full of me, don't you?" Her energy arced and began to move into his body through his fingers.

Fionna's grandmother was a genius. Dan was right. Garrett now knew as he began to work Kaimi with more force and give her the friction she so desperately wanted but was terrified to feel. She came again almost instantly.

Her hungry cries seared through him. She sought his strain with her hands and began to pull him and slide her fingers over the throbbing flesh that currently felt like fevered steel. Suddenly, she sprang and pushed him back. He watched her as she stared ardently at his package.

He was the one who felt like he was flying as the bed, the chalet, the entire world spun away as she licked up his shaft. She began to suck him timidly and then with more force. She pulled his erotic energy straight from its source. It flooded through her body.

"My god, that's fucking incredible," he gasped as his body thrusted upward into her mouth, and she moaned against him. She pulled away, her eyes curious and fierce in her need. Then she leaned back down for another taste of him. A rapacious growl echoed off the walls. It was absolutely incredible, and he hadn't yet entered her. "Stop," he commanded. "I'm hung too fucking tight for that right now. I need you." He grabbed her and jerked her underneath him.

"Are you ready, baby? Are you ready for me? I'm gonna take it slow, let you feel every inch, and if you want me to stop, I will."

"Please, just please. I need you. I don't want you to stop. I don't care if it hurts. I need you now." She clawed and heaved out her plea.

"I'm not gonna let you hurt," Garrett promised her as he rubbed some lube along his cock, pressed it to her clit, and focused on her rhythms. "God, you spread your legs so sweet for me. That little pussy finally crying for my cock. I'm gonna make it better, baby. I promise."

As she began to climb quicker this time, he prodded her with his head and then eased inside of her as gently as he was able.

"What do you feel?"

"You. It's so good. More please, more," she begged. It took every ounce of patient strength he had not to bury himself inside of the tight wet perfection that was slowly encasing him. He pushed in another inch.

"That still feel good, baby?" He had to make absolutely certain.

"Yes," she gasped and then bucked up, forcing him in farther.

"Oh, fuck yeah," he panted as he gave his first thrust and joined their bodies and their energy completely. His shield fused with her Occamist rhythms and lit the entire room.

After another thrust, he pulled back and rubbed more of the lube around his shaft and inside of her before he went back for more. That did it. That was all she needed. Her orgasms began consuming her as he transitioned from slow, gentle thrusts to pounding against her body, making certain to keep her wet.

"I know you can take more for me, sweet girl. I know you can."

"Oh god, yes," she gasped.

"Tight little pussy so pretty stretched wide around my cock. Such a sweet girl for me. Look, baby. Watch how I make you mine."

"Oh god, yes!" She leaned up to watch his cock pound into her harder and faster, but then she fell back against the mattress and spread her legs wider in an undeniable invitation.

Garrett had never felt anything so astoundingly perfect. It may take her a little while to get going, but my god, she was so tight he'd never get enough. She inhaled his body and then begged for more. The lube had their energy combining in heavenly waves of ecstasy.

Garrett shuddered, but he wasn't strong enough to deny himself the release his body craved. He wanted to fill her full of everything he was.

"I'm about to fucking lose it. You feel too damn good. Are you ready?" he begged.

A fervent moan was the only answer he received as her next orgasm licked like a consuming fire around his strain. He exploded inside of the only woman that could ever have made him whole. He clung to her tightly as he tensed and shuddered. As she stilled, he eased out as carefully as he was able.

"Are you okay?" he soothed as the erotic haze began to clear from his mind, and he could think again.

She was beaming as he guided her up onto his chest so he could cradle her in his shield.

"That was amazing," she whispered in awe. Garrett chuckled.

"I agree." He kissed the top of her head. He turned on his side and wrapped his arms around her closer. "I've never felt anything so amazing." He let what they'd just done replay in his mind in great detail.

"So, you liked it?"

"Liked it? That was incredible. *You* are incredible. I don't remember or even care what my life was like before you, but you're all I want now. Please just say we can keep doing that and you'll be mine and..." he paused but wasn't able to halt himself. "Say you'll move in with me when I move out here. Just please."

He knew his family and his friends would probably call in psychiatric medios as soon as he told them he'd asked a woman to move in with him, but he didn't care. He needed to talk to Chloe and tell her once and for all it was over completely this time, but none of that mattered. His next life's breath depended on the answer she was currently debating.

"Please," he continued to plead. He could not be separated from her. It would kill him.

"The last time somebody wanted to be my boyfriend they wrote me a note. You know, check this box." She laughed.

"Then the only box on the note from me is yes."

"I want to say yes. Believe me, but this is crazy fast. I need to think about it. Just promise the long distance thing won't go on too long and please, please, please don't cheat on me. You'll be the only guy that hasn't."

Garrett raised her head until he was staring into her timid eyes.

"Never, ever. You think on it as long as you need to, but I know. If this works like I know it's going to, Miss Walyuo, I plan on making you Mrs. Haydenshire." He wasn't going back to the life he'd lived for too damn long. It was fruitless and stupid, and he was thoroughly done with it all. He had everything he would ever need lying naked against him, and he'd never been more certain of anything in his entire life. Cal had been right all along.

Her terrorizing fear must've been coiled deeply in her soul though. It flooded her rhythms. He would vanquish the fear, starve the self-doubt that inflicted its wounds so viciously, and show her the love she needed and deserved. He would tend to her and care for her in a way he'd never done for anyone else. He noticed that she'd given no reaction to what he'd just said. Another round of determination armored itself in his shield.

"Would you mind putting a little more of that stuff on me? I'm supposed to do that to keep from hurting the next day," she explained as her cheeks blazed in her embarrassment.

"Would I mind playing with that sweet pussy some more? Nope, I think I could definitely handle that."

She laughed as he scooped more of the coconut-scented salve on his fingers and tenderly massaged it into her lips and inside of her. Her breath caught again, and she swallowed harshly.

"You up for another round, sweetness?"

"I…wish I was. I'm just not sure. I just feel like I'm so much work," she confessed as her body shuddered slightly. Garrett had never willed his body to recover so quickly before. It never took him long, but he reminded himself that she needed to recover as well.

"You would really want to marry me? Even after all of that stuff you had to do?" The question seemed to echo from the recesses of her soul. She bit her lips together like she was trying to halt its exit from her mouth.

Garrett pulled his hand away and wiped the residual salve on a nearby towel before he cradled Kaimi against his chest again.

"Sweetheart, I didn't have to do anything at all. I wanted to do everything I did to make you feel loved. I wanted you to get lost in me. Like I told you, I've had a lot of sex, but that is the very first time I've ever made love with anyone. It was the most incredible experience of my life. And yes, I want to feel that and be with you through whatever is going to happen for the rest of my life. If you're willing to give this a shot, then I'm not looking back. There's nothing back there worth having anyway."

"I'm just gonna believe you because I want to so bad, and this day has been insane, so just please don't hurt me."

"Never. I wish you'd believe *that*," he urged fervently. "I'm gonna have to prove it to you, I guess."

He felt her smile against his chest.

"Let's get some sleep, okay?"

She nodded as she cuddled herself against him, making him smile. "If I sleep here, will you be able to sleep?" He caught the desperate plea in her tone.

"No other way I ever want to sleep again," he answered readily. He had no room for doubt. If he was going to combat hers, he had to lose his own.

CHAPTER 47

PLANS AND PREPARATIONS

The sun was high in the sky when Garrett awoke the next day. He smiled as he let his hand run down Kaimi's back, and he kissed her forehead. She gave a replete sigh and tucked farther into his embrace. It was right where she belonged.

"Want some coffee, sweetheart?" He cleared his throat and squeezed her luscious ass all in the same moment. She wiggled it for him. He gave her a lusty moan as he continued to grope her.

"If I open my eyes, the absolutely most amazing sex I've ever had plus the best night's sleep I've ever gotten will be over, so obviously, I can't open my eyes."

Garrett chuckled. He was thrilled she was just as taken with their new relationship as he was. "Not over, baby. Just beginning."

"See, I'm obviously still dreaming." She squeezed her eyes tight and kissed his chest. "This is the first morning in my whole life that I've had sex the night before, and I'm not hurting so badly I can hardly walk." She allowed her eyes to open hesitantly.

"You do understand that, first of all, I'm crazy about you, and second, that I'm an Ioses Pred. Like a damn strong Shield if I do say so myself. Whenever you tell me some guy hurt you, I want to hunt all of them down and fix it so that they are never able to have sex again, right?"

"Sorry." She giggled sheepishly.

"S'ok, as long as you're mine then I'll never let anything else hurt my baby," he vowed fervently.

"I really like being yours," she whispered as she braced slightly. "I feel so safe with you. I feel like I've known you forever."

Garrett kissed her head again as he kept her cradled beside him.

"I know. Me too." He'd never believed in soul mates. Hell, he'd never even wanted one woman at a time. All of the legends about Shields finding the one they'd protect above all others never made any sense to him until now.

It was overwhelming to be in the presence of the one he'd want forever, in the energy of the woman who was most definitely his soul mate, and the one he desperately wanted to wear his ring. And suddenly, he understood what had driven Cal back to Moscow despite knowing that the odds were against him.

"Stay right here. I'll bring coffee. I make killer coffee, just ask Maylea."

"Okay." She let her hands trail over his chest as he slid from the bed. "Can I ask you something?" She eased into a seated position. Her hair was in a wild mane around her head. Her eyes were bright from their extended sleep. Her lips were still kiss-swollen. He knew if he explored between her gorgeous thighs he'd find leaked evidence of his deep claim from the night before. She looked good and thoroughly fucked, and god, he'd never seen anything more gorgeous.

The kitchen was near the bed, so they could talk as Garrett casted the coffee maker and began dumping grounds into the filter.

"Anything," he allowed.

"Did you and Maylea ever date or sleep together or anything? She's so freaking beautiful I would hate her, but she's also probably one of the sweetest people I've ever met, so I can't hate her. But if she used to be your girlfriend, then maybe I could figure out how."

Garrett laughed as he shook his head at her. "Never dated her, never slept with her, never wanted to."

"Right." Kaimi rolled her eyes as if such an idea would be preposterous.

"Cream and sugar?" Garrett smirked at her assumption. She gave him a speculative nod. "Fi and I have been best friends since she came to Venton. She has also had a thing for Dan Vindico since the moment she put her designer shoes on the campus grounds. I love Fionna, but I love her like I love Emily and Abby—those are my little sisters," he added as he wasn't certain how much she knew about his family.

"No chemistry. Find her product, shoe, purse, lingerie obsessions annoying as hell. She's high, high maintenance, and I am not about that life. I have no romantic interest in her at all. But having her as my friend and being the best possible friend to her that I can is very important to me. Fionna and I get each other. She makes my world make sense, and I try to do the same for her. I wouldn't know what to do without her but only as a friend. You, however, I love like I want to spend the rest of my life being with you, don't ever see myself surviving without you kind of love." He tested her with his vow. He was doing this. He handed her a mug as she stared up at him like he had three heads.

"Did you really just say that you love me while you brought me coffee in bed? Because I may be little, but I have dancer legs, so I think I could hold you as my prisoner and never ever let you leave."

Garrett shook his head at her and sipped his coffee. "I've never said that before to anyone." He watched the shock of his vow wash over her. She couldn't seem to stop grinning.

"How are you sure? I feel like weird and different and so happy even though I should be so sad, and like there's some kind of buzzing nest in my stomach, but is that it?"

"I think so, sweetheart. I just know I don't want to go home. I don't want to go anywhere without you," he assured as he kissed her cheek and then leaned back so she could curve her body into his chest as she leaned against him and drank her coffee.

"Okay." She nodded as she tried to catch her breath. "Then I think I love you too. Maybe. Quite possibly."

"I'll take that."

Since it was already almost noon when Garrett coaxed her out of bed, Kaimi set to work. He held her in his lap out on the deck while she called her mother to tell her that her grandmother had passed away. He kissed away the tears the call elicited.

He drove her to the funeral home that was handling the cremation. When her eyes goggled over the price of everything, he offered to pay. She refused him and maxed out two of her credit cards instead. Garrett decided with the substantial pay raise he was going to be acquiring as soon as he helped Dan clean up Venton, he'd make her his wife and all of his family's substantial income would become partly hers.

Kaimi seemed exhausted after speaking with the Hawaiian Kahu who was going to perform the service Wednesday morning. They were to board the boat at nine. It had all been entirely too many decisions to make after the only person who'd ever really loved Kaimi had gone on.

Garrett couldn't fix it for her, as badly as he wished he could, so he took her back to their hideaway, after picking up fish tacos for dinner. He heat casted the tacos and left them on the counter, so he could lie down with Kaimi in the hammock on the deck. She fell asleep almost instantly, and Garrett eased himself out. He grabbed his phone and slipped into the chalet.

"Hey, Dad," he greeted.

"Son, are you okay? Where are you, and what is going on?" Governor Haydenshire demanded.

"I'm fine. I'm bringing someone home with me Thursday. I really want her to meet everyone, and then she's going to Rio with me to deliver the presents to the orphanage. She might want to stay on the farm while I'm in London with Dan. Is that all okay?" He would've given anything to see the look on his old man's face at that moment. But he just chuckled as he awaited a response.

"Forgive me just a moment, but this is my son Garrett who I am speaking to, correct? Second born. One commonly heard saying things like, 'One's just as good as another as long as they're racked,'" the governor quoted, and Garrett grimaced.

"Uh, yeah, but could you never say that out loud again?"

"I've been asking you that for years."

"Dad, please." Garrett rolled his eyes as he peeked out the front door to check on Kaimi.

"So, you want to bring your, dare I even hope to use the word, *girlfriend* home to the farm to meet your mother and me, and all of your brothers and sisters, and then she is going with you to Brazil?" the governor rephrased.

"Yes, and yes to the girlfriend part too. Oh, and tell mom no beef and no pork of any kind at all."

"Okay, medical, spiritual, ethical, or just strong-minded?"

"Medical and ethical and just awesome, okay? I'm serious. I know all of the shit I said in the past, but this is different."

"I need to sit down." Governor Haydenshire did sound faint. "Yes, son, of course. Your mother will be thrilled. Your brothers and your brother-in-law will harass you mercilessly, but you deserve that, so…" his father allowed.

"Great, see you Thursday. Gotta go. Kaimi's waking up."

"How old is Kaimi, son?"

"Uh, twenty-seven," Garrett recalled from one of the many phone calls he and Kaimi had shared over the past week.

"Gifted?" his father quizzed. "Not that it matters," he amended quickly.

"Yes. She voted for you."

"And smart. I like her already. All right, we'll see you day after tomorrow, and tell Kaimi she's welcome on the farm for as long as she'd like to be here."

Garrett quickly blocked Chloe's number from his phone and left it on the counter. He still hadn't responded to Dan and Fionna's numerous texts. He eased back into the double hung hammock.

"You went away," Kaimi fussed as she repositioned herself on his chest. Garrett grinned as he recovered her and sent soothing rhythmic pulses through her skin.

"I had to let the family know I'm bringing you home with me. I have to give all of my brothers time to come up with the shit they're going to say to try to embarrass me in front of you."

Kaimi giggled. It was a sound Garrett was quickly becoming addicted to.

"What if they don't like me?" Panic set in a moment later.

"They'll love you, baby."

"Do I need to go to the library and check out books on manners and stuff, 'cause I don't know any of that?"

"Breathe," he instructed. "My mother once served pie that my baby brother stuck his fist in the center of to the Australian Premier's son. The first time my kid brother Logan brought the girl he married several years later over for dinner, he dropped the butter dish in her lap and then poured tea all over Rainer, who is my sister's husband. My parents have eleven kids, and basically two adopted kids, so if we made it through one meal without at least two glasses of tea being spilled, it was a freaking miracle. They're regular, normal people, baby. And they will love you and love the fact that they can all harass me about you."

CHAPTER 48

VOYAGES

The next morning, Garrett held Kaimi's hand as she moved onto the beach to the small gathering crowd. Once everyone arrived, they boarded the boat that would take them out to scatter the ashes. The salty air and brine combined with the delicate, peachy scent of the plumeria flowers waiting to be dispersed with the ashes.

As they awaited departure, Garrett kept Kaimi close to him. Her own plumeria peach musk filled his nostrils.

A woman approached and Kaimi bristled. "Uh, Garrett, this is my mom, Carlina," she introduced hesitantly. "Carlina, this is my boyfriend, Garrett."

"Nice to meet you." Garrett offered the woman his hand. They'd been in the small crowd for over ten minutes, and this was the first time they'd spoken.

"You too," she agreed though she didn't look particularly thrilled. "I didn't know you had a boyfriend," she huffed as if Garrett wasn't standing right beside her daughter holding her hand.

"Well, I do. You don't know a lot of things," Kaimi spat indignantly.

"Whatever, this is Simon." Carlina jerked a nicely dressed man, who wasn't much older than Garrett, toward her. He gave a salesman smile as he studied Kaimi and then let his eyes slide to Garrett.

"You're the new deputy commander of Iodex, right?"

"Yeah, eventually," Garrett informed him. He didn't like the way Simon was eyeing Kaimi who did favor her mother.

The Kahu located Kaimi and told her that the captain was ready to depart.

"Are you okay?" Garrett whispered as he held her tight as the island disappeared behind them and they sailed out toward nothingness.

"I don't know what to think or do or how to be."

He planted a kiss on top of her head. "You don't have to think or do or be any certain way, sweetheart. I promise. It all just sucks. Some days it sucks less, some days more. Then you'll have a bunch of days where you think you're pretty okay with it all, and then it'll all come back in an instant and it'll bring you to your knees all over again. But I promise you, I'll be here for all of those days."

"Thank you," she whispered. "But don't say that. Because...you might not."

Before Garrett could combat her doubt yet again, the anchor was dropping, and the Kahu urged everyone onto the bow of the ship.

The deep sound of the blowing of conch shells reverberated through Garrett. He watched intently. There were prayers offered and several chants performed. The ashes were returned to the waters and to the earth, and Garrett held Kaimi tenderly as she sobbed.

Tutu and Papa looked on sweetly. All of the instructors from the dance studio were in attendance. Josh had taken off a few hours to attend with Malie. Kaimi's friends were also there and didn't really seem to know what to do with Kaimi's announcement that she and Garrett were in an exclusive relationship and that she was flying home with him the next day.

Her friends moved to the back of the boat. They, rather loudly, discussed their concerns over Garrett and Kaimi's abrupt relationship. Kaimi offered Garrett a sorrowful gaze as she glanced at the grouping of her friends.

"They're just worried about you, sweetheart. Little fast for them too, I imagine." He was actually pleased they were concerned. He wanted to know people were going to look after her while he was trying to figure out how to let her live five thousand miles away from him.

"I haven't really dated anyone since I moved here. Then Shaun told everyone what's wrong with me," she sighed out her regret.

"I really don't like him." Garrett threw a hateful glare at Shaun who was eyeing him speculatively.

"Me, either." Kaimi laid her head against Garrett's bulging bicep. He wrapped his arm around her mostly to annoy Shaun.

Tutu approached with a kind smile. Garrett found it mildly odd that she seemed to already have accepted Garrett and Kaimi as an item and seemed aware that he'd asked Kaimi to move in with him once he moved to the farm, though they hadn't told anyone.

"Now, Kaimi, if you want to come stay with us on the farm in your new hale, we would be so thrilled to have you. Garrett and Maylea and her family won't be in Virginia too much longer, but we'd be happy to look after you for a while. We did love Olina so," Tutu vowed.

Kaimi's energy soothed, and Garrett hoped she would take Fionna's grandparents up on their offer.

"I still have a month left on our lease but maybe after that. I don't guess I want to sign another contract," Kaimi explained confusedly.

"No, you definitely don't," Tutu assured her. "You come stay on our farm. Let us help you."

Malani approached with Kai and little Lanie. "I'm so sorry for your loss, Kaimi. Let me know if there's anything we can do."

"I'm okay. I was just talking to Tutu about moving to the farm before Garrett moves officially," she explained as she offered Tutu another appreciative smile.

"That would be great. Kai's there every day, and I'm over there all the time. We could talk about what we need to do for the hula studio."

Garrett grinned. Fionna had an amazing family and very kind friends, though he certainly wasn't surprised.

Kaimi nodded. She looked overwhelmed and deeply touched that she was being effectively adopted. Garrett was shocked that Carlina never spoke to Kaimi again. She and Simon left as soon as the boat docked. His heart ached as he began to really understand how alone Kaimi was.

CHAPTER 49

DECADENT DISTRACTIONS

He drove her back to the apartment she'd shared with her grandmother, so she could pack for DC and then for Brazil.

"I don't really have a lot of cold weather clothes. I got rid of them all when I left New York. I was so thrilled to be back here."

"I'll keep you warm, sweetheart." Garrett's vow elicited a slight grin. He moved around the room trying to help her pack and also learning more about the woman he wanted to make his wife. "Is Ringo coming along?" He lifted the frog from the wad of sheets in her bed.

Kaimi giggled. "Nah." She shook her head. "I have a new frog I'm sleeping with who might actually be a prince. Maybe."

Garrett grasped Kaimi's hand and pulled her to him. "I'm going to require way more blow jobs before we see if I'm a prince." He waggled his eyebrows as she giggled.

"I thought it was kisses that turned you into a prince."

"Nah, that's a common princess misconception. It's sucking us off," he assured her as she continued laughing.

Then an excited, mischievous light cast her eyes, and Garrett's heart picked up pace. "Would my prince like to be sucked off...now?"

she urged, and Garrett's eyes flashed and then closed in ecstasy as Kaimi's hand began caressing his zipper line.

"Only if the princess gets to come too," he panted as his abs clenched in anticipation.

"Aww, now I know you're a prince." She pushed him back toward her bed.

"This has to go." Garrett spun her and unzipped the floral dress she'd worn to her grandmother's funeral. "I want you naked. I want to see you." He growled as the dress slid from her delicate features and revealed her graceful body to his eyes.

She had his slacks unhooked and unzipped a moment later. He shed them quickly. Garrett popped the clasp of her bra with one quick move and groaned as he slid his thumbs over her nipples and then lifted their slight weight in his palms. She shivered from the sensations as they rose into tightened beads. Her breath caught quickly.

"You sure, baby? You sure you want me in your mouth?" He slipped his hands delicately from her breasts up her neck until he cradled her cheek in his hand. He brushed her beautiful lips, swollen and pert, with his thumb. They were the precise shade of a delicate pink wine set off against her deep olive skin. She gave him a heavy nod, and a groan thundered from Garrett's chest as he pulled off his shirt and sank back on the bed. Kaimi crawled over him.

Her nipples grazed his thighs, and his pelvis gave a hungry thrust toward her mouth. Her delighted grin had his body rolling in need. She let her hand tenderly tease his sack and then spin around his shaft and head. A desperate, guttural growl filled the air around them as Garrett fought not to plead for relief.

She bathed him with her tongue, and he writhed.

"Suck me, baby. Please." He couldn't halt the plea.

Her rapid breaths lifted her breasts against him, and Garrett's eyes rolled back in his head. She moaned and then drew him in her mouth, drowning his need and nearly driving him over with the first draw of his erotic energy straight from its source.

"That feels so incredible inside of me." She gasped as she licked again and then pulled him in, ravenous for more.

"Take it, sweet girl. It's all for you. Pull everything I've got," he urged desperately. She made another draw, and Garrett's body cinched tight. She sucked and licked rhythmically, as he laced his fingers through her hair and guided her in for more.

"Show me. Show me my cum in your hungry little mouth. Show me how much you like it."

Her moan was voracious as she opened her lips and did as she was told. Garrett's groan echoed around the room. She went back to work.

"Stop, baby," he managed though that was the very last thing he wanted her to do. But if she didn't want to drink him, she had to halt her delicious progress. Her eyes held the wildfire he loved as she released him long enough to drag her tongue up him and to shake her head.

"Oh, fuck yeah," Garrett groaned as she pulled him deeper this time. Her breasts pressed against his thighs. "That's my sweet girl. Lets me come down her throat," he groaned. He felt his energy unbind inside of her, and it filled her body just before he filled her mouth. His body twitched and shuddered from the heavenly sensations. "Drink me," he commanded. "Drink it all."

Garrett was simultaneously deeply satisfied and filled with carnal craving.

"Lie down," he ordered as he moved to her purse and removed the small jar of lube. He smiled as he pulled her panties away from her. They were already wet.

He'd learned several things in the last few days of being with Kaimi constantly, and something was clearly working. She was throbbing. Her inner lips were flushed a delicate pink, and the erotic energy from her mound was pulsing for him.

Garrett let his tongue lap over her belly button ring as he worked his way down. He moved back up her body as he dipped his index finger in the lube and began coaxing her open. She moaned as her hips lifted in desperation.

"That's my sweet girl," he soothed in her ear as he gently let his fingers explore farther. "Does sucking my cock make you wet, honey? Does tasting my cum make you needy?"

Her answer was a desperate groan. "God, yes," she whimpered.

"More please, more," she begged. Garrett's body gave a rapid shudder as he fought with his own desires and with hers.

"I fucking love to hear you beg. Love how greedy you get for me." He coated his fingers again and eased inside of her slowly and tenderly. According to Kaimi she'd had more sex in the last few days than she'd ever been able to before, and Garrett watched over her obsessively to make certain that she wasn't telling him she was fine when she wasn't.

She'd felt no pain, and he planned to make that his life's mission. Her breath caught as a luscious groan panted from her lungs. Garrett turned his hand and stroked his fingers over her G-spot. He circled his thumb near her clit, careful not to touch until she was soaked. She preferred clit-adjacent strokes. Her sweet little body responded so rapidly to him, it overwhelmed her if he wasn't careful. He teased the delicate bundle of nerve endings before he went in with his tongue.

She went wild. Her body lifted off the bed as her back arched deeply. He pulled his tongue away after a few strokes, still letting her body guide his every move. Her muscles cinched and pulled his fingers deeper, and he groaned in ardent desperation. Her breaths quickened as he fucked her hard and fast with his fingers.

"It's right there, isn't it, sweet girl? Feel how tight you clench for me. Feel yourself pulling me deeper. God, you're so fucking perfect." Her needy little moan broke with a gasp. "Do you want to watch, baby? Do you want to watch my fingers pound into you?"

The liquid form of her energy coursed around his fingers, as she lifted her head. Her eyes sought his. "It's right there. Just let it come for me," he ordered.

She bucked and writhed. He owned her.

Garrett eased his hand away and waited on her eyes to open. He stared her down and then sucked the evidence of her need from his fingers. Her desperate, needy moan fed the beast inside of him.

He slowly managed to calm and cradle her against him.

"Are you okay, sweetheart?"

"Perfect and happier than I've ever been except..." She choked up. Garrett kissed her forehead.

"Hard to be here without Nana." He already knew. Plaguing

sadness pulsed in her energy though she constantly tried to keep it at bay. She tucked her head under his chin as he let his shield encapsulate her again.

"Why don't you go on and stay at the farm if you want to come back here while I'm in London? Or just move in with me in DC for the next however long it takes me to clean up this shit at Venton. I've got plenty of savings, and I also have it in pretty damn well with your future boss. Fi will let you stay there until we all get moved. Hell, she'd even go ahead and pay you."

"Maybe I could fly back and forth some, but I have to pack and deal with everything here. Go through all of Nana's stuff." She shuddered from the thought alone. "All of the paperwork and bills. It's going to be endless."

"All right, let me go find this guy in London and then I'll fly back and forth. I'll help you do all of this, and we can get set up out on the farm."

"I need to work. I have to dance almost every day or I kind of start to go nuts. Plus, I need the money. I want to work on the stuff for the new classes Maylea is letting me teach. But maybe if Miss Leialanie does move and closes the studio before you move back out here then I could come stay with you, if you're sure you don't mind. I don't want to get on your nerves. I don't have any money left, and I still haven't even gotten the rest of the hospital bills," she admitted fretfully. "This is still all really fast."

"I know," Garrett agreed. "But it's also really good. My life hasn't been this good in a long time. I don't care how fast it is. I know you're who I've been looking for all of this time, when I didn't even know I was looking for anyone at all. Please let me take care of you. If you want to fly back and forth some, let me buy your tickets. At least let me do that."

"Let's just take it one day at a time. I don't want to think about your not being here with me. It hurts to think about."

Garrett's heart ached and his shield protested against his skin. "I know. It hurts me too, baby. Believe me." He hoped she didn't know that the pain his shield was wielding was a deep physical assault, but his heart ached as well.

CHAPTER 50
NERVES

The next day literally flew by. With every mile the Crown Governor's jet gained, they lost time, so Garrett and Kaimi stayed lip-locked for most of the flight. This made the loss of time to spend together much more manageable.

Kaimi had freaked out that morning and debated dying the red streaks in her hair back to its original dark brown. Garrett had spent several long minutes telling her how hot he thought it was and begging her not to change it.

He kept up constant reassurances that his family would love her, and he'd begged her again to stay with him in DC or at least on the farm with his parents and younger siblings after they returned from Brazil.

She'd panicked over all of the things that drove Garrett wild. Everything from her belly button ring to the numerous holes in her ears to her tat had been debated and discussed.

"They're not going to see your tat. That's all for me, and seriously..." Garrett had gestured to his own chest, arms, and back. This at least had soothed her panic momentarily. But she was frantic again as the plane began its approach to the Senate.

"They're going to love you almost as much as I do," Garrett vowed as Pete Namphis left the cockpit with a smirk on his face. "Kaimi, this is my dad's pilot and a good friend of our family, Pete Namphis. Pete, this is my girlfriend, Kaimi," Garrett introduced as Kaimi scooted out of his lap.

"I was worried you weren't letting her get enough oxygen. I came back to make sure you two hadn't passed out," Pete teased.

Kaimi blushed, turning back into Garrett's peach. He tried not to stare at her hungrily and let Namphis know what was on his mind. "Hey, she's beautiful and she's mine," Garrett teased, only deepening Kaimi's blush. Pete chuckled and shook his head. Garrett was certain he was shocked by Garrett's adamance but wasn't going to comment in front of Kaimi.

"We'll be landing in just a minute. Your dad called and said he was meeting you at the gate. He had Logan and Rainer take your Highlander to the farm for you."

Garrett draped his arm over Kaimi and scooted her closer to him. In her embarrassment, she'd moved two solid feet away and was hanging off the cushioned seat into the aisle.

"Thanks, Pete." Garrett remembered his manners as Pete made his return to the cockpit. "So, you get to ride to the farm in my dad's minivan which wasn't the image I was going to give you, but it appears I have no choice."

"He probably misses you. I'd want you to ride with me if you'd been gone for a while."

Garrett chuckled as he gave her a smirk. "I don't think he missed me. I think he wants to meet the girl who had me quitting my job and flying to Kauai." That had a broad grin spreading across Kaimi's face as she nestled her head on his shoulder.

"Your dad drives a minivan?" she asked a moment later. "I would've thought he'd have limo drivers and stuff." Garrett could tell that the thought of limos didn't interest her in the least.

"I told you my dad isn't into any of that. He doesn't think he's anything special, and if any of us got to thinking we were the shit growing up, he was the first one to take us down several notches rapidly."

Kaimi was biting her lip and staring wide-eyed out the windows of the plane as it touched down on the tarmac.

Garrett forcibly edged her out of the plane. "He will love you, and you know how much I do," was his constant spoken vow to her in what seemed a futile effort to soothe her nerves.

Governor Haydenshire wore his customary smirk. Garrett gave him a nod as they descended from the steps off of the plane. He was most certainly where all of his sons had learned the very same facial expression they so often sported.

"Dad, this is Kaimi Walyuo. Kaimi, this is my dad." Garrett kept his arm wrapped around Kaimi's shoulders as she seemed unable to both hold herself upright and walk.

"Nice to meet you, Kaimi." Governor Haydenshire extended his hand.

"Oh, uh, yes…you as well…Crown Governor…Haydenshire…sir. Am I supposed to curtsy?" she fumbled uncomfortably, and Garrett bit his lips together to keep from laughing.

"So, obviously, she's adorable," Garrett explained. The governor chuckled and shook his head at his son.

"Please never curtsy. Governor Haydenshire or Stephen is fine. And I can only recall once or twice that I had one of my sons' girlfriends banished because I didn't like them," he teased.

Kaimi shrunk back into Garrett with a terrified look.

"He was kidding, baby. Relax. For me, please."

"I'm sorry, I was trying to lighten the mood. We're thrilled you're here," Governor Haydenshire corrected.

"I'm just a little nervous, I guess."

CHAPTER 51

INAPPROPRIATE INTRODUCTIONS

Garrett wasn't certain what to do as they approached the governor's Sienna. He knew Kaimi wouldn't want to ride in the front passenger seat with his dad, but he didn't want to be rude and put her in the middle seat like a child. With a shrug, he decided to remove Abigail's car seat and toss it in the back with the twins' so he could sit beside Kaimi in the middle.

"Have you ever been to DC, Kaimi?" the governor asked as Garrett laced his fingers in hers to allow her to draw from him if she wanted. She did immediately, and Garrett leaned to kiss her cheek.

"I love you so much," he whispered in her ear. He must've been slightly louder than he'd intended, however, as the minivan jerked to the left as his father stared in the rearview mirror in utter shock.

Kaimi didn't seem to notice. She gave a delighted shiver from Garrett's vow.

"No, sir. I've only ever traveled to New York. Actually, when I went for my auditions, I'd never even left the islands before. I got to JFK, and there were more people inside the airport than I'd ever even seen in one place. I had to try to find my hotel and then get to Juilliard. Nana kept telling me everyone who lived in New York was a mugger. I was terrified," she explained as she began to loosen up a little though she continued to draw from Garrett. He fought not to groan from the heady feeling of her drawing strength and love from his hand into her body.

"Garrett didn't mention you'd studied at Juilliard. You must be quite the musician."

"Oh, actually, I'm a dancer."

"Even better. I was worried for a minute Lillian might try to convince you to teach her piano this evening. My wife can do anything at all, but for some reason the piano has stumped her for the past forty years she's been trying to learn."

"I'm sure she could outplay me. Nana signed me up for lessons when I was a little girl, but I hated them. My teacher banned me from her music room when I demonstrated a grand jeté off of the piano bench."

The governor laughed, but Garrett knew he had no idea what a grand jeté was. Garrett himself hadn't known until he'd taken Kaimi to the hula studio the evening before because she wanted to dance. He'd leaned against a wall and watched her twirl and jump to the rhythms of the music. She whirled through the air like an angel.

Dance seemed to be the time when Kaimi had the most poise and confidence. She came alive under the lights and in front of the wall of mirrors just like she seemed to enliven under the tender caresses of his tongue and fingers and the prods of his length inside of her. Garrett's breath caught from the thought alone.

"One of Garrett's elementary school teachers told Lillian and me that we should sign him up for music lessons. She felt it would give him an outlet for what she termed his 'inappropriate energies.'"

"Dad," Garrett spat as Kaimi began laughing. "She's already aware of all of my inappropriate energies, but thanks."

Kaimi's eyes goggled as she began laughing harder which made the comment worth it.

"I assume she is also aware of your inappropriate comments then," the governor scolded.

"Yeah, she's good with those too."

A few minutes later, Governor Haydenshire turned down the gravel lane that led to the massive wrought iron gates of Haydenshire Farm. The lion crest was on prominent display.

"Your farm is so beautiful." Kaimi grinned as she took in the fields by the light of the sinking sun. "Do you have animals?"

Garrett suspected that Kaimi loved animals as much as he did. He'd debated getting a dog on numerous occasions, but the size and breeds that interested him would be miserable locked up in his apartment during his long, twelve-hour shifts.

"Other than the eleven kids, no," the governor teased. "With the kids, and the gardens, and the orchard, and then the additional kids, we decided that was probably enough." He pulled the minivan into the barn. Garrett wasn't surprised to see all of his brothers' vehicles already parked there alongside Rainer's Porsche.

"Are you ready?" Garrett helped Kaimi from the van and then transferred their luggage into his Highlander.

"No." She shook her head as Garrett guided her to the side porch.

"It won't be you they're after, trust me." He followed his father into the large farmhouse kitchen.

Mrs. Haydenshire was beaming as she eyed Garret and Kaimi.

"Mom, this is Kaimi Walyuo my...*girlfriend*." Garrett braced for the incoming harassment.

"Your girlfriend?!" Patrick sounded astonished as a delighted smirk etched his face.

"It's nice to meet you, Kaimi." Mrs. Haydenshire shot Patrick a warning glance.

"Hi. It's nice to meet you as well." Kaimi took in the myriad of faces all studying her.

"So, Kaimi, you know he's got tootsie rolls for nads, right?" Connor sneered.

"Yeah, Garrett, how many licks does it take to get to the center?" Logan leapt.

Garrett rolled his eyes as he pulled Kaimi in and cradled her to his chest.

"Do you all think you could act marginally human just for tonight?" He drew a deep breath of her—that lush plumeria musk that was all her own. "Okay, baby, you ready?" he urged as Kaimi turned her face back out with a giggle. "This is my older brother, Will, his wife, Brooke, and their little girl, Lily Ana." Garrett gestured to Lily

Ana who was in Emily's arms. "This is my little sister Emily and her husband, Rainer Lawson," Garrett continued. Rainer offered Kaimi a kind smile as Emily beamed. "Of absolutely no importance at all are the following line of Haydenshire men, Levi, Patrick, Connor, and Logan. And their significant others. Olivia, Lucy, Patrick Jr." Garrett's hand landed on Lucy's very swollen midsection. Everyone chuckled as he continued. "Reid, who is willingly putting up with Connor though none of us know why. We assume it's some kind of head injury. We're trying to get him some help." Reid laughed as he put an arm around Connor's shoulders and shook his head at Garrett. "And Miss Adeline, Logan's vastly better half. And this,"—Garrett lifted Abigail up from her playpen—"is Abigail." He concluded as Abigail kissed Garrett's cheek. He grinned at her and kissed her nose.

Kaimi grinned at Abigail as Garrett carried her over.

"Aww, hey Abigail."

Abby grasped Garrett's forearm and stared at him expectantly.

"Curious?" Garrett turned to Emily.

"She wants Kaimi to hold her," Emily explained.

"Oh, uh, okay." Kaimi started to panic. Garrett chuckled.

"She might try to tell you what she's feeling, so if she grabs your hand or your arm, just try to feel her rhythms," Garrett explained as he handed Abigail to Kaimi.

"Hi there," Kaimi offered in a slightly breathless pant. Abigail grinned as she settled into Kaimi's embrace. Abigail grasped Kaimi's hand, and Emily stepped in to help. She read Abigail easily.

"She likes you," Emily offered Kaimi sweetly.

"Oh, well, that's one of you at least."

The twins raced in from the living room.

"And to complete the ensemble, these are my twin brothers, Keaton and Henry," Garrett explained as he lifted Keaton into his arms.

"I'm name is Keaton. Why is your hair like dat?" Keaton probed demandingly as he pointed to a red section of Kaimi's hair. She turned a terrified gaze on Garrett.

"That's how pretty girls wear their hair, little man," Garrett answered readily.

"Keaton gets his etiquette from Garrett, Kaimi. Please excuse him." Mrs. Haydenshire rescued Garrett.

Kaimi seemed to revel in holding Abigail who was delighted with her.

"All right, everyone, let's eat," Mrs. Haydenshire urged. "Levi and I made several roast chickens, and I have potatoes and a few other things, so everyone grab something. Rainer, you and Logan put ice in the glasses, please, sweetheart," she directed the crew.

Garrett helped Kaimi strap Abigail into her highchair and then seated her as well.

Everyone settled in and began passing around chicken, carrots, potatoes, and braised mushrooms along with Mrs. Haydenshire's outstanding homemade biscuits.

"This is delicious, Mrs. Haydenshire. Thank you so much for having me," Kaimi offered. Garrett winked at her as he rubbed her leg under the table.

"We're thrilled you're here. We're so sorry to hear about your grandmother though. If there's anything we can do to help, please let us know. Stephen mentioned you might like to stay here while Garrett and Daniel are in London. You're welcome anytime. I promise to limit your exposure to Keaton." Mrs. Haydenshire chuckled.

"I'm name is Keaton," Keaton informed everyone as he squeezed a chunk of potato in his fist.

Kaimi looked truly touched, but she reached for Garrett's hand. She chuckled over Keaton's announcement but didn't seem to know how to respond.

"Let us get back from Rio and get settled, Mom. Then she can decide. I can take her back to Kauai as soon as we get back, or she can stay with me."

Governor Haydenshire looked extremely pleased with Garrett's care over Kaimi. His mother swooned. His brothers, however, looked stupefied to the point of being rude.

Patrick cleared his throat discreetly. Garrett slid his eyes to the side and raised one eyebrow.

"Is she pregnant?" he mouthed. Garrett rolled his eyes and shook his head.

Will clearly had the same question and gave Patrick a shrug and then offered Garrett a wry grin.

"Thank you though, Mrs. Haydenshire." Kaimi glanced around the table uncomfortably.

Adeline offered her a sweet smile and rolled her eyes at Garrett's brothers. Kaimi instantly liked Adeline. Garrett could tell.

"Kaimi was telling me that she studied dance at Juilliard." The governor shot all of his sons warning glares.

"Only for a year," Kaimi deflected. "I didn't get to finish. I moved back to Honolulu to take care of Nana when her condition got worse." Her voice lowered with every word she spoke as she shrank back against her chair.

Mrs. Haydenshire was visibly moved as she reached and patted Kaimi's hand.

"I thought you were moving to Kauai?" Levi quizzed.

"Oh, he is. I'm sorry. Nana and I moved to Kauai because Tutu helped her. Uh, that's Maylea's grandmother...no, sorry, Fionna, I mean," Kaimi tried to explain. "She was sick for a long time before we were able to move to Kauai."

"Fi's grandmother is kind of a natural healthcare genius, so between her and the medios at Wilcox, Kaimi's grandmother had excellent care," Garrett smoothed over the slightly confusing explanation.

"What kinds of things did Fionna's grandmother do?" Adeline was intrigued.

"Adeline is an obstetrics medio at Georgetown," Garrett explained her fascination. "She delivered Halia." Kaimi grinned as she nodded, but Garret noticed that she hadn't had time to eat much of anything.

She also didn't really seem to want to offer much on her Nana's care. Emily noticed and stepped in. "It might be a little soon to be discussing that," she whispered.

Garrett made a mental note to thank his little sister profusely when he returned from Brazil after Christmas.

"Oh, I'm so sorry. Of course," Adeline apologized.

"It's fine." Kaimi tucked closer to Garrett as she began consuming small bites of the delicious dinner. Garrett noted his parents' extremely hopeful glances as he kept one hand on Kaimi while he ate.

"Why don't you let us in on how you and Kaimi met?" Governor Haydenshire commanded the table. Garrett chuckled as Kaimi blushed. She stepped in on his behalf.

"Oh, Garrett was so sweet. He fixed my car battery for me. He's amazing," she gushed, and Garrett knew he was done for.

"I'm not sure *amazing* is the word I would use for Garrett," Logan goaded with a derisive chuckle.

"Oh yeah, Lo, I mean come on." Connor leapt on the band wagon. "Remember when he was so amazing that he snuck out when he was fifteen, casted Dad's car, got it out, but failed to notice that he had almost no gas and got stuck down by the Beechmans' farm at two in the morning?"

Kaimi laughed as she gazed at Garrett. He rolled his eyes and then shot Connor a warning glare.

"Oh, remember when he was in fourth grade and told Mrs. Coughman that she was too pretty to be so upset when he didn't do his homework?" Will cracked himself up.

"Thank you all, but if you'd shut your pie holes, my girlfriend could eat," Garrett sneered.

"Aww, Garrett, we love you and we want Kaimi to know all about you. Like the time you and Will and Dan were going to climb up on the roof outside my window and scare me." Emily giggled. Kaimi turned to Garrett with a delighted grin. If she was having fun, he would take the abuse.

"I might've slipped on the drain spout and fell into Mom's rose bushes."

Kaimi's hand flew to her mouth as she tried to quell her laughter.

"Yes, Lillian and I spent more time with Garrett in the emergency room than any of the others as I recall," the governor chimed in.

"All right, you all, let Kaimi eat," Mrs. Haydenshire said.

"I love you, Mom." Garrett elicited more giggles from Kaimi.

"Yes, well, you should."

A knock on the front door interrupted dessert and coffee.

"That'll be Tad and Nathan." Mrs. Haydenshire grinned.

"Yay!" Emily leapt to the door to let their uncles in.

Everyone stood to welcome Tad and Nathan. Garrett grinned as they approached.

"Uncle Tad, this is my girlfriend, Kaimi," he introduced. "Kaimi, these are my uncles, Tad and Nathan."

"It's so nice to meet you." Kaimi beamed.

"Oh, honey, don't worry. You'll meet somebody better soon," Tad tsked as he hugged Kaimi and made everyone laugh.

Kaimi shook her head as she reached back and took Garrett's hand. "I don't think so."

"Uh-oh, Garrett Haydenshire, believe you just might've found the one, now haven't you?" Nathan was visibly thrilled.

"Yeah," Garrett agreed as he stared into Kaimi's beautiful copper eyes. "Believe I have."

Mrs. Haydenshire clutched her chest as she visibly willed away tears.

CHAPTER 52

WALK THE DOCK

"Your family is so sweet," Kaimi gushed as Garrett swathed her in his Iodex heat-synced jacket and cradled her in his arms on the dock by the lake. The moon was bright on the cold, clear night and illuminated them.

"Sweet is really not what I was thinking." His brothers had done a decent job of not giving away the fact that Garrett had most definitely been a player most of his life, but he could have done without the stories of his more stupid stunts growing up.

Kaimi nuzzled her head in Garrett's neck. His heart picked up pace in his rhythms as he caressed her face tenderly.

"You know, there's a Haydenshire tradition with this dock." Garrett hoped she wouldn't think he was an ass. She lifted her head and studied him with a wry grin.

"What kind of tradition?"

"Well..."—Garrett winked at her—"the summer Dad decided we were going to tear down the old dock and build a new one, Will and I did a few calculations and drew up new plans to put the dock here instead of over there. That way Mom couldn't see us from the kitchen windows."

Kaimi smirked and shook her head at him. "And why wouldn't you want your mom seeing you from the kitchen?" The moonlight danced in her eyes and rippled across the water.

Garrett leaned and brushed a tender kiss across Kaimi's cheek that had her shivering but not from the cold. The air around them was hot with their energy dancing in its desire to be joined. It was filled with the heady scent of her and of sex that was just beginning to emanate its need. "Because if she can't see us, then I can do this." He let his hand move up the jacket to her stomach. He painted tender kisses along her neck.

A slight moan escaped her, and Garrett held her eyes with his own. "And I can touch these." He lifted the shirt tail and trailed his hands up to her bra as he began to grope. Her nipples throbbed against the slight cup, eager for his attention. He popped the front clasp of the bra, and a breathy moan echoed from her open mouth. "And if you want me to, I can suck you right here." His thumbs softly circled her areolas as her nipples strained to be tended and cared for.

"Please," she begged fervently. Garrett growled. Her desperate need drove him wild. He braced her body back in his arm as he leaned his head to the throbbing tips that ached in their desire for his mouth. They pulsated against his tongue, and he brought her relief as she writhed in his arms.

Crown Governor Stephen Haydenshire

"I don't know where you think you're going, but it better not be to walk around the lake," Lillian informed Stephen.

"Why?" He walked around the lake almost every night and most certainly that had been his practice for the last dozen years or more if one of their sons had a girl out on the dock. The setting was just a little too hidden away and romantic. They didn't want anything getting out of hand or going further than it needed to go.

"Because." Lillian sipped her tea in the soft light of the clean kitchen. Most everyone had gone home after the dishes had been done. Logan and Adeline were still snuggling on the couch, but they only had eyes for one another. Tad and Nathan had put the twins to bed, and Stephen had already gotten Abigail to sleep.

"She's the sweet precious girl I've been praying for, and I don't care what they're doing out there. You're not interrupting them." Her words were soft and full of her nurturing love, but Stephen knew if he argued, her tone would change. "He told her. Didn't you see it and feel it between them? He told her what he did and what happened to him, and she loves him so much."

"I know, sweetheart. I just wish he'd tell me," Stephen confessed the most gut-wrenching part of the horrific tale. He joined her on the window bench seat that overlooked the fields set off in the moonlight.

"I'm not sure he's ever going to do that. He can't seem to understand that he could never have done anything that would make us not love him or not want him with us."

Stephen nodded his understanding and his agreement, but the thought that one of his sons hurt so badly they could possibly think they were unloved robbed him of breath to use for speech.

He'd known from the moment Garrett had arrived home from his month-long journey to nowhere that something had thoroughly broken his son. But all of the clues and detective work Stephen had worked through couldn't have prepared him for what he'd found out just a few weeks before.

The Senate had hosted medios from around the globe to honor those involved in the joint Auxiliary and Valeduto Departments' Healing the Wounded program. Medio Craig Barnaby, out of St. Mary's hospital in London, had been in Stephen's office, which was on display for the event.

"Is this one of your sons, Crown Governor?" He'd lifted a photograph of Garrett in his Iodex uniform from Stephen's desk. Something immediately clicked in his mind. "Yes, that's my son Garrett. Do you know him?" Stephen's heart had thundered as he'd awaited the answer.

"Perhaps." Medio Barnaby nodded. "I never forget a face, and his is so familiar. Did he ever wear a beard?" Stephen's heart seized his vocal cords. The only time Garrett had ever let his facial hair grow more than a few days' length seared through his mind.

"Where did you say you volunteer?" Stephen had tried to be nonchalant, but he knew he'd been standing in the presence of the missing piece of the puzzle.

"Outside of Rio, sir. At the Xavier Aid Station near Rocinha."

"Rio, huh?" Stephen had feigned polite nonchalance. As soon as the luncheon had been over, he'd set to work. He was the Crown Governor of the American Gifted Realm, and people rarely denied him information.

Numerous phone calls later, Stephen sat in stunned disbelief in his office. His heart had ached physically. His throat swelled with grief at all that his son had done and had been through. He'd sent a photo of Garrett to the aid station via email and had struck upon a nurse who had cared for him.

"She's going to bring him back, Stephen. I can feel it. My precious baby boy is going to move thousands of miles away for her, and she's going to bring him home." Lillian's decree brought Stephen back to the present. "She's going to bring him back to us." Tears began leaking from her eyes, and they cut Stephen to the quick just as they always did.

"I know. I can feel it, sweetheart. I promise." He tried to reassure her. "Sam was right." Stephen realized in that moment as he guided his wife's beautiful face tenderly to his chest. "He's not running away. He's running to something better than we could ever have given him here."

His wayward son was coming home.

CHAPTER 53

VIEWS AND PERSPECTIVES

~GARRETT HAYDENSHIRE~

"So, this is casa de la Garrett." Garrett summoned and switched on the few lamps he owned.

"You have such a beautiful view of the city." Kaimi rushed to the windows and took in the DC skyline from Garrett's sliding doors that led to a minuscule deck.

"I think I have a hell of a view right here." He wrapped his arms around her and cradled her back to his chest. Her energy trilled.

She spun to lay her head on his chest. "I feel so safe in your arms when I can hear your heart beat and you hold me. It's like you'd never let anything hurt me."

"Never, baby," Garrett vowed readily. "Are you tired or do you want to look around and then go out somewhere? We could go see the city." He tried to gauge her desires.

"Being in three different time zones in three days is going to be a little crazy."

"I'm sorry." Garrett hadn't really factored in the toll on her that would come from flying from Lihue, to DC, and then to Rio.

"No." Kaimi shook her head. "It means so much to me that you wanted to share your family with me and the orphanage. I can't wait to get there. I like kids. I just never figured I would have any, so I didn't pay much attention on how to take care of them other than to teach them to dance. But I can feel how much the orphans mean to you, and I want to help you help them and see you with them. You're just amazing."

Garrett wished she'd stop saying that. He was far from amazing, but he could never quite hide his smile when she said things that made him feel like a king.

"I'm not really tired," Kaimi explained hesitantly. She turned back to the lights of the city set off by the darkened, winter night.

"Want to go get lost in the city for a little while?" Garrett asked though he already knew the answer.

"If you want to," she urged hopefully.

"I want to go anywhere with you, sweet girl, but then I want to get lost between your legs when we get back."

Her breaths shortened instantly as the wildfire stirred in her eyes. The curious, excited gaze she held just before her eyes darkened slightly whenever he stoked that fire drove Garrett absolutely wild.

"I really like it when you get lost there. I kept thinking about that when we were at your parents'. I couldn't help it," she informed him with a sweet giggle. A pronounced blush colored her delicate features. "That's why I kept getting so flustered, I think." Garrett laughed at her outright. He was certain she was the cutest thing he'd ever seen or held in his arms. "But I don't think you could get lost there." She continued her explanation with a wry grin. "I'm kind of tight and all."

Garrett gave her a low, shuddering moan. "Oh baby, believe me, I know. You're like heaven, and you're all for me. And I don't ever want anything else."

"Garrett," she whispered. Her rhythms tensed abruptly, and fear played in the energy that poured from her.

"What's wrong?" He was instantly concerned over whatever had her nervous.

She lifted her head and stared into his eyes. "I really, really love you, and I've never ever said that before to anyone but you. I feel it and I know that's it."

"I told you I've never said that either. I've never loved anyone before. But I know what I feel right now and I know it's love." He patted her backside. "Come on. Let's go see DC."

Garrett led her to his bedroom. He pulled one of his Iodex sweatshirts over her head and changed into jeans himself. A few minutes later, he locked his door and led Kaimi to the closest Metro station.

"Oh, wow," she trilled as Garrett led her to the Ellipse. He pointed to the Non-Gifted White House on the way. "That's so gigantic." She gasped as she stared up at the National Christmas Tree lit in full glory and standing reticent over the trees surrounding it.

"I kind of think it pales in comparison." He gestured to his own crotch and effectively cracked her up.

"You have a tree this big in your pants?" She feigned confusion as Garrett mocked insult just to keep her laughing. He grabbed her hand and led her farther down the park that contained romantically lit trees from every state.

"And the tree from your homeland, Miss Hawaii," Garrett drawled as Kaimi rolled her eyes. The Hawaiian tree was decorated with large hibiscus blossoms and smaller plumeria garlands that smelled heavenly. Garrett caught the scent of Kaimi in their sweet blooms.

She moved into Garrett's arms. He embraced her readily. "You know if you kiss in front of the hibiscus blooms then you have to marry the girl you kiss," she informed him but couldn't quite get out the tall tale without laughing.

"Is that so?" Garrett cradled her jaw and guided her face upward.

"No, I totally made that up," she whispered just as Garrett let their breaths mingle in the cold night air for the half second he was able to wait before he devoured her mouth.

"Come on, sweetheart. There are several things I want you to see tonight and then I might have to figure out some punishment for your just up and lying to me," he teased as he guided her back toward the White House.

Kaimi smirked but then pulled back slightly.

"I don't like that tie the girl up and spank her kind of thing." Panic flooded her rhythms.

"I was kidding. I swear. I would never do anything you didn't want to do, and I'm not into that either." The thought of someone tying up his precious and wild baby made Garrett furious. She had to fly free without restraint, and he of all people understood that.

Kaimi nodded and seemed to allow herself to believe Garrett's vow.

"I got set up with this guy once in New York. He was a violinist at Juilliard, and we went to this restaurant in Brooklyn near the river. He creeped me out, and then in the middle of dinner, he starts telling me how he gets off on tying girls up and the whole handcuffs, whips, and shit, or whatever." Kaimi shuddered as they walked, and Garret fought back the bile that flooded his throat. "I got really mad. I don't know why because I wasn't going to sleep with him, but I think it scared me. It did seem like he was just kind of trying to see if I was into that too. It irritated me that he wanted to know if he could tie me up on our first date. So, I dumped this huge glass of red wine right on his crotch when I stood to leave, only I accidentally sloshed some in the candle at the table and then I set the tablecloth on fire."

Garrett guffawed as they headed back toward the Metro station. "My God, I love you."

She beamed over his acceptance of exactly who she was. He didn't want her to change at all. All he wanted to be different was her address and maybe in a few months her last name.

He guided her to the west end of the National Mall. The sight of the reflecting pool from the Lincoln Memorial was very romantic, and Garrett sincerely hoped she'd engage him in a few more kisses before they moved on.

"It's so crazy how they still don't know." She stared up at the massive memorial of Abraham Lincoln—one of only four men to ever hold the office of Non-Gifted President that was actually Gifted.

"Most of them don't know about us at all, sweetheart. They certainly don't know that occasionally we've held their highest office, and they did still manage to kill him." He shook his head.

She gave him a sorrowful nod as she turned to stare out at the water. "This is so beautiful."

"So is this." Garrett stared down into her eyes as he backed her up to one of the columns around the memorial. There were a few tourists there but not many. It was too late in the year and too cold. He didn't give a damn anyway. They could watch him consume her if they wanted, but all he wanted was to join their souls and their bodies in a kiss that would unite them in eternity, that would seal their fates as one forever.

Garrett pulled Kaimi in his lap on the Metro for the next ride. They were going farther out. He guided her through the stone archway that led to Bishop Gardens just outside of the National Cathedral. They located a bench tucked away along the floral paths and seated themselves for approximately a half second before they began making out heatedly. There was no one around, and he wanted her like he wanted to draw his next breath. He sucked her tongue and then released it long enough to draw his thumb over the crotch of her jeans.

"I'm gonna take you back home, baby, and I'm gonna suck you here," he informed her in a breathless pant.

"Yes, now."

"Come on, sweetheart." He guided her into his arms. "Let's get you home and out of these clothes so I can wrap you up in me."

CHAPTER 54

CHRISTMAS DELIGHT

Before allowing himself any sleep, Garrett slid softly from the bed. He pulled his worn flannel sheets and blankets over Kaimi tenderly. He gazed down at her, and his heart ached. He didn't want her to go back to Kauai, and he didn't want to go to London without her. She was so small and helpless there in his bed, swathed in one of his T-shirts. She'd been curled up on his chest, sleeping soundly in his strong embrace. She needed him to keep her safe. His shield was going to be brutal after she left.

Garrett swallowed down the emotion that had come on him suddenly as he leaned and breathed a kiss on her cheek. She smiled slightly in her sleep, and his heart skipped a beat. He moved to his cheap particleboard desk in the room and summoned on his computer and monitor. He lowered the light as much as he was able and checked to make sure he didn't awaken his sweet baby asleep in his bed.

He worked quickly. He wanted nothing more than to get back in the bed beside her and watch over her as she slept. He had to get her a Christmas present though.

Garrett almost laughed out loud at the thought alone. He typically broke up with anyone he'd seen even a few times right about Thanksgiving and then didn't start dating again until after Valentine's.

You were such a fucking asshole. You should try to get her to marry you now before she figures that out, he chastised himself as he logged on to the Senate Flight website. He typed in his new badge ID number from Hawaii. As soon as he'd set up a new account and entered his credit card number, he made the rather expensive purchase. He decided to print them out in the morning when she was in the shower. He turned off the computer and crawled back into the bed.

～

"Come back," Kaimi whimpered the next morning. Garrett chuckled as he did as he was told.

"I was going to get you coffee, sweetheart." He slid back under the warm flannel and wrapped his arms around her as she immediately sought his chest.

"I love you more than coffee so hah. And believe me that is a huge deal!"

Garrett was growing quite accustomed to having hilarious conversations with Kaimi before she ever allowed her eyes to open.

"I won't make you choose between us."

"Good!" Kaimi yawned and let her eyes open slightly. "So, how does today work and Brazil and everything?"

"I'm sorry, baby. I should have already told you this."

"Just tell me now."

"If you think you can handle another Haydenshire meal, only this time will only be my parents and uncles and the little ones, then we'll have breakfast there. Dan and Fi and the girls are coming over to help me load all of the gifts and supplies. We'll take them back to the Senate and load up Dad's jet again. Tonight, we'll stay in a nice hotel, but tomorrow morning, we'll need to head out early to get to the orphanage to get the toys set up for them. It's a ways out. Staying there is a little rough. We won't be able to sleep together. I'll come check on you and everything before you go to sleep, and it's very safe, but probably no available showers because they need the limited water for the kids." He braced as he awaited her reaction.

"I usually just take a pack of baby wipes and extra deodorant with me when I go camping, and I've done that for weeks at a time." She shrugged. "We could take sleeping bags. I don't want to take one of the kids' beds." That was her only concern. Garrett was overwhelmed. He stared at her in rapt disbelief. Chloe's furious rants about working at the orphanage the years before rang through Garrett's mind.

"They have beds for the volunteers, and you're just absolutely incredible."

"Why?" Her brow furrowed. She looked embarrassed at the assessment.

"You just are, and I love you so fucking much. I need to talk to my uncle when we're there this morning."

"Uh, thank you, and what does any of that have to do with your uncle?"

Garrett chuckled. He'd never even considered asking anyone to marry him before, so he had no idea how something like that went down.

"He's a jeweler, sweetheart. The best in the Northeast actually." Garrett decided he didn't want to keep things from her, and he wanted to know what kind of ring she would like, since he suspected that massive diamonds weren't her thing.

Kaimi's head shot up off his chest.

"Oh my gosh, like a jeweler like you want to buy me a friendship bracelet kind of deal or one of those hearts that has two pieces that I hate or like a jeweler like, you know…you know!" She gasped, and Garrett laughed.

"I hate those stupid heart things. How fucking ridiculous is that? A girl at Langley tried to give me one of those guy bracelet things, and I flushed it in the bathroom."

Kaimi's mouth dropped open. "You probably broke her heart."

"I did feel kind of bad," he admitted, "but my God, I'm not a dog. Don't put a tag on me."

"Okay, got it. No tag for you."

"I might wear your tag, but I want to talk to my uncle about an engagement ring." He studied her to see what she thought of that. Her rhythms pulled together in abject bliss.

"Hang on just one sec while I have a moment of extreme girliness."

Garrett laughed outright as Kaimi pulled the covers over her head and squealed for a solid minute.

"Are you about done with that now?" he harassed as she wiggled back out and nodded though he'd never seen her so excited.

"I'll do it again while you're in the shower."

"What if I get you to take a shower with me?"

"Then you will have to suffer through."

"I'll manage," Garrett assured her.

She was thoughtful for a moment.

"Would you maybe be thinking about the kind of ring you'd like, in which case you should be talking out loud so your boyfriend has some freaking clue what to ask for?"

She blushed as she gave a meek shrug. "I always kind of thought it would be so cool to have tattoo rings done. You know, that either go with or under your ring, ring." The light that danced in her eyes told him that in that moment she felt truly loved. Garrett's heart swelled as he lay back down and pulled her back to his chest.

"Do you want that instead of a ring or with a ring?" He considered the best way to propose at a tattoo shop.

"I don't know." She looked unable to believe that they were having this conversation. "I don't like those massive diamond things plus I would snag it on everything because I am a complete klutz."

"Let's go talk to Uncle Tad." That seemed to be the logical first step.

CHAPTER 55
FAVORITES

An hour later Garrett guided Kaimi back into his mother's kitchen. Mrs. Haydenshire was rocking Abigail while Nathan prepared breakfast. Tad and the governor were involved in a discussion about state and Realm taxes in New York.

Garrett's mother offered them a kind smile which they returned. "Nathan, there's some turkey bacon in the fridge. Would you make that as well? Different pan," Mrs. Haydenshire urged as she held Abigail, who was trying to stand in her mother's lap.

"Thank you, Mrs. Haydenshire. I'm sorry. I hope I'm not being too much trouble." Kaimi fussed over the additional bacon being made on her behalf.

"It's no trouble at all. I've been trying to get Stephen to eat it. It's much better for you."

"I know, I know," the governor sighed.

"It doesn't taste better," Kaimi whispered to Garrett's father. She wrinkled her nose and the governor laughed as he nodded his agreement.

Everyone sat down at the kitchen table this time and began eating.

"Hey, Uncle Tad." Garrett helped himself to another helping of Nathan's fried potatoes, which were one of his favorites.

"Yes, my favorite nephew?" he teased.

"Man, I know you tell us all that." Garrett elicited laughter from everyone at the table.

"Well, for right now, it's you, so what can I do for you?"

Garrett glanced at his parents for just a moment before he laced his fingers through Kaimi's with his left hand, so that he could continue to eat.

"If a guy wanted to get an engagement ring that would go with a ring tat, you could design something like that, right?"

His parents looked overjoyed, and Kaimi blushed violently as she squeezed her eyes shut for a moment.

"I could definitely come up with something." Tad slapped Garrett on the back.

The Vindicos arrived a few minutes after the breakfast dishes were being washed. Fionna hugged Garrett for a solid minute before she moved on to Kaimi, whom she squeezed tightly with a mix of elation over Garrett and sorrow over Nana.

"Just go with it. She can't help herself," Garrett chastised as Kaimi looked mildly bewildered over Fionna's exuberance.

"Honey, let her breathe." Dan gently guided Fionna away.

"But I'm just so happy, and you live in Kauai, and you're going to live on the farm." Fionna wiped away tears.

"I missed you," Aida fussed as Garrett swept her up off her feet and kissed her cheek.

"I missed you too, Aida Mae. I'm sorry I haven't been over in a while."

"Ni-on-na," rang from Keaton as he made his way in and extended his arms up to Fionna. She giggled as she picked him up and kissed his cheek. He attempted to kiss her back on the mouth.

"You have a little competition there, fifteen mile," Tad harassed.

"Don't I know it." Dan laughed. Tad had taken to calling Dan fifteen mile. When he'd phoned Tad about crafting Fionna's engagement ring, his orders had been that every man in a fifteen-mile radius should know that she belonged to him. Tad had certainly accomplished that directive. Garrett gave a slight eye roll as he took in Fionna's left hand dripping with enormous diamonds.

"Kaimi, do you have a minute to flip through these with me while

Garrett loads up?" Tad gestured to several massive, leather three-ring binders with the Latus logo on their covers. Latus was the name of Tad and Nathan's shop in New York.

"Oh, uh, okay, but don't you need my help?" Kaimi looked torn between Garrett and Tad.

"Dan and I will load. You look," Garrett urged.

"Oh, Garrett," Mrs. Haydenshire remembered suddenly. She handed Abigail to the governor. "Rainer and Emily left you a check. I put it on the bulletin board. Don't forget it," she reminded.

"I won't, and tell them thanks," Garrett assured his mother.

"Here's ours." Tad handed over an additional check for the orphanage.

When Garrett glanced at the total, his eyes goggled. "Uncle Tad, thank you. You didn't have to do this."

Tad and Nathan both shook their heads. "If it means something to you, it means something to us," Tad explained.

Abigail was smacking her hand on her father's. He wasn't paying attention.

"Sorry, baby girl, what is it?" The governor concentrated as Abigail grasped his knuckle.

"Do you want to go see Kaimi or Halia, Abby?" The governor studied her. She motioned her tiny hand to Halia who was asleep in her car seat.

"Baby Halia's asleep. You have to be gentle, okay?"

Abigail wiggled and leaned toward the baby. She was seated on the floor in front of Halia's car seat. Everyone smiled as she patted Halia's foot tenderly. Fionna was beaming, but Garrett knew it had much more to do with him and Kaimi than Abigail and Halia.

"My car's loaded down as well. Maybe we should load the stuff from the barn into yours, and Fi and I will go with you to the Senate?" Dan offered kindly.

"If you don't think we can get it all in mine." Garrett was watching Kaimi as Tad directed her back to the kitchen table and pointed to a binder full of nothing but tattooed wedding rings.

Dan grinned as he shook his head. He followed Garrett out to the barn. "Okay, what the hell happened to you, and just out of curiosity, did you really tell Sorenson to kiss your ass before you quit?" he demanded as soon as the barn doors were opened.

Garrett began hoisting boxes of toys into his Highlander. "She's just it. I know all of the shit I said in the past, but I was a dumbass. I guess this is how it was with Fi. You were ready to marry her when you got off the plane from Sydney."

"Yeah, but at some point in my life, I did want to get married. You have never wanted to."

"Now I do." Garrett shrugged. He didn't want his and Kaimi's relationship dissected and prodded apart. She was perfect. He was woefully undeserving, but he wanted her desperately. Somehow, she wanted him as well.

"I'm thrilled for you, and Fionna hasn't stopped smiling. We'll let you be in love, but at least let us harass you about it."

Garrett laughed as he nodded his acceptance.

"Can I ask you something?" Dan hesitated as he and Garrett lifted boxes of formula into the Highlander and slammed the back door shut.

"You can ask anything. Doesn't mean I'll answer." Garrett glanced back at the house, wondering what kinds of things Tad was learning about Kaimi.

"Did you tell her about Brazil?"

"Yeah." Garrett sighed. He certainly would never tell Kaimi's confession to Dan, not without talking to her first anyway.

"And that was all good?"

"Yeah."

"That's great. I'm really happy for you, and if we can do anything to help, tell me. If you want to go on and move out to Kauai, I can hand over the commander's badge and let you run things until I get out there. That way you don't have to do the long distance thing."

Garrett was shocked and honored. "I'm hoping I can convince her to stay here with me. I know Fi will rehire her. That way I can help you clean Venton up, and then we can all move together."

"Yeah, of course. Fi already adores her, and she's told me several times what an incredible dancer she is. She's got a job when we get out there if she's willing to let you take care of her here."

"I'm easing her into the idea, but we'll see. If she doesn't want to move here for a while, then I may take you up on that."

"Just let me know."

They returned to the kitchen to find Logan and Adeline had arrived and were devouring breakfast. Adeline and Fionna were talking about engagement rings with Kaimi and Tad. Aida was seated beside Fionna and listening intently. She crawled up in Garrett's lap when he joined them at the table. Her arms wound around Garrett's neck, and she squeezed him fiercely.

"You feel happy," she announced with a broad grin. Kaimi was astonished, but no one else at the table seemed to be.

"I am happy," Garrett assured her.

Fionna blinked back tears as she reached for Dan's hand, which he supplied readily.

"I was just telling Kaimi about that shop in Kapaʻa where we got the Haipai symbols. They do really great work. I'm trying to get Dan to let them fix my hibiscus flowers that stretched into an entire landscape when I was pregnant." Fionna sighed.

"And I'm fine with that as long as I get to come and cast you, and it's a woman who does the work," Dan informed her though everyone knew Fionna would ultimately get her way whatever that may be.

Kaimi grinned. "I assume it's somewhere I probably wouldn't have seen it."

Fionna nodded and then shot a smirk at her extremely overprotective husband.

"It was a good shop though. I was impressed." Dan agreed with Fionna's suggestion of where Garrett and Kaimi could get ring tats on Kauai.

Kaimi looked slightly overwhelmed by the amount of helpful suggestions she was receiving.

"We need to head out." Garrett tried to save her.

"Can I ride with Uncle Garrett and Aunt Kaimi?" Aida requested. Dan's eyebrows shot upward in question.

"Sure, baby girl." Garrett didn't comment on her title for Kaimi. It sounded like a perfectly logical conclusion to him. He saw no need to correct her. Kaimi looked thrilled with the idea that she could become a huge part of both Aida and Halia's lives. They couldn't have their own, but if she married Garrett, she was certain to have numerous nieces and nephews.

"Kaimi, if you decide you'd like to stay here with us for a few days while Garrett takes care of this insanity in London, we'd love to have you, sweetheart," Mrs. Haydenshire offered again.

"You could come stay with me and the girls. We would love that, and we could work on some ideas for the studio," Fionna interjected.

"Thank you. That's so sweet of both of you, but I need to go back home and deal with everything there. All of Nana's stuff and I maxed out two credit cards on the funeral, so I need to go back to work soon."

Everyone in the room looked devastated. Garrett shook his head as he saw the idea form in his father's eyes. He was going to offer to pay off the credit cards and to have everything taken care of for her in Kauai. Garrett knew that would only make her more uncomfortable.

"We'll take care of it. Let's just get to Rio and we'll talk," Garrett tried to reassure everyone.

"If we can do anything…" the governor offered.

"I know. I'll take care of everything."

CHAPTER 56

CHRISTMAS PRESENTS

A few minutes later, Garrett transferred Aida's pink flower car seat to his Highlander and loaded his goddaughter into it.

"Mommy says I can give you your Christmas present when you and Daddy get back from London," Aida explained to Garrett and Kaimi as he cranked the Highlander and backed out.

"That sounds good, and I'll give you your Christmas presents then too and your birthday gifts." Garrett winked at her.

"You got me presents too?" She gasped.

"Of course, you're my girl."

Aida beamed. "I know and that makes the sunshine in my tummy."

"What did you ask Santa for, Aida?" Kaimi asked hesitantly.

"I asked him to bring all of the children at the orphanage where I lived before I came to live with Mommy and Daddy lots of toys and books. And I think that Santa gave Uncle Garrett all of the lots of presents because he can help Santa deliver them. And I also asked him for a very special dolly that isn't a baby doll like Sophie. She's a little girl doll like me, and her name is Nanea, and she lived in Hawaii a long time ago. And I'm going to live in Hawaii soon. I've read all of her stories, and she's my very favorite, but I don't know if she can come live with me because she is very expensive, and Halia already came to live with us. She was in my mommy's tummy and then she came out. Do you know how that works?" Aida studied Kaimi intently. Garrett bit his lips together as Kaimi shot him a bewildered expression.

"Uh…sort of."

"Daddy said that God put Halia in Mommy's tummy, and I asked him if He was going to put another baby in mommy's tummy but Daddy said not for a while, and then I said if Daddy and God talked about that, or if Daddy just thought that another baby wouldn't come into Mommy's tummy for a while, and Daddy said that he just thought another baby wouldn't come into Mommy's tummy for a while, so I don't really think Daddy knows. But Daddy's face does this whenever I ask him about it again." Aida concluded her very lengthy explanation and turned her face up into a somewhat concerned scowl as Garrett tried to quell his laughter. Kaimi nodded her understanding as she tried not to laugh as well.

"I hope Santa gives you your doll just like you wanted." She tried to change the subject.

Aida drew an audible breath of exhilaration. Garrett gave Kaimi a slight nod. He knew Dan and Fionna had purchased the doll and all of her many accessories for their precious little girl, and they would be displayed lovingly in front of the tree when Aida woke up the next morning.

"I would take very, very good care of her, and put on her school dress on school mornings, and pack her lunch, and then I would put her play clothes on when I got home from school, so she could play with me, and she has a nightgown, and they have one that matches it that's my size, and she has her very own shave ice shop and a doggie named Mele." Aida was thrilled with the very idea of getting the doll she'd longed for since Fionna had first shown her the catalog back in the summer.

"That sounds like fun. Maybe if I come live with your Uncle Garrett on the farm then I could play with you some. I'm going to be your hula teacher this year." Kaimi beamed at Aida, and Garrett's heart swelled. It was the first time she'd spoken with any certainty about coming to the farm and living with him. Her wanting to spend time with his goddaughter had Garrett's love for her growing exponentially in a matter of seconds.

"Okay!" Aida sounded thrilled with the idea. "And Nanea also has a whole entire luau set and a dress, and if that comes to live with me then we could play luau. And she has a whole market like the one near Tutu's house," she added hopefully. Garrett grinned as he winked discreetly at Kaimi. All of the items she'd just enumerated were wrapped and awaiting Aida at Garrett's apartment.

"If you want to read Nanea's stories, they have them at the library near Tutu's house and they're very, very good and exciting. I've read them a bunch of times, and Daddy reads them to me when I check them out at the McCarron Elementary Beary Yourself in a Good Book library. They're on the Polar Bear shelf, but I'm allowed to check out from there because Daddy signed the note," Aida explained as Kaimi giggled.

"Maybe I could go check those out, since I'm going to be lonely while I'm back in Kauai and Uncle Garrett is here."

Aida's face fell. "I don't think you're supposed to go back to Kauai without Uncle Garrett because he feels happy when you're here, and I don't want him to feel sad anymore."

Kaimi gazed up at Garrett on the verge of tears. "She's right, and trust me Aida knows me better than just about anyone." If his eight-year-old saving grace could convince Kaimi to stay, then he certainly wouldn't hamper Aida's efforts.

Dan and Garrett loaded the boxes and boxes of gifts and supplies onto the cargo hold of the Crown Governor's jet.

"All right, you two have fun and make him behave," Dan ordered Kaimi.

"But I don't want him to behave," Kaimi teased as she began to loosen up around Dan. She was intimidated by his size and strength and his often gruff demeanor. Garrett had debated telling Dan that she was nervous around him, but telling a guy not to be who he was seemed ridiculous.

Fionna shook her head. "Yep, soulmates."

Dan lifted Aida up into his arms, and she squeezed her father tightly. This seemed to further Kaimi's comfort with Dan.

"Have a good Christmas, and Aida, call me tomorrow and tell me what Santa brings," Garrett urged.

"I will! And what he brings Halia."

"Of course," Garrett scoffed. Dan and Fionna looked utterly blissful to have two little girls to play Santa for that evening.

A little while later, Garrett fell back into the plane seat they'd ridden in the day before as Pete prepared for takeoff.

"So, there's a bedroom on your Dad's plane." Kaimi giggled mischievously. Garrett grinned as he pulled her into his lap.

"There *is* a bedroom because my Dad stays on the plane sometimes when he flies to other countries. But my dad hates to travel, so it doesn't get used that often. Although I do know that Logan and Adeline made use of it on their honeymoon."

"And would you have ever made use of it, Deputy?" she sassed.

Garrett debated. He hadn't ever made use of the bedroom on his father's jet. The Angels jet, however, he'd used more times than he could count.

"Uh…not Dad's."

"Ah, but you are a member of the mile high club I take it." She tried to hide her hurt but couldn't quite manage the task.

"Yeah, I am, but sweetheart, I told you I've had a lot of sex. I've only made love with you." This did seem to soothe her somewhat. "And if my girl would like to make love with me on my Dad's jet and join the mile high club then I can certainly make that happen."

Kaimi looked very intrigued. Garrett's heart began its familiar hammer. His blood quaked and hungered for her. His shield pulsed in need, and his cock rose to the occasion.

"I keep thinking that Nana can see me all the time now because, you know, she's in heaven. And I keep thinking about all the things we've been doing, and that she's probably up there covering her eyes and saying lots of Hawaiian words that mean shocked and appalled,"

362

Kaimi explained just before she cracked up. "And if we do it on a plane, that's even closer to heaven, so she'd have a front row view."

Garrett joined in her laughter as he drew her closer. He just needed her in his arms. That was all he would ever need.

"I hope Nana knows how much I love you, and that I'll always take care of you."

"Can I think about the bedroom for a few minutes?"

"Of course, baby. We don't have to do anything at all."

Kaimi nodded and seemed momentarily relieved. "Will you tell me what you're supposed to help Dan do before you can move?"

"Sure." Garrett began the story of everything that had been thrust in Dan's lap at the beginning of the school year.

Dan Vindico

"I really don't think we should get involved. I'm sure Garrett will talk to Chloe in a few days." Dan tried to soothe his wife who was quickly becoming frantic as she prepped Christmas dinner and avoided Chloe's rapid-fire texts demanding to know where Garrett was and why he hadn't returned her calls or texts.

"I don't want Chloe to do anything to ruin this for Garrett and Kaimi. I love her, and she's one of my best friends, but she's had a thing for Garrett for a long while. She kind of thought he was perfect because she didn't want a commitment either, but I think she also thought if he was ever going to settle down, it would be with her." Fionna restated the same thing she'd explained three times.

"I know, but Garrett is going to have to break it to her that he wants someone else. He already told her he was moving. I don't think she'll be too surprised."

"I just have a bad feeling." Fionna laid the lasagna noodles in the casserole dish and moved it to the oven where the sauce was bubbling away.

They stopped talking abruptly in the kitchen as they heard Aida telling Halia something in the living room. Dan had turned on a

Christmas movie, and Halia had been watching from her play mat while Aida kept an eye on her from the couch.

"If Santa brings me my doll, then we can take her on the plane to Tutu's house, and that way we'll already have a friend when we have to go to a new school," Aida explained as Halia cooed her complete lack of understanding. She waved her hands up and down rapidly as Aida kissed her little sister's cheek.

"My sweet baby, I wish she would tell me she's nervous about moving." Fionna sighed as she shook her head. "She can feel how excited we are, so she won't say anything."

"I'll talk to her," Dan assured his wife.

Garrett Haydenshire

"Dan and I are taking Rainer to London because he knows what this guy looks like. If we can confirm that he's been receiving an unearned paycheck for the last several years, then we'll call in London Iodex and have him arrested, but if he hasn't, then we go back to the drawing board with Will and see who has been walking away with hundreds of thousands of dollars."

"That sounds exciting and kind of dangerous."

"It's only one guy, and he has no idea we're coming for him. I don't think we'll be in any real danger, but I just don't think it's this guy. I think Wilshire's up to no good again." Garrett was shocked at how much he enjoyed talking about his work with Kaimi. For the last several months, he'd debated getting out of law enforcement altogether. Life had been getting to him, but now he felt the fire begin to roll in his gut again. It had been missing since Logan had pulled the trigger that ended Pravus's life last March.

"I wish I could go with you. It would be so cool to watch you work." Her pride filled Garrett's soul though he felt blood pool in his cheeks.

"Kaimi, baby, please just stay with me. We can go back to Kauai in a week or two, and I'll help you clean out your apartment. I just don't want to go back to life without you." He finally began his begging.

"I was just thinking that if I go back home while you're in London, I can kind of figure everything out. You know, like how I fell in love and am talking about getting married all of a sudden. I can deal with Nana's stuff and just let this whirlwind take effect, and then move in with you and just finally feel like somebody really loves me and sort of do that squealy thing I did in the bed this morning a lot." She blushed violently as she tried to explain why she wanted to go back to Kauai alone.

"All right," Garrett sighed. He stood and located the Christmas present he'd purchased her in the middle of the night.

"I didn't have time to get you more than this, but Merry Christmas. By this time next year, I want you to be Mrs. Garrett Haydenshire, okay?"

Her eyes goggled. "Is that a proposal?"

"No, because I don't have a ring, but it is the truth."

"Okay." She nodded, and he handed her the envelope.

"I don't have you anything," she panicked.

"You have everything, and you gave it all to me," Garrett vowed. "Just open it."

Kaimi stared at the envelope. Garrett knew she was frantically trying to figure out a way to get him a Christmas gift between now and the next day.

"What is this?" she quizzed as she revealed the tickets.

"They're three round trip tickets on Senate jets from Lihue to DC. They're open tickets so you can come back and forth anytime you want."

"Oh my gosh. Thank you!" She leapt into Garrett's arms and hugged him fiercely.

"I still don't want you to go." He hugged her tightly and wished he could feel her excitement, but all he felt when he thought of her flying back to Lihue was loss and dejected fear.

"Garrett, the way that I feel about you isn't going to change just because I go back home. I really, really love you. I love being your girlfriend. I want to be your wife, and I never thought I would ever meet a guy that made me feel that way. But I kind of need a few days to sort through all of this. Okay? It's a lot to process."

"Yeah, I know. I'm sorry. I didn't mean to pressure you into staying. I'm just gonna miss you so much." He began to consider having a few days to process. "I have some shit I need to take care of too. Just promise we'll be together in a few days, okay?" The conversation he had to have with Chloe began to take shape in his mind.

"I promise," she vowed.

<h2 style="text-align:center">CHAPTER 57</h2>

LOST

~DAN VINDICO~

"Daddy, it's me, Aida," Aida announced as she stared down over Dan in the bed at five forty-five Christmas morning. Fionna giggled from the sheets beside Dan. As they only had one child who could speak and move about the house of her own accord, the statement was highly unnecessary. Dan chuckled as he lifted Aida into the bed and snuggled her in. She was so excited Dan could feel it trilling constantly in her rhythms.

"Hi, me Aida," he teased and reveled in his little girl's delighted laughter.

"Do you think Santa came to our house?" She was very nearly squealing in her excitement.

"I don't know. Should we go get Halia and see?"

Fionna yawned and turned over to share a grin with Dan.

"Yes, I think so, and I want you to open your present."

"Okay, baby. Let's go get Halia, and then we'll go see if Santa came." Dan hadn't been so excited to get out of bed on Christmas morning since he was eight years old.

Aida was utterly overwhelmed as she flew down the steps and then gasped at the display Dan and Fionna had created the evening before once they were certain she was asleep.

Nanea was seated on her bed beside her shave ice shop and books. There were several Lego sets and a karaoke machine.

"Is all of that for me?" Aida's chin trembled as tears began to trickle down her precious face.

"Let's go see it, okay?" Dan tenderly guided Aida to her gifts and let her take them slowly one at a time and tell him all about Nanea and what she would do with all of her new toys.

Halia did seem to be fond of the rattles Fionna had put in her stocking though she certainly had no idea that it was even Christmas.

They let Aida absorb everything slowly and had breakfast before they opened the presents under the tree.

"Thank you." Aida carried the set of Nanea's stories with her as she hugged Fionna fiercely.

"You're welcome, sweetheart." Fionna kissed the top of Aida's head and then helped her change Nanea's clothes, so that she could wear her holoku dress for the day.

After the new presents had been stored in Aida's room, Dan settled on the couch beside her and handed her a cup of the apple cider Fionna had brewing on the stove. They were expecting both sets of their parents for dinner.

"It's warm, baby, so just sip it," Dan urged. Aida carefully set the mug on the table, then placed Nanea back on her bed, before she returned to the drink. Dan beamed. There would never be a more thoughtful child.

"You know, Daddy's going to have a whole new job once we move." Dan studied Aida closely.

"I know," she informed him. She refused to look Dan in the eye as she bit her lip.

"I'm a little bit scared about that," he explained.

Her head shot up as disbelief colored her features. "I didn't know you got scared."

"Everybody gets scared, sweetheart. We're moving far away, and we'll have a new house and a new job and new people and new friends and a new school...."

"But Uncle Garrett is going with us, and I was a little bit scared when he brought me to Washington, DC, but now I love it, and I have a whole family, and a little sister, and dollies, and my fairy princess bed, and books I can read, and a karaoke machine to sing, and you and Mommy, and I'm the luckiest little girl in the whole entire planet. So, I think this will be okay too." She seemed to have decided this as she spoke. "Because you and Mommy and baby Halia and Uncle Garrett will be there, and I love you all so much. You make everything be okay, so it will be okay." She patted his hand.

Dan realized his misstep. She was trying to console him instead of the other way around. She was a Receiver through and through.

"We love you too, sweetheart. You know, it's okay to miss things here or people here, and we'll be back to visit several times each year. And Harper and Sarah will be in your school with you, and Mommy will be at the dance studio with you. It's okay to feel scared or nervous."

"I haven't ever lived with you when Mommy had to go to work too."

Dan understood that there was more to her concerns than going to a new school.

"Mommy will go to work some, and Daddy will go to work sometimes, but we'll still be home with you and Halia too. And if we both have to go to work, then Tutu and Papa will be with you or Uncle Garrett or Kai and Malani."

"I like Kaimi too. Her hair is neat."

Dan chuckled and nodded his agreement. "I think Uncle Garrett likes Kaimi a lot. What do you think?" He wondered if Kaimi might be making his little girl feel insecure. Aida had certainly been Garrett's main concern for many years.

"I think he likes her a lot, and that they're going to get married, and maybe God will put a baby in her tummy like he does in Mommy's, but Uncle Garrett has to find her again first."

Dan's heart ached over the first part of her sentiment. He hadn't allowed himself to think about the second declaration, but Fionna heard her from the kitchen and was by their side a moment later.

"You know not everybody has babies just because they get married. You don't have to have a baby to be a family. And we shouldn't ask Garrett and Kaimi about that because whether or not people have babies isn't any of our business," she explained. "But why do we have to find Kaimi again? Is she lost?"

"Not yet," Aida stated knowingly.

"But she's going to get lost?" Dan asked.

Fionna had explained to Dan that she used to have premonitions as a child, but that her father refused to believe her. When he'd moved her off Kauai, she stopped having them altogether. Once a Receiver's internal shield was fully developed, partly due to the incredulity of adults, they only have a sixth sense about things that were going to happen based on the emotional energy around the event.

"Yes," Aida lamented dejectedly.

"Do you know when she's going to get lost?" Fionna asked.

"No." Aida shook her head.

"We'll help Uncle Garrett find her when she gets lost, okay?" Dan assured her.

"Okay, because he needs her." She drew another sip of her cider and then went back to playing with her doll.

Dan and Fionna shared a horrified expression though neither of them knew what was coming.

ABOUT THE AUTHOR

J.E. Neal (aka Jillian) vastly prefers coffee to tea, guac to salsa, the beach over anywhere else, and the world inside her head over the one outside her front door. She also loves not having to choose.

Driven by the question 'what if,' J.E. Neal's world began to manifest. What if there were people with powers the rest of us couldn't see? What if the energy of our world could be summoned and used at their will? Characters with these amazing abilities took shape in her mind. She created—and continues to create—an endless number of stories full of delicious escape from our reality where emotions are visible, desire is palpable, and danger is universal.

Learn more about J.E. Neal at JillianNeal.com

facebook.com/jilliannealauthor
twitter.com/JillianNeal_
instagram.com/jilliannealauthor

ALSO BY J.E. NEAL

TANGLE OF MAGIC

Tangle of Magic Boxed Set (Books 1-6)

Tangle of Lies (Book 1)

Tangle of Chaos (Book 2)

Tangle of Desires (Book 3)

Tangle of Fates (Book 4)

Tangle of Trust (Book 5)

Tangle of Ruin (Book 6)

ENERGY OF MAGIC

Shield and Shattered Cages (Book 1)

Shield and Faltered Steps (Book 2)

Shield and Splintered Oaths (Book 3)

Shield and Humbled Crown (Book 4)

Shield and Vile Serpents (Book 5)

Shield and Coveted Splendor (Book 6)

Shield and Guarded Shadow (Book 7)

Shield and Worthy Sinner (Book 8)

Shield and Sacrificial Heirs (Book 9)